CW01269791

Goldengrove

BY THE SAME AUTHOR

Poguemahone
The Big Yaroo
Heartland
Hello and Goodbye
The Stray Sod Country
The Holy City
Winterwood
Call Me the Breeze
Emerald Germs of Ireland
Mondo Desperado
Breakfast on Pluto
The Dead School
The Butcher Boy
Carn
Music on Clinton Street

Goldengrove

Patrick McCabe

unbound

First published in 2025

Unbound
An imprint of Boundless Publishing Group Ltd.
c/o Max Accountants, Ketton Suite, The King Centre,
Main Road, Barleythorpe, Rutland, LE15 7WD
www.unbound.com
All rights reserved

© Patrick McCabe, 2025

The right of Patrick McCabe to be identified as the author
of this work has been asserted in accordance with Section 77 of the Copyright,
Designs and Patents Act, 1988. No part of this publication may be copied,
reproduced, stored in a retrieval system, or transmitted, in any form
or by any means without the prior permission of the publisher, nor be
otherwise circulated in any form of binding or cover other than that in
which it is published and without a similar condition being imposed
on the subsequent purchaser.

While every effort has been made to trace the owners of copyright material reproduced
herein, the publisher would like to apologise for any omissions and will be pleased to
incorporate missing acknowledgements in any further editions.

This is a work of fiction. Names and characters are the product of the author's
imagination and any resemblance to actual persons, living or dead,
is entirely coincidental.

Is That All There Is
Words and Music by Jerry Leiber and Mike Stoller
Copyright © 1966 Sony Music Publishing (US) LLC
Copyright Renewed
All Rights Administered by Sony Music Publishing (US) LLC,
424 Church Street, Suite 1200, Nashville, TN 37219
International Copyright Secured All Rights Reserved
Reprinted by Permission of Hal Leonard Europe Ltd.

Text design by Jouve (UK), Milton Keynes

A CIP record for this book is available from the British Library

ISBN 978-1-80018-359-9 (hardback)
ISBN 978-1-80018-361-2 (ebook)

Printed in Great Britain by Clays Ltd, Elcograf S.p.A.

1 3 5 7 9 8 6 4 2

For Ian Morgan

With special thanks to Damien Brennan for his generous support as a patron of this book

Contents

Dramatis Personae — ix

Chapter 1	??	1
Chapter 2	!!!	31
Chapter 3	Speshul Intelligence Shervish	54
Chapter 4	Joan Collins	63
Chapter 5	Lovers in the Penny Arcade	70
Chapter 6	Em-Oi-Foive, Pshaw	82
Chapter 7	The 'Colonel O' Solution	104
Chapter 8	Nurses' Parties	128
Chapter 9	Plinka Plonka	144
Chapter 10	Bowsiness	155
Chapter 11	A Steam Iron	164
Chapter 12	The Truth About 'Colonel O'	169
Chapter 13	Even the Monuments Shall Not Remain	188
Chapter 14	Roll Over, Bubbles	197
Chapter 15	A Night out at the National	207
Chapter 16	Biddy Mulligan the Pride	216
Chapter 17	The Hydrogen Bomb	230
Chapter 18	Are You Certain It's Yours, Biddy?	245
Chapter 19	Heaven's Gates	261
Chapter 20	The Upside-Down Man	270
Chapter 21	The Rules	285
Chapter 22	The Man from Del Monte	314

Acknowledgements — 322
Supporters — 323

Dramatis Personae

Chenevix Meredith	*MI5 agent bearing more than a passing resemblance to Max von Sydow*
Henry Percival Plumm	*MI5 agent and theatrical agent, Billy Bunter lookalike*
Rosie Dixon	*Proprietress of the Woolsley Bay Hotel, on the south coast of England*
Ambrose Roland	*MI5 Command and Control*
Alex Whiteside	*MI5 agent with a penchant for 'Joan Collins'*
Valentine McBoan	*Actor, star of popular radio series* At Home With the Tomeltys *and Minty's regular*
Hugh 'Barney' McRoarty	*Actor, star of popular radio series* At Home With the Tomeltys, *former saxophone supremo and Minty's regular*
Charlie Kerrins	*Actor, star of* The Confessions of Brendan Behan *and Minty's regular*
Maurice Norton	*Renowned stage actor who toured with the legendary Anew McMaster*
Deirdre Norton	*Singer and wife of Maurice*
Clement Grainger	*Theatrical and musical wunderkind*
Máiréad Curtin	*Feminist director of the radical Little Matchbox Theatre Group*
Peter 'the Bowsy' McAuley	*Apparent inebriate with hidden motives*

Beatrice Coogan-McDonaghy	*Beloved late wife of Chenevix Meredith*
Joanne Vollmann	*Aspirant young writer and former lover of Chenevix Meredith*
Captain 'Hushabye' McVeigh	*of the Ulster Defenders, bloodthirsty scourge of Fenians and Teagues*
Dolores 'Dils' Pratt	*Would-be Ulster starlet and companion of Captain McVeigh*
'The Reverend' Passmore Stout	*Slavering, intemperate, revivalist preacher*
Jacqui Harpur	*'Dublin's finest columnist' and Peggy Lee impersonator*
'Uncle' Leslie Courtney	*Noted pervert, teacher at Mandeville House College*
Peregrine Montgreve Masterson	*Golden boy and egotist of Mandeville House College*
Nabla Cooney	*Freckle-faced innocent of the National Ballroom*
Miss Mulgrew	*Sex worker, astray*

Chapter 1

?？

Yes indeed, you may very well ask.
 Blowing up pubs – why bother?
Or what precisely one's lifetime colleague thinks he might be playing at – lying splay-legged in a bathtub, with a ludicrous parade of soap bubbles evacuating his you-know-what. Ah yes, a charming sight indeed – there really can be no doubt about it. The last of poor old Henry Plumm – or 'Plump', as I preferred to call him – that sweet, old, gentle, profoundly loyal dearest of hearts.

Now, sadly, departed this world for ever.

He really and truly will be missed. Because there simply can't be any denying the fact – that when it came to poor old Plummsers, you could always be sure to rely on him for a bit of a chuckle.

Yes, old Plumpy would always provide what you required in that department. Whenever you felt you might be in need of cheering up – to ''ave yourself a larf', in the time-honoured traditional manner. What might be described as a bit of your average old 'carry-on'.

Because, of course, on top of everything else, old Henry – he really could be the most convincing impressionist. There wasn't a mimic to touch the man. You name it, believe you me, he could produce it. Sitting right there beside you in the pub, he could effortlessly generate anyone at all.

On one memorable occasion, at a function in the ambassador's residence, of all places, it happened to be Alec Guinness in *The Man in the White Suit*, a selection of attire for which I distinctly recall him exhibiting a preference – which I actively dissuaded, considering it just a little too 'ostentatious', attracting unnecessary attention, I cautioned. Which, of course, it inevitably did.

But, honest to goodness – what a performance! With everyone present collapsing in stitches as he became, in every possible aspect conceivable, Sidney Stratton from the celebrated Ealing comedy.

'I have to say that that's a funny outfit,' he declared with impish diffidence, cradling his elbow in his left hand.

'Oh yes? What's funny about it?'

'It's so luminous, I mean, to be perfectly honest, it looks like it's wearing you!'

Before directing his attention, with comparable aplomb, towards a role from a TV advert which had become just as popular, albeit much later on – 'The Man from Del Monte'. Announcing, with a wide sweep of his Panama hat: '*El Hombre Del Monte* – he say yes! *El dice que sí, caramba* hur hur hur!'

Without a doubt a most memorable and successful show – in practically every respect. Buoying his ego up even further.

Which is why he tended, whenever he felt it appropriate, and on that evening he did, to concentrate his attentions on myself, if you don't mind. That is to say, his spontaneous, note-perfect representation of my accent. Predictably enough, with more than a few elegant flourishes – not to say exaggerations – thrown in for good measure.

Why, it were as though, in his reading, poor old Chenevix here, gustily interpreted as being attired in a straw boater and striped blazer, resembled nothing so much as a repertory actor in a touring production of *The Boy Friend*. With the voice in particular, I must acknowledge, being the most impressive aspect. A delivery of 'languid elegance' comes to mind. Somewhat stagey, slightly aloof.

His observations on that occasion at the embassy had included some aside referring to the cruelty that resides within the English nature. A contention best left to others to pronounce upon.

For both Henry Plumm and I – regrettably, I have to admit, we won't be examining the pros and cons of such topics any longer. What with his poor old valiant, honourable head having only recently been comprehensively stove in. Thanks to the effectiveness of a sturdy old weathered spruce oar.

What a way to go, as the Americans like to say. Or used to. Back in the time when the likes of Walter Kerr held sway – and Ray Milland too. In their day, communicating in that very same vein which dear old Plumm had effectively made his own that day in the embassy. No wonder I'd been embarrassed – I mean, he had sounded almost exactly like me, for heaven's sake!

'Dearest Chenevix!' he winked, delicately plying his long thin Wintermans cigar. Before proceeding in that decidedly non-rhotic timbre he had now established, in other words, what might just as easily have been the voice of a pre-1939 announcer, habituated to primitive microphone technology. Concluding what remained of his provocative little monologue. Deploying that manner which many in the audience assumed to be an affectation – one adopted in the hope that the formal delivery and round, even tones might be perceived as commensurate with the speaker's presumed degree of exceptional intelligence. And, of course, delicate sensibility.

Ray Milland more than anyone, really – with that clipped voice and slightly aloof manner, which, of course, he had appropriated from yours truly, for where on earth else would someone of my unfortunate colleague's modest station ever have acquired it?

Oh yes, without a doubt. Old *Dial M for Murder* Henry

Plumm – but for the fact that, on this occasion, it is none other than he himself who transpires to be the victim. Honest to goodness, though, as I say, what a way to go.

As the Potato Heads liked to put it, back at the beginning of our careers in dear old Erin: head down, arse-about-face. Although, at this point, I really do have to say – not exactly noble, is it? Whether for Regina Imperatrix, or anyone else.

No sir.

Not in the slightest.

Ah well.

But anyway, as I was saying – as regards M'sieu Plump – and this is right from the beginning, believe you me – tapping that cigar, he would just turn around and come out with it, right out of the blue: 'Meredith, my dear boy, what in the devil is wrong with you now? For, as God is my judge, in all my life I have never encountered anyone so frustratingly taciturn and glum.'

I seem to recall him announcing on one occasion – no doubt in some dreary Liffeyside public house or other: 'You know, more than anyone else I can think of, Merry, you seem to remind me of the Scandinavian Max von Sydow. It's that still, ineluctable way that you have of standing. Yes, just standing there in that habitual manner of yours, in a doorway. Clad, as ever, in that same drab old raincoat. And, in common with von Sydow, perpetually seeming to gaze out windows.'

Although I have to admit that, after all these years, it certainly looks like he got that right. As I remain here, quite motionless, albeit sans overcoat, surveying the surrounding bay in all of its bluish haze. Appropriately, perhaps, if one is to be cast in the cold Scandinavian mode, through the prism of this high Gothic window.

There's not a sound.

Only that familiar, peculiar stillness which is so much a feature of the off-season Woolsley Bay Hotel. And which seems to surround me, covering my body from head to toe like a cold skin. Scaly. Somewhat appropriate, I suppose, for individuals such as we are – professional assassins. Not that I would ever admit to being one in public.

'I mean, honestly, dear!' as old Plummsers might say, 'to even consider such an ill-advised, not to say intemperate, revelation. Honestly, really, there are times when you can be such a toot!'

He used to make these silly words up – as I do myself from time to time. Yes – 'toots' and 'bosh barnacle'. All sorts of things. Whatever just happens to come into your head.

But now, however – not so much as a word out of the poor unfortunate, with his poor bonce, as he might describe it, caved in beyond redemption. As he lies there in silence beneath the silver taps. With his two arms outspread and that poor old Cupid's bow mouth hanging wide open – giving the impression of some exotic, exsanguinated marine creature. Before jerking unexpectedly and going blub blub blub. And then, just as dramatically: pop! As out drifts another marble-sized bubble – through his protruding bottom, I mean.

Providing what can only be considered the most fitting end for someone who was proved, ultimately, to be very little more than a self-serving, amoral, mendacious nonentity. For, at this point, I can think of no other description.

Even if, certainly at selected intervals throughout our shared lives, that might well have been considered a description of none other than my good self, Chenevix Meredith. And one which poor old Henry – incontestably, at least towards the end of what you might call our little 'drama' – would not have hesitated to articulate.

And it may well indeed be the case that my inherent caution and, at times, irritating tendency towards reticence – as opposed to his bonhomie and almost legendary flamboyance – might well have earned such a categorisation. With one's close-clipped greying moustache and raincoat still, almost obstinately doing precious little to disabuse any putative surmiser of such unflattering perceptions.

Were the question, however, put seriously to myself, I should have to admit that I find the Max von Sydow comparison – to be prefectly honest, not a little . . . well . . . somewhat fanciful, shall we say. A tad indulgent, even, certainly when compared to the uniquely theatrical and colourful Viscount Henry P. Plumm DSO, EGM, MBE, who, by his very existence, rendered one's presence in company really quite unstriking, to say the least. Almost to the point of invisibility, indeed.

Although, conceivably, a case may be argued for quite the opposite being the effect where Mr von Sydow was concerned in the seventies feature *Three Days of the Condor*. Which starred none other than Robert Redford, if you recall. In which Max can be viewed remarking, with characteristic coldness, to the eponymous Condor, played by the blue-eyed matinee idol: 'What you don't know for sure is how exactly it will happen. Well then, permit me to be of some assistance in that regard. You may be walking. Maybe the first sunny day of spring. And a car will slow beside you, and someone you know, maybe even trust, will get out of the car. And he will smile, a becoming smile. But he will leave open the door of the car and offer to give you a lift. That, you may be sure, is how it will happen.'

'Dear heart,' I often used to sigh as I clutched my umbrella and turned around to Henry, 'imagine if something comparable were to happen to you or I. Hmmph?'

He had snorted as usual. Yes, here it comes again, that great whinny-laugh.

Hur hur hur, responded that sweet old Plump.

As I returned to my thoughts of Max von Sydow – or Joubert, which was his actual character name, if memory serves. Observing him closely as he appeared once again out of nowhere – edging with his back to the damp brickwork of the darkened alleyway, advancing stealthily like a cat. Before ascending the rusted metal staircase of a fire escape, and sliding into a room where his unsuspecting quarry was waiting.

'Would you mind moving away from the window, please?' was all the raincoated assassin had to say. In a register which, on reflection, was not at all dissimilar to that clipped, aloof manner so familiar from the work of Ray Milland. Yes, it definitely seemed to possess those very same mellifluous, distinctive, plummy tones. Over-enunciated and remote – calling to mind the vanished age where lay its origins. Almost as though it belonged to some pompous-sounding broadcaster of yore. A stagey, neutral voice.

'I won't scream,' he found himself being informed.

'I know,' he replied.

As von Sydow – Joubert – levelled his weapon, complete with gleaming silencer. Before folding it up and disappearing into the murk. In the very same manner as I am about to do myself. Through the curtains.

You know, I often think of what we, as people, have in common: assassins, state actors – men-of-the-shadows of various kinds. Variegated, certainly – but also with a great deal in common. Hitmen. Thespians. Honestly, I ask you – really and truly, what a genuinely incorrigible crew.

You know, I think I'll treat myself to a cigar. A Henri Wintermans, if you please. There – that's better. Ever so soothing and conducive to contemplation. There are times when I'm having a puff when I feel like I belong more to the era which succeeded that of dear Henry and myself, the one in which the formal delivery of our earlier years had all but been supplanted by the sensibility of what has been described as the 'cool-cat era'.

I don't know. I couldn't really say.

But there can't be any denying that the formal style of the fifties and early sixties, that is to say the period to which we both belonged – it was already ceding territory to a world we were no longer in a position to recognise. Even on that damp little offshore island where it had been our misfortune to spend so much of our professional time. Which, back then, was largely populated by inebriates only recently hauled up out of the ground.

'Yes, the Potato Men of darling good old Erin,' as Henry used to describe them. He could be so funny! With me finding it impossible not to laugh – whenever I think of those arse cheeks protruding in the bathroom. But I really will miss him. Just as I will our soujourns in good old Erin.

Yes, our intermittent dalliances on the atoll, serving Regina. But most of all in dear old dirty Dublin, city of rain and compulsive, shifty liars. Primed and ever-ready to abase themselves in the pathetic pursuit of would-be charm. A tendency, more than any, which I think got Henry's goat.

Because I can remember him remarking one day in the Scotch House back bar: 'You know, Mr Churchill had at one point given serious consideration to the deployment of anthrax. In the case of these more recent insurgents, I am inclined to think that he may well have been right.'

That would have been in the early seventies. With 'that old nuisance', as he called it – and with infuriating tedium – having sourly declared itself once again.

The rain has begun again over Woolsley Bay and what few remaining cars there may have been have already departed for the city. And now, in their absence, hovers that unmistakable melancholy which always seems to descend whenever a bank holiday comes to an end – in a specific type of British coastal 'home from home', at any rate.

A description more than appropriate to the surroundings in which now, after all this time, I have found myself. Ah yes, that old home from home. Which is how Miss Rosie Dixon – the famed proprietress of what was, once upon a time, an 'entertainment hotel' – elects to promote her once-upon-a-time magnificent edifice.

In all honesty, a testament to Victorian overreaching. Now, in fact, little more than a birthday cake slowly but surely sinking into the ocean.

Not that Madame Dixon appears to care very much – snoring her head off, as is her wont, lying there helplessly slumped across a deckchair and not caring a damn about being caught out in another shower.

Reminding me, actually, as I stand here looking out at her, of no one more so than the grand dame Beryl Reid, another old stager, if you happen to remember any of her performances. Such as, for example, *The Killing of Sister George*.

The Killing of Brother Henry, ha ha. Forgive me, will you – just my silly little idea of a joke. In poor taste, I acknowledge. Pray please, if you would – let me continue. With my little seaside story – concerning Mme Dixon and our adventures chez Woolsley Bay.

Rosie's father was Alderman Whitney Dixon. Along with a considerable complement of tics and neuroses and a tendency to give utterance without any significant degree of consideration, the Woolsley Bay Hotel had been his parting gift to his beloved daughter. Who had nursed him through to the end of his life, for the best part of twenty-five years – after his wife had flung herself across a balcony. Regrettably, the coroner had never established the precise sequence of events. Not with any degree of certainty, or so Dixon told me.

Standing here watching her, it occurs to me that it would probably be for the best if I went out and summoned her inside – for I fear that the rain is not going to abate. As a matter of fact, I would venture to suggest that there well may be an electrical storm in the offing. Certainly by the looks of those clouds just beyond the cliffs. Such a brooding cumulus as presents itself before me.

There isn't – at least, not yet – any great need, however, to be overly concerned about the fortunes of poor old departed Henry, aspirant OBE. For a start, I've taken the precaution of pocketing the bathroom key. And, in any case, poor old Dixon – as I say, by now she's so intoxicated she could barely establish a barn door directly in front of her. Still snoring. You can hear her from here, gagging through the swathes of rain.

Such quiet, though, apart from that. Ho hum.

I realise, of course – on some level, at least – that I ought to feel guilty over what has taken place with Henry. Indeed, there are those who would bullishly insist upon it, considering what the pair of us have shared throughout the years. And not just in Clod Land.

'After all, you were a team, were you not?' I can hear them object. And which is true – after a fashion, at least.

'Did you not share serious responsibilities together – for the organisation of atrocities and such?'

I can imagine that being one of their more strident assertions. A perception to which they are more than entitled – how am I in a position to complain? With the facts, of course, being that in our line of work, what often appears to be the case very rarely is.

Especially on the atoll where the pair of us stout hearts soldiered together – often at great risk to our personal health. And that is putting it mildly – over there in what he habitually referred to as Terra del Swede. Aka Ballyturnip, as I used to say, weighing in with my own little tuppenceworth.

Its official name, at that time, was of course: Éire. Ireland, in other words.

'I'm sure you've heard of it,' old Plummsers used to say, whenever his intention was to raise another laugh. And which, to be honest, was pretty much every single day of the week.

'Harrumph! Harrumph! Hur hur hur. Land of mist and persistent moral evasion!'

Gut-wrenching at this point, I really must concede, to think that now, after all the entertainment we enjoyed – and we did enjoy plenty! – that this is how events have concluded.

Perhaps it was always going to be that way, I found myself reflecting, knowing only too well how beneath that layer of Henry Plumm's golden charm there had always lingered a substratum of conceit. Those little piggy eyes set way back in his head, missing nothing through the winding, uprising horns of the Henri Wintermans' smoke. No wonder I'd experience a brief, involuntary shiver.

However, in any case – back to business. I'll attend to the disposal of the body later on, and whatever else must needs to be done. Just as soon as old Rosie has decided to abandon her sodden deckchair and laid, at last, her sozzled old curly head upon the pillow. Fingering the key where it's resting deep inside one's pocket, I descend the great big oaken stairs and make my way in the direction of the vestibule.

In a way, this place reminds me of the very first office we established in our beloved Éire. It was located in a backstreet just off the South Circular Road, and festooned with portraits not unlike those which decorate these very walls and alcoves. Although, in the case of the Woolsley Bay Hotel, the images concerned are mainly of nobodies everyone has long since forgotten. If they ever knew them in the first place.

Not that I haven't enjoyed my tenure in 'Old Mouldy', as I call it. Most definitely not. Because I absolutely and 100 per cent have adored it – and been grateful too for the opportunity that I've been granted. For the ministry was under no obligation to do it. Transfer me here and see to my welfare – all those many long years ago. Which is how it seems – although it can't be actually more than two or three.

So, make no mistake – I remain thoroughly and comprehensively grateful to Her Majesty and staff for their consideration. Their largesse, really – over and above. Because, since moving in, I haven't so much as paid a penny's rent. But, then, that's always been the way here at the Woolsley Bay Hotel – a location especially designated where those concerned, on Elizabeth's behalf, can make it their business to look after those who have 'served Her Majesty well'. Of that let there be not a soupçon of doubt. Or 'smidgereen', as the Potato Men might call it.

So attests, at any rate – hopefully with the appropriate degree of humility – your dutiful correspondent Chenevix A. Meredith. Whose remit – indeed almost from birth – has been to deploy an approach of both inherent caution and maximum deniability. And which, of course, has always been one's traditional modus operandi.

Without risking dramatic escalation or political embarrassment, one pinpricks away at the target's authority by exploiting weaknesses, undermining the economy, promoting dissension and spreading distrust.

'This is how, in a world of players, we as gentlemen are expected to behave,' as Ambrose Roland was fond of repeating – ad nauseam, to tell the truth. With denial and diversion – but perhaps even more importantly, delay – always being recruited whenever possible. Sometimes, of course, responsibility being admitted – but always accompanied by a concomitant questioning of the standards applied to evaluate the particular action. With doubt and uncertainty never ceasing to remain one's allies.

Speaking of players, as I pass a portrait at the turn of the stair – just to my left on the main landing wall – who do I become aware the artist has depicted? Why, really quite unexpectedly – and I am amazed that I have not noticed it before – a still, pensive rendering of none other than a certain 'Mr Pinter'.

No, not of the celebrated, if controversial, playwright. Who did, apparently, lodge here in Woolsley on a number of occasions during one of his many tours of the south-east while in repertory. However, no – as I say, it was not him. But, in fact, Leonard, his older and much lesser-known brother, looking smart in his military tunic.

There's a little printed card at the bottom containing his biography. Before his death, sadly, it reveals, Harold's brother was blown up in Africa. He had succeeded in attaining the rank of Lt Colonel. A warm glow of pride went coursing, ever so briefly, through me, reading that. And I felt like reaching out to the man. No, obviously not for him the sullen nonconformity of his 'conscientious objector' sibling. Absolutely not for Leonard.

'A disgrace to the family' was what he used to call his brother. 'A total and utter bounder. A self-serving, bad-humoured, arrogant cad.' With their differences, apparently, on occasion having extended to fisticuffs. Oh yes, that 'old 'Arold' and Leonard could often be seen rolling around the floor – whenever Pinter Senior would arrive home on two weeks' leave.

'Take that!' Leonard would say – because he was his regiment's welterweight champion. And I didn't blame him – not one iota. For, brother or not, like myself, he profoundly loathed the other man's politics. The other man, that is, who, just moments before had been fulminating yet again – 'sounding off' as Leonard had described it – in the back kitchen of their cramped East London home.

Much to the mounting chagrin of the phlegmatic, somewhat more prosaic, but arguably more gifted Leonard.

A contention which the following anecdote will presumably do much to support.

Because this type of altercation was by no means uncommon at all when Leonard came home. But, by all accounts, this was even worse than before. With the arrival of Leonard Pinter seeing the future Nobel Prize-winning author pacing up and down the length of the kitchen, frothing at the mouth as he repeatedly opened and closed his fists. All the while grimacing and wincing to a really quite absurd degree. At one stage, he had actually punched the wall above the radio.

'The first image of the play, not that the likes of you would ever understand!' he barked at his brother, referring to *The Birthday Party*. 'Yes, the very first thing that was put on paper – about a year ago – was a kitchen, Meg, Stanley, cornflakes and sour milk. There they all were – they sat, they stood, they bent, then turned.'

'Oh do shut up, you great big, self-regarding twit!' had been the response from an already irate Leonard Pinter. 'Because if you don't, I've a good mind to turn you through that blooming window, I really have. For you absolutely are becoming the most infuriating, sententious old windbag! It really is the truth, I'm sorry to have to be the one to tell it to you, our Harold. Yes, an arrogant, bumptious, inflated blooming windbag!'

Windbag or not, it has to be admitted that the particular communist ingrate concerned, when it came to it, could certainly tell a good story. Particularly if the material happened to involve his time as a jobbing actor during the period of the late fifties, when he had toured a miserable and moist, quite unpromising Éire in the service of the legendary actor-manager Mr Anew McMaster.

Who, he proceeded to explain, without any form of request whatsoever having been solicited, had been in the process of presenting *Oedipus Rex* by Sophocles in the unremarkable midlands town of Mullingar, and was building up to his blind climax when one of the locally recruited extras went and had an epileptic seizure on stage before collapsing. And who then was subsequently dragged into the wings, where he was attended to by various women. The sounds of their ministrations seeped onto the stage. McMaster, by all accounts, had halted – then turned to the wings and, with all the extravagant fury of which he was capable, vented: 'For God Almighty's sake, you people – or can't you see I'm trying to act!'

All of which is now by the by. As indeed are the creative efforts of Lieutenant Colonel Leonard Pinter. None of which are celebrated now – if indeed they remain in the memory at all. 'Confections' – which was how the exceedingly humble (breathtakingly more so than his sibling) Leonard had elected to describe his oeuvre. A parcel of offerings which had contained such efforts as *Pow! Who Goes There?*, *Mr Harbinson's Delight*, *Not So Fast, Bernie Wilkins!* and, probably the most finely and authoritatively executed of all, *Assignation Beyond Hackney Marsh*.

Not one of which, at least to my knowledge, has ever received anything approaching a professional production. A state of affairs which is really quite unacceptable – considering the breadth and extent of the dramatic abilities on view.

'I've read them all,' Henry Plumm used to say, 'and so far as I am concerned, even the weakest of his efforts leave that other fool, that loud-mouthed narcissist, without question, in the halfpenny place.' Meaning the future Nobel laureate, of course.

'Intemperate barrow-boy, for that, when it comes to it, is all he is, dear Chenny,' I can recall him observing on more than one occasion, 'and I make no apology for advancing such an appreciation.'

Not that the younger Pinter's talents unduly bothered his sibling. It was more his politics, which he routinely and resolutely despised. As a matter of fact – in what can only be described as the most extraordinary coincidence, in the circumstances – on a day when they happened to be up on Hampstead Ponds, enjoying a day's boating, during the course of yet another dispute, this time over Harold's repudiation of his National Service. When the unfortunate Leonard, by this stage at the end of his tether, had threatened to 'this very minute smash an oar right across your back!'

Considering what has just happened here in Woolsley Bay, it remains a tad difficult to suppress the wryest of smiles.

'Yes, across your dashed bloody back, you infuriating twat – even if you are my brother!' he had bawled yet again. But, unlike myself only just recently in our bathroom – and, of course, a certain Colonel 'O', which is of course where I got the idea, and of whom more later – the essentially mild-mannered Leonard hadn't made good the threat.

In marked contrast to the hopelessly volatile and egocentric Harold – whose public reputation in this regard, I feel pretty certain, is in very little need of repetition here. And whose lack of social graces, and manners, generally, were by any standards really quite deplorable. Containing no suggestion whatsoever of the soft-spoken Leonard's consistently admired social grace and unimpeachable politics – buoyed by fidelity not only to the Conservative Party but the essential institution of the monarchy, and of course Her Majesty in particular. To whom he was to remain unwaveringly consistent in his deference – prior to being tragically blown to pieces out in Africa. Where, precisely, I cannot for the life of me at this moment quite remember.

In so many ways, their relationship for me tends to mimic that which existed between myself and 'Old Plumpy', as I used to call him, whenever I was in my cups. You should have seen how red he used to get! Just like that 'old 'Arold' whenever Leonard, yet again, trumped him. The very same as when I trumped old Plump!

'Don't you dare do that again, do you hear? Mimic my accent, because that's offensive!'

Before me turning around and doing the same – mimicking him, only twice as bad. Oh, it really was such fun.

'Oo-ah I doo-ah like a naice cee-gah!' I would enthuse.

'Iddint it a naice smuk, Plumpy?' I'd chuckle.

And which I know, of course, that I ought not to have done. Should I, Old Plumpy? Because it really isn't – is it? – on. Such indulgent behaviour, I mean. So ungracious. Plumpity plumpity pum pum pum. Have another drink, dear boy.

What a pair we were, when I think of it – back in those long lost days at the posterior of Europe, stationed in a country without so much as a cent to its name. And not even so much as a morsel of civic order.

I mean, really and truly, by any standards, it was a laughably failed state. With it only being a matter of time before they, abjectly, invited Regina back. Just as soon as they accepted the error of their ways – taking a long, hard look in the mirror for the purpose of appraising what was patently obvious to any reasonably intelligent observer. That they belonged, without exception, to a hopelessly distracted nation of ingrates and inbred agitators.

Ah yes, myself and good old Plummy back in the land of whiskery old potatoes. Not unlike 'The Pinters', I suppose, the relationship we enjoyed was of an essentially protean and somewhat theatrical nature. With the pair of us, in our turn, being defined by certain thespian inclinations. Affording expression, I suppose, to those exclusive and often contradictory natures within.

With, as has been illustrated earlier, something of Max von Sydow's rather austere and unforthcoming personality commingling on a daily basis with that of, shall we say, the more baroque and rococo Anew McMaster himself, for heaven's sake. Possibly – indeed, most definitely! – when old Plumm would go and get himself all drunk and inebriated again. An occurrence which wasn't at all infrequent, I am afraid to say.

So, small wonder the poor fellow would end up with his bonce caved in, lying there sprawled like a mantis in the bath.

It was only a matter of time, really – considering some of the outbursts of which he was capable. Not that his behaviour wasn't in some ways understandable – what with the high levels of stress incurred by the nature of our profession. But, really and truly, was there any real need for some of those irksome melodramatic outbursts to which he was prone, right from the outset?

It was the first thing, really, that I noticed about him. 'That fatal thespian tendency' as I prefer to call it. The nature of which I guessed straight away – leaning a little in that direction, as I do myself. Ah yes, that fatal thespian tendency. Dear oh dear. As they used to say in Potato Land: 'There was the pair of us in it.'

Yes, there really was.

Why, in common with those dear old Pinters of theatreland, we might have starred in our very own self-penned episode of *The Bruvvers*. A nod, of course, to the popular ITV series, if you remember it – starring Frank Finlay and the delectable Kate O'Mara. Scrumptious, I'll say! And in which – as so often before – I can effortlessly visualise an intemperate Harold Pinter as myself, chasing Leonard 'Lenny' Plumm around a capacious, carpeted drawing room. In the process of flinging a variety of expensive crockery and political insults in equal measure after my so-called 'brother'. With little difficulty – I momentarily crave your indulgence of my egotism – contriving an imaginary country-wide repertory tour.

Of which *The Bruvvers* would form the centrepiece – packing out rep all across the land. Especially in locations not entirely dissimilar to where I have spent the past three years of my life. That is to say, Woolsley Bay. In the company, the greater proportion of it genial, of my once beloved but regrettably now deceased old loyal comrade, Lord Henricus Percival R. Plumm.

The highlight of which transpired to be – as you all will now be aware – what I like to think of as a sprightly and vigorous but most of all comical, Edgar Wallace-style bagatelle. Entitled *Bubbles in the Bath* by Percival Windybottom. With that great big, white-haired, unstoved head plastered all over the cover of the paperback.

Ha ha – that's a laugh, it really is – and I genuinely do hope that none of you will consider it unnecessarily gratuitous or in any way unkind. With my primary excuse being that, as a consequence of one's experience in the service, there still remains that impulse to massage one's assertions, tailor them with a certain type of audience always in mind.

Hardly surprisingly, considering the fact that the very same is true when it comes to the execution of certain selected state operations – even the most routine clandestine manoeuvres. Not that the unquestioning acceptance of such a situation is going to impress everyone. Far from it, as I know only too well. Recalling, as it does, a rather caustic remark from an old associate back in Ireland – a genial fellow, and himself a Potato Head. Even though you might not have thought it, for he had spent a considerable amount of his time in America. As a matter of fact, I think this was in the US Embassy in Dublin.

'I am consistently underwhelmed, Mr Meredith,' I remember him saying, 'by the world-weariness of your people. What has become of the British, I often ask myself, for what they seem to be doing is involving themselves in a lot of shit, none of which appears to mean anything, in fact, nothing more – here in Ireland, Indonesia or wherever – than playing games. Successive governments have turned to covert action to prevent or mask decline. It is a form of fancy footwork to meet Britain's global responsibilities and try to assert some control in an uncertain environment.'

But, whatever the truth of that particular speculation, 'we're a considerably long way from old Ballyturnip now', as Plumm would often observe in the old times. Long after we'd completed our 'tour of duty'. If – when it comes to Ireland – it's ever really properly completed.

He was always complaining about having had to go there at all. But then, as they say, that's actors, ha ha! I can imagine him doing it yet, if he was still alive. Moaning and groaning about how abruptly it had ended. Not to mention the crass ignobility of it all, for heaven's sake, face down in six inches of poorly heated water. Yes, complaining, to Plump, I'm afraid, had become a way of life.

More than anyone, he was always on at poor old Biddy Mulligan (he himself had christened her that, on account of her being the maid, and Irish to boot), giving off yet again about the sorely inadequate facilities. Particularly – and you'll appreciate the irony of this – where the heating of the bathroom water was concerned.

'There never seems to be enough!' you would often hear him bawl, usually around about six o'clock, which was when he liked to schedule his daily scrub.

'I shall resign my commission!' was a commonly voiced clarion call. At least in the early days. Before he became wearily suspicious and circumspective. Hostile, even, especially towards

Biddy – making regular threats to 'abandon this accursed establishment, once and for bloody well all'.

'I intend to leave the hotel this evening,' he would declare, 'and for good this time.' He never did, however. Not that anything was ever done about the water or the temperature. And certainly not by Miss Rosie Dixon. Who, of course, was in no position to do so, being three sheets to the wind, as always. Even before breakfast, if you can believe it. When you would often espy her shrouded by a cloud of steam in the kitchens, already tippling away at her crock of gin – under the impression that she wasn't being seen.

That, of course, would be attributable to the 'Lady Potato' part of her character. Her mother, you see – she'd given me the whole interminable saga, and on more than one occasion – had been born in some flung-together village of mud and bits of sticks, situated on the west coast of County Clare.

A goodly long way from poor old Harold Pinter's beloved south coast of England.

Most visible, perhaps, in his play *The Birthday Party* – a piece for which I, personally, retain an enduring affection. Where the grannies in their flowery frocks used to arrive in their droves, and dear old Dad with his pipe fast asleep in a deckchair, and somewhere in the distance far along the esplanade, a Salvation Army band boisterously oompah-ing its way through 'The Dambusters' or some similar rousingly appropriate melody.

All of which has little to do with our story, I must admit. That one which may be called *The End Of Plumm*, if not *Exit Agent Windybuttocks*. Although it also must be accepted that many people in the services have tended to end up in remote and forgotten locations such as Woolsley Bay. Places which, like themselves, have seen better days. Almost as grey and indeterminate as, dare I say it, Max von Sydow. Standing alone by a tall Gothic window – often unperturbed – for hours at a time. With the only reminder of one's former existence – and indeed that of

Henry Plumm, RIP, who was with me every step of the way, for he had to be throughout our secondment in dear old dirty Guinness-drowned Dublin – being another faded portrait, this time on the lower landing.

And which turns out to be a likeness of yet another former resident – this time none other than an esteemed fellow thespian, very much feted in his time. Strikingly handsome, as it transpires – gazing out from behind that gilt frame with broad, high forehead and smooth, flat, boyish face. Looking every bit as sophisticated as he did during his heyday on ITV, distinguishing himself weekly in the profound and mysterious part of David Callan. A former Queen's employee and devotee – just like myself and you-know-who. And whose preoccupation, once again exactly like my own, has been that of maintaining extreme vigilance and ensuring the rigorous suppression of sedition. In other words, a solidly dutiful defender of the realm. And perhaps, once more in common with my own good self, however reluctant I may be to admit it, just that little bit, shall we say, eccentric.

However, let us not delude ourselves on this point. That, whatever distractions there may be – whether of the comical sort, as with Henry, or otherwise – one's chosen occupation has never been, at any time, anything other than difficult. And often downright perilous, to be honest.

Which explains why so many – including His Eminence Dr Windybuttocks-Slurp-Of-Woolsley-Bathroom – are, heartbreakingly, no longer with us. Then there is Ambrose – 'Control', that is, to accord him his proper official title. Yes, poor old Ambrose Roland – he too has passed away. Only last weekend, as a matter of fact. Stroke.

I came upon his obituary in *The Times* by chance – an impressive piece of writing, I thought: chiselled, precise, not unlike the man himself. It itemised, of course, all of his many official honours. Delicate decisions, obviously, have to be made involving recommendations for awards and dedications – former employees have to be trusted, or paid, not to publish memoirs, for example. And widows and orphans must be taken care of. Although this had not been an issue in the case of Ambrose Roland, Control.

He had been proud, or so at least he had publicly claimed, to be granted his honour. Celebrating, gustily, in my very own presence with a rendition of the tried and trusted late-night club favourite:

> Their assets, their accents, their undies laid bare
> Then, only then, can we apportion the share:
> BEMs may be spared for intelligence chores
> But OBEs are reserved for the silkiest drawers.

In the event, he had been awarded a KCMG, albeit towards the end of his career – in the prestigious Order of St Michael and St George, normally reserved for ambassadors, colonial governors and the like.

However, I digress – because I was telling you, wasn't I, about my old actor friend, the suave and diffident Edward Woodward.

'Usual, Chenny?' was how he used to greet me when we met in Ben Chitwell's, our habitual West End watering hole, just off Piccadilly.

Ben had been in drama school with Eddie – but, thank heavens, they never talked shop. And, as for myself, well you know me. As a matter of fact, you don't, but, as a rule of thumb, perhaps try returning to the eminence grise represented by old Max von Sydow. Who, throughout the course of his artistic life, had made caution almost a work of art. An approach which might have served Agent Windybuttocks well – especially during our time sur Bog. Yes, back in the anti-Côte d'Azur.

But no – I suppose he became like those we moved among. With it being a weakness he'd developed over time. 'The Paddy Factor', I used to call it – when I first became aware of his growing, excessive loquaciousness. Blathering, I believe it's called. Gossiping, yakking – call it what you will. Either way, in our profession, as ought to be obvious, it can often prove to be fatal. Which, in his case, it certainly appears to have done. Yes, that was what had undone old 'Windy' in the end.

'Come along, step into the car,' I had murmured that day in central London, as the car glided alongside the kerb. And in he went. Never suspecting a thing until the end – when he found himself, as I say, discharging copious bubbles, arse about face.

I hadn't expected it to be so easy. But, of course, hubris had always been another of his failings. To the end, remaining under the illusion that he was some kind of impenetrable, lone-wolf warrior. Well, goodness me. Step into the car. Come along, Henry.

Anyhow, as I was saying, about old Edward, my friend – although I'm certain many people will probably have forgotten, along with his acting career, Mr Woodward had also always been in possession of the most exquisitely fine tenor voice. And, without a doubt in my opinion, could easily have forged a career for himself in that aspect of showbusiness. During the period when he and I were associates – by which you may take it that I mean avid consumers of Hennessy VSOP brandy – he had released a number of long-playing records which were set to become extremely popular. Especially at the height of his television career.

I have never before spoken publicly of my association with Edward – discretion, as always, being uppermost in my mind. But – it chills me even yet to think of it – there could be no concealing any of one's private and most personal secrets from a certain strange and inscrutable individual who once resided in Woolsley Bay. And who, in fact, was my next-door neighbour. In room 202, in fact. Now, like so many, sadly deceased.

In spite of her wig, paint, rings, bracelets, necklace and, it seemed to me at least, a most cumbersome profusion of scarves and other gaudy accessories, she had seemed nimble, almost witch-like. According to her own testimony, the permanent resident of 202 had first begun her career as a fortune-teller in the late forties. 'Right here on the Bay', many years before, she had been spending 'never any less than twelve hours a day' in her clairvoyant's tent on the beach – emblazoned, as might be expected, with constellations of moons and stars.

There will be those, of course, who would evaluate her as amounting to little more than a lot of old flim-flam, poppycock and whimsy. But I would not be so sure. For a start, it did not take long before I became aware of the fact that, along with much else, she appeared to know a very great deal about me, had access to facts that she really ought not to have done. And there was that knowing manner of her steadfast scrutiny.

To be perfectly honest, the sheer breadth and extent of her knowledge – it turned out to be really quite distressing. Chilling, even.

'I know all about you, Mr Smiley Chenevix Meredith,' I remember her declaring sharply on one occasion, 'and your impressively practised modus operandi. Having people believe that you're of little consequence, crafting, as you do, a presence of the most dreary anonymity. A lacklustre fellow, that's who you'd most like to be – because it suits your purposes. Quite the opposite of your colourful friend Henry. No, you would prefer to be perceived as of scant consequence. Bona fide state actor, as you are, a good deal more than proficient in the art of disinformation and maximum deniability.'

It took me aback, as I'm sure you can imagine. As she took her time, dexterously arranging a pattern of playing cards on the baize surface of the table. And then, just for the briefest of moments, looked away.

'However, now, if you don't mind, I'd like to tell your future,' I found myself being warmly informed.

'You will be surrounded by gentlemen who mean to do you harm. But ultimately what's going to happen is that you're going to be blown up by your very own agent of destruction. Which, more or less, is what I should think you deserve – after what you will do to someone who, for many years, considered himself your confidant and friend.'

'Don't be ridiculous!' I found myself laughing boisterously, when, to my surprise, I looked up and saw that she was gone.

As off I went along the beach to mull over my thoughts.

'Does the name Valentine McBoan mean anything at all to you, Mr Meredith?' I could remember her querying softly – with the fixed intensity of her gaze, I must confess, having had the effect of making me stiffen. Because I really don't like it when I become – over-alert, I suppose. I quite loathe it, actually. But that's how it is – I fear that it is my nature. As it was now, while I plodded along the foreshore.

She had looked right at me, again across the table, her eyes penetrating. Ever so slowly, turning a jack of diamonds.

'Hmm,' she murmured – as if knowing that it got to me. 'Hmm, my dear fellow.'

As my natural instincts for self-protection and subterfuge came into play.

'Ah yes, now that you mention it! Val, old Val McBoan. He really was a great old character!' I beamed again. Secure in the fact that I was actually telling the truth. Because he was – incontrovertibly. A great old character.

Val McBoan had worked with the RTÉ Repertory Company in Dublin for years. As a matter of fact, while sitting there, I listed off all the shows I could remember in which he'd participated – down to the most minor of parts. What was sad about Val was that, in spite of what he might have thought himself (as far as he was concerned, he was Peter O'Toole!), he had never attained the leading man status to which he'd aspired.

However, let's face it, old McBoan was damned good at what he did – even on one occasion coming close to achieving the acclaim he'd sought for so long. With his portrayal of the writer

Brendan Behan in a dramatisation of *Confessions of an Irish Rebel*. First mounted in the year 1966, if memory serves correctly – two years after the author's tragic death.

Other notable productions with which he was involved, as I recall, include: *Ready When You Are, Seamus McMurtry, Bridie Boylan Married Pat Heffernan, Not Now, Alison Moody*. And, of course – for some the best of all – his long-running trademark radio show, the lunchtime soap opera *At Home With the Tomeltys*. In which he had played the part of Peter, or 'Paythur' as the Potato People prefer to pronounce it.

It has to be said that he really was a great old raconteur, Val McBoan. And, of course, although as a fact it may not have been very widely known, something of an impressive cinephile. Oh yes. Val knew his 'flicks'.

The first I knew of that was in Minty's – the theatrical pub that we all frequented just off Grafton Street, near the office. He was already in full flow as I came breezing in the door. Expatiating on yet another 'continental' film. *Torso*, it was entitled. He was wearing his customary brown coat – an ash-stained, beaten-up, houndstooth sports jacket with leather elbow patches. Stroking his chin as he paused for protracted periods. Before launching into yet another torrent of admittedly knowledgeable words. I never saw anyone smoke so furiously – you could barely make him out behind the billowing blue fug. Minty's, as always, was packed to the rafters. Not that he would have noticed – or cared, as he continued.

'Oh, a piece of unmitigated trash beyond all shadow of doubt,' Val went on, 'but, as always, Chenny, me auld flower, as tends to be the way with these European directors, containing some small but significant aspects of interest – influences shamelessly borrowed from the masters. This one in particular had all the routine characteristics of the *giallo* genre, characterised by extended murder sequences featuring excessive bloodletting, stylish camerawork and unusual musical arrangements – from what might be described as "crime jazz" to sleazy bossa nova played in a melodic and multi-signatured style, with fuzzy Rhodes piano and Hammond organ remaining prominent. Like a lot of such attempts, I have to confess I admired its impertinence!'

Some of the things that McBoan would come out with. It genuinely never ceased to amaze me.

Perhaps not unexpectedly, he had viewed the feature flick concerned in the notorious Majestic Cinema, which was situated in Mountjoy Square and represented that infuriating little backward town's sole approximation of what might, at something of a stretch, be designated an 'underground arthouse'. In spite of the fact that, in truth, it wasn't a great deal more than a flea-infested soft-porn venue, which hosted all-nighters but had become a reeking dosshouse, distinguished by the presence of tramps and the acrid aroma of Jeyes Fluid disinfectant.

In common with the neighbourhood where it was located, its peeling, saturated walls of baroque and gold echoed a time of long-since-vanished splendour. A gilded palace fallen on hard times, where the rent was paid by art and 'continental' features such as Peter Barnes' *The Ruling Class*, Peter Nichols' *A Day in the Death of Joe Egg* and Joe Orton's *Entertaining Mr Sloane*. Often on the same bill as *Torso*, *Blue Movie Blackmail* and *Truck Stop Women*. If you could tolerate the ammonia stench that issued from the lavatories, along with the flickering strip-lights and filthy, fly-spotted windows, the Majestic Cinema was a home from home.

As we chatted away there, half-choked by the swirling smoke of Minty's and having to roar to be heard, little did Val McBoan or myself suspect, indeed possess the slightest inkling, that the Majestic Cinema was also destined to be the location where some of the best people I have ever known, whether in Ireland or anywhere else, were going to meet their deaths. Being blown to pieces by a savage anti-personnel device.

Placed by – well, let's not get into any of that, shall we? Not right at this moment, at any rate. Perhaps later on. Because here at the end of summer – with all the cars having at last made their tired but satisfied way back to the city – it's something I should really prefer to forget.

But that, of course, is easier said than done.

CARNAGE IN CITY ESTIMATED AT LEAST THIRTEEN DEAD

I had been particularly affected, I remember, by Máiréad Curtin's photograph on the front page of the *Sunday Champion*. Which showed her wired up to a variety of monitors, IV drips and tubes – with it already plainly evident that the poor girl's chances of survival were minimal to non-existent. And which, at no point – ever! – you have got to believe me, had been my intention. With that unfortunate episode back in the Arabian Gulf, expedited along with Gracefield Urquhart (Lt), being the only other one of such a bitterly regrettable character.

However essential.

And which had occurred not long after I'd taken my leave, fortunately for the very last time, of Queen's College, Oxford. When, largely due to the carelessness of Urquhart, we'd got ourselves in a spot of difficulty with an associate, I suppose is one way he might be described.

Hussain was his name – or 'Bud', as he'd generally become known to the squaddies in the barracks. Yes, there goes comical, genial, hail-fellow-well-met Budr Hussain. Who ran an illicit backstreet booze shop in the village – where he habitually turned a blind eye if you slipped a couple of riyal into his grasping paw and ushered some local floozy out the back.

At least until he turned against us – so far as I could make out on account of some possibly imagined slight. Of which Urquhart would have been more than capable, I willingly concede. In any case, little fool saw fit to contact the barracks and report certain ill-advised errors of the commander of Reconaissance Platoon (Recce) – even going so far as to name the local girl in question. Who couldn't, if I recall, have been more than sixteen years of age.

Being implicated, I didn't have much choice, watching as Urquhart – having successfully lured him to the compound – set about wiring him to a battery, whipping him this way and that, all the while doing the best we could to get him to admit it.

But not so much as a word could we prise out of the lank-haired miserable ingrate – which was how, I suppose, it happened in the end. Not that I'm particularly proud of it, but at least it was quick, the implement chosen scarcely making a sound. As neither did he. A mere whimper.

We deposited him in a crate of fish along the wharf, covered in blocks of ice that were already melting, exposed in the heat. Breathing his last, I regret to say. So far as I know, there wasn't anything more about it. The whole blessed affair represented an entirely unfortunate and quite unnecessary episode – especially considering how popular 'Bud' had been. Not least among ourselves. It pains me, even yet, to have to recollect it – with it being, as I say, the only really surgically clinical, unemotional decision I've ever taken in such matters. Irrespective of wherever it was that I found myself.

Gracie Urquhart, of course, had always thought of himself as something of a comedian, and for years afterwards, whenever we'd meet, drunk or sober, at some point in the evening he would inevitably catch my eye and chuckle as he muttered under his breath: 'Right a bit, left a bit, up a bit, down a bit! Bernie the Bolt!'

Referring, of course, to the means by which the intemperate Hussain had ultimately met his end – the treacherous little judgemental bastard, after all we'd done for him. Which, at the lieutenant's suggestion, due to its being untraceable, in fact had been a crossbow.

Familiar, of course, from the popular Bob Monkhouse game-show of the time, *The Golden Shot* – the source, obviously, of my erstwhile colleague's amusement. And which had involved what was called the 'Tele-Bow', a crossbow attached to a television camera guided by a contestant. The most difficult task was to fire the crossbow bolt to cut a fine thread holding a small door closed. Breaking the thread – or in this case, oesophagus – opened the door, producing a shower of golden coins. As, in a way, we had done ourselves – after a fashion at least. Or, as Urquhart had mischievously described it, heading back towards the town, 'an absolute bloody red penny cascade!'

All, however, at this stage, best forgotten. For, after all, I've got old Windy to dispose of.

Chapter 2

!!!

Ah yes indeed, !!! is right.
You can say it once or twice or all you like – over and over again, if you so wish. For very appropriate indeed such an exclamation might be – what with some of the events which have occurred throughout the years. All of which involved both myself and poor old Henry, RIP. Back in that dear old Dublin, where we were posted long ago. Where the thing that struck me most was the rain – which never seemed to cease. And I don't think it could have been my imagination – for Henry had often passed comment to that effect. In fact had conferred upon it a nickname. Watertown, he called it. Which I suppose is ironic, considering how he ended up himself, base over apex and with his chops chock-full of the stuff.

Ha ha. No, I don't mean it. Look at us – a pair of agents! Dumped over there, at Her Majesty's service. Whenever we'd get down – which I have to say was often – I'd do my best to raise my counterpart's spirits. Yes, back in old Watertown, city of dreary damp limestone and gurgling drains.

'My dear puppy,' I would often exclaim, 'I fear you might have a tendency to underestimate the endurance of old Pat and Biddy. I am not at all certain that you have what it takes for this position. Are you going to last the distance, puppy?'

In spite of my genuine concern, however, he did. So thank heaven for that. Even if things mightn't have worked out exactly as I'd planned. Because it hadn't been my intention that anyone ought to lose their life – not unnecessarily, at least.

But there you are.

'A bloody curse on this crepuscular backwater!' he never ceased complaining, shaking his newspaper stiffly in the back bar of the Scotch House hostelry, positioned between a portrait of the Manchester United team that had succeeded the tragic 'Busby Babes' of Munich and a truly hideous engraving of Mary, Queen of the Gael.

'Can anyone tell me what sin it is I have committed to merit such a cruel and unforgiving sentence?' Prior to embarking on yet another of his fiery denunciations, which really used to amuse me. This time it was the turn of none other than Nye Bevan – really quite unforgivable comments on the Labour Minister's less-than-recent remarks on the Conservative Party. Alluding to them as 'lower than vermin' and attacking the non-socialist press in Britain as the 'most prostituted' in the world.

There were occasions – and this was one of them – when his countenance would grow so livid I genuinely feared that poor old Plumm might sustain a stroke.

'There are times since arriving here,' he would typically continue, 'when I remind myself of those innumerable wafer-thin "colonels" living on five hundred a year with their dusky mistresses, the flotsam and jetsam of our receding empire. Without the benefit of the mistress, of course.'

'But at least,' I offered hopefully, 'we do find ourselves positioned in the field, employed in the role of full-time operatives, rather than competent staff officers sitting, office-politicking and dreaming in SIS room thirty-nine or forty. Hmmph?'

He simply grunted and made no effort at reply.

I myself had already been in the country for over ten years and had succeeded – in so far as might be possible – in coming to terms with my situation. Thereby doing the best I could to assist Henry Percival Plumm in that regard.

'To create a service,' I suggested behind a floating cloud of cigarette smoke, 'to counter their methods and inclinations requires an intimate knowledge of their constitutions, methods and resources. Which can only be obtained by experience and a prolonged study of their habits, pamphlets and documentary evidence available.'

Plumm himself hadn't arrived until, why it must have been close on six or seven years later, in 1965 or thereabouts. At the personal insistence of Commander Ambrose Roland, or Roley as we called him – head of the section at the time.

'We've been acquainted of various rumblings. Something regarding a planned assault along the border. It might be nothing, just Paddy Potato running off at the mouth again – but best to be on the safe side all the same.'

I remember it so well – meeting him at the passenger terminal in Dún Laoghaire – known, of course, as Kingstown when it had belonged to us.

'I don't know about you, Mr Plumm,' I recall remarking as I took his case, 'but I could bloody well use a drink.'

He nodded eagerly and off we sped in the direction of my favourite established watering hole, the Scotch House, located on Burgh Quay, where the gulls screeched fiercely high above the Liffey at low tide.

'To Her Majesty,' we declared, sotto voce in the gloom, with old Plummy professing himself amused, if not even a little embarrassed by this sudden, unexpected exhibition of really quite unnecessary jingoism – but still holding up his glass before bursting into laughter.

He had the facility of reciting relevant official documents by heart – which he did now, for no other reason than that of our own amusement.

IRISH REPUBLICAN ARMY
Political Attitude

Principal aim is the reunificiation of all Ireland in a Catholic Irish Republic through military means.

Headquarters

Dublin

Regional Organisation and Concentrations

Although based in Southern Ireland, strongly represented in Co. Donegal and border counties. Its main concentrations are in the Catholic areas of Belfast other than the Lower Falls area.

Membership: Strength and Composition

Not accurately known. Estimated at between 1,200 and 1,500 either trained or under training to bear arms or engage in acts of sabotage. Organised in small, military-type units under command of local brigade group. These are supported by unknown numbers of Southern-controlled Republican clubs.

Activity Patterns

Responsible for numerous acts of sabotage against government installations and public utilities in Northern Ireland.

IRISH REPUBLICAN ARMY – LEFT-WING FACTION
Political Attitude

Marxist-orientated socialist, Republican, aimed at securing the unification of North and South Ireland by political means, reinforced by military activity.

Headquarters

Dublin

Regional Organisation and Concentrations

Groups throughout Southern Ireland. Main concentrations in Northern Ireland are in the Lower Falls Area of Belfast and parts of Londonderry.

Membership: Strength and Composition

Not accurately known. Estimated at between 600 and 700 active members capable of bearing arms. A greater number, members of various Republican clubs throughout Northern Ireland, are in support.

Activity Patterns

Very active politically in the field of civil rights and militarily in opposition to British security forces.

ULSTER VOLUNTEER FORCE

Political Attitude

Violently anti-Republican. Its main intention is to preserve the status quo by the use of violence if necessary.

Headquarters

Not known.

Membership: Strength and Composition

Not known.

Activity Patterns

Bombings were frequently carried out under the guise of IRA outrages to provoke a Protestant reaction and to heighten tension between the communities.

Other Remarks

It is doubtful whether the UVF has any genuine corporate existence, and the name, which is a historically emotive one in Ulster, provides cover for a number of virtually autonomous groups, largely criminal in character.

'There's really just one thing I'd like to say at this point,' I heard myself begin, loudly blowing my nose into a hankie, 'and that is, as the great Clausewitz has observed: in war are all acts of philanthropy a gross and pernicious error!'

'Is that a fact, my friend?' I heard him chiming wickedly as he sank what must have been his fifth or sixth golden Hennessy. 'Quite the philosopher, aren't you? So here's health to our Queen, that long may she prosper along with ourselves – you and I, my dear Chenny Chenny Chen!'

Beyond the window, as we sipped our libations, a squad of great grey herring gulls swooped over O'Connell Street, where numerous thin itinerant children were begging. As brown Anna Livia went sluggishly flowing past, with the birds still shrieking high above the stink of low tide. At the end of the counter the elderly, grey-haired barman continued polishing glasses, patiently whistling a scarcely audible, subdued, melancholic tune.

For one reason or another, I seem to remember, I must have drawn some attention to his speech, for I can vividly recall the dramatic and unexpected reddening of Henry Plumm's cheeks. I think I had remarked on his accent – but in a not at all insensitive manner – at least I thought so. I had not expected him to take offence. It had just amused me, that's all – the way he elected to pronounce his own name. With the episode illuminating an almost attractive glimmer of fragility.

'It's not my fault I have this accent,' I heard him complain bitterly. 'I've had to live with it ever since my days in that blasted Mandeville House College.'

'Did you attend old Mandy too?' I mused abstractedly, but clearly not all that particularly interested – since I was already more than aware of the fact from his files.

And, as for Mandy, I knew all about it. For had my so-called uncle, the former drill sergeant Leslie Courtney, over many years not laboured there? Initially I had adored 'Uncle' Leslie Courtney – a wonder to me, as a boy, that man was. I had absolutely worshipped the fellow. It was a pity he died – but then, of course, these things happen.

Drank paraquat in the boathouse, apparently – or so I had been told. The very same boathouse that, sadly I suppose, we both knew well. I knew that his suicide had taken place in the aftermath of his dismissal from Mandy. Which, really and truly, had only been a matter of time. Given what the rogue was up to with the students. Poor thing.

Then the most abrupt and unexpected thought occurred to me – as I raised my glass and elbowed Henry ever so gently in the ribs.

'Speaking of Mandy, my dear puppy,' I suggested, 'perhaps one day you and I might get together – along with a selected number of our former school colleagues. And, with all the fervour of which we find ourselves capable, together recite our glorious school anthem. Do you approve?'

I cleared my throat and commenced in my reasonably acceptable tenor voice:

Are you grieving over Mandeville unleaving?
Leaves, like the things of man
you with your fresh thoughts care for, can you?

Goldengrove, Goldengrove,
Fare thee well!

I lifted my head, becoming aware that we'd been noticed. As the barman jerked his thumb towards a sign directly over my head.

NO SINGING

Difficult as it might be to believe, the barman's name was actually Paddy Murphy. Henry said he couldn't believe his ears. Scarcely two or three hours in the city and what does he find?

'For heaven's sake – Paddy Murphy! I give up.'

But it has to be admitted he was a kindly old soul, and, as on many previous occasions, ever so helpful. Something which I considered as we sat there watching him gliding along behind the counter like a ghost, clad in a grubby, white, knee-length apron.

'No,' I whispered to Henry, 'old Murphy – he never gives me any grief at all. Just lets me sit here any time I want, minding my own business.'

'I'm not surprised,' Henry said, nursing his cognac, 'that he doesn't bother you. Because, to be perfectly honest, to me he looks like he's more or less dead already and wouldn't be in possession of the energy required.'

There was a band, finishing up playing outside the gentlemen's convenience: 'The Floral Dance'. Crucifying it, actually.

'So much for the musical nation we've heard so much about,' I heard Henry mumble irascibly under his breath.

'Believe you me, you'll soon get used to such surprises,' I heard myself respond, catching a glimpse of the flyblown wooden clock, mounted above a yellowing photo of some backwoods football team – each one of them built like 'blooming brick shit'ahses', as Gracie Urquhart was fond of remarking long ago over in Aden. At any rate, I think he did.

'Harrumph!' grunted Henry, sneezing loudly before shoving a massive handkerchief back into his blazer pocket. There ensued then a protracted period of silence.

Tick-tock.

Tick-tock.

As the wooden clock went: bong.

Already it seemed an absolute age since my own personal leavetaking of the city of London. And here now beside me was old Windybuttocks-of-Bathroom. Only just arrived, in the Year of Our Lord 1965. Not, I could tell already, having the faintest apprehension at all of just what it was he might, in fact, be in for.

But, as I was soon to discover, that, whatever else he might have been, old undercover operative Henry Percival McPlump OBE (in his dreams) would soon prove to be the most engaging character. And, unlike myself, quite the flâneur.

A most energetic, flamboyant and outgoing character. Who, within a very short time indeed, had managed to surround himself with the most attractive cohort of comparably life-loving, ambitious and colourful fellows, all, obviously, associated with the profession.

Most of whom, of course, he had encountered through 'the Agency' – not Her Majesty's, of course, but its sister, I suppose one might say, established for the routine purpose of dissembling, etc., among other functions. Yes, that was largely where he met them all – in Grafton Mews, just off the main commercial thoroughfare. The Grafton Theatrical Agency – haunted by the aforementioned Valentine McBoan, along with many others. Whose names remain too numerous to mention. But whose number included – at various intervals coming pounding up the stairs – Charlie Kerrins, Maurice Norton and the hugely popular star of Ireland's much-loved afternoon radio soap opera *At Home With the Tomeltys* – the one and only Hugh 'Barney' McRoarty. Collectively representing a really terrific little gang with whom he declared himself privileged to be associated – once I began succeeding, obviously now with old Plummy's help – in once and for all establishing my long-gestating bolt-hole in the Dublin theatrical and bohemian world, such as it was back then.

Because poor old Turnip-and-Turf Land at the time – it really was the most godawful, hopelessly deprived place: both culturally and economically. Yes, it really had been the most difficult time.

And I have to be honest and state here quite plainly that before arriving anywhere near Erin-go-Bragh or whatever the devil those old Potato Heads wanted to call it – I wasn't really 100 per cent sure if I'd ever be able to get over Bea. My poor departed, loving, darling wife. Beatrice. Beatrice, my beloved – my life's sole companion. She had passed away, you see – quite torturously, in fact – of cervical cancer. Took her over fifteen months to die. But I was by her side each and every day. Or as many of them as I could humanly manage.

It must be said that the pair of us, we were happy. Not for all of the time that we spent together – which was close on thirty-five years, in fact – but as much as any ordinary couple had a right to expect. If nothing else – and Beatrice herself would have been the first to acknowledge this – I made her laugh. 'Yes, you definitely did succeed in amusing me, my dear husband Chenevix Meredith. Whatever else, that much most emphatically cannot be denied.'

There were one or two associates who, perhaps a little unkindly, had suggested that she bore a significantly strong resemblance to Doris of *On the Buses* fame. I suppose because of the perennial apron, which she literally never took off, in combination with those hideous milk-bottle glasses. Dear Sweet Specky, I used to call her sometimes – echoing, I suppose I would have to acknowledge, some measure of my teasing of 'brick-red' Henry. Certainly in his cups.

Brick-red, I mean. There were times when I thought he was going to explode. Veins would protrude in the centre of his forehead. Large blue ones. Just the very same as poor old Bea.

'Ah, Bay-thruss! Auld Ploddy McDonaghy, what am I goin' to do wit yew a tawl a tawl!' I would, occasionally, quite out of the blue, declare. She was Irish, you see. Although you wouldn't have had to be an agent or a detective to deduce that. Not with those bow legs and the unfortunate profusion of freckles on her poor pasty face. I couldn't quite properly imitate the accent. But she didn't seem to mind – or at least she said she didn't. And, in actual fact, on occasions found it somewhat liberating. Maybe because of the dull lives we led. But anyhow, she often laughed – and continued to do so, right up until the time of her death. After which I missed her so.

Heavens, could it be quiet when I found myself alone now in the house. With Beatrice gone, not a single whisper. No more huffing and puffing, squawking and complaining, 'Lift up your feet!' No more sweeping or hoovering. Which she always insisted upon – quite unnecessarily, at least in my view. Screwing up her nose in that maddening and wholly disapproving way that she had. I remember it as though it were yesterday.

This was how she would generally commence – just that little bit provocatively, but not so much as you could identify it.

'Mr C, The Mystery Man'. That was how she liked to address me. 'Mr Chenevix, "The Mystery Man" – is that how I'm expected to address you now? Or are you styling yourself otherwise, perhaps, on this occasion?'

'Mr Mystery,' she would retort acidly. With that, regrettably, sometimes being her way. As I have told you. In the aftermath of which I would find myself musing: 'You know, she really is lucky, my nearest and dearest. That I'm not, actually, John Reginald Christie or some of these other peripheral members of society. Otherwise she could have found herself ending up underneath the patio.'

Like poor Joanne Vollmann, God rest her sweet and beautiful soul. About whom more later, as they say. When the time, as they also say, is right.

But, going back to Beatrice, in spite of the sunny times, we'd sometimes experience the bitterest, most vicious rows imaginable.

'You are making a very big mistake,' I would say, 'yes, a very big one indeed, my dear.'

But then she would recruit that old tried-and-trusted – what I like to call her 'Cabbagehead' charm – that old vitality they speak of in the eyes. D'Oirish twinkle. You know what I mean. And I'd hear her calling out to me from the kitchen, 'I wonder, bejapers, would me husband be partial till a scone now with strawberry jam?' Which, of course, she knew I absolutely love! 'Maybe, perhaps, with a grand wee blob of butter?'

And then, just the very same as poor Joanne Vollmann, God rest her, I'd become light-headed and melt in her arms. And maybe she in mine. Such a lovely girl as she could be at times, dearest old lovely specky Beatrice. Bay-thruss Coogan-McDonaghy, to accord her her full title, Baroness of Turnip-on-Shannon. May our God this night gaze once more down and upon the meadow of sheep where they graze, her loving head attain its final slumber. As the Right Reverend Passmore Stout, an old acquaintance of both Henry Plumm and I during the course of our tour of duty, might have observed. Had he been engaged to perform the official duties. Which, thankfully, he wasn't. The slavering, emotionally intemperate, unimaginative, donkey-headed buffoon.

I didn't want any of that ilk there. All the same, it was good of Commander Roland to have taken time out – to indicate solidarity, if nothing else. Especially since, as I know, he himself hadn't been in the best of health. And had better things to do than attend yet another funeral. But yes – there he was. Standing beneath his umbrella in the rain, with those long, greyish-silver, winding tendrils of hair reaching down his neck – bearing a not at all insignificant resemblance to the hopelessly discredited and inept former Labour politician Michael Foot. If that is someone whom you might remember. Although, at this late stage, I'm sure few do.

Any more than I do myself remember clearly those drifting phrases which intermittently return in the night, echoing the remonstrations of one's former spouse. Although it couldn't be her. Because my Beatrice was not what you'd call a 'harridan'. Occasionally, they can even be relentless. To the extent that I'm tempted to cover my ears.

'Don't think I don't know what you're up to – coming home here at all hours of the night. I know too well your secret desires and the tricks you get up to in order to keep them concealed. Wandering at all hours in those public parks.'

Tssk! Thunderous apologies for these unpardonable digressions, puppies.

And without further delay, returning, in your company, to the once imposing fastness of salt-wracked 'Old Mouldy', i.e. the premises here in good old Woolsley Bay. Where it really is so pleasant – a humble, albeit weathered, paradise by the ocean. With very few sounds to be heard about the place, apart from the shuffling and muttering and mumbling of the now-arisen Madame Rosie 'Tattyfilarious' Dixon.

Who, with her panoply of chins and really quite attractive deep-set hazel eyes, for me never fails to recall the illustrious star of such music-hall-inspired gems as *The Square Peg*, *School for Scoundrels* and *Make Mine Mink*. In other words, the distinguished Hattie Jacques.

Yes, wobbling Rosie Madame Jacques who, in spite of all her atrocious snoring and copious consumption – and she could, as the Spuddies of old Erin no doubt would remark, without turning a hair have drunk Lough Erne dry – it has to be admitted never once has she disturbed me at my work. Aware, as she is, that I am in the process of preparing my memoirs. The only time I see her, generally speaking, being at breakfast. She even brings me supper late at night – shuffling off down along the corridor without so much as even a whisper. Except on occasion maybe the odd little humming of a faintly familiar tune from the old days – the theme from *Bulldog Drummond*, perhaps – maybe even *Round the Horne*.

However, I was telling you, wasn't I, about dear old Henry Plump, RIP. I can just imagine if he was still alive and happened to hear that. 'Don't call me Plump!'

Yes, Plump, dearest puppy, sub-Billy Bunter. And long-time esteemed former associate in the vicinity of dear old, dirty, conspiratorial Dublin back in the fanlit amber of long ago. In that rainswept city of perpetual drizzle and creaky arthritic bones. To whom I remember bidding goodbye on that very first day of his arrival – in the Year of Our Lord 1965 – in the doorway of the Scotch House bar on Burgh Quay after we'd had a skinful.

Like some reverse emigrant bursting out of his buttoned-up raincoat, catching the bus to his appointed digs on Hollybank Road – located in a leafy suburb to the north of the city, in Lower Drumcondra, a place occasionally used by the Agency.

Principally for new arrivals. Yes, that was old Plummy's first introduction to the place they called 'Éire' (pronounced 'Ay-Ruh') – or 'The Atoll of Despair', as Ambrose used to call it.

Not that old Roley was alone in his less than uplifting apprehension of the place. For in the year 1965, although the so-called country was already over four decades old, so far as I could ascertain, there appeared to be a general undisputed consensus that after all that time, poor old 'Éire', or whatever it happened to be called, seemed pretty much on the point of vanishing without trace. Yes – quite literally disappearing off the face of the earth.

'A kind of Calcutta of Western Europe,' dear Plumm used to say.

But now – especially since Brexit – all of that seems like centuries ago. Almost medieval. As I'm sure I do myself. Even old Rosie has suggested from time to time that she finds my manner just that 'little bit old-fashioned'. Which hits the spot hard – what with herself being no spring chicken. But I'm of an age (seventy-eight next birthday) when such perceptions cause little or no offence. Indeed, as a matter of fact, more than anything they tend to amuse me.

'Aye! Dat me, alroight!' you'll often hear me respond on such occasions. The very same as Henry used to – and I really can reproduce his voice. Why, I'm nearly as good a mimic as he. As good as that old Plummy affecting to be Irish.

'Aye! Dat me, alroight, so 'tis, hur hur!'

Delivering the mocking brogue of my former acquaintance as he used to do when we drank together – back yonder on the shores of that beaten-up, out-of-date atoll.

It's hard not to chuckle. I mean, it really is. I have to cover my face with my hand.

'Just what are we going to do?' I squeal. 'Our famous darling Henry Plumm. The world will be a quiet place without him, that's for sure!'

The one to miss him most would be Maurice Norton – our mutual friend. I seem to hear him calling out his name – just as he used to when we'd meet in Minty's bar.

More than any of them, I think that good old Maurice – he really used to enjoy all those rumours that had begun to circulate around the city as regards the true intentions of poor old Plummers and myself. Or, to accord us our proper titles – now lovingly rendered in gold leaf on the office door: Dublin's Premier Theatrical Agents. Certain 'whisperings' that included assertions that we had been recruited by Her Majesty's government for the purpose of – I mean, can you believe it? – strategic disruption, elaborate deception and downright flat denial.

'Now we know,' a particular barfly by the name of Marty Furlong – a former stagehand who hadn't been employed for years – had muttered behind his hand at the counter one night, 'what was meant by Harold Wilson when he promised to transform Britain from a nation of gentlemen into a world of players. Yes, we can see now what he meant – and the kind of "players" he had in mind.'

I used to laugh whenever he'd make these less-than-veiled declarations. As, if I'm honest, did practically every other right-thinking individual in Minty's bar, otherwise known as the Minstrels' Rest. Which was where I'd first become aware of these random imputations.

'The Intelligence Men,' I – so brazenly! – used to laugh it off. 'Yes! That's me and old Henry, beyond the shadow of a doubt! Living our lives as though it were a playlet scripted, say, by Leonard Pinter. "Cor, mate! This bomb here in the front looks like it's going to go off before we reach our destination! Ah, go on out of that, will you, Henry, me auld mucker – sure, after all bedad and bejasus, don't we have anudder one de very same in de back!"'

Boom boom. Wot a larf.

But if that was memorable, it was nothing to Charlie Kerrins' 'counterreaction' soliloquy. Offering an admirable defence on our behalf – only this time more volubly. Yes, Kerrins' speech from the dock, it really was most effective and eloquent.

Regarding a certain historical episode he had elected to describe as 'The Paythurlux Massacray', improvised for the sole single purpose of embarrassing yet another ubiquitous drunkard. Who was now, at this point, facing me fiercely and in the process of making further outlandish accusations. Of what might best be described as the predictable, pedantic character.

'You needn't think you'll pull the wool over my eyes, you slimy, limey English bastards,' he spat, before elaborating expansively, although still not making a great deal of sense. The subjects largely featured Saxon perfidy and skullduggery, with a great deal of attention being paid to 'bogus agencies'.

However, Mr Kerrins, I am happy to be in a position to report, succeeded commendably in 'closing the fellow's gob once and for all', as he'd subsequently, and colourfully, phrased it himself.

'Aye, this would have been around the time of the Croppy Boy,' Charlie Kerrins began, 'if you ever happened to hear of him – maybe even a wee bit later. Well wasn't there a "stirring",

God bless us, down, I think, in County Carlow. Aye, a riot of sorts that was got up by a band of brigands – in a little garrison town as went by the name of Paythurlux Cross. And, glory be to God, if it wasn't a relative of this very man here, aye, Mr Chenevix Meredith standing there beside you. Wasn't it his very own self, in his capacity of field marshal, that was drafted in for the purpose of putting down the dangerous mob – mudcaked Fenian Patricks, without exception, all. Would you like to hear about it, friend? Because it seems to be by your expression that you would – fond as you are of trickery and the bellicose arts. Not to mention making claims with divil the bit of substantiation. Anyway, God help us, weren't the 15th Hussars drafted into poor old Paythurlux – and what they did, the rascals, and didn't do. Slashing and burning for all they were worth and them drunk till the nines in the middle of all they were doing. Look! Here comes a worker, sabred to the gills. Did you ever in your life see so much blood? For I'll wager that you didn't. God bless us, look over yonder and what do you see – yes, he of the thin Saxon lip and implacably ruthless eye. Sure, who else could it be – after all, what else have the British government got to do, aye, and its enforcers, lackies billeted above in Whitehall – only dispatch good old Pater Chenevix the First over to Carlow with his instructions in his pocket. Aye, and what are they – only to start the "stirring" and then, like they'd told him, read the grumbling mob the auld Riot Act from a window.

'Over there, look – a woman trampled by a horse. And such a hail of bricks that's coming flying. The Yeomanry had already dispatched rebels in their hundreds – some of the soldiers were easing their horses' girths, others adjusting their accoutrements, and several more wiping their sabres. Several mounds of human beings still remained where they had fallen, crushed down and smothered. Some of these poor creatures were gasping for breath – others moaning pitifully. With just as many who would never breathe again.'

It was a stunning performance. I thought his eyes were going to pop out. But then Charlie Kerrins, he was one of Ireland's premier character actors. As on he went, with blood-red image mounting upon blood-red image – evoking powerfully the sound of ringing steel and pleading, gut-opened women fleeing across Sacred Heart Square. And it getting worse and worse, rivers, indeed, running out of wounds right behind them as they raced.

'As Pater Chenevix – this man's antecedent – sweeps the sheet of the Riot Act in the air and laughs and laughs till his stomick is darn near fit to burst – and him thinking of all the heads that'll soon adorn the castle walls, not to mention the quality of the seed and breed that's set to follow him down through the generations – and they up to the very same tricks and shenanigans, even down to disseminating the most worsest pack of lies – that they've given up disembowelment for the giddy attractive life of the theatre! Do youse hear me now?'

The bold Charlie – by this stage he himself was in stitches.

'As onward plough the cavalry through struggling bodies and snorting animals. Then along comes the 18th Infantry Regiment – led by none other than this man's great-great-grandfather, yes the one and only Major General Pater Chenevix Meredith. But of course it is – because, after all, have you not nailed his truthful colours – is that not the case, my friend? The very same as you've done to every damned slaughtering military Saxon as ever soaked the fields of old Ireland with your flowing crimson fluid. Bejapers, such a slaughterhouse as old Paythurlux has turned into – small wonder they made a ballad and it every inch the equal of the poor old "Croppy Boy". This is a Waterloo for you – a Waterloo for Paddy and Brigid – now die, you eternal scum! As poor old Paythurlux turns into your very own Paythurloo!'

At which point he thrust out his chest and bawled out in a lusty tenor voice:

Oh Payhturlux, where are you
In grim mire lying swathed
Your guts for garters oozing sweetly
Rivers red in old Car-loo!

He called for another drink, snapping his fingers as he tipped me a wink.

'Yes, it was you did that – wasn't it, Chenevix? But of course it was – for, after all, you're English! At least according to that loudmouth over there at the counter, Marty Furlong! But of course it was Chenny the cold-blooded Yeoman – even though he wasn't even born yet! Aye, him and the seed and breed of him, along with every other limey that's fit to walk. Or so our learned friend Furlong would have us believe. So with a lineage the like of that, is it any wonder your superiors would send you over for to make this poor man miserable – setting up agencies to keep tabs on Biddy and Pat?'

He bawled anew as the former stagehand Marty Furlong, flush-faced and humiliated, commenced a sullen pilgrimage towards the door. With this to say before he finally made his exit: 'No end to their chicanery, and you've gone and fallen for it again, haven't you? Yes, poor old Pat and Biddy, always wanting to think the best – anything to be liked and well thought of, you lot. Which, of course, they're more than aware of, that and all your other weaknesses. Yes, they'll tell you, the British, that it is a national characteristic of theirs to dislike and distrust secret organisations working on their behalf in peacetime. But despite that, their national interest will often override such caution and inherent reluctance. British covert policy is defensive and not aggressive, they'll insist. Such a collection of innocent babes. Man alive, you credulous fucking pricks!'

'Hey! Don't be like that, Marty! I'm sure Mr Meredith would like to buy you a drink – for it's not very often we get to meet the likes of you – Marty Furlong, our homegrown spycatcher, ha ha!'

'Maybe you should try and go fuck yourself, Kerrins!' shot back the disgruntled ex-stagehand. 'Might be an idea to try doing that!'

The bar was alive with whoops.

'I'll see you get what's coming to you yet!' were the last words spoken that night by Marty Furlong.

Not that it mattered, because Charlie wasn't listening. Being much too busy informing me that he 'loved' me, and not to be bothered with 'morons' the like of that. I'll never forget his voice. It was wonderful, as he started up again.

> With standards high, they made their way
> Onward through the falling dew
> The Yeomen bloodied but still proud
> Across the corpse-laden fields
> Of old Carl-oo!

He clapped me heartily on the broad of the back.

'You can't, in the end, beat an auld song. But, in the end, sure, that's all it is. Who cares about history or what happened in the auld times? Am I right, do you think, good old Chenny – in thinking that?'

'You are absolutely one hundred per cent,' I returned, as we set about some serious consumption of gin and vodka. And that, more or less, was the end of 'The Paythurlux Massacray'.

Which Val McBoan, later on, suggested ought to have been incorporated into a stage show, so hilarious had it proved. Not to mention succeeding in having the desired effect. Just as a drink – a double gin, as it happened – came sliding along the mahogany counter towards my good self. Before coming to rest, with a wobble, at my elbow. And I looked across the counter to see Val McBoan's upraised thumb.

'The bloody effing Paythurlux Massacray – the best I've ever heard in Minty's, as God is my judge, this frigging night, I swear – and that's saying something! And one thing is for sure – it sure did close that idiotic eejit's mouth – covert operations, in the name of God did you ever hear the like! Haw haw haw haw bleeding haw-whoop!'

Yes, it had certainly been a night to remember.

But more about good old Minty's later – legendary hangout of weathered thespians and self-styled lefties, it has to be acknowledged that, by any standards, it definitely was a watering hole to be envied. With the idea of that blooming old Henry Percival Plumm, poor fellow, never mind myself, being anything other than a bumbling, bibulous – albeit entertaining – theatrical representative inducing bouts of hysterical laughter in so many of those in the profession who had become our closest companions.

Principally, I would have to say, the aforementioned Maurice Norton.

'Some chance!' he used to say. 'Way too old-fashioned. You'd stick out like a sore thumb!'

Even in Dublin, I presumed he was implying. And it was true. Why, even dear old Bea – God rest her poor heart, as the Spuddies like to say – baggy-bottomed slacks and frumpy blouse notwithstanding, she actually seemed more modern and up-to-date than I did.

That, at least, was how it seemed to me. With the speed things appeared to be moving at back then. What with the Beatles, Carnaby Street, John Profumo, etc., etc., and every pampered Tom, Dick and Harry practically spitting in the face of their parents. If only the little idiots knew what they were in for! Especially in the land of what Control used to call 'those poor misguided claymunchers' over there in 'The Ingrate Archipelago'.

'Ay-Ruh,' he would smirk, shuffling some files on the surface of his desk, 'what a damned bloody nuisance.' A so-called country for whom 'liberation' in the end, you'd hear him mutter behind his hand, had delivered little more than rickets and theocratic mania, not to mention hopeless civic and social ineptitude. Still, all of that is history now – with an approximation of peace having broken out at last in the misbegotten place.

Leaving me, I'm happy to be able to say, with very little resentment of any real style remaining – indeed, if I'm honest, harbouring no small quantity of good-natured, happy memories. Indeed, I shouldn't wonder if one day I shall be tempted to pay a return visit to old 'Ay-Ruh', Land of Thankless Orang-Utan Hysterics.

But where was I?

Yes, there she is, having sobered up at last. It's Rosie Big-Bum humming over in the garden – working away with her trowel again. Do you know what I'm going to say? And please forgive me if you find it offensive, especially in these fraught times of political correctness. But I'm going to say it anyway, because – at least from this vantage point – I think her rump is even more expansive than that of my poor deceased wife.

Two Hattie Jacqueses.

As down now she bends – sober, at least for half an hour – crooning as she picks herself out a selection of weeds from the lines of seashells decorating the border.

'Bless 'Em All', I can hear her singing. And which is exactly how I feel myself – as regards everyone I encountered who happened to be involved in one way or another. Job well done is what I say. Look! She's leaving! With a bluebird in the hedgerow nodding its approval. At the very least, I think that's what it is – making no claims to being a prolific birdwatcher. No, not in the least like Billy Bunter Plumm. Yes, old Plump the Ornithologist. There wasn't a thing he didn't know about the blighters. Indeed, he had been a long-standing member of the Royal Ornithological Society of Arundel, where he grew up. Or so he claimed. That first day I met him, in late March '65.

I've never in my life encountered anyone so irascible as he was that day on the south pier in Dún Laoghaire. But then, to be fair, the ferry had been delayed by over five hours.

'Typical,' I'd hissed as we gathered up his luggage, 'welcome to the banana republic. Held together with pieces of string.'

The way he looked at me – I swear I thought he was going to self-combust.

In any case, however – more about all of that later on. Because I want to tell you about some builders that we've had around here recently – with every man bloody jack of them being from you-know-where. That bloody, accursed, omnipresent archipelago. Mother 'Ay-Ruh', land of petrichor and overcooked cabbage, Georgian city of horse manure and stout. Not to mention the drizzle that creeps, ever so relentlessly, into your bones. Destroying you, daily, from the inside out.

Wearing you away. What were they doing here, was, obviously, the very first question I asked myself. Just who had invited them?

'They'll lie in wait for years,' Roland once remarked in his office – completely out of nowhere. 'But, make no mistake, they'll never forget. That's the inheritance of the hurt mind, you see – the colonial wound. And, most of all, don't be in the slightest way deceived by their laughter, because be assured that all their jokes ripple over the surface of fanaticism. It has been said, and often, that Irish laughter is without mirth, being rather a guerilla activity of the mind. You may persuade yourself it's not – that is your prerogative. But, believe you me, then, when you least expect it . . .'

I remember being shocked as he drew a line across his throat.

Chapter 3

Speshul Intelligence Shervish

It was one of these particular workmen – that hulking monstrosity who, to my mind at least, as I say, was the identical twin of the actor Arthur Mullard. Complete with regulation boxer's pug nose and off-pink cauliflower ears. Or perhaps you don't remember the fellow? Very well then, I'll enlighten you, being in possession of so much knowledge concerning his life and times that I might even have retrieved it from an official file, ha ha.

The author of *Oh, Yus, It's Arthur Mullard* was actually born in Islington, north London, to a humble background. Eventually forging a career as a cockney character actor in film and TV comedy, he started work at the age of fourteen as a butcher's apprentice and joined the army at eighteen.

Mullard was now quite enormous – he must have been close on twenty stone. And now here he was, having turned up unexpectedly – in the process of hoisting a shovel over his shoulder, having just been recruited by Madame Rosie Dixon for the purposes of completing her proposed 'Old Mouldy' extension. Of which I knew nothing, for she hadn't spoken so much as a word to me about it.

It was Arthur who had actually been first to do the recognising. Of which I soon became aware, having observed him pointing surreptitiously over at me. From behind a free-standing sheet of galvanised metal which they themselves, for some purpose which escapes me, had only just recently erected. With his companion – a skedaddling little Charles Hawtrey type, who kept on nodding away in enthusiastic affirmation.

I wasn't, of course, supposed to have noticed any of this. However, in my own time, I made quite sure to let them know – appearing one day out of the blue right behind him and tapping Arthur firmly on the shoulder.

'Hello there,' I said, 'it's very nice to meet you. In a way, to be honest, I'm just that little bit flattered that you and your murdering colleagues would even think someone like me worth it any more. So, thanks again, both to you and all your IRA associates, or comrades, if that is a term which you might prefer.'

As is my own tendency where serious matters are concerned, he initially made a laugh of the issue – running a few fat fingers through corrugated waves of gleamingly over-lacquered hair.

'Oh now!' he grinned. 'Quare times and that's for sure!'

This burgeoning deceit, I must say, I found amusing – aware as I was that Arthur had featured in a movie called *The Counterfeit Constable*, in which he shared billing with the equally ample Diana Dors, England's very own Marilyn Monroe.

With those prominent lugs of his waggling in the breeze, I really did get such a kick out of observing Arthur hauling that ubiquitous barrow around. He had developed the habit of grunting reluctantly whenever he saw me coming around, pushing past impatiently as he ferried his load of gravel.

Grunt and mumble as much as he might, however, it was clear that, ever since our initial conversation, he had been longing to engage me in more meaningful, presumably menacing, significantly more formal conversation. But simply couldn't locate the resources or engineer the appropriate situation within himself to do it.

Not that it bothered me significantly, I have to say. No, so far as Chenevix Meredith here was concerned, that old pug-nosed offence-against-humanity could continue going on about his business until the sky over Woolsley Bay came collapsing down on top of him.

I knew – almost immediately, of course – that I'd encountered the fat moron somewhere before. And when I remembered, it alarmed me, to be honest. It had been approximately a year or so previously – standing at the counter of a particularly drab public house in north London. Where he'd been observing me keenly until I had finished up my drink. Before taking it upon himself – along, of course, with the backup of others, none of them now members of his 'team' – to pursue me out into the ordinary, unremarkable, gritty London afternoon.

And, in spite of one's Herculean efforts to elude them through the stratagem of availing myself of goodness knows what number of buses – succeeding in their concerted efforts to do what, presumably, it had been their intention for some considerable time to do. Terminate one's tenure upon this earth, I suppose it is fair to say – with their efforts, happily, proving unsuccessful. Although it really quite emphatically did come close, with their assiduous ministrations resulting in my subsequent stay in Northwick Park Hospital, confined to the intensive care ward for what, I think, must have been close on three weeks.

Anyhow, I happened to be coming down the stairs on this particular evening when I bumped into not only Arthur but another of his fellow workers – a squat little chap that I like to call Snudge – with thick black bushy eyebrows, the very spit of Alfie Bass (*Bootsie & Snudge*, *No Hiding Place*, *Alfie*, etc.). He kept on looking out from behind Arthur Mullard. Those shifty eyes, that familiar, evasive body language. A proper backslider and no mistake. And Bootsie, his pal – the very exact same.

'So then – what do you think of our resident Irishmen?' Madame Rosie had enquired, arms folded. Exhibiting a certain new-found, almost childish giddiness which had recently become apparent any time she happened to be in their company, 'I've just been busy making them a spot of tea.'

I chatted with Mullard and Snudge for a while – oh, about football and the like, along with the imminent vote on Brexit. But, to tell you the God's honest truth, throughout all our jibber-jabber, all I wanted to do was just get away. As he regarded me out of the corner of his eye.

'I'm nearly sure that I've seen you before,' I heard Snudge suggesting behind his hand – much to Mullard's evident displeasure.

'Have you, by any chance, been up around Kilburn or Willesden in your time? That is to say, NW6?'

'Not at all,' I retorted light-heartedly. 'To tell you the truth, I rarely venture far from this fine old home I have made here for myself in Woolsley Bay!'

'Oh, I see,' he nodded. 'Well, that's a good thing anyway!'

Whatever he intended to mean by that – practically climbing up on top of a not at all unenthusiastic proprietress, squealing wildly as she swatted some clay crumbs off her apron.

However, it really is time to return to more serious matters. For there is only so much that one can say about those two gurning narrowbacks. Silly fools. So, pray let me proceed. And elaborate further one's post-marital association with a certain other beautiful lady – practically forty years my junior, in fact. Believe it or not. I know poor Bea, God rest her soul, wouldn't have.

Anyway – my beloved's name? It was Joanne Vollmann, aged twenty-three. It had been the day of her funeral, you see – and to tell you the truth I was feeling a little down.

Having gone to visit her parents, Mr and Mrs Vollmann – an elderly couple who resided in Golders Green.

'We hadn't been aware of your relationship with our daughter, Mr Meredith,' I remember one of them saying – to be honest, I cannot be certain which. 'Because dearest Joanne, you know – in many ways she could be so private.'

'I know that,' I agreed, 'so much of her life went into her work.'

The bound typescript of her novel, *Hegira from Jerusalem* – as yet unpublished – had not escaped my attention on the living-room table.

I had remained in their company for the best part of an hour. Before returning on the bus and alighting just outside the public house on Willesden High Street. It was called the Case is Altered. So christened after a phrase made famous by a sixteenth-century lawyer, on foot of evidence received dramatically changing the course of proceedings, but also a popular Ben Jonson 'comedy of humours' – and which, like Minty's in its time, saw it favoured not only by gregarious theatrical imbibers but dissolute strays of every stripe. And where, as I have already indicated, I had the misfortune of encountering what one might describe as one's nemesis – or nemeses. Because there were, in fact, three of them on that occasion – all equally silent and glowering menacingly, at the end of the bar directly facing the gentlemen's convenience.

To this day I can't be 100 per cent certain precisely which was the one who struck the blow when they cornered me in the alley down by the side of the Prince of Wales Theatre. In the West End. They'd followed me on the bus. All I can really remember is the small crowd beginning to gather as I lay there, face down in the gurgling channel alongside the pavement. With the noise of the churning liquid seeming so absurdly loud – before I became aware of the scream of the approaching ambulance, and the crowd began parting to admit the paramedics.

'I tink I moit have kilt da kunt!' is all I can remember – faraway in my mind as the medical people loaded me onto the gurney. By this stage my assailants had long since fled the scene. How I should have wished to have dearest Joanne there, holding my hand.

I had happened to meet her quite by chance in Ray's Jazz Shop, in fact, situated on Charing Cross Road, directly above

Foyle's world-famous bookshop. With her pale makeup and mascara-daubed eyes, she'd reminded me of no one so much as Liza Minnelli in what must be her most celebrated role – that of Sally Bowles in the demi-monde seventies musical smash-hit, *Cabaret*.

One of the most sensible and intelligent people I think I've ever known, Joanne – she had to be. No stupid lumpen Arthur Mullard-style Irishmen there, I can assure you. Although I was only, much later, to discover that some of her pronouncements, in spite of the conviction of her delivery, well, they weren't what you might call entirely original. Which brought a smile to my face, I have to say, when I happened to be browsing – I mean, honestly, yes – in Foyles. And happened upon a volume by a certain *wunderkind*, a progenitor of the radical feminist movement. Or so the biographical note on the dust jacket claimed.

Along with this: 'I have had to train myself out of that phoney smile which is like a nervous tic on every teenager. My dream action for the Women's Liberation Movement would actually be a smile boycott. Yes, an entire boycott of the whole idea of smiling.'

And so there it was – word for word, the very same statement as she had offered to me that disputatious afternoon in the flat. Because she really liked arguing. Impressing me considerably, I have to say, in doing so. I mean, all I could see right in front of me was this frowning, considered, hopelessly earnest expression. As she wandered about half naked in the flat, looking beautiful, as though concluding a scintillating, groundbreaking lecture at the Oxford Union or the London School of Economics.

That little faux pas aside, however, there could be no gainsaying her incisive intelligence and extraordinary breadth of knowledge. And not just in the world of politics, either. She could recite the entire script of *Cabaret* verbatim. I just can't tell you how much I loved that picture. As I did so many from that era – especially those of Alan J. Pakula. The director who Ambrose – also being an aficionado – would bemusedly describe as 'the Nabob of

Paranoia'. After *All the President's Men*, etc., etc., *Three Days of the Condor*, blah blah blah.

However, in actual fact Pakula himself didn't direct that – although, given its style, he might well have done. With its hero Max von Sydow – aka Joubert, aka oneself – seeming murderously present in almost every frame. Lurking there in his raincoat, shadowed beneath his trilby – with infinite patience teasing the hairs of that distinctively downturned, neatly clipped moustache. Which now seems appropriate, I really do have to say, in light of the conversations I'd been having with our platoon of blustering navvies. With those consistent sidelong glances and occasional mutterings inducing into the surroundings a most definite seventies-style sense of incipient catastrophe and paranoia.

Not that I oughtn't to have expected as much – after all, it isn't as if I haven't been in the business long enough. As well as having listened incessantly to Roland & Co. for so many years on the subject.

'Because they're simply not the sort who give up. That's something you'll notice after you've been there for a while in the Kingdom of the Whispered Conspiracy.'

There couldn't be any doubt that I knew what he meant – that constant, gnawing sense – the feeling that you're at all times being watched.

'After a while, it becomes second nature,' old Roley used to say – and in the end he was proved right. There wasn't very much Ambrose Roland didn't know. Because you always are. Being observed, I mean. Which isn't all that surprising, really, when you think about it. Because, after all, old Erin-go-Bragh, when it comes to size, it really is the most absurdly tiny country. Minuscule. Not a country at all, attested Control.

Reflections which were still on my mind when I heard a gentle but firm knock on my bedroom door, followed by the dulcet, mock-ingratiating tones of that good old Rosie Dixon enquiring as to whether or not I might happen to 'like some supper?'

This was most unusual – her knocking, I mean, which could only lead me to the conclusion that her curiosity, finally, had managed to get the better of her. I could see her squinting at my manuscript on the table. The memoir, I mean.

With her, no doubt, in retrospect, somewhat even further intrigued by the precise details of my personal life and just what 'our gang' – that is to say, Mullard & Co. – intended to do.

Perhaps, I considered – and then became comprehensively convinced. Because even a blind man, not to mention an inebriated pensioner like the poor unfortunate Madame Rosie, couldn't fail to determine that there was definitely something untoward afoot. Something really quite nasty, at that. Thereby concluding that there appeared little alternative open to me but to nip her proposed investigations in the bud.

'No thanks, dearie!' I called aloud, 'because unfortunately, you see, I'm already in bed!'

'Very well then – tatty bye!' I heard her call back. For just the briefest of moments reminding me of my poor wife Bea – something on which I really did not want to dwell.

I switched on the TV only to find that the channel had already been tuned to Gold. Which never was the case. And which I have to admit did little to contribute to my already under-threat sense of calm and composure. What were the chances of that? I repeated to myself – quite hopelessly transfixed by the dark, brooding countenance of the stunningly familiar actress Kate O'Mara, in distorted lime-green colour consuming the entire screen.

Just like in the popular series *The Brothers* all those many long years ago, when Maurice Norton's wife had been murdered, practically sliced in two by an AK-47 assault rifle. In what the *Sunday Champion*, yet again, had described as 'another night of shameful carnage'.

'Even by the standards of little psychopathic "Ay-Ruh,"' as Roland was heard to comment.

I remember not sleeping a wink that night. All those dreams I used to have, in the suburb of Lower Drumcondra, situated on the northside of the city. Or, as dear old Plumm, in one of his habitually amusing moments, called it, 'the apogee of all dead-and-alive holes'.

Now those dreams, they were beginning to return – here in this bedroom, in the dim light of Woolsley Bay. Except that this time, they were real. When the phone, late at night, would often ring with a sudden, actually quite distressing clarity – and you'd hear that taunting, muffled voice at the other end. It was Mullard, of course, hopelessly intoxicated.

'Speshul Intelligence Shervish!' you could hear him snort. 'We'll soon see who's Em-Oi-Foive. We're going to kill you, ya kunt, so we are! Dat's why we came here – but den I suppose you suspected dat, didn't you?'

Before, all of a sudden, the instrument going dead.

Chapter 4

Joan Collins

Not that I was ever going to say anything about that. Because, for a start, after all she's done for me, I shouldn't like to offend poor old Rosie McTattyfilarious.

Not in any conceivable way. For, ever since the commencement of my tenure here, she has offered me nothing but the height of consideration – quite aside from providing me with no end of diversion and amusement.

As a matter of fact, she may even be aware of the fact that I have appended the alternate title of Hattie Jacques, star of the Carry Ons, to her personage. But, as Biddy Mulligan the maid has often pointed out to me, 'Not being a bit like us auld Irish ones!' she is infinitely too demure and reserved of character to even dream of broaching such a subject. Continence being the acknowledged virtue of we English, I suppose – even if she definitely has a teenshy little bit of the 'Irish cabbage' in her. Which can often manifest itself in the most unexpected and subtle of ways – that is to say in would-be self-abasing jokes, and curiously abstruse and overwrought contortions of language, dissemblings of each and every stripe.

Why, only the other day she approached me in the lobby and, as meek and ingratiating as you like, enquiring as to whether I might be of a 'little assistance', and permit the storage of some items of sentimental value in my quarters.

'Just for a while,' she explained, slurring her speech, 'well out of harm's way.'

Safe and secure, in other words, from the possible splashes of paint and distemper which might be the inevitable consequence of the labours of Mullard & Co.

The next thing I knew, I found myself standing there watching – actually giving them a wave as they set about rearranging various throws and step-ladders here and there at the end of the corridor.

'By all means, my dear,' I agreed – knowing instinctively that there was likely a great deal more to these 'stored pictures' than might have initially been anticipated.

And at this point I have to make a confession – on behalf, you might say, of the Woolsley Bay Hotel. Which really, in terms of the hospitality and heritage industry, not to say entertainment, remains in possession of ideas and aspirations really quite inappropriate to its station. But then – at least judging by the faded brochures I had found abandoned in a drawer in my room – that, more or less, had always been the case. Promising, as they did, 'an experience of the modern go-ahead England, exclusively for the swinging set'.

And who knows, maybe in the early days, it might at one time actually have been – but I have to say that not one image, not one single item of the lumber that our 'guests' continued to ferry boisterously into my room – for 'safe-keeping', as Rosie had said – not one picture meant anything in the slightest to me. I'm afraid all I can say is that if this sad, spotted and bleached cargo of 'entertainment stars' was anything to go by, then the so-called UK 'jet set' of the 'switched-on' 1960s must have been labouring under some very heavy delusions indeed. For not a single portrait of these 'modern pop groups' did I recognise. All of whom seemed to me to be the bargain-department, off-season, end-of-the-pier variety.

And, as for the collection of 'cabaret crooners', whose virtues

Rosie had elaborately extolled, they were individuals of an even more profound obscurity, if such could even be imagined.

As the heavily perspiring, grunting procession of Mullard & Co. proceeded unabated with their deposits, I continued, in vain, with my search for recognition.

Although I have to admit that a number of the shots were very well taken. Excellent studio portraits, in truth – in spite of the fact that both the flies and time had commendably done their work. These prints, however, were few in number, and did little to mitigate my mounting irritation. After all, I thought – just who on earth were Nicholas & the Beatnik Wonders? Or, for that matter, Bobby Strange, so-called 'No. 1 popster' and 'unique interpreter' both of 'Blue Moon' and some other long-forgotten sugarpuff ditty entitled 'Walking by the Shore'.

Soon the place was filled with these once-upon-a-time hopeful nonentities. Whose sad number included Tony & the Starlights, who had once featured the aforementioned Bobby Strange in the role of lead vocalist, Louise Trepowlski, Maurie & the Dreamboats, Fossi Winton & the Drills, Billy Dankin. Which was why I heaved a sigh of relief when in arrived a pair of thick, bushy eyebrows – Snudge, of course – barging in without knocking. Ferrying an enormous promotional photograph for *The Stud*. Starring Joan Collins, if you happen to remember.

He managed the hottest disco in town – but she managed him. Satisfaction guaranteed.

'Leave that over there by the wall,' I remember calling, somewhat sharply, over to him, 'I have to have a proper look at it.'

Heaven knows what gibberish he offered by way of response. But he set the specified item reasonably neatly by the side of the window, and then went off, touching his forelock, blah blah blah. Not a single syllable could I manage to decode. Yes, mush mush blah was all I could hear – and that's coming from someone who has spent the best part of four decades as a resident of what he and Mullard liked to refer to as their 'beloved homeland'.

I had overheard them when they were drunk, talking a great deal of this so-called 'homeland' – most especially his treasured County Mayo, which he'd insisted on telling me he was from. Outlining, in what can only be described as a phonetic stream of dissociated divulgement, the distinctive topographical details of the western seaboard, along with the unmatchable friendliness of the people, until I had practically felt like screaming aloud right there in front of the poor unfortunate, over-animated cretin.

Which I regretted, in a way – that it had to be like that. It was just such a pity that, from the very first day I had set foot in the countryside which clearly meant so much to the fellow, I had found it an almost sinfully untended place. A description, although I didn't mention it to old bushy-eyes Snudge, not entirely unapplicable to so many of Potato Land's many wintry crevasses.

'Over there you can be certain,' Roland always used to say, 'that the very first casualty of our little skirmish will be the truth. Because all of them – believe you me, without any exception – they're really quite unreliable. In so many ways like veal, dear boy. Try to remember that, if you can, in whatever dealings you may have with the duplicitous buggers.'

An observation which, in retrospect, is in itself not without a comparable degree of the levity which he had also informed me I should come to expect once I had landed upon 'sweet "Ay-Ruh's" shores'. Considering that old Roland, in passing the foregoing observation off as his very own – and not, in fact, one of the practised salon witticisms routinely dispensed by none other than Noël Coward – was effectively confirming his own fallibility in this regard.

Indeed, it has to be said that there are those – and I consider myself among them – who might suggest that the middle-class English in general, let alone Ambrose 'Roley' Roland, could well be considered the greatest dissemblers of all. And that may include myself and old Plummy. That is, if Henry Percival Plumm can even be said to exist. Properly, at any rate, in the way that the rest of us do. But of course he does! For heaven's sake, don't be silly. How could he not? As some of the clientele in Minty's used to say, when the rumours would rear their heads again: 'De loikes of de pair o' dem two belonging till Em-Oi-Foive. Are you out of your bleedin' auld mind, you big fool?'

However, as I was describing, with regard to the very final photograph that they had to place in storage – I must confess that I have always been particularly fond of its subject, Joan Collins. Especially her work as a screen actress – and now here she was at the height of her fame. Curiously enough, in the aftermath of my enjoyment and visual indulgence of the black-and-white representation of 'the Dame' in question, what I found myself recalling was in fact not the sumptuous extravagance and baroque elegance of that 'certain night' which she brought immediately to mind. But the truly dreadful, to my ears at least, percussive persistence and sheer unbeararable cacacophony of the musical riot which I experienced on that – in many ways best forgotten – actually deeply troubling occasion.

Bumph-bumph-kickacao-kickacao-bumph-bumph! I mean, honestly, really and truly! I am talking about a club called the Chaguaramas, which in 1974 was situated in Covent Garden. It was the first venue of its kind in London that I personally had experienced, at any rate. What had brought my former colleague Alex Whiteside there, I could only imagine – but I was soon to find out. He had a habit of roaring into your ear with that squeaky voice of his – exactly as he was doing now, reasserting his attitude to his position regarding Roley, 'the station' and the overall scheme of things.

His speciality was the burglary of embassies and ambassadors' residences – executed with such a precision and finesse, in most cases, as never to have been discovered to have taken place at all.

'A diplomat,' he continued to insist, cupping a hand over his mouth as he spoke, 'and never forget this. A diplomat has as much right to be insulted if he is called a spy as a soldier has if he is called a murderer.'

My eardrums were close to bursting with the accursed thumping of the relentless percussion and the sweeping shafts of ultraviolet, which on occasion had come perilously close to blinding me.

Whiteside's paramour – yet another of his preferences, a drag queen – of course, didn't notice a thing. Or, at least, didn't seem to. But then, I suppose, poor old Whitey, given that pathetic stout and suetty appearance – the truth is that most likely he was glad to find himself with anyone at all who might give him even an approximation of love, however fleeting that might be. I forget the name of the overpainted dolly in question – but she couldn't have been more than sixteen years of age. I stared at her in revulsion and disbelief – dolled up to the nines, the absolute dead image of Joan Collins. With no expense or detail spared – an overabundance of silks, sequins and satins. Obstinately batting her fake eyelashes at Whiteside, draped indecorously across the arm of a red banquette. We were all – really, quite hopelessly, I have to admit – plastered.

Even to this day I can still hear that maddening thunder that they liked to call music, with not so much as a hint of respite, repeating chunka chunka over and over in a locomotive, haemorrhage-inducing, pulverising rhythm and hissing hi-hat.

Paradoxically, if I remember, there was also something inscrutably clean about it – ebbing and flowing as those extended electronic beats varied between drop-downs and euphoric peaks. With the deejay moronically waving from the inside of his perspex booth, proudly surveying his mirror-panelled fiefdom with its plethora of mirror balls, stacked heels and polyester. As his clients gyrated to the highly mechanised and sensual sound of now and tomorrow.

'Can't get enough of your love, babe!' sang the great big booming voice of the soul form that was popular at the time.

'Barry White!' I could hear the dolly girl yelping. And which Whiteside, mad to be appreciated, claimed he also loved. Although, at the time, I couldn't have determined whether, in fact, it was the vocalist in question he was actually referring to, or the exaggerated wriggling movements that his sixteen-year-old companion was making in his ear with his tongue. All the while batting those heavily laden eyes at me, chuckling foolishly as she squealed again, falsetto, 'Eeksters! I love this one!' Hauling poor old Whiteside onto the tiled flashing floor again – in the face of a flurry of unconvincing protests. Before he toppled, and in the process succeeded in losing every single item that his pockets contained – keys, wallet, you name it, the lot. Maybe even secret information – *qui sait*?

With this Baby Joan more than excited as she flung herself, histrionically, into the scene. I mean – what on earth else would a Joan Collins do? Going 'poo poo poo' and 'mum mum, sweetgums Alex', like some deliriously wanton catamite preparing them both for the end of the world. Which, in a way, as it turned out, was true – beneath the fluid whorling purple of the Chaguaramas Club neon sign, in the centre of London 1974.

Poor Alex Whiteside. Dear old Whitey. Because I really did like him. Still, as stern old Ambrose Roland never seemed to tire of saying, 'If it must be done, then we must needs do it, Chenny and post-haste, if you please. You hearing me, Chenevix?'

Or, should I say, 'puppy' Max von Joubert, fearsomely inscrutable eminence grise of Em-Oi-Foive. Ha ha ha ha, honestly! Really and truly.

Chapter 5

Lovers in the Penny Arcade

It's gut-wrenching, honestly, having to recollect so much of this material. Whether for a memoir or anything else. Especially the manner in which my old comrade met his end. So rest in peace, poor Alex 'Whitey' Whiteside. Former soldier, friend and colleague. How could it have possibly come to this? I wondered.

But it just goes to show, doesn't it, when you think about it – that, one way or another, there has always been a kind of ineffable magic, dark or otherwise, attached to the personality of the screen star Joan Collins. That irrepressible, quite bewitching Queen of All Dames. I remember once reading an article which, I have to say, captured her essence really – by which I mean 'charming, flirtatious, stylish, politically incorrect, iconic in her own lifetime'.

She was his heroine, the author had frothily elaborated, St Joan of *Dynasty*. He had dreamed of calling her but could never summon up the courage – luxuriating in the thought of her ever so delicately picking up the phone – and in those precisely sculpted, aristocratic tones, examining her nails before politely enquiring: 'Hellay! Who is this, please?' in a voice that went on to be both flirtatious and expectant, but not without a hint of possible treachery – and with a savoir faire that was equally alluring.

Whether or not it was absolutely necessary to depict Fontaine Khaled, the character played by Miss Collins not only in *The Stud* but also its sequel *The Bitch*, as quite so callous and self-serving, I really do not know. But such was the decision of the film-makers, and they may well have had their reasons – yet it seemed to be even more outré than might have been necessary, highlighting at every opportunity the woman's sheer unadulterated selfishness – poisonousness, indeed.

The good-looking new manager hired by Fontaine Khaled soon begins to realise that his job includes more than just running her nightclub, funded by her wealthy husband. His duties also include managing her insatiable sexual desires.

Oliver Tobias. Do you remember that name? I'm sure you don't. Probably the same as Arthur Mullard. But that doesn't matter. Because what's important is that I do. Remember it, I mean. As a matter of fact, I'll never forget it.

Just as I won't every single thing that's associated with that Joan Collins lookalike boy. I mean, it's not often you encounter the former resident of an orphanage in Belfast attempting to create the illusion that he is the living image of the female star of two popular sex films. Particularly when that person has only just barely turned sixteen years of age. Although this, I must say, probably thanks to the extraordinary amount of time the individual in question had devoted to the task at hand, what with the selection of clothes, meticulous application of makeup, etc., the transformation was most convincing, not to say compelling.

Certainly, in the beginning, I have to admit that I had indeed taken the former resident of a Belfast orphanage, Danny Douglas, to be what he claimed he was: a genuine, natural-born and extremely attractive female. When he'd arrived at first, quite unexpectedly, at least as far as I was concerned, sidling in beside us there in the corner booth – wrinkling up his nose and waving a tortoiseshell cigarette-holder in that trademark, mock-confrontational Joan Collins manner – there were quite a few eyes on him, I have to say, in the Chaguaramas. But, as he kept on whispering into the besotted Alex's ear, he was 'all yours, darling'.

It was pitiful, really, to observe the effect it was all having on poor old Whitey. There just was nothing he could do as regards these unfortunate compulsions of his. And which I'd known all about, really, for quite some time. Which of course was the reason why Roley had selected me, putting in the request that I shadow him over a period – knowing as I did, from our friendship, not only his tendencies but the locations in which he assuaged them, Covent Garden being the principal one.

Not far from another haunt, which he liked to frequent because of the level of sulphurous jeopardy involved: the all-night amusement arcade Playland in Piccadilly Circus. He wasn't the only one of our fellows to be observed on the premises concerned. Or the military, either, come to that. Yes, a very popular old arcade was Playland. And most appropriately named, I would have to say. Because I had acceded to Roland's request, and due to the diligence and persistence of my observations, over time I became more than aware of these facts.

When I say 'request', I'm afraid that's merely nominal. A fig-leaf, you might say. Demonstrate even the slightest hint of reluctance or disapproval, and Roland gave you one of those legendary looks. Arctic might be the appropriate adjective. So let us, if we may, be honest here: I didn't have a great deal of choice in the matter. Becoming, thereafter, a true man of the shadows.

It was difficult for anyone who didn't personally know him to comprehend what appeared to be the near-suicidal behaviour of the unfortunate Alex Whiteside. Particularly when combined with the evident emotional instability of his most recent companion. Which manifested itself, variously, in outrageous exhibitions of brattishness, public rows and an astonishing lack of self-awareness. He had actually once torn off his long curly wig, screaming hysterically as he flung it across the floor on another occasion in the Chaguaramas.

But, when pressed, 'to his great shame', Alex Whiteside had confided in me that it 'somehow' added to both the 'excitement and desire'. To be perfectly honest, I had actually been there since the very beginning. When he'd met 'Miss Collins' one wild and wet stormy Saturday night on the premises of Playland. It was in there, according to the usually more than reliable Ambrose Roland, among the flashing lights, clacking flippers and lightning reverb of the pinball machines that 'some of our fellows preferred to idle. Where they elected to meet their lovers, if you want to call them that.' Enjoying the 'golden wonder' sweetmeats, he sighed, of the all-night West End penny arcade.

'What possible attractions such a location might have retained for otherwise capable fellows, I shall not for the life of me ever understand.'

Those were the words Roley had issued as a parting shot – not without a thin sneer of unmistakable contempt.

All he had requested was that I 'keep an eye' on Whitey.

'After all, I've warned him three times – and he really is beginning to try my patience. Especially with those Ravensbrook chappies.' Meaning, of course, Ravensbrook House, the boys' home in Belfast. Where 'Miss Collins', presumably, had been admirably tutored.

Quite by coincidence, an old associate of ours from the Agency in Dublin, a fellow by the name of Clem Grainger, had also been present in the Chaguaramas Club that night. And although I knew it was he who broadcast whatever rumours there were regarding my involvement with what subsequently occurred, I have to be honest and say that to this day I bear him no ill will. Indeed harbour nothing but sympathy for anyone who happened to be close to the fellow.

Although, having known Clem Grainger for a reasonable

length of time, I have to concede that I had always considered him – as had a number of others, including Maurice Norton, who never said a bad word against anyone – to be, how shall I put it? Just that little bit. Unstable.

But there cannot be any gainsaying his abilities – which had seen him, and on more than one occasion, described in the pages of the *Evening Herald* as a living, breathing 'theatrical *wunderkind*'. By 'Dublin's finest columnist', Jacqui Harpur, no less. Someone who herself was more than well qualified to make such a judgement. Especially considering her occasional performances – usually 'in her cups', as Maurice Norton used to put it – in Minty's. Delivering, inter alia, the most powerful and enigmatic impression of the chanteuse Peggy Lee. As Maurice Norton applauded, gamely introducing, 'The star, Miss Jacqui Harpur!' Gliding out from behind the counter, having doctored the sleeves of her dress to create the illusion of Peggy Lee's trademark 'balloon sleeves' – seeming for all the world like a human chalice as she cooed into the face of a helpless Val McBoan.

Charlie Kerrins called out from the back of the bar: 'Is that all there is?' Before Miss Harpur obliged by continuing in a near-perfect rendition of those flat, unsettling tones so characteristic of the exotic nightclub diva, loitering by the piano as she contrived to ease herself onto the instrument's glossy white curve, eerily crooning the melody in question while attired in an explosion of black-beaded fabric and ostrich feathers, with a foot-high black plume rising out of her wig.

'Is that all there is?' she'd repeat in those flat, almost remorseless tones, 'Is that all there is?'

There had been many other nights like that in the Minstrels' Rest in the company of famous people who wandered in and out over the years. But none, I think, to compare with the occasion when none other than Jack Lemmon had happened to drop by – not long after having competed the movie *The Out-of-Towners*. Having travelled to Killarney for the purpose of enjoying a spot of golf – something which he, and quite regularly, was prone to do. Usually when he had just completed a project.

He had been drinking and carousing there in the Minstrels' until well past three in the morning. Holding an appreciative – and, it must be admitted, not unsurprisingly inebriate – audience rapt with a tongue-in-cheek rendition of the hokey old Irish tune 'Mother Machree'. No one that night gave any indication of harbouring any intention of forsaking the Minstrels' Rest until, as Val McBoan observed, well past dawn.

'H'ho!' he chirped as Charlie Kerrins climbed up on the counter. Clearing his throat to begin yet another 'reci-mi-tation!', as he called it.

Without a doubt, it really had been a night to remember. But, spectacular though it might have been, it would never have been anything like the hoot it was but for the combination of Charlie and Val. Famous throughout the land for his characterisation of Val 'the Chiseller', a walking, talking jokebook of 'native songs and stories'. They both took the floor for over half an hour. Holding the visiting American in thrall with their delightful performance (or sections thereof) of their already celebrated interpretation of Brendan Behan's *Confessions of an Irish Rebel*. With Jack Lemmon doubled up, when, at one point, Charlie Kerrins performed his legendary Chaplin walk all along the length of the counter. And then, twanging his braces as he tossed his forelock back and forth, Val McBoan gave an almost perfect impression of the young Irish felon. Much to Jack Lemmon's continued delight.

'Not that I have any particular affection for the memory of Cromwell, you understand. Who, as is popularly known, would not be one of our national heroes. I didn't mind him cutting off the king's noggin, because that just showed that a king's head can come off like anybody else's. But his actions at Drogheda were like those of a Heydrich and a Himmler combined. Then in the town of Wexford he massacred 200 women grouped around the

Cross of the Redeemer, and delighted his soldiers with the slow process of individual murder, stabbing one after another. When his soldiers were running their pikes through little babies in between psalms, they would shout: "Kill the nits and there will be no lice."'

The star of *The Out-of-Towners* thought this, in particular, absolutely hilarious.

But not nearly as good as many other of the 'acting stories' when the pair of them, eventually, got into their stride. And, as if that wasn't enough, Maurice Norton and Deirdre, his wife – both of whom were solid, long-standing pros in the business – came close to upstaging the two 'Behan boys', as Jack Lemmon called them.

Especially with their stories of their time in repertory, when they had toured the length and breadth of the country with Anew McMaster and the 'fit-ups'.

'We were doing *Othello* in Newcastlewest, County Limerick, Mr Lemmon,' Mrs Norton told the actor, 'and I, of course, was playing the part of Desdemona. Then what happens, I'm coming out of the tent, into the fair green after the show. And doesn't this woman take me aside and she says, "I can't for the life of me, ma'am, understand how you could possibly have anything to do with that fellow!"'

'There are plenty more where that came from!' her husband interjected. But not before Charlie Kerrins launched an outrageous ski-jump right off the top of the counter – eventually landing squarely on the taller man's shoulders.

'Irishmen and Irishwomen!' he bawled in a perfect interpretation of Behan's raw, working-class accent. 'In the name of God and the dead generations from which this blessed little country of ours receives her auld tradition of nationhood, will someone for the love of Jaysus be a dacent man and get up there and buy poor auld Charlie here a drink. Whoop!'

The night ended with Charlie and Val outdoing themselves with a performance of 'Dark Rosaleen':

O, the Erne shall run red
With redundance of blood,
The earth shall rock beneath our tread,
And flames wrap hill and wood,

And gun-peal and slogan-cry
Wake many a glen serene,
Ere you shall fade, ere you shall die,
My Dark Rosaleen!
My own Rosaleen!

'Which, of course, as you probably know, Mr Lemmon, being a man of scholarly bent and a theatrical one to boot, is by James Joyce's favourite poet, James Clarence Mangan, who died of the cholera fever in the Great Famine of 1849.'

This was what Val McBoan had to say. Before Charlie Kerrins succeeded in elbowing his partner out of the way and, croaking hoarsely in a great big swirling blue fug of cigarette smoke, was to be heard declaring: 'And who also wrote this, which I give you for your pleasure, Mr Lemmon, sir: "Roll forth my song, like the rushing river . . ."'

Failing, however, to proceed when someone shouted out from the back: 'Pull the chain and in a jiffey, your shit is floating down the Liffey!'

It was to pass into folklore as the best night ever. Or at the very least one of them. Never to be forgotten by Jack Lemmon, Oscar-winner and treasured star of the much-loved *The Apartment*. With the gloriously gamine Shirley MacLaine, of course. I mean – who else?

The only other occasion to rival Mr Lemmon's visit was the completely and utterly unexpected evening when Phil Silvers, well-known frontman of the popular television series *Sgt. Bilko*, had arrived in – already, like Lemmon, a little bit sozzled, sporting the yachting cap he had worn in his film *The Boatniks*, a section of which had been shot in Dublin. In the small, picturesque fishing village of Howth, to the north of the city.

What a night that was – with Maurice, fortified of course with goodly portions of Jameson whiskey and Dutch courage, pointing out the similarity, physically, between the Yankee comedian and the British poet Philip Larkin.

'The pair of them,' he declared, holding court up at the bar, 'have heads on them that'd put you in mind of duck eggs – with goggles on!' Not that Bilko was about to take any offence – subsequently, like Jack Lemmon, going into sentimental raptures about the 'strange and mystical literary heart of Dublin, that ancient city of Joyce and Shaw and Swift'.

Which normally would make me laugh and provoke a derisory comment or two – but it was clear to everyone present that there had been really something special about Maurice's entirely unanticipated recitation of Larkin's poem 'Dublinesque'.

'Like the end of something and the beginning of something,' I remember someone saying – I think, in fact, it might have been Val McBoan, 'occurring at the same time, without anyone realising.'

As Maurice Norton took a bow to a round of appreciative applause – while another well-known inebriate by the name of the Bowsy McAuley stumbled temporarily, attempting to make his way towards the lavatory. Batting away some imaginary impediment as he grunted impatiently: 'Just who the frig is Philip Larkin? Because if you're asking me, that fellow's the spit of Eric Morecambe!'

Which, when you think about it, is absolutely true as well.

'Bring me sunshine!' chanted the Bowsy, stumbling awkwardly onwards, smashing slap-bang into a wall.

As, also hopelessly inebriated, I granted permission to my good self to produce from its case my trusty Selmer saxophone. Yes, I do play, since you ask – however sporadically. And then proceeded to segue enthusiastically, if not quite precisely, from

'Stranger on the Shore' to the roistering tune 'Yakety Sax'. With the latter, perhaps predictably, bringing the house all around us down.

I think we eventually vacated the premises at dawn – resting, if I recall, on a rolltop wooden bench situated along the banks of the Grand Canal, in the process of consuming soggy chips from a bag. By this stage, Phil Silvers had long since returned, seeming extremely contented indeed, to his appointed hotel. As the two of us sat there, both Maurice Norton and I, in the tremulous silence of the gradually approaching daylight, a chugging barge beneath a plume of smoke was making its way steadily and evenly towards the city. Leaving us there as it proceeded onwards towards the west – just as the slightest little drizzle began to fall. And it definitely did, in that instant, seem that whatever sensations Sgt. Bilko had experienced throughout the performance of Philip Larkin's crystal-shimmering verse – there could be no scouting their veracity and sheer authenticity.

I mean, the place had clearly moved him – albeit in his own peculiar and individual way. Having, perhaps, been arrested by what one could only describe as the noble, unassailable grandeur of that place which had once been described, without even the slightest hint of irony, as the greatest, most beautiful 'second city of the empire'. And as we both sat there with the raindrops splintering noiselessly on our cheeks, there can be no doubt about it – but that I felt myself really quite overcome with regret. For ever having denigrated, or even for a second having doubted its uniqueness – a provincial city-town the colour of claret with redbrick Georgian mansions boasting fine doors and those little wrought-iron balconies standing back from the road in well-bred reticence.

Town of alleys filled with suppressed, conspiratorial whispers, certainly – but also with bars of the most beautiful barley sugar wavering upon brown water at evening. And where the Liffey, of which its greatest artificer of all had remarked, just flowed Anna Livia on and on. Larkin had written of a small-town city which was already in the process of giving way to the modern world with its out-of-town shopping centres, ring roads and American ways. But in many respects the drizzly grey town written of by Joyce was still very much discernible and present, in spite of the growth in population and ongoing construction of the modern housing estates of Howth, Clontarf, Rathfarnham and many others. Which had stealthily succeeded in eroding the open commons and small green fields.

Yet, somehow – you could feel it – the spectral echoes of his time and that of the Act of Union, mysteriously they still remained. With their ethereal representatives never seeming so far away, their crinolined half-forms to be apprehended at the head of the stairs in a gone-to-seed Georgian house, or disporting themselves on swings between neoclassical pillars beneath richly stuccoed ceilings. In the distance you could make out the Dublin mountains rising ghostily from the water, with that beautiful false innocence in their violets, greens and golden rust of bracken.

As the two of us, for all the world like children, fell asleep together without so much as another word beneath those wide, pleasant, eighteenth-century buildings gleaming like glass in the drizzle. Before waking up to the sound of Brendan Behan's beloved ever-resonant Christchurch bells.

'How are you doing now, Em-Oi-Foive?' I remember poor old worse-for-wear Maurice chuckled as he took out a handkerchief and rubbed his throbbing forehead.

'Oh not so bad,' I replied with a mischievous little tinkle of a laugh, 'not so bad at all, thanks for asking.'

As, through the open window of a car stalled close by, came drifting the flat, existential bleat of none other than Peggy Lee: a song for which both of us, in our time, had professed no small degree of affection.

Is that all there is?
If that's all there is, my friends
Then let's keep dancing!

Why, the pair of us, dazed, might have been suspended as though in a dream.

Chapter 6

Em-Oi-Foive, Pshaw

'In Town To-Nite!' trumpeted the *Evening Herald* tagline in livid red above a full page of adverts, majestically crowning the most-read showbusiness gossip column in the city.

'It's Your City!' it read, 'with Jacqui Harpur.'

Complete with a cheeky, Dublin-style imitation of *The New Yorker*'s monocled gadfly, the one and only Eustace Tilley.

Look at him there with his nose in the air, a monocled Regency dandy with nothing better to do with his time than observe through his monocle the sweeping trajectory of a butterfly in full flight. Chosen, of course, by Jacqui – alert as ever – for its suggestion of whimsy, an appropriately elegant emblem of wearily sophisticated detachment. How does he speak? one can only but wonder. With the only conclusion possible or plausible being some approximation or other of studiously non-rhotic engagement. That which, post-war, had soon become known as 'that weirdo announcer accent'. Which ultimately found itself becoming displaced by the coming era of the fifties and sixties.

A long way indeed from the golden age of broadcasting and those pompous-sounding narrative commentaries which might just as easily have been delivered by guess who? Henry Plumm. Who could, just as easily, when one thinks about it, have been a hybrid, an eccentric fusion of Ray Milland and Cornelius

Vanderbilt IV. Some unborn admixture of maybe Roley and Westbrook Van Voorhis, if you ever happened to hear of him. Which I'm sure you haven't. A most distinctive, plummy broadcaster. Even plummier, perhaps, than Henry P. Plumm, ha ha.

Yes, I can conceive of it without effort – old Henry presenting as the embodiment of the stentorian phoney-British voice that dominated newsreel narration, stage and movie acting, and, indeed, much of public discourse, certainly in the United States during the first half of the twentieth century. Think of William F. Buckley, perhaps. The Round Table group in the lounge of the Algonquin Hotel. Or Westbrook and his series *The March of Time*.

Do you recall the authority, that overwhelming sense of someone who knows their subject inside out and appears to be in complete control? That gives you the idea.

Reminding you, perhaps, of the over-enunciated style. And, of course, that sense of urgency. Which, like so much else in this world, is premised on some kind of illusion or other.

'And which really does become us, dear boy!' I can hear old Roley shouting in my ear. 'Why, there are times when I sometimes think that, when it comes down to brass tacks – why, we are almost in our own way just as bad as any Paddy!'

With that distinctive hint of wry amusement, and the long silver forelock hanging down over his leathery face – hunched in the debilitating grey gloom of the Scotch House along Burgh Quay. Where the two of us, presently, were due to be joined by Henry. For the purposes of what we called, laughingly, a 'debriefing'.

I mean – can you imagine? In that coffin stood on its end that they called a public house? With our surroundings being just about as far as one could possibly imagine from the wit and sophistication of the Round Table group or, indeed, any other life-embracing New York establishment.

'You can almost feel it everywhere, can't you, Plumm?'

I remember observing as Henry and I both stood there in the doorway, my colleague shaking the drops from his brolly, 'The atmosphere of seediness and decay about the city. Not to mention that damned ever-pervasive sense of provinciality. I have often felt there is something almost doomed about the people one encounters here in this neighbourhood of ruin and need. That they have the poetry, almost certainly, is not in doubt. But they require our organising genius to prosper. Us mercenary philistines – without which Wales, for example, would irrevocably revert to the same, uninspiring type of arableism. Don't you think?'

'Indeed, my dear Meredith.'

As we bade farewell to Ambrose Roland, our superior, and strode along the length of the would-be thoroughfare christened in honour of 'the Liberator' Daniel O'Connell.

I enjoyed Henry's company. But such blustering as I had to listen to as he wobbled along by my side! Just about as far, to be honest, from the sprightly, dandified figure of the butterfly-spotting figure of Eustace Tilley as might conceivably be imagined. Billy Bunter OBE. That's what I used to think. Knowing as I did how, ever since joining the service, he had set his heart on being a recipient. Because that's who Henry Percival Plumm wanted to be. A Dublin version of Eustace Tilley OBE – complete with ebony cane and high white collar.

Maybe one day he might read about it in the paper – specifically in Jacqui Harpur's column. With his big face beaming under arches and waving pennants, in the process of receiving yet another award in recognition of his dedicated service to Her Majesty. Yes, gazing out, snooty as ever, at his abject and adoring public. In shameless emulation of the eponymous cartoon urbanite who strode across the top of 'In Town To-Nite!' and Jacqui Harpur's extravagant *Evening Herald* prose.

Which I happened to be reading now – having seen Plummy off to his digs on Hollybank Road. I had just nipped to the

Scotch House for a swift one. And was very much enjoying the picture she was painting of the latest goings-on in Dublin's world of entertainment. Identifying, most fulsomely indeed, it has to be said, a certain youth by the name of Clem Grainger as 'very much the one to watch in the world of Irish entertainment'. He was, she claimed, 'already making serious waves'. This youth called Clem Grainger. 'Moving in a new and exciting direction' was how it was described, a 'burgeoning movement' through which he and a number of like-minded others intended to reinvigorate 'this stultified theatrical backwater'. A city, he asserted, in an interview with Jacqui, 'almost irretrievable in artistic terms. But we in the Little Matchbox Theatre Group – make no mistake but that we are up to the challenge.'

Thanks in the main to their work with this 'extraordinary grouping' (Jacqui Harpur's words), a number of other talents had also been attracting close attention. Yes, apparently with these new and groundbreaking productions, alternately helmed by Grainger and fellow Trinity College graduate Máiréad Curtin, the Little Matchbox Theatre Group were, without any doubt on the part of this highly respected columnist, 'already on their way'. With a roster of shows including 'quite striking', 'shocking' and 'really quite unforgettable' renderings of heavyweights such as Genet with *Querelle de Brest*, Poe's *The Tell-Tale Heart* and *The Lark* by Jean Anouilh. They had also, Miss Harpur had pointed out, in more recent times, turned their attention to a number of neglected Irish playwrights – including George Fitzmaurice. Whose *Dandy Dolls* had caused a sensation – not least because of their Dada-esque presentation of the material.

When I showed the article concerned to Henry during the course of our perambulations the following day, I was a little surprised to hear him confess to being 'somewhat aggrieved' by this report. Explaining how, in spite of her undoubted accuracy and perception in many other aspects of the subject, she had somehow omitted to include the fact that it was none other than he himself, Henry Percival Plumm – under the auspices, obviously, of the Grafton Theatrical Agency – who had actually given 'Dublin's Coming Man' his very first theatrical opportunity. He harrumphed again as he shook his umbrella.

'Not that I myself care enough at this juncture to solicit even the slightest of plaudits for so doing,' he continued, 'for, as I will readily concede, my dear Meredith, it was more than evident from the outset that the talents of the young man concerned were not only notable but formidable. As were his charm and style, dear heart. Most striking of all was his metropolitan character – not a characteristic immediately accessible anywhere that I've found in this little pile of creative dust that's called Dublin by the River Liffey.'

I knew, of course, that he was only partly serious. Aware as he was that poor old Stinktown – and, at low tide, believe me, that water, it really did pong – was only at that time really finding its feet in the modern world. It was certainly a long way from the one that we ourselves represented. That is to say, the one which had made us: an imaginary psychic principality, I suppose in one way – best defined by a pose of amiable, disengaged worldliness. That, at least, was how I perceived myself. And, in the end, was better at it than Henry. Knowing, as I did, how to keep my mouth shut! Never mind being so stupid as to go and write things down. At least until now.

Ah yes! I can hear myself sigh: honour, loyalty, handmade suits, strong drinks, deep leather armchairs in smoky clubs – that had always been my particular vision of England. A world to which this young man, Clem Grainger, appeared to represent almost the exact polar opposite. Considering his youth – he had just turned twenty-one – it would have to be accepted, as regards artistic global influences and current trends, that this Grainger had been quite remarkably ahead of his time. Why, he apparently had even constructed a fabulously modern recording studio, something quite unheard of back then. At the bottom of his suburban garden, no less, in the southside suburb known as

Terenure. Something that, as I say – and not only for young people – would have been the stuff of dreams at the time. With the national TV and radio station barely out of nappies. I remember, I was still experiencing considerable difficulty in pronouncing the damned name of the bloody network concerned: Radd-Dee-Oh Tell-Eh-Feesh Ay-Run!

I hadn't been all that long in the office before our paths, as was inevitable, eventually crossed, and Grainger wandered in off the street into our office at the Grafton Theatrical Agency, which was located in Grafton Mews – just a stone's throw off the main thoroughfare of Grafton Street. Where I had been sitting, chatting away to Shivaun at the switchboard. I was handing her over some memo or other when in he strode without even bothering his backside to knock. Attired in his customary Bertolt Brecht peaked denim cap, brown hair reaching down to his shoulders.

'Hi!' he said impertinently, wiggling a couple of fingers. 'I'm Clem!'

In common with all our prospective clients so far, he expressed admiration both for the office and the sheer imagination of the venture – the very first of its kind in the city.

'As a matter of fact, in the country, north or south,' he pointed out. Before tossing his shoulder-bag along the wall and plonking himself down right there in front of my desk. Proceeding to act like the couple of years that he'd spent in London conferred on him the authority, more or less, to tell us how to do our job.

He was young, however, and I allowed him that. Although the more he kept looking around him, making observations and saying the first thing that came into his head, the more I kept being reminded of F. E. Smith's (later Lord Birkenhead) observation as regards Michael Collins of the Irish Republican Brotherhood. 'I am sorry to have to say that his conclusions appear to exist solely in the realm of his own rather overheated imagination.' But the lad continued to amuse me, I have to say, and so I made no effort at all to interrupt.

'What you've got going here has the potential to take poor old sleepy old Dublin by storm, guys, it really has. And I have to say that I find it most exciting – me personally, I've been waiting a long time for this.'

Then he went off on a solo-run monologue, describing in great detail his experiences on the Strand.

'Where I worked for a time with Cadogan Enterprises, if you ever heard of them. Women flocked through the door. Actresses, models, debutantes and shopgirls threw themselves into action. I guess it was because the scene over there, when I started – the whole thing was really only in its infancy, to be quite honest. The Rolling Stones were making a name for themselves in Richmond. The club we used to go to, the All-Nighter, had a regular flow of bands and musicians: the Yardbirds, Led Zeppelin. John Mayall would often drop along with Eric Clapton in tow. Meanwhile, back at the ranch – the office, I mean – my boss had only just gone and signed up a funny-looking young girl called Samantha Eggar – how about that? You've seen *The Collector*?'

'Yes,' I nodded, 'why yes of course, Clement. William Wyler. Dear John Fowles.' I had actually, somewhat mischievously, used his full name.

'Anyhow, I was having coffee with her this day in Dandy Kim's, one of the poshest coffee places along the King's Road. When in walks – who do you think?'

'Paul McCartney,' I offered, not listening to a word he said.

As he beamed from ear to ear.

'No,' he replied, 'Chris Stamp – Terence's brother.'

I don't know how long he'd been rabbiting on – although, thankfully, unlike so many of dear old Erin the Atoll's residents, in an accent that didn't immediately call to mind a certain beast of burden in the process of eagerly consuming turnips.

It was equally important to both Henry and I that the front door of the office, at street level, was always kept open. So that the writers, actors and various other aspirants who felt they might have something to offer us could feel free to call at any time. The open door was a reminder that the Agency existed, first and foremost, for the benefit of artists. This accessibility was in keeping with our policy of informality – and of course we had already acquired something of a reputation for playing the role of men about town. With both of us being seen as regulars at the nightclubs and restaurants of the city centre. Which was liberating for the clients, allowing them to jettison the protocol and enforced politeness that normally besets the Agency business. Past the front door, framed studio portraits of such thespian luminaries as Gretta Dawson, Bourke Devlin, Giles Plunkett and Craig 'the Dame' Tuohy beckoned our visitors from the walls of the pinched stairway leading up and into the offices, which were festooned with further pictorial testimonials to our clients' achievements.

In the inner office we had surrounded ourselves with plants, scripts, books and yet more posters, as well as a number of awards won by some of our clients. Not that there were so many of those, as yet. Visiting Grafton Partners, I think, gave the clients a sense of identity, of retaining an individuality yet within a prestigious collective. Belonging to the Grafton Theatrical Agency soon became a passport to being noticed in the necessary and appropriate circles in the city – and most importantly of all, being taken seriously.

So that was what the premises looked like. And now the staff. Well, apart from our effervescent 'Girl Friday', Shivaun Carmody, there wasn't any. Just me and old Plumm. Apart, of course, from the unfortunate visits, at intervals, of that godawful nuisance from Whitehall – the ghastly Lionel Harbottle. Whom Henry, in one of those intermittent flashes of spectacular insight, had perceptively christened the Patagonian Banana Slug.

Harbottle had contracted malaria during a posting abroad – with that distended neck being a by-product of some other undiagnosed tropical ailment. And which, it really has to be said, was more than a little arresting, certainly the very first time you set eyes on the idiot. Although, to be honest, so far as I can remember, Clem Grainger hadn't seemed in the least put out by his extraordinary appearance. Or, indeed, his behaviour. Which was similarly repugnant. For, along with everything else, what determined the presence of the Slug in any room was his consistent hysterical chatter on disparate and hopelessly unanticipated topics. The man was a ball of nervous energy, which possibly may account for his sexual proclivities. The Slug on the phone – along with everything else – was quite a sight to behold.

Animated even while seated, he would thrust his glasses up onto his forehead, shift his legs about and continue to gesture effusively throughout. Partly perhaps because of his own comparable tendencies in that department, Clem Grainger didn't appear to take much notice. With his attentions, perhaps, being more than significantly captured by a cornucopia of black-and-white theatrical luminaries which now adorned the walls in their thick black frames.

Henry had spent the best part of the weekend making it look the best he possibly could – an array of famous faces which saw the young actor opposite voicing fulsome and enthusiastic approval. But now the energetic Clem Grainger was actually sitting cross-legged on top of my office desk, with his Brecht hat tilted back on his head. Flicking through a script which he 'felt certain' might be suitable for our agency.

'Because it's far and away the best thing I've written,' we found ourselves being loftily informed. 'An Irish interpretation of the Scottish company 7:84's profoundly political but also extremely successful *The Cheviot, the Stag & the Black, Black Oil.*'

It was the first time, actually, that I'd become aware of Grainger's relationship with left-wing politics. Because, unlike so many of the others who came in and out, or were associated with the Máiréad Curtin set, Grainger actually seemed to know a lot of serious people, associated with various freedom splinter groups and so on. It was only much later on that I discovered just how well he knew Ambrose Roland's deep-cover boys.

'That pair of Scottish oafs,' as Ambrose himself had called them. During that period, he had been pulling the wool over my eyes, for whatever reason. But, of course, with Roland, you were never going to know.

Saor Éire, meaning Free Ireland, was one of the subversive groupings Clem Grainger was known for certain to be associated with. And who featured regularly in the pages of the *Sunday Champion* – robbing banks, destroying electrical installations across the border, and so forth. Grainger occasionally authored pamphlets on the means to achieve socialism, and was a great admirer of the activist and writer he was speaking about now, one John McKenzie.

'Seven per cent of the population, as you know,' we were once more informed, 'own eighty-four per cent of the wealth. This is a play we have really got to do, Mr Meredith. Really and truly. Honestly, Chenevix – you have simply got to trust me on this one.'

There existed a temptation, so assuredly did he speak, to share with him the view that he was now beginning, whether he knew it or not, to embody all that disgusted me about communism – its intolerance of opposing views, its divisive class hatred.

But experience wins the day, and one always elects to keep one's counsel.

I should explain that the Grafton Theatrical Agency – being the only enterprise of its kind at the time, had actually been none other than Henry Plumm's brainchild. Which, given the essentially prosaic nature of the man – I mean, he could be funny but was more reactive, if you know what I mean – came as quite a surprise. In any case, he had somehow succeeded in persuading not only Roland of the idea's long-term validity, but also a number of serious F4 doubters too. With the idea being that we were to maintain 'a watching brief' in dear old Éire.

What we were given to understand was that our policy, essentially, was the one I have already described as 'pinpricking'.

For his part, Roland – and I, for one, had no reason to doubt him – ever since the war, had been convinced that 'something of significance was inevitable on the island'. In any case, that suited him, I remember him musing, before suggesting that such an approach – one, essentially, of 'defensive framing' – when followed through into implementation, created a strategic weakness. Because merely reacting to events, lacking initiative and leaving things subject to drift, was both perilous and ill-advised.

'Anyway, by my reckoning, it's only a matter of time,' I remember him insisting – with that characteristic taciturnity in the Scotch House back bar – 'and when it does, as it will, eventually, any operations which may be deemed necessary against the IRA and their sympathisers shall be described, whenever possible, as "counter-action".'

Before adding, as he drew on his slim panatella: 'It may not, of course, come to pass. But it always seems to, doesn't it, one way or another – where ourselves and that bloody lot are concerned. But, as always, we'll lead them on as we've done so often before. Until what we want eventually begins to take shape. When we'll arrange for poor old Paddy and Biddy to become just that little bit fearful and confused. Erase all possibility of its being confused as a political problem and more, you understand, of what we might call a moral one. Because, in the end, they're all that little bit uncertain in that way. Especially when the atmosphere of tension is heightened. They'll become more careful about what they do and say. It tends to be quite productive from our point of view, as I know you're aware. That feeling you get in a place when all around you there's this sense of, I don't know – constant watchfulness. Then deviance tends to be less tolerated. When their Special Branch, inevitably, as it must, eventually falls in line. And not one single socialist, Republican, or militant trade unionist will be able to so much as move without us knowing about it.'

'Em-Oi-Foive, pshaw!' I remember Henry chuckling behind a swirling blue cloud of smoke, 'I mean – did you ever in all your whole life hear de loike?'

He really was quite proficient when it came to imitating the accent.

'De loike!' he repeated, as we both collapsed into laughter.

'An agency hiding in plain sight in Dublin,' I remember Roland observing as he rose up from his desk, 'an idea so absurd it simply has to work!'

And it certainly was that. Absurd, I mean. Seeing as, at that time – when I'd first encountered the *wunderkind* Clement Grainger – there was precious little sign of anything approaching what might be described as the 'Troubles' in the country. Certainly not of any significant kind. No, none at all. The place was as dead as a morgue, for heaven's sake. Which was why, when he had arrived that day into the office, the 'force of nature', as Jacqui had described Clement Grainger, had stuck out like a sore thumb. Yes, Mr Clemmo 'the Man' Grainger – artistic go-getter and creative enterpreneur, rabbiting away on who knew how many different subjects, waving his arms like a talking windmill. Bertolt cap pushed back on his head.

To be honest, it would have been difficult for anyone, experienced or otherwise, not to find themselves taken in by such a performance of invigorating, youthful enthusiasm. As he sat there before us clad in an expensive brown leather jacket and black ribbed woollen polo neck – with the brown hair washed and those twinkling eyes darting all around him, taking in everything. Why, he might have been a young Albert Finney. Nothing, it seemed, was going to stop him. Whom he had actually referenced in his conversation, in fact – Albert Finney, I mean.

Wondering, 'just by the way', if it might 'just be possible' to entice the rugged Northern star of *Saturday Night and Sunday Morning* over to Dublin. For the purpose of assuming the leading role in a production which he and Máiréad Curtin were preparing, called *Citizen X*. A history of what he described as 'the faceless people throughout history, in Ireland'. Those who had been consistently written out of the story, he explained.

'I've also just recorded a single,' Clem then informed us.

By this stage we had spent close on three hours in his company. He removed his cap and gazed down into its depths. As he drew a deep breath.

'Yes. Play every single instrument on it myself. So if, for one reason or another, these theatre projects don't happen to work out – I may well go into record production full time.'

Something which, in fact, he eventually did. And made quite a success of it too. Before the awful tragedy struck. Something so dreadful that I can't – and won't – go into it here. Because it's too much to think about.

In any case, in between times, he had actually begun doing quite a lot of work for the Agency. On an informal basis. Proving, it has to be said, a tremendous asset in spreading the news of our existence around the city. As well as ensuring that we were now not only the first port of call for many of the older theatre people, but also those who might be considered at the 'cutting edge', as our talented new recruit himself preferred to phrase it.

'What you fellows need,' I remember Clem saying, 'more than anything is cred. Street cred, yeah? And I am the one to make sure that you get it.'

I have to be honest and acknowledge the fact that this generous offer represented an opportunity which I, at least – with Henry having already departed for the Scotch House and Lionel Harbottle being way too drunk to notice – had no intention of passing up. I shook his hand.

'Bravo!' I exclaimed. 'Top whiz, dear Clem!'

With the younger man's thumb already upraised as he slung his satchel across his right shoulder. And headed 'downtown' to meet 'the Máiréad'.

'Uh-huh, yes, to meet the Máiréad,' he called back with a grin – already on the stairs, taking them two at a time.

It was around that time that the Little Matchbox Theatre Group, with the assistance of a generous grant from the Arts Council – after much soul-searching, deliberation, etc. – had decided, at last, to go full time.

'Where else are we going to find them?' he'd said to me. 'Such a company of theatrical insurgents, like-minded individuals. A unique group of mould-breaking creative thinkers. So it's now or never – we go professional or we don't.'

Which was when the Rathmines Combination came into being – basing its style on the New York 'Actors' Studio'. Working out of a place called the Tramshed in Rathmines. It was an old abandoned transport depot which they had set about transforming themselves, and to which I became a regular visitor. Always in search of new talent, as Clem Grainger said, mock-heroically announcing me as I appeared through the doorway.

The place was already a hive of industry, Máiréad drilling holes into a lump of wood one side of a flat and Clem ingeniously converting biscuit tins into stage lamps. Some of the others were all set to go with paintbrushes and glue-size. The smell of the latter was really quite foul but addictive and, paradoxically, given their ambitious plans, synonymous with theatres from another age. No stage area smells the same, I have always felt, that has not had the canvas flats primed with that pungent adhesive.

'Mr Meredith!' I remember him laughing. 'You can always rely on Chenny to keep those vigilant peepers of his wide open!'

Already the influence of the Tramshed as an all-purpose experimental art space had become enormous. Throughout the theatre world in Dublin, practically everyone was talking about it. Clem himself had called it a 'creative freaking explosion'. It was part coffee bar, part arts centre, part flophouse.

The furnishings consisted of some floor-to-ceiling Donegal

tweed drapes on the windows, and several milk crates with old doors resting on them as coffee tables.

The classes he and Máiréad had initiated there, in a city previously starved of both modernity and artistic daring, were finding themselves routinely now being described as 'legendary'. Their volunteers had postered the city from top to bottom. There were flyers everywhere, flagging a variety of multi-purpose, inclusive 'Arts Lab' events, feminist discussion groups and 'confrontational' lunchtime theatre.

It was now 1971.

Various excerpts from the *Sunday Champion*, Ireland's first 'full-colour' newspaper, had been pasted in full view along the back wall – including a number of stories which I well knew had been planted by Roland and his boys (Roley, by now, was head of D section, responsible for propaganda and the dissemination of rumours). Why bother with such cheap and, arguably, irrelevant newspapers? Well, as Henry used to say, the execution of covert action, whatever form it may take, is generally designed with an audience in mind. They concerned mainly the 'renascent' IRA, devil worship, drug traffic, etc. Most of them made for interesting reading:

Are You Getting It Every Sunday?
Inexplicable Pentagrams in Kilkeel Graveyard!
Charlie's Angels Screwing Big Daddy!

All, of course, in the most lurid typeface:

Fianna Fáil Politician Caught Red-Handed in Sauna!
Another Day in Murderous Ulster!
A Young Irishman Claims: Seduced by Creatures from
    Another Planet!
Boot Boys Say We're People Too!
Is the Devil Loose in Northern Ireland?

'Theatre of Cruelty?' pondered another headline – alongside a particularly good photo of Máiréad Curtin. A snuff movie of the mind was what she had planned, she explained, for the company's next show. An ironic aspiration, one has little choice but to observe – considering the awful manner in which everything worked out. Eventually. Only a couple of short years later, in fact.

Around this time, collective art exhibitions also became a regular feature of the Tramshed – along with periodic mixed-media shows. They also ran a restaurant, while at the same time trying to repair the roof. Small difficulties such as the box-office telephone being cut off, because they didn't have the money to pay the bill, had to be somehow overcome. There were candlelight shows – always full – because there often wasn't any electricity supply.

Máiréad Curtin had single-handedly come up with all the graphics, derived mostly from the German expressionist style of the thirties. In her abilities and enthusiasm across a range of the arts she was almost the equal of Clem, and had successfully mounted one of her own plays – a provocative reinterpretation of the Greek myth *Oedipus Rex*, significantly narrated from Jocasta's point of view. To which Jacqui Harpur in her column had given yet another resolute 'thumbs-up!' Urging punters to be sure not to miss the Little Matchbox Theatre Group's latest 'creative explosion'.

'A dramatic depth charge and perhaps most successful experiment yet!' was how she described it.

They had even gone down a storm in London as one of the participants in a festival entitled A Singular Eye. Which was intended to promote a deeper understanding between the two islands. 'In what are,' the programme note had somewhat euphemistically acknowledged, 'difficult and problematic times, politically.' And which had actually been introduced by none other than my old friend and colleague, Whitey.

Yes, Alex Whiteside – this time inhabiting his role of cultural attaché at a specially convened function in the Concert Hall. With his circulated speech eliciting much favourable commentary as regards his articulate and sophisticated grasp of Irish history.

Whitey cleared his throat. I hadn't realised just how slight and insignificant he was. Almost as invisible as myself. He reminded me a little of the actor Tom Courtenay.

Who you might remember from the film *Billy Liar*. He certainly wasn't like Joubert, anyway. Because one of them is quite enough. More than enough. However, he went on:

'This performance sets the social context for the artistic events of the London-Irish festival, generously sponsored by both the British Arts Council and that of the Republic of Ireland, An Chomhairle Ealaíon. By emphasising the complexity of the social background in which contemporary Irish artwork is produced, we try to create a sense not just of Ireland but of the many different Irelands inhabited by those inside the country, and perceived by those outside.'

There were few present who might readily have conceded that they understood precisely what it was Big Janis Olssen, who had actually directed the excerpt performed on that occasion by the company, had intended as her prevailing theme.

But all were in agreement that, without a doubt, it represented the best of what was clearly a challenging conceptual movement taking place in that 'small but always vibrant city across the Irish sea', as Whitey had gone on to put it – with not even, can you believe it, the slightest hint of irony.

When it came to the time for the performance, Máiréad Curtin had suddenly appeared as a leper in a hooded cloak, swinging a clanging bell as she moved in and out among the increasingly discomfited guests, before scaling some supports and clambering onto the balcony, unscrolling a lengthy vellum parchment which she claimed to be written in the 'moist blood of all the traduced females of Irish history'. Which she then proceeded to read through a big grey metal bullhorn:

> In wonder ask, how could this be?
> Then answer only by thy tears,
> That ruin fell on thine and thee;
> Because thyself wouldst have it so—
> Because thou welcomedst the blow!

These words, she announced, had been authored by the nineteenth-century poet James Clarence Mangan. All the way through her speech, she continued to make the most elaborate, serpentine gestures – before, without warning, launching into an untamed contemporary dance routine, also largely composed of similar overwrought body movements. As two slide projectors projected a variety of photographic images from antiquity – monastic ruins, etc. – on opposite walls.

The projectors were twin-synchronised and programmed by a continuous tape on which an audio had also been recorded, with Éamon de Valera's unmistakable speech patterns – already somewhat machine-like – having already been electronically treated, overlaid with an eerie fizz.

It was really quite a display – appearing, as it did, to come from everywhere all at once. This was what the tape relayed:

> Certain newspapers have been very persistent in looking for my answer to Mr Churchill's recent broadcast. I know the kind of answer I am expected to make. I know the answer that first springs to the lips of every man of Irish blood who heard or read that speech, no matter in what circumstances or in what part of the world he found himself. I know the reply I would have given a quarter of a century ago. But I have deliberately decided that is not the reply I shall make tonight. I shall strive not to be guilty of adding any fuel to the flames of hatred and passion which, if continued to be fed, promise to burn up whatever is left by the war of decent feeling in Europe . . . Mr Churchill makes it clear that, in certain circumstances, he would have violated our neutrality

and that he would justify his action by Britain's necessity. It seems strange to me that Mr Churchill does not see that this, if accepted, would mean Britain's necessity would become a moral code and that when this necessity became sufficiently great, other people's rights were not to count.

Máiréad Curtin then released an auditorium-filling cry of protest.

'This,' she explained, proceeding to mime herself being wrapped from head to toe in an elaborate webbing variety of duct tape and cumbersome chains, 'for those who do not know – is the austere voice of the enemy of all Irish women, puritanical presider over what must now be known in our country as "the Devil's Era".'

Some observers were clearly uncomfortable as she finished – but I could see that Roland found it all quietly amusing. 'Honestly,' I could imagine I heard him saying, 'such fuss.'

The performance had been judged a modest success, though the evening itself was somewhat spoiled by the inevitable – at that particular time – evacuation of the building, as a result of a telephoned bomb scare. From whom or from where, no one seemed to know. However, Máiréad and the Rathmines Combination – they, indubitably, had succeeded in making their mark.

The Grafton Theatrical Agency (that is to say the local branch office of Em-Oi-Foive, ha ha!) consisted largely of two offices separated by a corridor – the outer one manned by our more than competent secretary-cum-receptionist Miss Shivaun Carmody. And then my own, much larger space with barely so much as a square inch of wall space remaining empty, ornamented by photo images of practically every UK actor and actress one could imagine – both major and minor, from Gielgud to Arthur Lucan, the thirties right up to the present day.

Already there were towers of applications squeezed into folders, from every aspirant actor, comedian and dancer in the city. Not to mention ever-growing bundles of (usually) badly presented playscripts, typed every which way. And, indeed, sometimes handwritten – just as often – in pencil, and generally quite illegible. Although I genuinely did do my best to read them all – with Shivaun turning out to be of infinitely greater worth than Harbottle in this regard, being as he was usually way too sozzled. Because she really did have an eye – a very intelligent lady, little old Shivaun. It was she, in fact, who had discovered *The Road to the Shore*, a powerful adaptation of an Irish short story which I lost no time in dispatching out to Clem and 'the Combination'.

'Howya head!' was Grainger's idiosyncratic traditional Dublinese greeting. 'So what's been shaking down Grafton Street direction?'

With it not being uncommon, as I say, for the door of the inner office to come flying open and introduce his buoyant, effervescent presence – windmill-waving his arms as he announced yet another flurry of possible projects. Then off he would go, with his exit proving every bit as noisy as his entrance. Just as it was doing now, as down the stairs he went, two at a time as usual – having just comprehensively demolished the script of *The Road to the Shore*. Dismissing it impatiently as 'a competent, workmanlike, not in any way admirable piece of work', slamming the typescript down on my desk, before embarking rapturously on what was to be their next 'amazing' venture – a drama which had 'seared' him.

'Yes! Right to my very soul,' he had continued breathlessly. Which he had recently seen in the Aldwych Theatre in London. *A Day in the Death of Joe Egg*, it was called, scripted by Peter Nichols. Máiréad was already hard at work on the mannikin, he told me – in its own right already 'something to behold', he insisted.

At the Patagonian Slug's own personal, specific request, we had recently installed a Gaggia machine in the office.

'Because I want it to impress the birds,' we found ourselves being informed – only half-jokingly. Previous to this, I had firmly vetoed his demand for an office bar, citing the fact that Minty's, aka the Minstrels' Rest, well-known haunt 'for Bohemians, fellow piss-artists and prospective clients', was only, just literally, around the corner.

Minty's, of course, was already famed far and wide – principally, it has to be said, for its lock-ins. Not to mention the ubiquity of 'curious happenings' between its walls. To say the least. Which happened to be the location of my very first encounter with Maurice Norton. Who, as I say, not only became a friend, and a lifelong one, but one of my most esteemed and trusted confidants.

Now some years retired, he had spent a considerable amount of his life as a travelling player with the legendary actor-manager Anew McMaster, journeying the length and breadth of the country, before securing, relatively late in life, a permanent position with the Radio Éireann Repertory Company. From which, as I say, he had now retired. I had also become friendly with his very beautiful and wonderful wife, Deirdre Norton. Or Dee, as she was called.

Even after all this time, I still find it difficult to accept how she died – really and truly in the most horrendous of circumstances imaginable. In Farnagh, north-west County Donegal. Not so very long after the 'Troubles', as they called them, had properly got into their stride.

To be perfectly honest, I can't even believe that I'm setting down such words.

Dee Norton and Maurice: what a pair of genuine friends. Truly wonderful individuals. So personable, you know? Just about the best one could ever hope to meet, literally anywhere.

'But then,' I remember observing to Henry in the Scotch House one evening, 'be careful what you wish for. Because this city, with its manifold subtle charms – it can, and has done repeatedly, play tricks with the best of us. Neither you nor I can ever afford to be complacent. You know what I'm trying to say?'

It was to be some time before the sheer accuracy of this analysis was to become apparent. When, over time, once more I would find myself becoming reluctantly acquainted with some of the particular rumours to which I alluded earlier. Which had the effect of making me feel uncomfortable – being, as I was, extremely uncertain as to who precisely might be responsible for their cultivation.

At no time, I have to admit, would my suspicions ever come to include Clement Grainger. But then, of course, Alex Whiteside had warned me – hadn't he?

'Be very, very careful,' I can recall him insisting, 'especially with those of whom you've grown most fond.'

I had even, actually, become extremely tolerant of Clem Grainger's disposition, and that way he had of addressing any number of disparate subjects at once – pushing back the Bertolt Brecht cap, hoisting the shades – furiously rotating his jaws as he chewed on another stick of gum. When he wasn't puffing away in an office already filled floor to ceiling with smoke. Yes, that was Grainger – turning in yet another exhibition of what I had come to realise was actually an expression of a seriously manic nature – one which, I have no doubt, was instrumental in his ultimate demise, almost certainly contributed to it.

Poor Clem. What a way to go. Outside a bloody caravan. In a windswept excuse for a fucking seaside resort. That makes Woolsley Bay seem like the Costa del Sol. They had found his ribcage underneath the towbar. I mean – can you believe that?

Chapter 7

The 'Colonel O' Solution

However, 'God bless us and shave us!' as poor old Charlie used to say – Kerrins, that is, one of my all-time favourite people. Yes, God be good to us, shave us and bless us, just how long ago it all seems now. As I stand sentinel here again at my tall Gothic window to the west of 'Old Mouldy', this once-proud fastness of the Woolsley Bay Hotel. Thinking back on the oh so long-ago. Through the good offices of one's own imagination, restoring it, however briefly, to the precise same splendour by which it was once characterised.

Which is why I can not only see but feel it – that very same bracing air of this bonny seaside wonderland. What can only be described as the wondrous watercolour magic of dear sweet Woolsley Bay – complete with its fairytale sea and spray. And unexpected gusts of windblown sand. Ouch! No – I'm only kidding. Just a little detail – a grace note, perhaps, one might call it. For one's memoir.

Where one's latest 'chapter of reminiscence' is to be entitled, albeit a trifle melodramatically: 'Return to Belfast'. Like one of those turgid monochromatic movies from the fifties. Starring, perhaps, Robert Mitchum. Decked out, no doubt, in a filthy old belted raincoat. Playing a retired bomber, now weathered and aged – overcome with regret. But that's not me, I'm afraid. And it isn't Henry, either. Certainly not the version I prefer to remember.

Ah yes, that old clubbable and talkative, at least in his cups, Henricus Percival Plumm. No. Because 'Quacktown Knockabout' might be, in his case, considered a possible, plausible title for dear old Meredith-Joubert's memoir. Yes: *Quacktown Knockabout: My Life as an Agent in Belfast.* Ha ha. And, of course, Dublin. But mostly Quacktown – that little miserable, largely Presbyterian red-brick port city to the north – as far as this particular chapter is concerned.

For yet another of Merry's 'latest adventures'. Which, at least according to dear old Rosie Dixon, is precisely how my long-planned catalogue of 'fanciful farragoes' ought to be perceived. With each one she hears about – at any rate so she claims – reminding her of something so outrageous, to say unlikely, that it might just as easily have emerged from the mouth of Ken Dodd or, if anyone happens to remember him now, the one and only Les Dawson.

'Or whatdoyoucallhim? Ronnie Corbett!' she'll often exclaim.

Not that she minds in the least how ridiculous or self-indulgent it might be. Being herself, as she never fails to point out, an avid fan of musical theatre. For which she knows I retain an unswayable, enduring affection and fondness.

'Don't put your daughter on the stage! Are you listening to me, I say, Mrs Dixon! Get over here at once, Madame Titty!' I heard myself laughing heartily only just the other day as she joined me unexpectedly on the wooden rolltop bench, where I was taking another breather in the aftermath of my daily post-prandial.

'When I was a staff nurse on the ward during the war, Mr Meredith,' she told me, 'there was nothing that I really enjoyed half so much as a trip with some of the nurses to see a show by Noël Coward. Oh, tops he was! He really had such a wonderful turn of phrase.'

Then she coughed, before squealing, 'Blimey O'Reilly – you've gone and bent me shuttlecock clean out of shape!' Wearily shaking her head as she vacantly discarded the hedge clippers, before reaching in her handbag and pulling out a half bottle of her beloved De Kuyper's. Down went another plentiful slug.

I met her there yesterday, again, after my dip. Unusually this time, I found her lying there prostrate on a beach rug. In the process of giving her full attention to a transistor radio, with that great big bum turned defiantly towards the west. Then what does she do only hand me a copy of the *Evening Standard* – shaking her head in exasperation as she did so. Indicating a full-colour photo of yet another crazed youth brandishing a petrol bomb on the cover.

'Renewed Brexit Riots in Belfast: Possible Return to the Bad Old Days?' ran the headline.

'You were over there for a while, weren't you? Way back when? What's it all about, Mr Meredith? I was under the impression that all of that old nonsense was over and done with,' she said. 'Wasn't there a peace process or something?'

It wasn't a subject which compelled her greatly, either now or then, I heard her insist. That distinction belonged to her love of theatre and concomitant sympathies with all aspects of what she described as 'the finer, more refined things of the spirit'.

'What's it all about?' asked Rosie Dixon, with her head slumping forward as she tried to decipher the words on the cover of the paper. Something to do with 'talks' and 'Northern Ireland'.

'What's it all about?' she repeated.

And I had to laugh, reminding one, as it did – how could it not? – of *Alfie*, the movie. When I turned again, I saw that she had fallen asleep.

I smiled when I saw whose face was featured in the paper. Then – when I recognised the name!

He was older now, obviously, and sporting a black dicky bow matching the Moss Bros-style evening dress. But there couldn't be any doubting the fact that what I was staring at was a picture of another familiar old friend from those days in Quacktown – that is to say, Belfast.

Yes. None other than Hushabye McVeigh, ex-prisoner and convicted killer. Or to accord him his full and proper military title, as would have been expected during those rather complicated and difficult times, 'the Captain'.

And who, by the looks of things, had travelled a very long way indeed from the early seventies, when he liked to swagger around East Belfast quaffing lagers and knocking back handfuls of Benzedrine, all got up in his trademark military fatigues.

Preparing himself for yet another one of his Saturday-night 'jaunts'. Which was how he liked describing his weekend field operations. When their modus operandi was to snatch random people directly off the night-time streets. Sometimes in a Cortina, others in his own black taxi.

Like so many of his associates, I found myself recalling, Captain McVeigh could exhibit traits of kindness – but could also be chillingly sly and manipulative. In that he liked to deploy, when he felt it appropriate, that old Quacktown 'street charm'.

Perhaps best defined by the character of what has become known as Belfast City's infamous 'gallows humour'.

For example, prior to dragging another unfortunate, hysterically mute and hopelessly stricken victim into what might be termed his appalling 'inner chamber', it was the habit of Captain McVeigh to good-humouredly rub his two hands together, inquiring as to whether this latest 'unfortunate' might be partial to a 'tasty wee cuppa tea'.

He spoke with a delicate, almost effeminate lisp – hence his nickname – before setting about plugging in his electric drill and, stripping his teeth in that distinctive, almost canine manner he had – chucking the cord as he revved the motor up. Then approaching, wielding the pneumatic drill. And, with a flourish, giving the cord another sharp tug – announcing that what was about to happen was: 'Showtime!'

Nothing less. Ha ha. Nothing less. Whether man or woman – absolutely fucking nothing less. No sir. Not for Captain 'Hushabye' McVeigh. Of 'C' Company, indefatigable Defenders of Ulster.

Had I been in a position to do otherwise at the time, I should have elected to have nothing whatsoever, in any way, shape or form, further to do with McVeigh and his ilk. Or at least as little as possible. A reluctance applicable also to a number of his friends and associates – specifically the revivalist preacherman known as 'the Reverend' Passmore Stout.

It was common for McVeigh & Co. to be almost erotically exalted for a number of days prior to another of these nauseating 'jaunts'.

'Saturday night and, once again, it will soon be showtime!' the Captain would announce in yet another of those dingy bars – skipping with that little banty hop across the expanse of the concrete floor.

Before getting behind the wheel of the black taxi and roaring off to the centre of the city. Then veering west, where yet another poor wretch, usually the worse for drink, was in their sights to become the next victim. Whoever he or she might happen to be – man or woman. For, as Captain McVeigh never failed to point out: 'At the end of the day it's all the same to us ones!'

Shrugging his shoulders as he gave the latest captive another vigorous shake – rousing them from their slumber with the addition of a bucket of ice-cold water.

As I say, I hadn't intended to be present at this or any of the other 'Romper Room' assignations, as they had recently taken to calling them. After an afternoon programme for toddlers being transmitted on the BBC at the time.

Another exhibition of the Theatre of Cruelty genre, one might observe. Never without its touch of black comedy, as I say. Ulster's answer to Harry Secombe – with those hanging jowls, McVeigh could have been his double. Especially when he sang a few verses of a song – though not, I'm afraid, from *Songs of Praise* – 'Dancin' on a Saturday Night'. Wailing away with his meat hook primed.

Also occasionally present on those evenings was his common-law wife, who went by the name of Dolores 'Dils' Pratt. With it nearly always beginning the same way – Dils letting out these would-be trepidatious squeaks. Which I have to say were really quite unconvincing. Lighting up another Silk Cut as she did her best to summon up the courage to face what was coming. Sure.

Then off we went.

'Ladies and gentlemen,' the Captain would begin, 'youse is all very welcome to another show here tonight. When poor old Brother Teague here is going to get it once again. And which is good. For, as you well know, he is no friend of ours.'

Brother Teague was a term unknown to me at the time. It was a derogatory, hostile term for Catholic. The native Irish, really – dating from the 'Troubles' of the eighteenth century. For theirs was a disagreement which really went back some time. Brother Teague was a pestilence for which there was but one remedy. Merciless extermination. For some, if not all – there really was no doubt about that.

And there could be no mistaking the worldview of Captain McVeigh.

No. None at all.

As he turned to the bloodied rag doll seated on the chair in front of him and enquired: 'You've been busy planting bombs, haven't ye, Brother Teague?'

Then he swung around again in order to address his audience. There were usually six or seven others present, including myself. I didn't, really, want to be there. But I had my instructions from Roland. So that was that. The Captain, by now, was warming to his subject.

'One of the worst taigs in all of Belfast!' he rasped. 'A beggar, so he is – hates anyone what has got to do with the Crown. So you know what has to happen. He does – and so do we.'

He stared right at him with the murderous implement clutched in his hand.

'Don't ye, Brother Teague?'

Curiously enough, and in stark contrast to my own routinely professed hesitance, Henry Percival Plumm approved entirely of the services available from Captain McVeigh HQ. Irrespective of the many undeniable risks involved. And, in doing so, advanced the theory that, in recent times, he had noticed certain changes in my behaviour and attitude. Avowing himself 'not just a little concerned' that I might possibly be in danger of developing what he described as a 'sentimental streak'.

Something which, I was aware, can often happen to people like us. The effects, perhaps, of a sustained and unrelenting torpor and lack of genuine stimulation.

In what to us was a peripheral, deflating, afflicted isle – a stultifying protectorate in which we'd happened to find ourselves. Remain there too long and you just might find yourself becoming the same as them.

'Really, dear boy,' I remember Plumm concluding his observations, 'to be honest, I would have expected a great deal more of you in this particular regard. Because what we are dealing with is a matter of efficiency, not emotion. So, please, if you would – dispense at once with any further such dalliances. Or any wilful indulgence in what seems to me nothing other than tedious, quite spurious, jejune moral analysis.'

And it may be, perhaps, that in some respects Plumm was right. But it wasn't just that alone. There was something – I don't quite know how to put this – almost primally abhorrent to me as regards McVeigh's antics and personality. And not just his camp behaviour. Although that too, yes. More, I mean that slyly invasive manner he had, which I had identified on that very first occasion when I'd met him. And which, in spite of the squat bulk, saw him kind of – creeping up on you. Almost mouse-like, in fact. But with the distinctive mannerisms of a nun. As he stood there right beside you, lisping breathily into your ear. Promising you yet another 'wee bit of crack'. Another euphemism with which I'd been unfamiliar.

It meant 'fun', apparently.

I have never liked being compromised. But, as Roland always liked to joke, and he did – 'Did you think you were signing up to a seminary?' Ha ha.

Anyway, as I say – I was. Compromised, that is. When I was recruited to assist the Captain and some comrades with their dispatch of an expired female one particular night – a moderately popular ballad singer, as it happened. Whose brother was also very well known in entertainment circles. Throughout the whole of Ulster – and indeed further afield. But particularly, as one of the party had explained in the car, in rebel nightspots.

This had made their 'catch' all the more appealing. A 'brother and sister' jackpot, ha ha. Teagues on the double. Both fine singers. Although Hushabye the Captain hadn't been in the slightest aware of this fact until he'd ransacked the unfortunate lady's purse and discovered her folk-club membership card inside. Along with some printed adverts for Mickey Full Tricky and his notorious 'rebel band of brigands'. Known far and wide as the 'Unrepentant' Mighty Felons.

'Hear them sing their hits,' McVeigh had read out in front of the now senseless detainee, '"Go to Sleep My Weary Provo" and, ha ha ha, "The Sniper's Lament".'

The latter appearing to drive him completely crazy – because then he insisted that the lady singer perform it for him.

'Because my own brother, you see – he was shot by a murdering scumbag Provo sniper – so as far as I'm concerned, it's the least you could do.'

So she did.

After which he had shot her three times in the head. But not before he went on to insist that I 'did my duty' and put another one 'intill her skull' as well. After she had expired, for heaven's sake.

Which I did.

Knowing that he wouldn't take no for an answer. It was a terrible business. But, you have to understand, by this stage all present were quite hopelessly inebriated.

In a stupor, really. And, had she been in the Saturday-night company, I feel sure Dils Pratt would have been prevailed on to add her assistance. She had, however, by this point, taken her leave – and wasn't there to witness us hauling away the body. Or the snorts of Hushabye as he shredded the well-worn 'Fenian' club card.

Before asking me whether we ought to 'you know what'.

I shrugged, non-committally – but to be honest that only appeared to incense him even further.

'You're not going to tell me you think she should go to waste?'

'But she's dead,' I remember protesting.

He had given an idle shrug and had actually appeared somewhat disgusted by the response.

'I don't know,' I heard him muttering under his breath, 'there are really fucking times when I wonder about you and all of your fucking English friends. I don't know how much, in the end, I can trust youse fuckers.'

He went on complaining in that vein for a while. However, in the end, he just gave up. I don't know exactly where it was we left the body. On waste ground someplace, in the northern district of the city. Rolling her, still inside the carpet, out the door of the battered old Ford Cortina.

In spite of everything – don't ask me how – some part of my character deep down inside succeeded in overcoming my initial resentment, reservation, or whatever you might like to call it, towards the man. Needs must, I suppose, as Roland liked to say. Certainly, at any rate, when the pair of us would find ourselves drinking. Which he always insisted, given the slightest excuse, we did.

'As an expression of both our friendship and renewed,

committed loyalty,' he would declare, 'along, of course, with what your bubbly fatty little pal – yon Henry! – likes to call our "mutual shared interest".'

How Plumm had laughed when I relayed that particular 'little nugget' back in Dublin, flinging his head back in the Scotch House's mournful interior.

'Yes – Whitehall's finest,' he had chuckled impishly when I relayed the details of these recent developments. Tee hee, he said.

'Yes, with allies the likes of Captain McVeigh & Co., the boffins back in Whitehall can always feel reassured. Loathsome little fucking toad that he is, ha ha.'

Apart from, of course, *Romper Room*, the Captain's favourite TV programme – or so I had found myself, almost proudly, informed – was none other than *The Comedians*. Which was also 'on show' every Saturday night. Although scheduled much earlier than the Captain and his crew. Round about teatime, if I recall.

I was offered this scintillating piece of information one ordinary afternoon in a hotel lobby. Over foaming tankards of Hushabye McVeigh's preferred libation – the popular lager known as Harp. Brimming over with the radiant pride of a slow-witted innocent as he delivered yet another long-winded joke. At the conclusion of which, as he struck his wobbling, rotund belly a mightly blow with his open hand, he brayed in the manner of *The Comedians*' well-known resident performer Frank Carson. Who himself, as it proved, was a native of Quacktown.

'It's the way eye tell 'em, sunshine!' mimicked Hushabye. 'You listening to me there, commander? It's the way eye tell 'em!'

As he sat there gormlessly with his back to the banquette's red imitation-leather upholstery – awaiting, or so it seemed, further fulsome praise. I didn't disappoint him – it wouldn't be fair, I found myself deciding privately, to deny that much to the excited, overgrown child.

'Quack quack!' he continued, slurping more slugs of the Harp down that rasping, rattling gullet.

As I gazed out through the window towards the millrace that had the nerve to call itself a city.

'Welcome to Wonderful Quacktown!' I used to say to Henry, to amuse him. Which it certainly did. Because Henry, being an avid reader – to a greater extent than I, most definitely – knew more about its history and culture than anyone. If you could call it culture, ha ha.

'That frozen industial nonentity further to the north,' was how the director Tyrone Guthrie (a long-time friend and associate of Maurice Norton's) had elected to describe the place, 'where the very air can chill the marrow, so ungiving and ungracious is its lowland penitential inheritance.'

'And,' quoted Henry from memory, 'as for the much-vaunted work ethic of the Protestant majority, their dully pretentious cathedral, which was begun in the eighteen-nineties – it hasn't even been finished yet.'

Then we proceeded to more pressing matters. Henry, that is, and myself – in the Scotch House. He didn't even know why we bothered with it, he mumbled – by which he meant the Crown, of course, and the ongoing relationship of Quacktown to it.

'Loathsome encumbrance. Where, one knows, deep down – and deny it though they will – in their heart of hearts they wish to be as us. Pouring the accent of the Surrey clubs over their own native cacophony of fowl-squawkings masquerading as speech and exchange. Even that poor old would-be capital further to the south, that quintessence of decrepitude, with its gay propensity for exaggeration and flight-of-the-butterfly metaphor, would appear to me to tower above this provincial outpost of baleful, enervating vulgarity.'

Those were among the kinder things he had to say about it. He winced with nothing short of revulsion.

'But so be it,' I remember him continuing, 'those are our instructions. And now that the so-called beggars down here are giving every indication of recommencing their aberrant, so-called political activities, we have precious little option but to meet them – and meet them fiercely with whatever means at our disposal. As before, as always. Only this time – if, for the purpose, we must needs recruit the assistance of Captain McVeigh and his dismal agglomeration – then so be it. But make no mistake – where these other border-hopping Irish Republican bastards are concerned – this time we intend to finish the job. Yes, comprehensively complete the task of centuries. And void the recusants exclusively from the realm.'

It could be dispiriting – all those long Sunday evenings in the back bar of the Scotch House. But there could be bright spots.

'Ah! There they are, sitting over there in the corner. Well, if it isn't Em-Oi-Foive!' you might hear Charlie Kerrins bawling as he came in the door. It was always good to see him.

Plumm liked to think of him as our 'defender'. Snorting, as he did, with undisguised contempt whenever yet another hopeless inebriate would buttonhole either of us. With eyes blazing fiercely, demanding to know 'the truth of what's going on!' Stabbing the air with a tobacco-stained finger as he went on growling, much to Charlie Kerrins' amusement.

'Aye,' Charlie would then interrupt, laughing his head off, 'of course there is something mysterious going on in Dublin. Like, I mean, the services in Whitehall are going to be that frigging stupid. To direct their clandestine operations from an agency located in the middle of the country's major fucking city. I mean, they might be bumblers, like you read in the books. But they sure ain't gonna be that dumb!'

With the idea, of course, being hilarious – as he elaborated later on – after the nuisance had departed into the night. Hilarious, yes. Not to say impractical. Which is the reason why, to this very day, I genuinely don't blame anyone for refusing to accord the entire enterprise any credit at all. Or to accept even the slightest details of our careers as would-be 'operatives' are distinguished by anything resembling verisimilitude.

Ha ha, reader – there are still even times when I lean towards a complete and utter rebuttal myself. Certainly in respect of what happened just as soon as the 'leash was off'. Which was how Ambrose Roland and Petersen – a new and entirely military appointment, with direct responsibility for the FRU (Forces Research Unit) – chose to put it. It was Petersen himself, in fact, who had instructed me on the rudiments of tradecraft and clandestine intelligence-collection operations: how to arrange a meeting; where to leave messages; how to detect if a telephone was bugged; how to spot a tail and how to lose one. It was he who had presented me with a new subminiature Minox camera and tutored me in the art of copying documents.

'The Paras, really – they lit the fuse,' suggested Alex Whiteside on a flying visit to Dublin. Not long before his impending demise. He had made the comment in the back bar of the Scotch. With the barman pacing to and fro in the distance, gazing out the window over the habitually aromatic River Liffey.

'Not that anyone is complaining,' he had continued, 'because after all, like old Blinker Hall of Naval Intelligence in his time, apparently, was fond of observing: "For heaven's sake lance the blessed canker. Lance the blessed bugger – get it out of the way once and for all."'

Obviously the motivation for the Emergency Provisions Act 1973. By virtue of this act, it read, the authorities 'may arrest any citizen and hold him for twenty-eight days under an interim custody order'. In practice, of course, the average detainee was held between seven and eight months before his case came before a commissioner. I remember all of those days so well.

Reading the *Sunday Champion* that morning after dumping the singer's body somewhere in northern Quacktown – God knows where – and feeling that all you could say to yourself regarding recent events was: 'This is a tedious and absurd situation. I mean, Chenevix Meredith, it really and truly is.' And who was about to argue?

On the inside front cover, 'the Reverend' Passmore Stout was pictured attending a prayer meeting, alongside his 'second-in-command', a former army major named as Barton McCausland, who looked on approvingly as his clerical associate once again insisted that he had nothing against 'our friends' across the border. Adding, however, that if he or any other loyal subject of the Crown were to be forced against their will into a united Ireland, he couldn't be responsible for what he might do.

'Or what he might get others to do!' I could hear McVeigh snorting into his frothy pint of Harp. Before raising his head in order to pay me a quite unexpected compliment.

'All the same, you're not a bad one,' he announced in his distinctive 'quack'. 'For an Englishman, I mean.'

Going on to deliver a protracted lecture on the British establishment's wisdom and good taste in acknowledging and supporting the Protestant class in Northern Ireland.

'Plain speakers that we are. People the like of us are firm and hit back hard.'

Unlike, he implied – a suggestion which I have to say genuinely tickled me, I'm sure you can see why – 'those twisting, no-good backsliders down South'. Whose trademarks, he suggested, were their natural-born games of evasion and indirection. Ha ha – amusing, *non*? Certainly given the present circumstances.

Ahem, oh yes. I mean, some of the things we get up to, Little Plumm! Do you hear me – little? Henry was almost sixteen stone in weight! And that's without water.

Johnny Fenian, McVeigh had called them. Brother Teague and his missus. Yes, old Brother Teague and his backsliding, open-legged mama. The prostitute. The Catholic lowlife. The master's plaything. Oh yes. The 'lowest of the low'. Open your legs, Biddy Mulligan. Ha ha.

Dils Pratt had also been present on that occasion, if I remember correctly. Yes, I can see it now. She was. Giggling and laughing away as she crossed the floor – doing her level best not to drop an already overloaded tray of drinks. Then draping herself exotically across his lap, peppering his bristly red face with kisses. Cooing as she coaxed yet another pledge out of him – that he would pay for her to stay in a hotel if the tape she'd already mailed to a big London agency were to meet with 'even the teenshiest-weenshiest ickle bit of success'. Before kicking off her sandals and launching into – I mean, can you believe it? – the theme from *Alfie*.

And the Captain, the one and only Hushabye McVeigh of the Ulster Defenders, encouraging her now for all she was worth. As he kept on hitting me with intermittent, playful jabs – impishly demanding, echoing the film, to know: 'What's it all about?' Until so much drink had gone down that, at the tops of our voices, we were all by this stage squawking insensibly in a corner of the lounge. Demanding if Alfie might be so accomodating as to acquaint us with what it might be 'all about'.

With the next development being, as we now came to realise, that both Dils and the Captain had tumbled awkwardly across the back of an armchair. And, with legs akimbo, were both lying there, spread out on the floor. As a harried barman came rushing over to their assistance – only to be treated to a by now totally familiar Frank Carson routine from *The Comedians*.

'It's just the way eye tell 'em, kawnt ye see? Eh? Eh? Tell the man, Dils. It's just the way eye tell 'em, daughter!'

It was dawn by the time I left. With only an hour or so before departure. The Enterprise train, however – thanks to the usual quota of bomb scares and general inefficiency – turned out to be over an hour late. Which was why I was feeling so overtired and melancholic as I sat there in the gloom of the Scotch House waiting for Henry. In that same old dreary back bar where the silence which ensued between us when he eventually came through the door seeming so protracted that it appeared to suggest that the same almost existential apprehension existed for my partner every bit as much as myself.

There were even occasions when his voice sounded remarkably

different. But whether that was the authentic one or not I couldn't tell then, and still can't say.

As he considered the barman, meticulously slicing a newspaper and folding the pieces up into squares, hanging them up on the back of the lavatory door.

'You think the world is one way,' I heard Henry sigh, 'and then something happens that gives you, as they say, pause. You know, of course, that I was once happily married?'

I shook my head. I hadn't, in fact. Not happily, at any rate.

'I worshipped the ground that she walked upon, to tell the truth.'

I said nothing and ordered another round of drinks.

'That'll be a pound and ten shillings, sorr,' whispered Murphy the barman. 'I'm truly sorry that we seem to have completely run out of De Kuyper's.'

'That's all right, Paddy,' I said, lifting the tray and putting the change into my pocket.

Henry Plumm – he seemed so worn out that he might have been there since the early morning or afternoon. Just sitting there, glazed, watching the winding tendrils of smoke as they languidly dispersed.

'No matter how much you prepare, no matter how many contingencies you lay, there will always be surprises. That, my dear Meredith, is one thing that I have learned.'

He tapped the ash into the tray and sipped his gin. Arching his brows as he indicated Murphy.

'Take him, for example.'

It was now growing dark and the beat of the rain was becoming so fierce against the window that it would have been tempting to remain there till the early hours.

Cosseted and comforted, many aeons distant from a city seeming so often drenched and depressed, so at odds with the sudden advent of those dancing shapes, so often appearing in the aftermath of the rain – reminiscent of the penny candle spikes evident in every Irish Catholic church.

As though reading my thoughts, I then heard him suggesting in the sombrest of whispers: 'It's not just because of the rain, you know.'

Before I could reply, he had summoned the barman over. Yes, Paddy Murphy. Who now stood there, a tray hanging by his side – with eyes that were instinctively and respectfully lowered.

'Among other things, Mr Murphy here is very fond of music. Would that be a fair thing to say, do you think, Paddy?'

'Yes, sorr, I've always liked to hear the odd tune. But we don't – management's orders, as I'm sure you've noticed – permit any form of singing on the premises.'

'No, but of course not. I assume it can lead to trouble.'

'That's right, sorr. After a drink or two, people can get restless. Not that often, but on the odd occasion, I suppose you might say that they often, too, can become excited. Feel things deep, if you get my meaning. English, Irish – Protestant, Catholic. Not that there's a great deal of harm in any of them old ballads, sorr. Mostly, to be honest, at least in my experience, it tends to be the alcohol talking. The drink, sorr.'

'And in any case, you don't like the ballads, do you?'

'No, sorr, I don't. A lot of old blather, them auld "come-all-yes". I prefer tunes that has got a bit of class.'

'Like what, for example?'

'Old Blue Eyes, sorr. Give me him any day. Me and the missus seen him in Las Vegas. One time we were over there to visit the brother. You mightn't think that, but we did.'

'And what did he sing?'

'He sang them all, sorr. "My Way" and all the rest. But the best of the whole lot, for my money, would have to be "Watertown".'

His use of the word gave me pause straight away – being aware, of course, that that was how Plumm often referred to Dublin. I mean, I never took anything for granted – I knew that, like so many of them, eavesdropping for him was a way of life, almost a duty.

' "Watertown", you say?'

'Yes. Some people don't like it on account of it being that little bit too – why, to be honest, almost unbearably sad. But me and the wife, we can't get enough of it. We play it over and over – any chance we get. Because we know what it means. What the Chairman of the Board was actually trying to say, even if people didn't buy the record much. About how people, sometimes without them even knowing – the love they once had, it can turn into a desert. Make them forget it had even once been there. But not us. We've been lucky. Fortunate, sorr. We're married forty-five years this coming March.'

'Thanks, Paddy. I think ourselves we've had enough. But why not have a little tipple yourself? Maybe a toast – to "love" and Old Blue Eyes, huh?'

'Thank you, sorr – but I make it my business never to drink on duty.'

'Maybe then you'd like to come to one of the shows with which we're associated? Val McBoan and Hugh McRoarty. They have a comedy premiering at the Gaiety this coming weekend. I'm sure it's something you and the missus might enjoy.'

Lifting some glasses, he treated me to an almost sickly looking smile. And it was after that I remember wondering – and not for the first time in this curious, uncertain principality – just who was manipulating who?

'Ah sure,' continued Murphy, 'I don't be all that bothered going out to the theatre now. Not since the old times, if you understand me, sorr. Do you see, me and herself – we tend to find the type of thing that you're likely to experience in the entertainment world now – to be honest, all this modern stuff is just that little bit too high-falutin' for the likes of us. Plays the likes of *Trilby* or *Love From a Stranger*. Her and me, do you see – we'd prefer the old stuff like *Oedipus Rex*. That, or maybe *A Long Day's Journey Into Night*.'

It seemed to take an age for him to make it back in behind the counter. Where he resumed his perch and gazed off out into the steaming, gull-screeching evening.

By now the rain had stopped. And Henry Plumm, almost miraculously, had opened up again. Even though he was still fixing me with that same old mournful expression.

'I was sitting,' he resumed, 'at our kitchen table in Kennington one evening when she came in, having been shopping. The kids were off at their friends', and as she sat down she said, "My dear – you and I, as you know, have always been friends. And, in spite of anything that might ever happen – that much, I know, at least I hope, will remain the case."'

A young student with a newspaper came bustling in, soaked to the skin – seating himself in the corner opposite the barman – as the low hum of fresh conversation began. The ash of Henry's Henri Wintermans had burned down to the tips of his fingers. But I didn't want to cut across his thoughts. He began anew.

'"I'll come straight to the point, Henry," I heard her murmuring as she poured out the tea, "I regret to say that I no longer want to be part of this marriage."'

Paddy Murphy had been making some remark which had amused the student – shaking his head as he swallowed a mouthful of Guinness.

'Man alive,' I heard the eponymous barman sigh, 'the things that you hear, would you credit now the half of it.'

The student shook his head in wonder.

As my colleague continued.

'Ever since that,' Henry explained, 'because I hadn't seen it coming, whenever I look back on the life that we had together, what it reminds me of most is a badly acted play. Yes, a shabbily directed, repertory-style bagatelle in some godawful provincial theatre, where night after night the lines are precisely and dutifully delivered.'

He paused momentarily.

'Sometimes I think the whole world is that way,' he said. Then lowered his head, with the result that I could only just about make out what it was he was saying.

'The lines of which, every night after that, before she eventually left for good, fell like fucking thin rain into a bucket.'

It seems strange to record it now, but it was one of the very few times when I had actually heard poor old Henry swear. In public, at any rate.

But which, I'm afraid, is not something I could have contended throughout what I suppose might be called 'the confrontation' – which, of course, had long since been planned. And was inevitable. Yes, all those many long years afterward – when I'd decided I'd waited long enough. To give the old cretinous bastard 'what for', as dear old Rosie of Dixon Mansions might have put it.

Because he did, and there's no denying it, there can't be. Betray me. It's a sad day to have to admit to that. But it's true. And, as much as any of us – perhaps even more than most – what Henry Percival Plumm was aware of were the Rules.

'The Rules, my lad. The fucking Rules!' I mean – how many times had we heard those words from Roland? Too many to count. And now here he was – not only discarding them but smashing the blooming things to pieces. Yes, it turns out, after all, that – of all the dissemblers in a profession which has come to regard such activity as nothing other than the finest of arts – he couldn't for once suspend his instincts.

'Never write anything down!' I had warned him. 'Do you hear me? Never!'

Little did I know that his project had already begun – and, consequently, his demise almost irreversibly guaranteed. No, there was nothing that either of us could have done. Even if Henry had indicated any willingness. No. Already it was over. And dear Plumm was under six fatal inches of water. Already in the process of 'for ever blowing bubbles'. RIP in the bath of 'Old Mouldy'. Except, of course, from the unappealing crevasse of his bottom. Regrettably, it must at last be conceded, the necessary 'deed'. Already it was done. Bye-bye, Henry, imaginary OBE. Knight of the Order of the Windswept Birthday Cake. Scion of the City of Bubbles, Woolsley Bay. Alas, he is gone. What a way to go, as the Americans say. Or used to.

We had been boating for the greater part of the afternoon – and already I knew it was going to happen. Rosie had departed – having gone up to London on the train, leaving a note. And also, as it happened – leaving the pair of us alone.

As a result, the coast remaining entirely clear for me to seriously consider administering what I like to classify as the 'Colonel O' solution. Smashing him, that is, over the head with the sturdy, weathered oar, which, along with the wooden dinghy, was actually the property of the hotel.

Yes, dispatching the treacherous apostate with one single, well-aimed blow of the wooden implement. Before delivering a goodly quota of, ultimately, fatal slaps. In the bathroom, of all places – where he had attempted, idiotically in my view, to seek sanctuary. But way too late – for the beater had already struck. With that promised, well-aimed, single, sturdy blow. Which saw the bastard tumbling wildly across the side of the bathtub – it was like the air going out of a dirigible. With all of the pages I'd torn from his ill-advised memoir, *The Hibernia Files*, floating all around him like a child's soggy paper boats.

'But it had to be done,' I suddenly heard a certain John Christie lookalike advise.

Disengaging from the body as though some entity or wraith, scarce with any substance – in what might have been some form of supernatural rite. Before closing the door of the bathroom behind him. As I pursued him meekly, taking up my position by the high landing window, polishing a pair of wire-framed spectacles as I murmured in a thin, low, nondescript register with the slightest hint of cockney: 'If anyone enquires after the welfare of Mr Plumm, you may employ the traditional strategies. No such person has ever been here. May, indeed, never have existed.'

It was remarked of John Reginald Christie that he was 'someone you wouldn't look twice at on a bus' – a figure who could juggle time and compress space through disguise and spectacles. A solitary presence who, in common with his victims, is habitually depicted in monochrome, adrift in a world of chiaroscuro tones of half light and shadow. From which the vital colour of life itself has been drained – and all remaining warmth of human endeavour. An accurate appraisal of how it has begun to feel, at any rate – here, at summer's end, in Woolsley Bay.

It was Virginia Nicholson, the Agency maid, who found him. Cause of death: stroke/advanced cortical atrophy. Severe bruising to the temple where his head had struck the taps.

'A complex feat,' I can hear Alex Whiteside observe in a characteristically rueful aside, 'if you never happened to be there in the first place. What a wicked fellow you are, Max von Sydow. Or Mr Christie, as I understand you are calling yourself now.'

Acute anxiety hysteria was what John Reginald Christie, apparently, had suffered from. As I do myself – here by this gleaming Gothic window, awaiting a rerun of the same dark dream which has haunted me for years: that of my own death.

It was just a pity I had to discover Henry's diaries. Maybe if I'd never found them. I winced involuntarily. Before finding myself, as so often, by the Liffey. There in the back bar, as of old. There was a shadow standing over by the window. But there wasn't a sound.

'Sometimes,' Henry murmured, 'you know, that fellow gives me the shivers.'

Meaning Murphy. I knew what he meant as he continued, 'Then a lot of them, as you know, are like that. I first became aware of how common such watchfulness actually is in this country – on the night we attended the prizegiving at the Gate Theatre. When Maurice Norton had collected his lifetime achievement award. You recall?'

I nodded.

'Val McBoan and Hugh McRoarty were there. Do you remember what the fellow said to McRoarty backstage?'

'Huh?'

'It was a government minister he'd been in prison with during the twenties. "I enjoyed your reading, Mr Norton, of Mr Wilde's excellent poem." "The Ballad of Reading Gaol" he was talking about. Then he guffawed – perhaps for my specific benfit, I don't know. But then, you see – you never really do.'

He didn't speak for some time after that. Then he resumed.

'I was in the bar when the minister in question came over to me. "I was telling you I liked Wilde's poem," he said, "but there's a good reason for that. Seeing as myself and Hugh McRoarty – myself and himself did a spell there for a while. But then, being who you are, you probably would be aware of that already. Wouldn't you? Yes, yourself and your colleague, Mr Plumm. That other fellow who acts like your shadow. What's his name? The Hush-Hush Man – that's what I like to call him." Then when I looked around, he was gone,' Henry said, 'the government minister.'

He had grown a little pale as he stared down into his glass.

'What did he mean by saying something like that?' I asked. 'Was he trying to be provocative?'

He regarded me with dead, rheumy eyes.

'I'm afraid, my old friend, I genuinely don't know. Because, and not only in this country, there are so many things that I simply cannot bring myself to understand. Like who is watching who – and why?'

Far away, a passing tugboat lamenting on the Liffey. Subsequent to that – not so much as a single sound.

Yes indeed – there are lots of things that we simply don't know about, I found myself reflecting on the verandah after taking my leave of Plumm.

I hadn't been expecting Rosie to come back so soon. And now, here she was, supposed-sitting with her gin bottle in a deckchair right beside me. For all the world resembling some hopelessly inflated version of the would-be Ulster starlet Dils Pratt. Now so drunk she could only just about say her name – even if she didn't bother to so much as utter a single word. Only snore.

Birds, eh?

Like something you might say when you've just interred your wife. Something, I'm sure, Michael Caine as Alfie would have been more than capable of. That is, of course, if the script had felt such an imperative necessary.

Please, Chenevix!

No no, please!

Poor old Beatrice. My sweet little darling Bea. As once was.

I mean – honestly, in the end, who on this earth ever succeeds in understanding anything?

Chapter 8

Nurses' Parties

Birds, eh? Just like old Alfie says in the movie. Michael Caine. My name is Michael Caine.

'What have I got, really? Some money in my pocket. Some nice threads. Fancy car at my disposal. And I am single. Unattached. Free as a bird.'

And I have got to say that I, at this juncture, I endorse old Alfie's sentiments. Being the very same as mine back in the good old seventies when Ted Heath was in charge and Roland and Whiteside and all the rest of them were the handsomest and most capable of young men in their prime.

As, indeed, were myself and a certain OBE-craving friend and colleague. Busier than ever we'd been in our lives. Yes, a right old pair of busy bees and no mistake.

Up all night, keeping tabs on subversives. You don't believe that, do you? You think it's not true. But of course it isn't – a pair of silly asses like us! For who, I ask you – yes, who on earth, in their right mind is going to put such a pair of donkeys in charge of such important matters?

Yes, perhaps running a third-rate actors' agency in an out-of-the-way city that no one gave so much as a damn about, whether in the entertainment world or anywhere else – that, I suppose might be a possibility. You might hand them over the keys of a ramshackle operation such as that. But that was all it would ever be.

A third-rate dumping ground – a talking shop for alcoholics and moderately talented but mostly failed actors. Always talking about 'going to London'. And 'breaking into the scene over there'.

That was what united them – ambitions way beyond any meagre little talent that they might have. Not that it mattered – for who, in their right mind, in the world of London showbiz, ever gave so much as a fig as regards anything which might be happening over in Spudland?

Certainly not in Grafton Mews. In a certain 'groundbreaking' theatrical agency.

Where no one was surprised to arrive in late on a Monday morning – only to find the Patagonian Slug passed out behind a filing cabinet, and with no prospect of anything being done at least until well after noon.

No. No chores or tasks or work of any form. No letters opened or phone calls placed. Absolutely no labour of any kind. Unless it involved knocking back a glass or two of gin. Maybe that might fit the description? Because that, in truth, was where the greater proportion of our labours was conducted.

Yes – right there at the main counter of Minty's bar, just around the corner from the office. The one and only Minstrels' Rest – where practically every deadbeat actor (and actress) in the city seemed to congregate.

Although, I have to admit, there were one or two who were of some merit. Including Hugh McRoarty, not only a character actor but also former saxophone supremo with the Bel-Air Showband. Who had actually introduced me to the instrument, and brought me up to Walton's music shop in North Frederick Street, giving me advice on which particular model to purchase.

A golden Selmer, as it happened. With the most beautiful keys of inlaid pearl. As soon as he heard me, he said I was a natural. In possession of a God-given talent.

'An absolute natural,' he'd whistled through his teeth.

A recollection which, this very minute, prompts me to pop back up to my room in the hotel and retrieve that trusty pearl-keyed wonder.

'The most beautiful tenor horn I think I have ever played,' said McRoarty.

Yes – go right in and retrieve it this very minute – and haul it down this very second onto the verandah. And, just for old times' sake, knock out one or two of the 'oldies'. Maybe even position myself by the water's edge and harmonise for a couple of minutes with the hush and sway of the approaching waves. Selecting for that particular purpose a very appropriate melody indeed – one of Maurice Norton's favourites, as it happens. 'Stranger on the Shore' – in other words, the signature tune of Mr Acker Bilk.

Ha ha, Max von Sydow standing on the sand, blowing his heart out on that old saxophone. But I think, for a moment, I'll leave the idea aside. For what I don't want to do is disturb the slumber of gentle Rosie Dixon – who just this minute has gone and conked out again. Lying sprawled there in the deckchair, at home in the comforting arms of Morpheus. Snoring away like a pig, bathed in the orange, sinking glow of the sun. With the brim of that old straw hat pulled down to cover her eyes. Such a racket!

I mean – honest to goodness, in spite of those chiselled cheekbones and that haughty imperious air, who would ever have believed that she was once a high-born lady bred of Ascendancy stock? Dame Rosamund Dixon? I can imagine her interpreting such a part with aplomb.

Not in real life, however – but over there on that run-down stage, in what remains of the Seafront Apollo end-of-the-pier theatre, once the gleaming jewel of Woolsley Bay. Why, indeed, old Max von Sydow here might just take it into his head to accompany her. As Herr Joubert and his dandy saxophone, maybe I'll go over and suggest that to her now?

B'DURP PARP PARP!

With its shiny bell pressed right up against her ear – and the little pink shell coming close to disintegrating as up it goes again and: B'DURP PARP!

As I assume the stage and declare, in my imagination: 'Shake your cleavage there, darling titty Rosamund! Or didn't you know that the show is about to start? And that you have been selected for the inaugural performance of this year's summer show! In which you now are on the point of taking your rightful place in the company of some illustrious vaudeville luminaries – quite a number of which are long since deceased. I speak, as you may anticipate, not only of the venerable Charlies, Hawtrey and Drake. But also dear, dear Alma Cogan and Vince Hill. Why, even Ronnie Hilton and his orchestra will be appearing – just as they did when all of them were alive. And before the Apollo itself was disgracefully permitted to run to dereliction. Yes, absolute rack and ruin, I fear – for what by this stage must be three whole decades! But not any longer – as now, for your pleasure, "Old Mouldy" Productions request a big hand – for Longfaced Meredith's Merry Melodies! Starring – how could they not? – Her Majesty's most efficient and elusive secret agent – the one and only Henry Percival Blump!'

Yes – 'Longfaced Meredith' – a nickname first conferred on me by none other than Captain 'Hushabye' McVeigh. On yet another grim evening back in Quacktown, not long after we had vacated the Woodlawn Social Club in East Belfast. Where he'd attempted – with the assistance of Dils Pratt – to force my participation in yet another of his obnoxious Saturday-night 'jaunts'. And when, initially, I'd demurred – a consequence of boredom as much as anything else – I remember that disdainful hiss from out the side of his mouth.

He nudged her in the ribs and she threw me a filthy look.

'Never mind, Dils. It's no surprise. For he's like all his kind. When it comes to it – always make sure to keep their own hands clean. Isn't that right, Longface? What do you say, Mr Meredith? Might the Captain be right about that?'

With that profusely perspiring mush of his pressed as close to mine as it could go.

'Are you listening to me, sunshine? Is that, at the end of the day, the story? A right old treacherous colonel, are we? Go on – admit it!'

Which of course may have been the case. Not that it matters a great deal now.

Not when everyone thinks . . . When everyone happens to be of the opinion that you're a . . .? What's the term they used to use back in Spudland? Teague an daw tayve.

That was what one of them had called me in Minty's. *Thaobh* meaning sides. *Ar an dá* meaning on both. A man who walks both sides of the street.

'That's what you fucking are!' he had hissed. Whoever he was.

'And we fucking know! More than that – the people who are fucking important know!'

'*An fhírinne*,' he had added just before he left. The truth.

'Because, sooner or later, it will come out. *An fhírinne*. The fucking truth – make no mistake!'

And which it did in the end. There can't be any denying it. Except that I wasn't just using two voices. Or working a meagre two sides of the street. No wonder it got to be way too much. Initiating, as it did, a series of unsustainable events. Occurrences which eventually led to both myself and poor old Plumm eking out what remained of our days here in an out-of-season, long-past-its-prime, south-coast seaside resort.

Alone here together, I think its fair to say, like a pair of little model figurines placed on top of a great old mouldering wedding cake long ago. In a world which seems so distant it might have been, one day, swallowed by the sea.

Yes, that is now how it seems, I am sorry to have to say. Although I won't pretend that I didn't see it coming. With it actually having been very much on my mind – that day in north London when they discovered me, at last, in that cold-water flat just off the Willesden High Road. Not far from the station. NW6. Lying there on those dusty bare boards, really quite demented, I really have no choice but to accept.

Not imitating Max von Sydow now – but Harry Caul, Gene Hackman in *The Conversation*. In the middle of playing 'The Old Longface Blues' on the Selmer. And all the while arguing with oneself – raving, really, to be honest – over the Captain, the Reverend – this, that and the other. Hunger strikes. Suicides. Booby-trap bombs. And so many other, really and truly, hopelessly muddled aspects of the political situation in Northern Ireland. As it had been – oh, goodness heavens, years ago now!

This was the year 2001, and I was far from the buoyant young theatrical agent I had once been. As Murphy the barman from the Scotch House might have phrased it: 'frothing at the mouth, the gentleman, so he was!' But not only that – covered, unfortunately, and this is a mite embarrassing, from head to toe in human waste. One's own, I regret to say.

Fingering, if you don't mind, a hopelessly erratic and entirely unintelligible melody on the aforementioned Selmer sax, muttering about people long since departed – for all the world, not in the slightest like Max von Sydow. More some bottom-of-the-bill Glasgow Empire tribute version of the enigmatic Harry Caul in Francis Ford Coppola's film *The Conversation*.

Quite how long I'd been lying there, rancid in my nakedness, before realising that the door to the apartment was now in the process of actually being forced open, I could not, certainly with degree of any accuracy, say. Apparently Roland's section had been trying to reach me for days. Without, I'm afraid, making a very good job of it – the whole sad affair resembling nothing so much as the Keystone Cops.

Which of course, in the old days, was what Henry Plump had

christened the Gardaí. For those less informed, that would be the Irish police.

'Embarrassing,' was his routine appreciation of their efforts in the security line. Not, it must be said, without some degree of justification.

For all the difference it made in the end – to poor old Henricus Percival, I mean.

With the poor fool contracting vascular dementia – which accounts for his presence here on the coast as permanent resident of 'Old Mouldy' in Woolsley Bay. But that's not how I liked to think of him, any more than I do of him dead inside a bathtub. Any more than I have any desire to revisit those memories – of him standing stock-still in the middle of the dining room, repeating the word 'Roland' to himself. While arranging matchsticks on the table or lining up serried ranks of dominoes on the lavatory's wooden seat.

Yes – I'm sorry to have to say that it actually got that bad. Now the poor fellow was quite oblivious of the life that had once been lived by both of us. Dublin or Quacktown – they might as well have not even existed.

Not that I was a great deal better during the 'Willesden period', I suppose one might call it. Why, compared to what was left of me back then, Caul in *The Conversation* was a paragon of virtue, discipline and cleanliness. But with the help of Roland and his men, I did in the end succeed in weaning myself back towards recovery. Quite a triumphant feat, I would have to say – however unlikely.

Ha ha. Better than winding up waterlogged, anyway – dispatching platoons of bubbles from one's crack. Yes indeed.

And now, in the heel of the hunt, as Maurice Norton used to say, I find myself in total and utter blissful health. Something which I honestly did not expect – and for which I must say I remain eternally grateful. Enabling me, as it did – even for just a small period of time – to offer whatever assistance I could to dear old Henry. Yes, help him in whatever possible way I could. I can see it yet – the pair of us standing there on the beach, a right-looking pair of old codgers and no mistake.

He's even sporting a Kiss-Me-Quick hat. I mean, for heaven's sake! You can even see him smiling in appreciation as I fumble helplessly with yet another deckchair. You'd have thought I'd have mastered the blooming things by now! But another sharp clack and down goes the blessed thing again. Like something designed by Heath Robinson, ha ha!

'Look!' I can hear myself crying out. 'This one here is especially for you, old chap!'

But with Henry giving not the slightest indication of ever having heard me at all.

'State actor?' Charlie Kerrins used to say, whenever the famous rumours would show signs of starting up around Dublin again. 'All I can say is that those security fellows across the water, they would surely have to be stuck if the likes of Henry Plumm is the best they can come up with. State actor? Fruity old piss-artist, maybe, more like!'

While I'm standing here by the window, surveying what passes for activity on the beach – check single dog, fluttering newspapers – I like to amuse myself by listening to the radio. Old Time Comedy Radio, with its selection of goodies on rotation, remaining my absolute favourite.

Sometimes – it seems uncanny – yet another old standard will erupt and almost succeed in wringing a tear from one's hardy old eye. 'The Wibbly Wobbly Walk', for example – a musical-hall standard dear Rosie professes to have a great affection for also – but to be honest, she can also be a right old fibber. So her enthusiasms may well just have been yet another clever little ploy to amuse and please me. Because I still have this feeling that – advanced in years though we both well may be – the impish little minx still carries a torch for me. And has even, on occasion, suggested that she might be persuaded to include my name on a certain legal document entitling one to a 'little piece of birthday cake!' as she put it.

Meaning, when the time comes, part-ownership of 'Old Mouldy'.

Not, mind you, that it is a subject yet to be approached in any great depth – simply because she would not be capable. Preoccupied as she remains with the consumption of bottles of gin. As she lies there, slumped in her blue-and-green deckchair, releasing another tornado from a distended, pink, fleshy nostril.

Sometimes, you know, Henry dressed up like Tony Hancock. Why, I don't really know. Maybe simply because he liked him. But talk about attracting unnecessary attention. He had sprung it on me one day, unexpectedly. And I can see him yet – there in his homburg, larger than life. Filling out a three-quarter-length sheepskin, twirling that ebony-handled, rolled umbrella.

'Why!' I can hear him giddily exclaim in the back bar of the Scotch House, 'It's the lad himself!'

He had even mastered the Tony Hancock walk. It brought the house down that first time in Minty's, it then being 'the heart of a Saturday night' and all the would-be thespians, drunks and assorted politicos already in situ. Yes, those familiar Minstrels' Rest-style reprobates of all shapes and sizes.

'Here, look, you fellers – it's the lad himself!' Charlie Kerrins had shouted up from the end of the counter – before arriving to join us, ferrying two tasty-looking, foaming pints.

We had a good laugh then – with Henry giving as good as he got, I have to say. And a darn fine impression of 'the lad' concerned, to boot. Which, of course, in retrospect, ought to come as no real surprise, Henry and 'the lad' Hancock sharing as they did what can only be described as an intense vulnerability. Along with certain other physical similarities. Most significantly, perhaps, that rotund build and a comically mournful expression.

It was as if both men flaunted a persona that represented a composite of all human weakness – those distinctively weary and exasperated tones which could turn the most mundane of lines into a rib-tickling observation. Yes, Henry Plumm might indeed have doubled for 'the lad himself'.

And no one, certainly by this stage, knows that more than I. Frustrated pretender and buffoon that he was. Not to mention 'betrayer'. Infidel. As well as 'idiot'. For no one should ever have done what he did. Knowing, as he did, that it – more than anything other imaginable – was completely and utterly fiercely prohibited. And 'against the Rules'. The Rules, Henry! The fucking Rules. Don't – ever! – write anything down! But you did, didn't you? Although, in spite of everything – as I stand here by the window, listening to the radio with those drifting songs from a faint, almost forgotten time, I still have to concede that, in some vague way, I loved the old fellow.

Knowing him, as I do – and always have – more intimately, perhaps, than anyone else I've ever known on this earth. More than anyone I could even dream up. Perhaps even more than myself, ha ha. Old Plumm. Yes yes yes, that old tubby Henry Plumm. Plummsy-Wummsy, colleague in arms. A blood brother of sorts, I suppose one might say. Knocking back his Canadian Club and Schweppes, as he tossed it back yet again, he chortled – that same old helplessly lugubrious head.

And braying in that now-familiar Hancockian register.

'Good evening!' and, 'Stop your old messing about, ay?'

No one enjoyed him more than Maurice. With whom we both spent so many lunchtime drinks. Not that the retired actor himself didn't possess a fund of stories! As a matter of fact, Maurice Norton had quite a reputation in that regard himself. He could be really entertaining and engaging when he got going – especially with those often scarcely believable accounts from his days with the fit-ups.

When, in the company of the legendary actor-manager Anew McMaster, they'd wandered the length and breadth of Ireland. Out in 'the sticks', in the depths of the sleepy, post-war countryside.

Where they'd mounted almost everything from *East Lynne* to Virginia Woolf, in a variety of astonishing locations from derelict haybarns and haggards to old schoolhouses.

'One of the funniest things that ever happened,' I remember Maurice recounting, 'was the time the nanny goat ate McMaster's codpiece.'

By which time, as you can imagine, he actually had me in stitches. If you could contrive a combination of Anthony Quinn and John Gielgud, arrayed in blue club blazer with silver buttons, regimental tie, white shirt and red-spotted pocket square, then you have some idea of the figure Maurice Norton presented. Of a type which I hadn't before realised existed in Ambrose Roland's torpor-afflicted archipelago. But, unlike a lot of the other stray, disconnected gibberish that generally passed for speech in the neighbourhood (you ought to have seen how Plumm used to morosely raise his eyebrows – particularly if the speechifier in question happened to be inebriated), I must confess to having found Mr Norton's gentle manner and those mellifluous vowels extremely persuasive and easy on the ear.

Particularly considering some of the lawless, not to say downright treasonous, episodes he was recounting from that between-the-wars period. Days defined by a romantic individualism.

'I had just terminated my contract with Mac,' I remember him elaborating one lunchtime, 'when I was informed that this other young actor from your neck of the woods had already been engaged to take my place. A Mr Harold Pinter, no less – of whom I am sure you are no doubt aware.'

As indeed I was – that particular playwright's *The Dumb Waiter* having been the very first production I'd attended in Máiréad Curtin's Little Matchbox Theatre.

'Anyway,' Maurice proceeded, 'as I was saying, Meredith, old chap – being a fellow of the theatre like myself, I'm confident that you will allow this story the appreciation I feel it merits.'

He cleared his throat and squeezed my shoulder firmly.

'I'd been taking the lead role at this time in a piece called *The Lodger* – a play based, really, on the Jack the Ripper story. Anyhow, after the performance was over, I went back to my digs in the main street of this little godforsaken out-of-the-way hamlet. Only to find that I'd been literally locked out of my digs. With all my belongings flung out on the path. The next thing anyhow a window opens up – and I look up to see the landlady looking livid. "Please will you let me back in, ma'am?" I shouts. "For, after all, I'm only the lodger."'

As he smiled, a little ruefully, patiently smoothing back those wisps of thinning grey hair.

'Oh no you're not!' we heard him mimic. 'Oh no you're not, my fancy, syrup-tongued friend. For I seen what you were at tonight up there on that stage in the Temperance Hall. And you couldn't have done it if it wasn't in you!'

All those memories, returning now on the beach. In the afternoon peace of dear old Woolsley Bay. As I sat there, grinning in my deckchair – twiddling my thumbs as Ma'am Dixon snored away. What a pity, I reflected, that she just wouldn't wake up in order to enjoy the show. My own personal *Seafront Apollo Gala Presentation*. With no end of anecdotes of comparable quality to succeed that colourful nugget about Maurice Norton's time with McMaster. And all being delivered, stream-of-consciousness style by my own good self.

All that was missing was my very own homburg hat – then I'd be the lad himself again! Along with my dark glasses and that old three-quarter-length sheepskin coat. Which had assured old Henry a high profile in Dublin's theatreland. Which, at that time, if one is perfectly honest – at least in the year 1965, before Clem & Co. started to shake things up – had been limited to more or less three or four hotels and pubs. And the jewel in the crown, obviously, being the Minstrels' Rest.

Yes, dear old Minty's – how could it not be? Patronised, as it was, by lots of old theatrical queens and would-be raconteurs. Swanning in and out among the wicker-clad Chianti bottles, red-and-white-checked tablecloths, heavy red drapes and glowing liqueur bottles. With myself, over time, it has to be admitted, having become rather ubiquitous. And, I must confess, just as often – in common with dear old Henry – being, somewhat unwisely, that little bit 'tipsy'.

Reinforcing the idea – as Maurice Norton was so often to, good-naturedly, point out – that the possibility of our agency being anything other than it claimed was one which could only be considered as nothing short of ludicrous. Hilarious, even – as he always used to add, tossing back his fine, noble head.

'Like something out of antiquity, carved in bronze,' I used to think, echoing Churchill's appraisal of Kevin O'Higgins, the first government minister gunned down by the insurgent nay-sayers (also known as the 'sea-green incorruptibles') in the early days of poor old Éire's administration.

'Hmm!' he replied when I told him, and you could tell that he was chuffed. Because Maurice and I – we really did get on like a house on fire. So much fun did we have together, it was not surprising that scarcely within a year the lunchtime gatherings enjoyed by our little 'gang' had already attained the status of legend.

Although there had been a number of 'hiccups'. Once, during the course of what was purported to be a 'script meeting', I seem to recall a dispute spectacularly concluding with Val McBoan taking umbrage at some small, throwaway comment – flinging my saxophone out the window.

Not that snoring old Madame Dixon appears to care – about Selmer saxophone, scripts or anything else. As she lies there, jerking just a little – her knitting basket tilted sideways on her lap. Snoring like an etherised hog. But I still consider it a genuine pity – her not bothering to wake up. To catch at least a part of my imaginary *Seafront Apollo Gala Presentation*. As I tip the brim of my dark velvet homburg and perform a little twirl with one's elegant, bone-handled cane.

'Yes, ladies and gentlemen,' I then commence with considerable brio, 'here on this brilliant sunny Sunday afternoon, I am proud to announce that it's myself here once again – the one and only, the lad himself. None other than Longfaced Chenevix Meredith. And, to borrow a phrase from one of my colleagues: "Wakey wakey!" So we now, at long last, proceed with the conclusion of *The Woolsley Bay Extravaganza*!'

An appeal to which, I'm afraid, dear Rosie gave no indication of interest whatsoever. Continuing to remain like a sack of potatoes in her deckchair. With the delicate little portholes of her nostrils still whistling and twittering away – one white arm dangling limply by her side.

'Oh, you nincompoop, Mrs Rosie Dixon!' I carped indignantly. 'What you are missing, you are just not going to believe! For this performance of carnival magic, believe you me it is sure to run and run. And not just for a mere weekend, let me assure you. No, not for Longfaced Meredith here one single inconsequential season on the coast. Ta-ra-ra-boom-dee-ay, yes Madame, off we proceed into posterity without question! Or don't you believe me?'

And I really do hope that what I had to say is true. As off we trot now with the intention of bringing down the curtain. Yes, once and for all, for what has been nominated 'The Woolsley Bay Special!' entertainment of all time. How is it possibly going to end? Don't you think she'd have demonstrated even the teenshiest little bit more interest or curiosity? She didn't, however. For whatever reason. Perhaps I am simply not adequate as a performer. Maybe Henry was better.

He certainly thought so – the bubble-producing old twister! Although I think it more likely to be the quality of the material. Maybe, in her judgement, a little substandard. Or unlikely.

Not possessing the appeal perhaps anticipated by ladies of the calibre of sweet old Mrs Rosie Dixon. Lingering there as she does, prone in the reassuring arms of Morpheus – reconstructs herself as 'Her Ladyship Rosamund', lingering on days that had been spent by her and her childhood friends on the village green, cavorting around the maypole. Enjoying tumblers of ice and fizzy lemonade, along with the peals of other little children far distant at evening time. Then off she would wander, in her mind, to her time in the nurses' home, as a staff nurse during the war.

Not that those little 'angels of mercy', selfless servants of humanity, didn't, in their own way, have their share of fun. For they did, believe me. As Rosie has related on many occasions over time. Because, after all, what is a young girl going to be in need of more than a little irresponsibility and 'down-time' relaxation, after having spent the day looking after some poor squaddie who's had the misfortune to have both buttocks blown off? Her descriptions of the parties which they'd enjoyed in the nurses' home had really tickled me.

'Oh, what a giddy lot we were, Mr Meredith!' she had chuckled. 'Filled to the brim with delicious, clear-lit, sparkling bubbly. Capering around and not giving a care, dolled up to the nines and pretending for all the world to be making love beneath the moon, and all to the sound of Frankie Laine's "Jealousy". Oh, the bounce of that orange-coloured tango, my dear Mr Chenny, and us with our plump forms close to bursting out of our oyster satin blouses, in our tight slacks and attenuated skirts. Yes, prancing and wiggling, goodness gracious, in our cheeky legs without stockings. Why, Mr Meredith – one's recollections, quite simply, they leave one aghast!'

I'm sure they do, Madame Cleavage, I remember smiling wryly. Yes indeed, I'm sure they do. Those quasi-provocative stories, to be honest, I didn't really mind. My only wish is that she hadn't reminded me of Beatrice as she slept. With that awful, dangling turn of her mouth. That had always troubled me about Beatrice and was the reason, in the end, I'd been so taken with the really quite delectable Joanne Vollmann. Who didn't so much as have a hint of such things. At all.

Which is why I got up and left her there – 'Bosoms' Dixon, I mean. Not Beatrice.

So yes, that's what I did. Forsook dear Rosie, left her snoring there on the sand. And returned back upstairs to do some practice here – positioned at my perch, as usual, by the window. Yes, spend a little time with my Selmer – in order, maybe, to calm down a little. Fingering away on that beautiful, golden, pearl-inlaid woodwind.

Did you ever think how Joubert – that is to say, Max von Sydow – and Harry Caul resemble one another? Both, effectively, nondescript middle-aged men, so bland they could easily go unrecognised. Introverts, both – unlike the often overbearing and exhaustingly loquacious Henry Plumm. You can almost feel the loneliness pouring out of them. If loneliness, that is, can be said to pour. Shed, more like. You can almost sense them shedding their loneliness. But not me – thanks to the Selmer.

As I close my eyes yet again and press the keys. And out flows the melody, shedding from the wide-open golden bell.

It's like a moon of happiness is melting somewhere deep down inside. Both of its body – and of mine.

Chapter 9

Plinka Plonka

Speaking of those nurses' parties, there is one person in particular I can imagine enjoying them more than anyone, throwing her very heart and soul into the 'carry-on', as it were. And that is none other than Dils Pratt herself. You remember her, don't you, reader? I mean, how on earth could anyone forget Dils 'Babs Windsor' Pratt, she of the spun-sugar hair and ample you-know-whats, common-law wife of Captain 'Hushabye' McVeigh.

I can see her yet, on another highly charged Saturday night round about eleven or eleven thirty, egging him on as she threw back her head and laughed in the back seat, passing around the bottle. Then the following morning, still laughing her head off just the very same way as she'd been doing in the back of the Ford Cortina – concluding, as always, with that spectacular nasal whinny – when the pair of them had dropped me at the station to connect with the Enterprise. That would have been in April '74.

I was glad to get shot of the pair of them – and would have read anything when I'd boarded the train – even that successor to Shakespeare, the *Sunday Champion*.

Which – I nearly threw up – actually had featured a full-colour photo of Pratt on the front page. It must have been taken about two or three years before, I thought. But I could have been wrong there – being still a bit shaken after our backstreet escapades the night before. They had been the worst yet, and I won't pretend otherwise – I could still hear the cries of the victim. The awful pleas and pathetic appeals as he sat there, clothes torn, strapped to the chair.

There was a buzzing inside my head. I shook the paper.

'Ulster Beauty Says No to United Ireland!' read the caption. As Dils turned and blew the camera a kiss. She was bursting out of a white cotton blouse, her elegant coiffure protected by a black-and-white panelled headscarf knotted babushka-style. Behind her, in the distance, the smoky blue of the Mourne Mountains of legend. Even I knew about them. And I cared little about the archipelago and its trumpeted so-called 'wonders'.

The photo was connected with some beauty pageant in which she'd, apparently, recently triumphed. In yet some other godforsaken hole, some sour and resentful outpost of the grim atoll – only kept alive, as Mr Churchill had always insisted, by the sheer, unutterable doggedness of its infuriating, ancient quarrel.

However, as regards our own sweet bosomy little Babs – whether or not she always made it her business to accompany the Captain on his weekend 'jaunts', to tarry awhile with him in the various dentists' surgeries, lock-up garages that he favoured, one genuinely couldn't report, not with any verifiable degree of certainty. Nor describe in detail – whether in longhand or some ancient beast of a typewriter, like fucking Henry Plumm – any further venues where they liked to stage extended bouts of their quaintly named 'rompering'.

A diversion which, by this stage, had become so commonplace that they derived scant amusement from it themselves. Simply going through the motions with a dreary, automatic sense of duty. I can remember, it must have been the fourth or fifth time I was there, in one of the disused dentists' surgeries, McVeigh momentarily leaving aside the Black & Decker and taking his wife by the hand as they both intoned, almost dully: 'And bend and stretch/and stretch and bend!'

'Aye, that auld rompering, Mr Meredith,' he had said to me in the car. 'Once they get a taste of it, swear to God they can't get enough! But to tell you the God's honest truth, me, I've done it so often I'm beginning to get just that wee bit fed up. You know?'

But there wasn't any let-up, every weekend, in their 'jaunting'. How they could not be apprehended by the authorities, no one seemed to know. But, then again, as Ambrose Roland used to always point out during our debriefings in London, 'Of course the police are overworked. What with their hands being full with those other insurgent, border-hopping twits. Yes, it's those other malignant saboteurs that are causing all the trouble. If they hadn't started all of this, as usual, there wouldn't be any disappearances on the streets of Belfast.'

'Security was stretched to breaking point,' he had added, in what was a relatively small city. Yes, little Quacktown. Ho hum.

'We must do what is absolutely necessary.' That was the 'mantra' or 'constant refrain' of that old Roley back in Whitehall. And it has to be said that, in spite of his initial reluctance during that period when I'd met him first on the pier in Dún Laoghaire in the year 1965, there was none more assiduous now in pursuit of Whitehall's intentions than His Royal Highness Henry Percival Plumm OBE (not). Certainly when it came to the exigencies of what was his most recent obsession, 'efficiency'. And, of course, doing what was considered 'absolutely necessary'.

These were the matters which preoccupied me all the way back to Dublin on the train. I couldn't keep from thinking about Hushabye and his chins. A trio of wobbling, unshaven red chins. And that great big ingratiating Harry Secombe-style smile. I could also hear his voice. Hear? It wouldn't go away. Particularly the manner in which he tended to pronounce the word 'catch'. Ketch. Beside me, in the window, I could make them out, wobbling. The chins.

As off he squeaked.

'We were talking about *The Comedians*. Would ye like to know which of them ketchphrases is my favourite?'

Those beady eyes, as usual, drilled into me as he spoke.

'Well – would ye? Would ye?'

I could imagine him leering over the rim of another foaming pint of Harp.

'Go on there, Longface. Have yourself a bit of a guess. Which ketchphrase?'

Primarily to humour him, I ventured a number of random candidates. Including: Hello honky-tonk.

You dirty old man.

It's the way I tell 'em.

Just like that! The tried-and-trusted Tommy Cooper staple. But then, Cooper wasn't a participant in *The Comedians* show, was he? Which probably accounted for the expression of thin-lipped loathing I experienced looking back at me, quite angular and distorted, from the train window.

As regards the rompering and their general modus operandi, it wasn't actually all that unusual for McVeigh and his associates to pause for a while during the course of their labours. To enjoy a cigarette, cards maybe. Or a game of pool. Even, on occasion, giving their attention to a black-and-white portable television positioned on a shelf high in a corner of the disused dentist's surgery. Which transmitted *Van der Valk*, one of the Captain's favourite programmes, most Saturdays. It was a popular TV detective series, set in Amsterdam.

It used to amuse me, for reasons which for the life of me I still cannot bring myself to understand, that manner in which Hushabye kept on rocking back and forth. Rhythmically squeezing both hands beneath his armpits. As he kept on repeating, in that curious falsetto which emerged whenever he became excited, 'Ack aye! Smart boy, surely, aren't ye, Van der Valk? But you'd never ketch me – whether in Belfast or Amsterdam. No, you'll never be able to arrest the Captain. For he just can't be ketched!'

Then he guffawed – rocking back and forth as he looked across the room towards his wife.

'Blondie smart alec skittering about Holland. But he'll never ketch Hushabye. No, never in a million years – not the Captain. So, dream on, fucker!'

Dils, however, wasn't paying very much attention. Nor, indeed, were any of the others. Too busy sharpening knives, and various other hideous-looking implements. As McVeigh took another drag of his cigarette, squeezing his hands as he whistled along with 'Eye Level', the lilting woodwind theme to the programme he was avidly watching. Before sighing, 'Back to work, then!'

Their labours soon punctuated by the shrieks of diving seagulls, skimming in and out the eaves of canal-side, tall Dutch dwellings.

All the way back home on the Enterprise train, I had been contemplating numerous other Belfast adventures.

'Anything strange or startling above in Quacktown?' I could already hear Val McBoan or McRoarty gamely enquiring – eager, as ever, for any fresh scrap of gossip, however meagre. But when I arrived in Minty's – it must have been around teatime – to my surprise there wasn't so much as a single sinner around.

As I sat there up at the counter, considering the baleful, almost small-town quiet that seemed to define the city at such times – but to an extent that was almost troubling now. I don't know quite how, because no matter how I tried, I couldn't seem to find the words. I glanced at the clock. It was now coming on for seven o'clock. How different it seemed to London, I kept thinking – as the spitting rain recommenced against the window. And I found myself mulling over the very first thing that I had said to Henry, that very first day when I'd met him off the ferry in Dún Laoghaire.

'There's another thing you'll have to get used to, and like the rest, probably won't have been expecting. You think that the weather will be pretty much the same as what we're used to across the water. All I can say to you is, Mr Plumm – forget about that. Because if there's any other thing that gets me down as regards this country, it's the godawful, ceaseless, soul-devastating rain. I'm sure, you know, that it affects the development of character. It's that grimness, the unrelenting pessimism and obstinately infuriating incapacity to expect the best. Yes, the climate really must have something to do with it. All I know is – it damned well gets you down over time.'

What had also seemed strange, and does even yet, when compared to London, was the fact that, no matter in whatever part of the town you might find yourself, somehow or another you could always smell the sea. Sea or no sea, it was beginning to assert its sly, subtle power – and was getting me down, as so many times before. So I finished up my drink and headed off southward, walking in the direction of Rathmines.

I stood there hunched in my overcoat, leaning across the Liffey wall. Where the river was at low tide. I closed my eyes, inhaling the tangy aroma of the hops as it drifted from Guinness's brewery. Trying not to think about the dentist's surgery, the pleas and appeals, pitiful screams and all the rest of it, back in Quacktown. Not to mention that sweet disarming smile which seemed to be a permanent fixture on Dils Pratt's countenance. Before deciding, on impulse, to pay a call to Henry, in the neat and compact apartment he now maintained on Brighton Square, Rathgar.

It was difficult not to wonder, right up until the moment of his death, whether or not he remembered any of the details regarding what I'd told him, the information I'd shared with him, later on that night.

As I remain here, twitching involuntarily, imagining him in my place gazing out to sea – as though suddenly recalling something of the most extreme importance. But never speaking – and then returning, once more, to that default position he seems comfortable in, of profound stillness. By this tall Gothic window, gazing out across the azure, unmoving ocean. In the smoky grey dawn of Woolsley Bay. How could two people be the very same and yet so different? I wondered. The greatest mysteries of all lie here within ourselves, I concluded. And it made me sad. Because part of me was sorry over what had happened to Henry. Whether or not, in the words of Roland, it had actually been 'necessary' or not.

Anyhow, after my extended conversation with Plumm in Rathgar, I felt considerably better. Fortified not only by his solidarity and comradeship, but also, I suppose, by his charm and wit. Which was in full view on that occasion. As a matter of fact, I have never seen him in such high spirits – with the jokes and light-hearted stories about this and that, our shared experiences – coming out of him thick and fast. In a performance Mr Hancock would have envied.

He'd been remarkably understanding regarding my misgivings concerning what I'd experienced the night before in Belfast. An occupational hazard, he'd suggested, offering me another drink.

'Time, as always, will take care of that. Don't worry, old fruit. For we've both been there before. You know the drill. It's always hard at first – but then it fades. As the days pass into weeks, then years.'

He sparked a match and lit a Henri Wintermans.

'It wasn't us who made it necessary. That, more than anything, Chenevix, you understand. Or don't you?'

I understood perfectly, I assured him. Which was true – I did.

'Very well then,' I said, and went off about my business feeling a little better, with it having been of considerable assistance just to share the burden of my discomfort with someone.

The next night in Minty's was a completely different kettle of fish – so crowded I could just about push my way in through the door. And who was standing there up at the bar? Only 'His Majesty' – as he called himself – yes, the one and only Hugh 'Barney' McRoarty. A character actor, as I think I have already mentioned, of no small renown in the city of Dublin. And a playwright, albeit as yet unproduced, of considerable insight and ability. Our legendary confrontation at the script meeting I have told you about – when he'd taken my saxophone and hurled it in a fury out the window of the Agency office – like so many 'artistic confrontations' in the city, had evidently now been completely forgotten. As had been predicted, wisely, by Maurice Norton.

'I have seen many such disputes,' he had advised me, 'many of them, I have to say, involving Mr McRoarty. Because that's the way in our little town – that's the world of showbiz 'n' drama!'

'Och, God blassus!' was Hugh Barney's salutation as he spotted me coming through the door. Already he had his big arm around me. He might have been a Donegal builder that you'd meet in one of the scruffy Irish bars in London. Such as the Case is Altered, perhaps, in Willesden. Yes. That was his type. Big old red-faced, bristly-chinned McRoarty.

'Well if it isn't the Binkie Beaumount of Dublin. How the hell are you, my auld British chum? Step right up here, don't be hanging back. And permit auld Hugh the privilege of standing Chenevix Meredith his favourite tipple, a Canadian Club and Schweppes.'

His hand was already sunk deep in his pocket.

McRoarty, without a doubt, could at times be infuriating. With an ego the size of Liberty Hall. But, nonetheless, considering the mood I'd been in the night before, I must say it was still great to see him. And enjoy a few 'scoops', as he called them, in his company.

In spite of his jocularity, not to mention the seemingly limitless fund of 'plots' and 'possibilities' that he had in mind for 'future productions', no matter how I tried, throughout these interminable monologues, for the life of me I couldn't keep from thinking about what had happened in the surgery. And where it was all going to go from here.

Belfast locals, of course, knew best what signs it was wise to avoid on dark nights.

Because Quacktown had its codes, and you either made yourself familiar with these dark codes or you didn't.

McRoarty by now was just two vibrating lips. And to make matters worse, we'd been joined by Val McBoan, who was now insisting on delivering excerpts from recent dramas in which he himself had featured.

Yes, those old Quacktown codes. A black taxi parked in an unusual spot. They usually followed a predictable pattern. That said, however, their methods could also tend to vary. And they didn't always stick to one type of victim. I suppose it depended on how drunk or drugged they actually were, the Ulster Defenders.

Once they were overpowered and dragged into the back of the cab, the captives would find themselves being mercilessly teased – in the Captain's Tony Hancock version of a military interrogation.

It was Dils who had related the most arresting of these particular episodes. If you'll pardon, that is, the unfortunate pun. Yes, it was she who had told me all about another 'wee singer', as she called her.

'To tell you the truth, I forget her real name, Mr Meredith. All I know is – no matter who she was, she was a damn fine musician, so she was. Far better than me, and that's the truth. But then, I never said I was any good, did I? That's the truth – they can say what they like about Catholics. But they're good at singing. She even had a banjo with her – aye, inside her case. You'll never guess what Hushabye did – made her play, so he did. Aye, asked her to give us a tune right there.

'"Go on, will you, Missy – open up the case. Open it up there like a good wee girl, and give us a bit of plinka plonka plink. There's a lass."'

After she had performed, as instructed, Dils informed me, they had used a sash cord to bind both her hands.

Pratt had been really quite drunk when she'd told me – weaving her way towards the counter as she slobbered abstractedly, 'Although, to be honest, I'm not really sure for definite if it was a banjo. It might have been one of them other things – what do you call them? A ukulele. But I think it was a banjo. She was good on it anyway, so she was. Plinka plonka plink. You see I remember the tune? Ha ha! Yes very good indeed.'

Not that poor old Dils Pratt knows all that much about music.

'Plinka plonka, very good. Yes, very good indeed – plinka plonka.'

Later on, she described how McVeigh sometimes did 'the telly'.

'Like they were on *Opportunity Knocks* or maybe *New Faces*!'

Because he really liked doing it – when I wasn't around.

'It's just that he thinks you're a wee bit dry. Like so many of your kind. No offence, Mr Meredith.'

Calling out to everyone, as he stood there clapping his hands in mock applause: 'Ladies and gentlemen, eyes to the front. Because it's Saturday night – and once more it's showtime!'

She claimed she herself never waited around when he started 'that'.

'Och, sure I couldn't watch the like of that, Mr Meredith!' she said. 'Not a flipping chance. Showtime, indeed.'

These days, standing here by the window – after all I'd told him, I often get to wondering just how much of it all Henry Plumm actually remembered. In the end, I mean. Before the cortical atrophy struck. Maybe, even yet, it's not too late to launch an appeal. Yes, cry out to my colleague across the sea and the depths of time. And put on a show for the benefit of good old Rosie and Biddy Mulligan the maid – the very last people on earth, it would seem. Apart from myself in 'Old Mouldy' here in Woolsley Bay. Now that we have but one season remaining – here on the coast at the end of the world, mount a spectacular final 'summer show'.

In the hope of jogging my old partner's memory.

'Is that you, Plumm – are you out there, Henry? You listening to me, old fruit? Very well, then. Because the time has come. For us together to perform a season on the coast. So, shake out those cobwebs, old friend – because the time has come for our final performance. Our day, dear heart, at long last has arrived. And there is no one more qualified than ourselves to perform it. For, after all, it's the way we tell 'em!'

There are those who would say dementia is a manifestation of a living ghost. And that's what Chenevix Meredith resembles every day – statue-still as he remains there, reviewing his life by those glinting, evening-gold panes. With the inside of his head, like Philip Larkin said, as some sort of lighted room. People in them are acting, you know, he said. Everyone. Especially you. Especially you, Henry Chenevix Percival Plumm. Ha ha.

But, at long last – at least! – your allotted share of gibbering is done. Now, dear heart, that you've left it all behind. With the gulls lining up outside the hotel window – declaring their rapturous approval in falsetto. For all the world like a Friday-night crowd at the Glasgow Empire. Or the beer-swilling oiks of *The Wheeltappers and Shunters*. Which used to give Mac the barman in Minty's a heart attack.

'Jaze, man alive – but how I love this!' he always used to say, as he clutched at his sides with the tears running down his face.

'Nearly as good as Les Dawson,' he chirped.

Which I also remembered well – it was transmitted on Sundays, not very long after *Songs of Praise*. When I was seated, as usual, gazing down into my drink and somewhere, not distant, the first muffled clap of summer-heavy thunder. And *The Les Dawson Show* being interrupted by breaking news of the latest atrocity.

Chapter 10

Bowsiness

Unlike poor old waterlogged, dementia-afflicted Henry – for whose outcome one must bear sole responsibility, let's be honest – this God-given poor old memory of mine is, happily, still functioning. But, try though one might, it still remains well-nigh impossible to avoid lingering on those more regrettable, darker occurrences.

So many of which, it has to be accepted, were unavoidable – defining those 'bitter but necessary times', as my old colleague had described them on more than one occasion.

Most memorably, perhaps, during the course of a certain interlude involving Clem Grainger. One particular midweek evening in Mulligan's public house of Poolbeg Street, just south of the Liffey.

Mulligan's was a pub I frequented only occasionally – preferring the Scotch House around the corner. To be honest, I hadn't even spotted Grainger at the bar – sitting there in the company of some of his music-business cronies.

By this stage he had been making quite a name for himself, it has to be said – working his way up from entry-level sound engineer to topline producer and manager. He was a handsome fellow, Clement – in that Joe Orton style I have already described. But by now the Bertolt Brecht cap was gone, the hair filling out, being considerably longer now. In what I tended to construe as a type of 'Oirish' approximation of California, I suppose. Then there were the glasses. Aviator shades, I do believe.

Standing louchely up at the counter, clad in his white silk scarf and studded leather jacket. Skinning his trademark Old Holborn rollies.

'I'll come straight to the point,' were his first words to me.

With it soon becoming apparent that he was more than a little drunk.

'It's not that I have anything against you,' he continued, 'but I know this for sure, having observed your curiously eccentric behaviour over time in this city. That you're not, by any stretch of the imagination, who you say you are. But I'll give you this – you're canny and you're fucking bloody clever. Still, that's nothing new – for have you and your ilk not always been that way? And all of these people, civil servants and the like, department functionaries who know no better. Charm them into collusion, do you? Is that the trick – credulous fools who know no better tend to think the best of you? I know of one old retired civil servant in whose company you've been identified from time to time. (Even at this point I'd prefer not to name the individual concerned.) Where exactly does he fit into the picture? It's not, as I say, that I have anything against you in particular – just that I'm puzzled by certain things that have been going on this past while. Here in this city, and in the country generally. Then there's this other thing. What can you tell me about a certain pair of Scottish chaps that have been nosing around of late – and acting very oddly indeed, if I may say so? They've even paid Máiréad a visit. Yes, once or twice they've been out to talk to her and the Rathmines Combination. Claiming that they're businessmen looking to invest. I saw them one day coming out of your office. You remember them, don't you – the two McClelland brothers? Who exactly, if you don't mind me asking, might they be when they're at home? Can you enlighten me, Mr Meredith, please?'

'Why, undercover subversives and state-employed dissemblers!' I almost replied, right there on the spot.

'Yes! The very exact same as myself, Mr Grainger. Only nowhere near as important in the pecking order! And, if you don't believe me, then just ask old Roley. Yes, please do. A telegram of enquiry over to the bods in Whitehall, ha ha.'

I would, of course – if I'd been foolish enough to come out with it – have been joking. Because the 'Twa Shortbreads', as Alex had christened them, their only function had been that of a 'gull'. Although, however it happened, they had, in actual fact, been moderately successful in some of their assigned operations. Having comprehensively pulled the wool over the eyes of the public in general.

And, indeed, many of those in authority – and the media. Why, they had even had a rebel ballad composed in their honour!

> The twa' Shorties they gang tae th' town ae the brown river
> for tae cause some disturbance 'n make puir folk shiver
> night noon and morn till the brae dawn dun she bruk
> For Erin go Bragh till they ran outae luck.
> Gang ye alive, twa' Shorties frae Clyde!

With that elongated simian jawline and his fondness for colourful tank-top sweaters, Teddy McClelland resembled no one so much as Robin Askwith – star of numerous saucy screen comedies popular at that time in the early seventies.

As did his brother, being an identical twin. The name of the sibling in question was Jackie. Already, as Grainger had suggested, they had both become well known in Dublin. They were in and out of Minty's all the time. Not to mention many other similar watering holes. Great characters, was the general appraisal. Except, as we have seen, for those of Clem Grainger's cast of mind. Left-wingers, politicos, insurgents, etc.

'Ah yes,' I laughed in response to his mini-interrogation that night in Mulligan's, 'I know who you're talking about now, Clement – it's old Teddy McClelland, isn't it, and his brother? The twins, yes. And I have to admit that the pair of them are a tonic whenever they get going. Almost as good as Cannon and Ball.'

This was when, as is so often the case whenever I deem it necessary, I literally become Henry. And watch as Max von Sydow bows, retrieving his rolled umbrella as he turns and, literally, exits the room. With, lo and behold! Henry Percival Plump taking the stage!

'Ey you, what you saying? That's my mate Tomma, that is. My mate Tomma! Ha ha. That's my mate Tomma, that is.'

I think that Grainger was afraid – as can often be the case with Henry, of course – that I fully intended to run right through the roster of ITV superstars. Which, presumably, was why his convenient insouciance began fading.

'So who the fuck are they, then, will you tell me? What are they up to – and how is it you seem to know them so well?'

'Oh, they're just like so many who come in and out of the office, like yourself. Heard there might be a bit of work going – but to tell you the truth, they're just not that talented.'

'Just not that talented?'

'Yes, that's right. Just not that talented. They're actors, you see.'

'Actors?'

'Or think they are.'

I motioned as I made my way towards the back of the pub, to 'join some people', rather unconvincingly.

Not that it mattered, for he soon made it clear that this explanation was going to be less than satisfactory. As he pushed in between us with uncharacteristic aggression – manoeuvring himself alongside me, squeezed against the back wall. Before leaning across to whisper in my ear: 'I know you're up to something, Mr Meredith – so don't go thinking I don't. I read about that fellow Alex Whiteside in the paper. And I know that you are connected with his disappearance. Even if I can't rightly say in what way or how that might have come to be. And I also know something else. That some people – political types – you might say, have similar suspicions.'

He produced a tin of Old Holborn tobacco and proceeded to look me directly in the eye. With it being the strangest thing, that as he ran his tongue directly along the paper's gumline, all I could see was this tiny image there inside his iris. As I did, the pulsating chunk chunk chunk of disco music. Which I immediately recognised as the soundtrack from *The Stud*.

As, right in there, tilted sideways in Grainger's gleaming eye, it formed itself in front of me. An image of poor old Alex Whiteside, as he did his level best not to be, for God's sake, any further besotted by the simperings and cooings of a sixteen-year-old Joan Collins lookalike, heavily made up to carry the role of Fontaine Khaled. Circling the bed where poor old Alex, now completely starkers, released the most pitiful and pathetic of whimpers. As Fontaine Khaled teased him with a scarf – a great big long item of the palest blue chiffon. As 'Mr Whitey' – that was what she called him – pleaded once more for her 'not to do it'.

But wanting her to do it.

So she did it.

'Do you remember the first time we met in Belfast,' she whispered, 'just you and me in the orphanage dormitory, back in sweet old Ravensbrook? Do you remember that?'

'Yes, I remember,' replied Alex Whiteside. 'Yes, I remember.'

Oh so well.

Before going on to utter those very same words that I had anticipated at the time of making the phone call which would see him ruined. Just as Roland et al. had instructed.

'I want to set you up in a house. I want you to be just for me and me alone. More than anything, I want that, Joan. Do you think that, somehow, that might be possible?'

He was a very mischievous and quite charming boy, oh but

yes. Which was why she said: 'Oh but yes, I think it might be very much possible. Very, very possible indeed, Mr W.'

Then what happens – more splashes in Whitey's eyes.

It was I myself who had contacted the police. I had made the call from a phonebox on Whitefriars Bridge – emphasising that it wasn't just a 'domestic dispute'.

I don't know how long it took them to get there – but they found them anyway, apprehending them both in flagrante delicto.

'I'm married,' Whiteside had choked. 'Will you please not do this?'

I looked up at Grainger. It was at this point Clement suddenly blinked and the image, already distorted, eventually swayed off into space. With Grainger edging in closer to me – vigorously flicking the ash off his roll-up – in a manner which I really could not have perceived as anything other than wilfully provocative. And, much as I dislike doing so, I really have to confess that by this stage, Clement Grainger – he really was beginning to get on my nerves.

But that was when Peter 'the Bowsy' McAuley stepped in – a part-time actor who regularly frequented Mulligan's. And who, as a matter of fact, had played the part of Brendan Behan with Val McBoan in a show which, although Grafton Partners had only been involved in a minor financial and advisory capacity, had been something of a spectacular success for the Hibernia Theatre, a little newsreel place located in the heart of Dublin city centre.

But that, of course, is all by the by. Because the Bowsy (the term means ne'er-do-well) by this point was certainly living up to his nickname. Behaving in an unnecessarily robust manner. Practically elbowing Clem Grainger in the face – in the process knocking his tin of Old Holborn onto the floor.

'Ah, for fuck's sake, Bowsy!' shouted Clem Grainger.

But to no avail – the roly-poly miscreant was now in full

anti-social flight – with none other than myself now the focus of his hoarse pronouncements:

'There he is, as I live and breathe this night – the one and only hero of the hour, who is there to match me auld segocia, man alive, but if it isn't great to see ya, auld Merry Chenny! How the bloody bejasus are you? And who's this sitting here with a face on him like a plateful of mortal sins? Well, glory be to God and His glorified fucking mother if it isn't young Grainger, the one and only son of Joe and Anne. I hear you're making a bit of a name for yourself, Clem! Shove over there to fuck and give, do you hear me, the woman in the bed more porter! Are you listening to me?'

Not that he – or myself, indeed – was about to be offered any great deal of choice in the matter. The drinks beginning to come thick and fast after that and the hopelessly crowded bar so inpenetrable with smoke and uproarious chatter that it was a close-run thing for one not to literally pass out.

Particularly when all you could think about was Alex Whiteside's 'sweetheart' – as he often called her – bawling her helpless adolescent eyes out. Swaying hysterically there on the doorstep as a burly officer led his paramour away.

For ever, as it happened. Although that hadn't been what I'd intended.

I almost came close to getting sick a number of times – the more I thought of him handcuffed in the paddy wagon, pale and shivering as he repeated over and over: 'How could you do it to me, Meredith? How in the devil could you bring yourself to be responsible for such base and contemptible treachery?'

My greatest wish on earth being – if only I could somehow have explained to him that the question, so harrowing in its validity – that it ought to be addressed to Roland and not to me. After all – it was he who had said it was 'necessary'.

When Mulligan's had closed, I lingered for a while on the quays to pass time – having arranged to reconnoitre with the Bowsy McAuley much later on. A couple of hours, as a matter of fact. On Portobello Bridge, after leaving the Mandarin Grill. Where I, like so many others in the city, used to go for soakage: their mixed grills were legendary.

Not unsurprisingly, the Bowsy by this stage was sober as a judge.

'How did you get on up north?' he inquired straight away – so we chatted about that. Although, to be perfectly honest, he didn't seem all that interested.

To disinterested readers, it well may seem really quite absurd that someone of the calibre of the Bowsy should turn out to be one of ours. But then, as Clem Grainger had remarked just before I left him – tugging at my elbow as he gazed up blearily: 'Lots of things do, don't they? Seem absurd.'

To be honest, I don't know where or indeed when exactly McAuley came into the picture and in any case he was more on the fringe.

'Just there to keep an eye on things,' as Terence Petersen had commented, 'a good one to have looking out for us, you know?'

In spite of what people might assume, it was actually a complete and utter coincidence that Grainger happened to be present in the Majestic Cinema that unfortunate day in Mountjoy Square when it was bombed. With the pedestrian facts being that he sometimes attended matinees there on his lunch break. And, being a sort of art-cum-grindhouse, the Majestic would, of course, have been absolutely up Clement's street. No, his being there on that dreadful occasion – when, I think seven people altogether lost their lives, including Máiréad Curtin – it was just one of those occurrences that no one could, ever, possibly have predicted.

Dreadful. Truly and utterly dreadful.

And, as I say, a complete coincidence that Grainger happened to be there. Although he wasn't hurt – he had left the show early, needing to get back to work.

Not that the Bowsy McAuley cared, one way or another.

Having no time whatsoever for Clem Grainger, as he had made abundantly clear.

'Or that mother and father of his. Joe and Anne Grainger, mortal enemies of the union, make no mistake about that, my friend. Every blackguard running-dog recusant has been in and out of their house. Rebel blackguards to the core, be under no illusion about that. No matter what image they might take pains to cultivate – aye, and that swaggering son of theirs to boot – let you be making no mistake about that, Mr Meredith.'

In some ways, the Bowsy reminded me of an overweight Edward Woodward. With those beat-up barrister-style tweed suits that he favoured, along with distinctive, broad-faced, boyish charm. You never knew where you were going to run into McAuley – always finding him either completely plastered or just this side of inebriation. Never sober. But with the truth being, however, that, 'He absolutely misses nothing,' I remember Henry remarking, 'and actually, when it comes to it, one of the very best of our people. Roland swears by him.'

Yes, one of the absolute best, he attested.

Which, coincidentally, happened to be one of McAuley's very own catchphrases. Or should I say: ketchphrases. Ha ha. As he came lunging right at you, swinging his arm around your neck. And those rheumy, rum-sozzled eyes looking right into you as he insisted: 'You're one of the best – are you listening to me, Chenny, my man? One of the absolute fucking best, and that's a fact!'

As off he strolled – yet again having convincingly contrived pathetic intoxication – swinging on his heel, still with both fists squared. Once more defying an impatient but somewhat bemused crowded bar.

'And any fellow who says to the differ, of this be assured all you bastards in here. That the Bowsy McAuley will be prepared to take him on. Do youse hear me, do youse? Up Ireland, now and for ever, to the damn and blasted latter end of the day! Hurr hurr!'

Chapter 11

A Steam Iron

Honest to goodness, tragic though recent events might have been, with poor old Plumpie and other things, the more I gaze upon that lapping turquoise ocean as it makes its way forward and back, with those exquisite and delicate lace-fringed waves exerting their mesmerising magic, the more I am tempted to insist on Mrs Dixon opening those gin-sozzled peepers and listening to what it is I have to tell her. And not only that, advise her as to the sheer magisterial beauty of the spectacle which she is missing. What a backdrop for our last season on the coast – like a Donald McGill postcard, for heaven's sake, come alive!

But not only that – because don't forget we also have Old Time Comedy Radio at our disposal. And all the jolly japes that memory will also provide. As, right on cue, here he comes – yes, the one and only Captain McVeigh, pirouetting out from the wings. Once again got up in that trademark cutaway shirt – ready to take the 'showtime' world by storm. Starring, as always, him and his 'wee honey'. Our wee girl Dils.

Wee Dillsley Pratsy.

Because, make no mistake – though an idiot he might be, Captain McVeigh – he could often be quite funny. His quips, on those many occasions when I met him in the Woodvale Inn, never failing to provoke the wryest of grins on my part.

As that leering, unshaven face with its orchestra of wobbling chins leaned once more across the table. With his eyes blazing fiercely in the artificial overhead light.

'Do you think they'll ever ketch me out? Shut down my Saturday-night showtime?' he wondered. 'I mean – you that's aware of things. Knows where all this is going. Mr Meredith who misses nothing. You that has the ear of yon fellow beyond in London. Yes, Mr Roland at your service. You reckon the rozzers will ever get around to ketch the Captain? Because, do you know what I'm going to say to you, Mr Meredith? Because, if you're asking me, my opinion would have to be that I don't think they ever will. And you yourself know just why that might be. Why that actually might be the case. Because, I'm afraid – I'm way too well protected.'

Then, for some reason best known to McVeigh himself – and of which Dils Pratt remained blissfully unaware, lost in her own private world of cabaret and Ulster screen stardom – he thrust himself over and jabbed me hard and firm in the chest. But the eyes hadn't moved – flashing, penetrating.

'Because I know all the detectives,' he growled, 'each and every fucking one, Commander Meredith. Even better than the ones I know off the telly.'

At which point, not entirely unexpectedly, for there was nothing McVeigh liked better than playing games.

Cat and mouse.

He was beaming from ear to ear as he slurped.

'Which of them all would you say's your favourite?'

Then he began listing various names in a singsong voice. No, not those of prominent CID personnel – but TV characters. Including Cannon, Mannix and Banacek. With his own personal favourite, he went on to insist, being Tom Selleck starring in the role of Magnum, PI.

'Cannon,' he chuckled, 'what a big fat useless fucker. Whadd-you say, Merry, are you listening to me now? Such an absolute sonofabitch. Worse than me, he is. Aye, even worse than me, Cannon is. Because all he ever seems to do is wheeze and stumble about. But all the same, he still seems to make enough to pay for his big fucking gourmet cooking, and keep a fucking Lincoln Continental on the road. He's got to weigh in at at least nineteen stone – which means that he'd probably, more than likely, be well fit to do a job on poor old Hushabye, you think? Yeah, he's got to be that – 'cos he's plain obese, close on three hundred pounds – stumbling out of buildings and him with hamburger and cigar still lit. Still lit, the fucker, can you believe it – stuck in the middle of his stupid fucking gob. I ask you. With bits of the burger still flying out of his paw.'

He swung around and shouted over to Dils:

'You listening there, darling? You hearing what I'm saying over there, you bitch? Never pay attention, do you – not unless it's to do with money. For that's all they care about, isn't it, Mr Meredith? Women, I mean. That and getting their lashes stuck on – like they're about to audition for *New* fucking *Faces*! Hey there, pussies – listen up, 'cos it's showtime!'

You could actually hear the idiot's teeth grinding.

'Well, you'd do well to pay attention, Dils. Aye, fit you better that you'd lend a body an ear when he's talking till you.'

But his common-law wife wasn't listening to a word he said. Being much too preoccupied endeavouring, as best she could, to isolate the elusive words, the recalcitrant lyric of one of her favourites when she'd had a few too many: 'Roll Me Over in the Clover'.

And which remains in my head, bell-clear as I stand here. Unmoving by the tall Gothic window as I spy on Mme Dixon. Grunting as she wakes and searches around for her basket of knitting. And, of course, her *Bella* magazine ('Is it all over for Ant & Dec?'). It's hard to believe the way it's ended up. I can still hear her scream when she discovered old Windybuttocks lying in the bath. Like something out of a horror movie. She had even looked like Bette Davis – hand up to the mouth and everything. But no sound coming out. Which wasn't, of course, surprising – considering that old Henry – he wasn't as yet . . . well, you know.

Expired.

Dead.

Not that it would have made a great deal of difference. With dementia, more or less, having done that anyway. Still groaning away in the bathroom, inside the tub. Ah well. It's funny the way life turns. What with Henry, in his time, having distinguished himself so admirably – in the naval service, for heaven's sake – and then finishes up discharging bubbles from his posterior. Yes, exiting out of that flagrantly thrusting aperture. But then, when you get this far in life, you are always more or less assured that, when it comes to the third act, there is generally a comical or farcical conclusion to everything.

Although not for a moment am I attempting to suggest that the average citizen is likely to find the Captain or his ilk – including his 'be-oo-ti-ful' lady or any of the others, including Battler Shaw and Winky – in the least bit amusing. Certainly when 'Wee Hushabye', as his lieutenant Winky Hardman elected to christen him sometimes, starts pretending in the surgery that he's none other than William Conrad. In the process of waving an imaginary cigar around – shrieking falsetto on a stage where off-white walls (the surgery hadn't been used in years) are splattered with great big whorling maps of blood.

And which Dils, bless her heart, always laughed about – especially over our drinks in the hotel – all the while, however, disavowing serious personal involvement. Claiming not to have been present at the majority of the 'rompering' occasions – and certainly not when certain ballads were being sung. Whether 'Mother of Mine' or 'Me Auld Skillara Hat'.

When, in fact, she very much was.

Finding it particularly hilarious, as I seem to recall – having actually been present for that one myself – when Hushabye, who by his own admission had already consumed twelve pints of

Harp, had released an absolutely unmerciful whoop before leaping three feet in the air and commencing to bark like a dog. Now crawling around as he tugged at his female captive's leg – imploring her to join in.

There could be hell to pay on occasions like that. Especially if his appointed lieutenants Battler Shaw and Winky happened to arrive, or any other members of the 'battalion'. Battler Shaw tended to exert an adverse effect on everybody. Being wound-up by nature – and, in any case, partial to the excessive consumption of amphetamines. There would then be bickering and consistent, if sporadic, arguments. The worst of which, in my experience, being that connected with some teenager Shaw had apprehended and with whom they didn't know what to do when their work was eventually completed.

It was only later on that it dawned on me that the corpse I'd seen in the laundry basket was him – the teenager, I mean. On the same night Shaw had been searching for the iron.

'Where the fuck is it? I always put it here – youse know that! Are youse listening to me, fuckers? I always make sure it's under these stairs! Give it me!'

It was an old-fashioned steam model – one often used to brand a victim on their hands and feet, in the manner of a rudimentary crucifix. There was an awful bloody mess when they finally got the job done. And Battler Shaw went back to watch the televison. The old Toshiba small-screen portable – where, completely by coincidence, William Conrad was crashing through yet another municipal market behind the wheel of his Lincoln Continental. But he wasn't saying anything now – yes, as quiet as a mouse, sipping away at his full glass of vodka.

'Man, but he is one contrary bastard,' snapped the Captain, 'Hushabye' McVeigh. 'Gets on my bloody nerves, he does.'

Chapter 12

The Truth About 'Colonel O'

The Mandarin Grill was situated across the river in South Richmond Street, Dublin, and was frequented mainly by theatrical personages and showband players who arrived at all hours of the night to order huge plates of greasy food and pints of milk. 'The works!' they would declaim, with a snap of their fingers. 'A full fry and the wine of the country!'

The Witnesses Showband were regulars there – which is how I came to be acquainted with them in the first place. Other familiar faces included DJ Grogan, the showband manager, Maurice Norton of course, Val McBoan and Gretta Dawson – both stalwarts of the Hibernian Players. The Special Branch was also known to pop in and out – and whenever they did, were usually to be identified in one or other of the alcoves. Doing their best and, as a rule, failing miserably to blend into the surroundings.

In terms of layout, the restaurant was partitioned into two distinct areas. There was a front section with a Formica-topped counter and wooden stools, and then, behind the dividing twin doors, there was the dining room with its more conventional café arrangement of tables and chairs. Traditionally, going back to its heyday in the fifties, the front lounge was a favourite haunt for gays, lesbians, cross-dressers and camp individuals in general. Who, of course, would have felt comfortable congregating there, in no way under threat. In one of the alcoves stood a vintage Wurlitzer record machine, a perennial favourite with the musicians.

The notorious Bud Mulholland had also been known to take a look in from time to time – whenever he happened to be over from London, where he owned a pub.

And where his outrageous moneymaking schemes and exploits had attained some considerable measure of notoriety. Having featured on no fewer than three occasions, in fact, on the cover of the *Sunday Express*: 'Irishman Spends Three Days Underground.' He had also staged world-class boxing tournaments in the National Stadium on the South Circular Road.

Built like a couple of beer barrels bound together, it was reported that he had laid out 'three cockneys' side by side – with one blow each, in his pub the Inn, located on Shepherd's Bush Green – before slugging yet another overzealous and misguided miscreant, sending him flying through a plate-glass window.

The menu in the Mandarin consisted of everything from beans and chips to chargrilled steak with lashings of onions, with endless variations on the fry-up-and-chips concept in between. Every night the rush began at around 2.30 a.m., when the first wave of sweaty nightclubbers came streaming through its welcoming doors.

It was full of surprises – some of which I was in a position to witness myself. Being privileged on one particularly memorable occasion to encounter Maurice delivering a rendition of one of his own favourite songs, 'I'll Walk Beside You', in his really quite beautiful tenor voice – to a hopelessly intoxicated but oddly appreciative, near-rapt audience. It was that kind of place. With even old Plumm at his grumpiest having to concede that on occasion, miserable old 'Oireland' of the leaden-grey skies, nosey housewives and its unimaginative, largely uneducated peasant clergy could actually 'catch one on the hop'.

'Yes – it has its own, rather unpredictable ways,' I remember him nodding.

Certainly brought a tear to my eye, that's for sure. Because I really had come to like Maurice Norton — and his wife. Loved them, really, in a way.

Whenever Plumm would suggest that the pair of us ought to treat ourselves to 'something a little more cosmopolitan', we would make our way towards the New Delhi in Camden Street. Where, as a matter of course, he would commence deriding whatever fare might happen to be on offer.

'What is the point of even coming here, then,' I would find myself complaining, 'if you're so sure that the quality is going to be below par? Why, it seems to me that before you even got your hands on a menu, you were ready to be dissatisfied! You know, there are times when I think Pat Murphy has a point. And by which I mean the Irish people in general. When they talk about the tediously predictable hauteur of the Saxon.'

'Oh no, my dear, it's not up to scratch!'

'Oh do, for heaven's sake, Plumm — shut up!'

'Damned bloody backwater,' would be his invariable response — as he dabbed those Dubonnet-dappled lips with a napkin, before adding: 'What could it possibly be in a former life that I have done to be sequestered here in this torpor-crushed atoll that has the nerve to call itself a republic. And which, in spite of what you may say, remains the home of every God-blasted beggar and counter-jumper in Christendom. For there's not one single soul in this city that I'd trust. Did you see where that government minister has been caught red-handed? It's all over now. The balloon's going up. So you had best get your Sunday suit on, my lad. For this is the time we've been waiting on all along. Yes, I'm afraid, Comrade Meredith — this is the moment towards which everything has been leading. So, go on then — eat up! Devour whatever they call this muck!'

Tiernan McGilly was a cabinet minister who'd been arrested late one night by the Special Branch in a country house — not just any old ordinary country house, but one infested with 'every cursed wily beggar and counter-jumper' you could imagine.

'Who ever desired ruin and misfortune to descend upon our realm!' spat Henry. And I don't ever think that I've seen him so angry.

'Hedge-killers, recusants. Casual backwoods destroyers of life and limb. Iniquitous maledictors of the very worst stripe,' he had added. 'And McGilly's the worst.'

There ensued a long silence. I saw no place to disagree – nor even to comment that his tie was hanging into his curry.

'Yes. That, I'm afraid, is your elected representative, Mr McGilly,' he snarled anew.

It had been all over the papers. There was even talk of a possible lengthy prison sentence. I had seen McGilly one night in the Mandarin – neat, conspicuous in a sharp pinstripe suit. Eyes ever watchful. A former health minister, now foreign affairs.

'He has been in our sights for quite some time,' Roland had told me, 'ever since the destruction of Nelson's Pillar back in 1966, as a matter of fact. Which he, or those close to him, perpetrated. We had even considered arranging an accident. But Petersen, ever the cautious one – and indeed maybe he had his reasons – in the end he decided against it. Yes, vetoed the proposal – which, coincidentally, had initially been introduced by our friend Alex Whiteside. Who at that time was an up-and-coming operator of unquestionable worth. He put a stop to the whole idea on the grounds that what was being suggested was nothing more than an exhibition of quite unnecessary and most likely counterproductive emotionalism.'

'I know what I'd have done with him,' I remember Henry declaring with particular vehemence, 'given him a taste of what "Colonel O" was fond of, way back when – in the days of Lloyd George and the "Irish Murder Gang", as the old Welsh Wizard called them.'

I knew immediately to whom Henry was referring. He had spoken to me on previous occasions regarding 'Colonel O', whom he had known for a while during his earlier days in the service. It was Colonel Ormonde de Winter he meant. Who'd been drafted into the city of Dublin directly after the massacre on Bloody Sunday, on 10 July 1921. The day directly after the Twelve Apostles, as the assassins in question had been so charmingly christened, had expedited their own personal, lethal bloodbath on the direct orders of the guerilla commander Michael Collins.

Brigadier-General Sir Ormonde de l'Épée Winter KBE, CB, CMG, DSO was a British Army officer who was posted to troubled Ireland, a country to which he was no stranger. He had, however, already gained some degree of notoriety over an incident which had occurred in the year 1904. When he and another officer had confronted a group of youths who had been repeatedly harrassing them while they were boating.

Colonel Winter had consistently warned the individuals concerned – 'Don't you know I'm "Colonel O",' and so on. But, his advice being so brazenly ignored, he had eventually, reluctantly, made for the shore. Where an altercation of some form had ensued. 'Colonel O' had fended one of the youths off. Eventually, as it happened, beating him senseless with an oar before he died. Finishing him off with one single blow. As it happened, also of the sturdiest spruce.

What a coincidence!

A development, in any case, which saw 'Colonel O' subsequently charged with manslaughter. But, as one might have expected, considering his position, acquitted of all charges. On his very first night as chief of intelligence in Dublin Castle, 1921, serving as a replacement for General Tudor, he had remarked on his unconventional introduction to 'this business' when, apparently, his mess steward had shot himself dead in the kitchen.

'Did you know,' remarked Henry Plumm out of nowhere – in his cups, in Minty's, very late one evening, 'I mean – were you aware that this venerable "Colonel O" nurtured a predilection for extravagant dress-up and disguise? Bordering almost, one might suggest, on that of the cabaret burlesque? I myself would happen to be of the opinion that that is very much the case. There is a photograph of him, extant, in which he bears – I kid you not, dear boy! – a distinct and really quite convincing resemblance to one very familiar from the world of music-hall entertainments! Yes, none other, I must tell you, than the dear old Arthur Lucan. Otherwise known as the Irish Washerwoman! In other words, my dear fellow, fabled star of stage and screen, Old Mother Riley! That would have been his modus operandi.'

'Colonel O', at least in Henry Percival's account, had given that very impression on calling late at night to the home of a 'well-known saboteur and counter-jumper' – soliciting alms with an extremely practised and convincing obsequiousness. Wringing her aged, old, liver-spotted hands as she bowed and scraped and pleaded in abjection: 'Ah, japers, sorr, but plaze would you tell me have you any munny? Arra God love you and keep you, just a couple of dacent wee pennies. Even a halfpenny would suffice. So it would, so it would.'

Then retrieving from under the skirts of his nightdress a small but effective revolver fitted with a silencer. Which would have been most unusual at the time. Shooting the individual three times, twice in the chest and then the head. Before stringing a crudely-painted placard around his neck. Which, too, was a gull of course. The crude letters read:

SPIES AND TRAITORS BEWARE: IRA.

A deceit which, as he well knew, would prove very effective. Inducing the requisite degree of doubt and confusion among the ranks of well-known rebel papists and nay-saying, contemptible recusants. There were many others who met the same fate.

'He really was my kind of man,' I remember Henry observing at the story's conclusion – catching Mac the barman's eye as he ordered us both another round.

Then he continued.

'Yes. A hero of the realm. Stout defender. Committed in whatever way might be possible to bring peace and decency and ordinary God-fearing civic manners to this hopelessly distracted nation of inbred, lowborn, amoral agitators.'

That, at least, is how I remember it – listening to the plash and swish of the rain outside. Although there are times – even yet – when I can still anticipate the onset of a certain alarming – I don't know, uncertainty. Sometimes even feeling – that I made old Henry up!

But why on earth would anyone do such a thing?

In spite of how unutterably tedious life in such a miserable city might eventually come to be? Approaching something close to – yes, unbearable, maybe. Becoming so tedious that, solely for the purpose of diversion and amusement – with perhaps the smallest soupçon of undirected self-aggrandisement – one might find oneself casting a nonentity such as the likes of Henry P. Plumm in the role of some hopelessly delusional, dapper-dandy version of what might be considered the prototype, Eustace Tilley. When such may not have been the case at all – belonging perhaps more to the world of 'Colonel O' & Co.

I cannot state for definite.

All I know is that for me he was vaster than anyone I've ever known. And not the same person who completed those ill-advised memoirs. The pages of which are still floating downstairs in the bathroom – with Rosie being too drunk to even notice. And blowed if I can be bothered. Because, to tell the truth, I wouldn't even touch the blessed thing. Don't ever write anything down, I had warned him. Not so much as a single fucking word! But do you think that he'd listen? Obstinate blighter.

Now look what's happened. Through the fault of no one except himself. It's a pitiful legacy, of that there's little doubt. Huh-huh-huh-huh Henry Plump, RIP – a pulpy, waterlogged mess. Blowing fucking bubbles – as the world sails on, oblivious.

But now that he's gone, I do have to concede, out of respect as much as anything else, that there still are periods when I simply cannot be without my old comrade.

Which shows what a hold, unfortunate or otherwise, he tends, and tended, to hold over my poor, world-weary, bruised imagination. Which is not surprising – for we've both been through a lot. Like so many in our profession.

Not that such developments ought to have come as any surprise, not to anyone who had the faintest idea of the journey on which they were about to embark all those years ago. With the writings of Lewis Namier being paramount among the prescribed texts for our studies, in which had been emphasised many times the unassailable fact that: 'Legends naturally surround all "secret service"; its very name inspires fear and distrust and stimulates men's imaginations.'

And why ought the initiators themselves be exempt, unaffected? The truth is that they aren't. Being, perhaps, even more vulnerable. Don't you think so, Henry?

We used to sit in the back bar for long periods at a time – in complete silence. Before Henry's contemplations would end with a startling suddenness and that bitter, impatient side of his character would, once again, be in evidence.

'A few more like that weasel McGilly, we'd soon have the whole wretched business tied up. In less than a week, I'm pretty sure, Meredith. Oh, and by the way, now that we are on the subject – I want you to return to Belfast and reconnoitre something for us. It's connected with that vile so-called captain of theirs. Something, you might say, to deflect attention away from the "main event" which, as you know, is now inevitable. Yes, the forthcoming Dublin business has been cleared from the very top. Anyway, this McVeigh fellow – I am more than aware that of course, the same as myself, you find having the slightest thing to do with him really quite appalling. But, and you know you can believe me, this time it will be a one-off. And, as you know – I wouldn't even dream of putting it to you if I didn't consider it absolutely necessary. Yes, very important indeed, my dear friend.'

I hadn't given the request so much as a second thought – being a little bit lubricated myself, as I recall. Which would, of course, have been of assistance.

Anyhow, it was this decision which led, ultimately, to what he had called 'the Dublin business'. And the deaths of God knows how many people, including Máiréad.

Damned misfortune.

My first port of call was his arranged meeting with 'the Reverend', Passmore Stout. Without him, there would have been no Majestic Cinema incident.

And Máiréad Curtin would still be alive. Along with who knows how many others.

But, heavens above, what a meeting location to decide on – outside the gentlemen's convenience in Ranelagh. What in the name of blue blazes did 'the Reverend' Passmore Stout think I was? I asked myself.

As I made my approach across the street towards the Triangle, I could see he was already standing – looking furtively about him, tugging at the belt of his white gabardine. As regards weight, I have to say this – the Presbyterian preacher was certainly aptly named – safe to say, he would have given William Conrad a run for his money. He pumped my hand and began walking briskly. Such enormous bulk, I thought, smiling faintly as I considered it no wonder Roley's nominated handle for the fellow had turned out to be 'Equus Incarnadine'.

Like so many Ulstermen, Stout prided himself on not wasting words. Though they depended on us, it required no particular powers of perception to deduce that when it actually came down to it, in truth they actually despised the English. Perhaps an inevitable consequence of their pathetic need. They viewed us, essentially, as coarse sensualists who ate too much, were sex-mad and conventional.

Given the slightest opportunity, they would declare that in Ulster one has to stand firm and hit back hard. 'Up here we tend to be plain speakers,' you would be told – whether or not you had ventured any enquiry.

'What a spurious boast,' Roland used to say, 'but then, whether Protestant or Catholic, what do those inbreds have to bray about?'

Unless they happen to be born and bred a donkey, in which case of course they find themselves with little option, I found myself thinking as I followed Stout all the way along the main street in Ranelagh village. Making our way to the appointed destination, the Pronto Grill.

Soon to be seated facing the Reverend across a red Formica table. Where it occurred to me that he didn't just bray after the manner of an ass – but rotated his jaws and shuddered like one also. With sprays of saliva flying all over the table as he wielded his cutlery like the crudest of implements, as though going into battle – bashing and chopping and licking up grease, with a devastation of peas and beans all around him.

'Hurr hurr hurr,' he repeated – shoving down another great mugful of steaming tea.

'I love a mixed grill,' I was informed by the Reverend – spearing a great big rhombus of liver.

'Hurr hurr hurr, there's nothing as is better – aye, and all washed down with a great big mug of tay!'

He whinnied again, swiping his chops with an enormous white handkerchief.

'English,' he called me – in a manner which I found quite taunting, but most of all resentful.

'Some say that I'm a violent man, English. I'm sure you've heard them making that remark – haven't you, Meredith?'

I didn't say anything.

Nothing at all.

As he resumed.

'But what, also, of the Christ,' he said, 'if I might crave your indulgence for a moment or two? If you'll just listen. Genesis Three, are you familiar with that? "And I will put enmity between thy seed and her seed."'

His eyes by now were bulbous, red-veined.

'Because until the Antichrist is vanquished, there can be no peace. Christ was not that type of man. No matter what they say or try to tell you, do not believe it. Because Jesus was not a namby-pamby! We must follow his lead and bring violence to the men of violence – just as he did in the temple. Christ was a violent man! We must attack the people who uphold rottenness – as Christ attacked the money-changers! The people who represent the Antichrist in our midst. And you know who they are, English. Every single one of them, Mr Meredith, is known to your people. And, one by one, by dint of our not inconsiderable, combined efforts – make no mistake, we will eradicate them!'

Rarely has it been my experience to bear witness to the unalloyed nature of something very close to pure ethnic hatred. Certainly at such a close range.

With nothing but the advice of Ambrose Roland to console me. And which now returned as the fish and chips turned to dust inside my mouth.

'That, my dear fellow, is the price we must pay. And continue to pay it, if such be considered necessary.'

Half a lamb chop disappeared down the Reverend's throat.

Then, I watched as, out of nowhere, he produced a Bible.

'This is not a book of peace!' he spat into my face. 'This, my English friend – whether you know it or not, or care – is a book of war! War against Christ's enemies, against the deceits of the devil, against the snares of ecumenism. We must listen to the call to arms and not be afraid. And Christ will fight with us, as he overturned those tables, and will be proud to see us as we go forth bravely to attack for him. Christ was not a syrup-tongued softie sentimentalist. More than anything, Christ was a violent man.

Violent for good, to stamp out wickedness! Please will you try and remember that!'

I think he had been noticeably nervous while waiting for me there on the Triangle because of the rumours which had surfaced regarding a friend of his deputy, the former army major, Barton McCausland. Who had once been employed in the Ravensbrook orphanage. An institution shrouded in rumour – one to which, as I was already aware, Alex Whiteside had already made numerous visits – and, according to some of these rumours, had apparently been threatening to 'spill the beans'. Out of guilt, presumably. No wonder Ambrose Roland had wanted him out of the way. Whether or not the suggestions were true was impossible for me to say. But I presumed they were, having personally encountered a certain very informed individual who'd been present at one of the Captain's Belfast jaunts.

Not so much as a word had this Mr Wilson spoken in the backstreet dentist's surgery all night. Because he knew better. Having, along with a number of others, also implicated in the Ravensbrook goings-on, reputedly been involved in the murder of a teenage boy. The boy's body had been dismembered, burned over an open fire and dumped in the Lagan River, which runs through Belfast. I had met Wilson, in actual fact, once or twice before. The previous time being that night in the Chaguaramas Club, where he had been hovering around. I had seen him conversing with 'Joan Collins' in an alcove.

But enough of that – because, to tell you the truth, it gives me the shivers.

It is much more appealing to reflect on Maurice Norton and his 'acting' activities. In particular those afternoon radio dramas for which he'd recently been coaxed out of retirement. Some years ago, he had actually come up with one of his own – an entirely original popular afternoon serial with which he had approached BBC Ulster. It was based on the lives of an ordinary small-town working-class family in the midlands. And, over time, had become an enormous favourite, both north and south of the border.

At Home With the Tomeltys, the programme was called. Or 'Tumbletys', which was how they tended to pronounce it in 'Ay-Ruh'.

'Are yeeze lishnin' to *The Tumbletys*?'

With a number of its catchphrases becoming common currency.

Such as, for example: 'You're a right old comeejan, so you are!' and, 'Oi tink oi'll have some shloup with vegabittles!'

Although he would never, initially, have dreamed of it ever becoming the case, those popular episodes of his homegrown radio series were set to run for years. With the final two series being directed by another friend from the fit-up days, one Paschal Honan. Who had also been a considerable trouper in his time. And had provided us all with a never-ending fund of entertaining stories and yarns – all of course aired late at night in the Minstrels' Rest.

'I'll never forget Bartle Noonan the night we played in Trim. We were performing *Napoleon and Josephine*, you see. Now Bartle – as you yourself know only too well, Maurice – to put it mildly, he was a very rotund figure of a man. And when the uniforms were brought for Pat Corcoran, who was playing the main role, they couldn't get one to fit him properly. As you can imagine, Bartle's borrowed costume, which was the one they eventually put on him – to say the least it was baggy, with the pants only coming halfway down and leaving a space in between which was covered by wrapping an orange sash around the middle. With bandsmen's hats on their heads, they cut the most peculiar sight. The lights were switched on, the audience went quiet, and all was ready. As the bold Pat Corcoran, a senior general in Napoleon's army, marched in to make the opening speech. That, I'm afraid, was as far as he got. The audience collapsed in uncontrollable laughter. Pat did all he could, standing and staring right at them – but the more he did, the more they laughed. Finally when they stopped for a moment, he stepped forward and, struggling for words, he came out with: "Right then, laugh at me – but wait till you see bloody Napoleon!"'

This Paschal Honan had nurtured ambitions in the world of playwriting and drama himself. Although it looked, to be honest, as though twenty years as senior producer on *The Tumbletys* had eventually got the better of him. With his nerves being in a rather bad state – his problems with alcohol, too, having plagued him.

Not, however, that you'd be aware of it most of the time. Whether in Minty's or any of the other pubs, where he tended to hold court as something of a resident eccentric. Squatting on a high stool, chuckling to himself. Arguing and disputing with himself as he set about working out plots and counterplots. Gesticulating and chuckling as he prided himself not only on the amusement but the sheer ingenuity of his creations. Perhaps most notably – if you'll forgive me, Mr Hitchcock – as regards an episode which might, a little mischievously, be entitled 'The Trouble With Harry'.

He was driving Mac the barman clean stone mad, as I recall. With Mac, unfortunately, being someone who was not in the least possessed of the even temperament which defined the barman in the Scotch House, Paddy Murphy.

Who would happily have indulged poor Paschal Honan and his quest for the ultimate 'Harold', the motivation central to the drinking game which, for reasons best known to himself, he had 'just this moment invented', as he claimed. After his fifth or sixth double brandy.

'First,' he had commenced, 'you got Michael Caine who plays 'Arry Palmer, don't you? Then you got Steptoe, whatshisname, 'Arry H. Corbett. To be succeeded, with your permission, by old Scissor-Limbs 'Arry Worth. After that, then, one of my own personal favourites – supreme practitioner of the thespian craft, who else but 'Arold Pinter. With the closing role to be assumed, if I may, by someone dear to all our hearts in this jolly good old town of Dublin – yes, the fabulous 'Arry Gregg, world-famous keeper of dandy old Manchester United. Who distinguished himself so extraordinarily well on the tarmac at Munich Airport on the day of that awful, terrible crash, when so many of poor old Busby's Babes met their untimely end. Do you know what he said, that old 'Arry, on that occasion – are you listening to me, Mac? Are you listening to me, barman – and give me another double while you're at it! Because this very minute I'll tell you what he said. I'm no fucking hero, said 'Arry when all and sundry were going around praising him. No blooming hero, and that's the God's honest truth. And would you like to know why that is? Because on any other day I might have done something completely different. I might have run away and done nothing at all, do you understand? Yes, done absolutely sweet nothing at all. And isn't that the truth, barman, when you think of it, of us all? It's true of me, anyways, ha ha ha ha fucking ha! Cheers, my loves!'

And so, indeed, had it proved.

Paschal Honan had hung himself the very next day, beneath a bridge in Portobello – discovered by a neighbour and his dog the following morning.

'Consistently overwrought,' was the grim, implacable verdict of Henry Plumm. 'The way that fellow drank, he would always have been playing with fire.'

Not, to be honest, that Henry Percival could be held up as any shining example in that particular regard. No, no paragon of virtue he – considering the amount of gin and brandy he himself was capable of demolishing.

Indeed I'd often found him on his doorstep in Beechmount Avenue really quite stupefied. Yes, totally insensible, raving about his dead wife Bea. I mean – where on earth did he go and get the idea that it was he who was married to my lovely wife Beatrice? Why, the next thing, I remember thinking, he'll be slobbering about sweet Joanne.

In any case, Maurice's friend Paschal Honan was dead. But, in true Dublin style, he enjoyed a great funeral. As we all stood there under our umbrellas in Glasnevin Cemetery. 'Sorry for your trouble,' and all the rest. And, unquestionably, he'd bequeathed an impressive legacy. Some of which was actually hilarious.

The officiating clergyman had even included a number of memorable quotes from *The Tumbletys* in his panegyric – not least 'whur's me vegabittles!'

One or two of the episodes – not that the priest adverted to the fact – had turned out to be extremely controversial in their time. Most memorably, perhaps, a somewhat off-colour segment entitled: 'Visitors Come to Town'. During the course of that particular episode, two hoity-toity-type English ladies had been accused, not only of being in possession of 'French letters', but also of appearing in a 'saucy' magazine.

'Effing blow-ins!' an irate neighbour was heard to complain. 'Them and their slacks and all that swanky perfume. Don't talk to me about Protestants.'

The piece had even been featured as the main story in the RTÉ Guide. With the headline reading: 'Saucy Sweethearts in Tomeltytown – Say Hello to Our Pin-Up Girls!'

'Saucy Sweethearts,' one of the regulars was heard muttering up at the counter in Minty's, disdainfully tossing the paper away.

'All I can say is – where in the fuck is all this going to end? This isn't why we faced up to Churchill. Michael Collins didn't die for the likes of them to be peddling rubber johnnies.'

But it had turned out to be one of the most popular episodes ever – in spite of causing an utter scandal in almost every pulpit in the land. Ah, those old Tumbletys.

'What a crew, what a crew, what a crew,' sighed Plumm – snapping his fingers to catch Paddy Murphy's attention in the Scotch.

'Is there nothing to be done with the irredeemable Irish Catholic?' he wondered.

'I mean, I ask you,' continued Henry. 'I blooming well ask you, Meredith, you know? These poor old backward Irish – what on earth are we going to do with them?'

Yet he had always made sure, all the same, never to miss the serial in question – chuckling away to himself as he tuned the dial.

'Look at *The Tumbletys*!' you'd often hear him say. 'Because at least you have to admit that it's accurate. Because that's what they're really like, the silly buggers! With these old Spuddies, damn and blast them – you simply never know just what's going to happen next. Do you know what I'm going to tell you, Meredith? They are completely and utterly unreliable. Just the very same as veal, as Noël Coward has always insisted!'

The number of mourners attending Paschal Honan's funeral was estimated as being in the region of five or six thousand.

'I'll give us this as a nation,' someone remarked later on in the Gravediggers pub, directly opposite the gates of Glasnevin Cemetery, where so many of the bones of dead patriots were laid, 'that if there's one thing we Irish are capable of doing right, it's holding a good funeral.'

On that occasion, I remember, Henry Plumm had smiled and nodded. But there could be no mistaking the sheer naked contempt in his eyes – having, on many previous occasions, derided the 'orgy of sentiment' he had observed at many such gatherings. Although, in spite of this, it has to be conceded that the Honan ceremony was almost a model of its kind – possibly as a consequence of Maurice Norton's unmatchable reading.

'Of all the poets, Paschal Honan revered Philip Larkin,' he declaimed, 'and no man has written better of the deceased's native city.

'There is an air of great friendliness but of great sadness also.

'And that is how we feel today,' concluded Maurice – just before the rainstorm broke and everyone headed straight across the road.

'They're all in there,' mumbled Henry as we entered – gazing out through the window towards the cemetery, where the rain was lashing mercilessly against the trees, sweeping in swathes above the grey-and-white marble of the tombstones.

'Yes, they're all in here now,' he continued under his breath, 'every last treacherous fomenter who imbibed sedition with their mother's milk. They have left us with our Fenian dead, the impassioned insurrectionists like to tell you. Any blessed chance they get, bloody recusants. The Saxons, they say, have laid our golden land waste. But they were in that condition long before we came near the place – just ask James Joyce. Or, better than that, take a look around.'

Which I did.

By now, an absolute silence had dramatically descended on the bar. As someone called out for 'Paschal's favourite song' – subsequent to which something of a faltering effort was attempted. Being suddenly interrupted by the sound of a woman sobbing fitfully.

'Did you happen to notice,' I murmured softly to Henry, 'just who was buried in the north-eastern plot? Did you remark upon the gravestone?'

'No,' replied my colleague, 'who is it you mean?'

'"Colonel O,"' I told him, ordering another gin as I started to shudder with laughter – describing what I knew to a somewhat taken-aback Henry, who hadn't been aware of many of the details. I kept it as quiet as I possibly could – after all, one doesn't want to upset poor Potato Pat when he's in the process of burying his patriot dead.

'He bashed the little fucker not once but fifteen times with the oar. Then went and set about him all over again. In spite of the fact that he knew he was almost dead.'

'You mean the young boy who was guilty of impertinence?'

'Yes,' I continued, 'because I'm sure, as you know, dear old "Colonel O", he had seen his share of horrors in the service. So he wasn't about to permit something such as that to go unpunished.

I think, in fact, he was ably assisted by his colleague on the occasion. A damned good job of it, in any case, they made. By all accounts, there was even cerebral matter located on some of the trees.'

'An oar,' reflected Henry, 'a rather unusual implement in the circumstances, but I expect it could be quite lethal if wielded with the appropriate expertise.'

'Yes,' I replied. 'I suppose that it could.'

As I lifted my thumb, catching the barman's eye – and the rain against the window continued on pouring down without cease.

Chapter 13

Even the Monuments Shall Not Remain

So vivid do they seem, one's memories by this tall Gothic window overlooking the bay, they might properly belong in the colourful pages of the *Sunday Champion*.

With those orange-and-amber shades being the very exact same as the manner in which they return to me now. For all the world like a Kodachrome photo. Which couldn't, of course, possibly be authentic. Because that's what memory does, isn't it? Relaying events like shimmering home movies. Ah yes, like an 8 mm moving picture postcard. Rendered, perhaps, by Mr Hitchcock and Donald McGill.

Ha ha!

Just as it was doing now – featuring grannies in flowery frocks, resembling nothing so much as great big turnover loaves. Not entirely, in fact, unlike Rosie Dixon – who is out there lounging in her swimsuit and strappy sandals. Dear heart, who she thinks she is, I don't know. Perhaps Jayne Mansfield, leafing desultorily through her magazine. Alongside pipe-smoking dads with odd cliffs of hair supervising boys in saggy knitted swimming trunks sailing wooden model ships and little girls with buckets and spades. And, somewhere far away, in this land of Watney's Red Barrel, *Z-Cars*, tartan blankets and golden spaniels reclining on the sun-warmed upholstery of an Austin Countryman, a Salvation

Army band oompah-ing away, following the trajectory of a conductor's baton.

Not a place ever destined to become the playground of the world's wealthy, a perpetual marvellous party where the beau monde and demi-monde from across the globe would meet to exchange witty repartee on the decks of yachts or over gaming tables. No, this ordinary little seaside resort of Woolsley Bay, in all its humility tucked away without ceremony here on the south coast of England – it makes no claims, whether in dreams or otherwise, to being any form of nouveau Mediterranean paradise. Where, nightly, on yachts, a sea of champagne was . . .

'Blooming Ada!' squeals Rosie at the very top of her voice – before returning once more to the comforting into the arms of Morpheus. Realising her presumed disturbance belongs to the country of her dreams. False alarm. As – analagous to the bubbles of dear old Henry Plumm – yet another distended string of whistles is smoothly released from her left-hand nostril, and the slightest of breezes flutters through the pages of the *Bella* periodical lying by the side of her deckchair.

However, prior to my continuing, I must avail myself of the opportunity to announce the arrival of another middle-aged lady upon the scene.

'Merciful Hour! It's Biddy Mulligan!'

Who, of course, is not Rosie's 'maid' at all, as I think I may have earlier asserted – but the Agency nurse, who comes in every week. Or used to, for the express purpose of looking after Mr Plumm. Ever since he got the you-know-what. And I have to say that I really do enjoy her company – that silly old giddy-goat way she has about her.

Lord only knows what age she is, Mulligan. But whatever it might be, it must still be admitted that she remains quite attractive in that eternal wobbly plump-and-mumsy kind of way. Quite incorrigibly maternal, always fussing around with towels and scrubs and who knows, the devil knows what.

'Stop, nurse, you're killing me!' I'll often giggle.

And, heavens above, does that pretty little giddy colleen respond! She hails from Dublin – but, like so many from that old wetland-by-the sea, has been over here for years.

'I've been contracted by the Agency for to look after Mr Plumm, the Major,' I was told.

'Poor old Henry. You'll find, I'm afraid, that he's in a bad way,' I said.

'I know,' she replied, 'cortical atrophy.'

Very impressive, I thought – for an Irish maid.

'Poor fellow,' I explained, 'I'm afraid, after everything that has happened over the years, that he doesn't so much as remember a single thing.'

Which, in my innocence, was what I genuinely thought. How innocent we can be, in spite of all our purported wisdom. Cheeky bugger! But I'll never forget his face when it happened. Why, loathsome is just about the only way I can think to describe it. As we sat there in the dinghy, swaying from side to side – and, out of nowhere, he said to me suddenly: 'You wanted me, didn't you, to end up like Whiteside. That, all along, has been your intention. Hasn't it, Longface?'

'Pshaw!' I replied, drawing the oars in and out.

'Lately, you see, I've been experiencing this awful, apprehensive feeling. That everywhere I go, no matter where it happens to be – that you are standing directly behind me. And you don't mean to do me good. That is to say, your intentions – they're not honourable.'

'Pshaw!' I repeated, grinning from ear to ear.

Fully intending to answer the fellow – but by this point, Mulligan was beckoning. As she bellowed out, indecipherably, in her brogue:

'Ah but bejasus, are youse going to stop out there all of the day? Tay's ready!'

Such a lugubrious expression Henry's face wore. I've never

seen it quite so extreme. Happily, however, when we got back to shore, it was clear that he didn't remember a thing about it. Because that is the way cortical atrophy works.

Poor old dementia. It hits us all, sooner or later. It must be similar to relocating in an underwater country – observing the world, as it passes, through portholes that are blurred. As the quotidian, although still manifestly present, teasingly ebbs and flows like waves. Being defined, of course, also, by that dread poor Henry spoke of. That hideous apprehension. That someone is going to creep up behind you.

And maybe beat your brains in – not, of course, necessarily with an oar. With anything.

Not that such a feeling, believe me, is what one might describe as in any way alien.

Far from it. For, to tell the truth, I used to experience it every Friday evening – just before catching the Enterprise to Quacktown. Knowing, obviously, what was in store.

More than anything what it was like – what it resembled, being the interior of the Scotch House on one of those November Sunday evenings. With Paddy Murphy over by the window in the corner – robotically polishing glasses with a tea towel. Staring out at – where Murphy was concerned – who knew what? Before, half-turning, remarking sotto voce to no one in particular: 'Does it ever do anything else in this city except rain? In the name of Christ, will it never end?'

Had we been elsewhere, the scene might well have been appraised as possessing a certain shimmering, silvery beauty all of its very own. A magic town of glass.

'But not here,' Plumm blurted, fingering out a handful of change, 'not here in this dire land. Where the dead seem more traditionally alert than the living.'

Although not, however, it has to be accepted, where a certain Mrs Tubby Mulligan is concerned. Because I have to say, even at this late stage of my life – that of all the people that I've met down the years – she really is an imp and a character. Yes, none other than old 'Merciful Hour!', who goes by the name of Mrs Biddy Mulligan! And who I would, absolutely truly and genuinely, have no hesitation in describing as just about the funniest care assistant alive! Oh yes – the worst of the blooming lot, I would say. That giddy little rascal, Madame Biddy Mullsers! Ha ha. With her idiom-peppered speech, more than anything, bringing to mind the programme which used to feature every Sunday morning on Radio Éireann during the period when I tenanted in an impressively appointed Georgian property located in Merrion Square. Not long after I'd vacated the house in Hollybank Road, Lower Drumcondra – where I'd been experiencing a series of the most unsettling dreams.

The Maureen Potter Show, I remember it was called. With 'merciful hour' being the presenter's Dublinesque catchphrase. Or, as a certain blowlamp-and-pliers expert might have preferred, 'ketchphrase'. It being a Sunday, usually with a hangover, one would switch on the set and out it would swim: 'Merciful hour!' Exactly as our new care assistant would pronounce it, with it seemingly being applicable to each and every situation imaginable. Especially if she happened to be under duress – as she was this particular day, so hopelessly out of breath as I watched her approach, loaded down with her shopping.

'Come over here and give us a kiss, you jewel and darling of the auld sod!' I called.

As I would often do – just for a laugh. With the pair of us enjoying great old chats – not just about Henry.

'I've finally lost my patience with the fellow,' I told her. 'He's up there in the bathroom breathing his last. Because, to tell you the truth, I've had it up to here.'

Then I chuckled and said: 'I'm only joking!'

'Because,' I continued, 'do you really think you can kill a bad thing like Henry?'

She looked at me, aghast.

'Oh merciful hour!' she exclaimed. 'You're only after giving me the fright of my life, so you are, Mr Meredith! Lord bless us and save us – to pretend to have done such a thing to the Major! And him in the bad state he's in, these times. I'll go on away up and give him his milk in a cup.'

As off she trotted, with her dumpy bottom waddling. Not unlike Madame Rosie's – who, by now, was snoring away even louder, like a brace of rusty foghorns. Yes, myself and dear old Biddy Mulligan from Éire. I used to love to see her coming. And the chats the pair of us would enjoy in the evenings – sipping our teas in the lobby.

'Like nobs,' I can hear her say, 'like a pair of grand old nobs, tee hee!'

I have to say that she really was a tonic. And if she swore like a barrack-room squaddie – then what the devil was surprising about that? Considering the fact that she was a 'biddy', and where she came from.

'Oh Paddy and Biddy, an inscrutable pair!' I used to say.

And what do you think she might have offered by way of response?

'Merciful hour!'

You're 100 per cent correct.

Even if there are those who continue to insist upon her complete and utter lack of real existence at all. Being yet another product of a distorted and maybe irredeemably bruised imagination. But that is not how it seemed to me. Chuckling away – merciful hour, merciful hour! – as she flitted incorrigibly from subject to subject. Such as – as a matter of fact, she had actually squealed: 'Bernie the Bolt!'

Straight away, I knew what she was referring to. So, obviously, I didn't pursue it.

'Merciful hour!' I responded, a little meekly. Doubling over with laughter as she shook her scullery-maid curls, crying: 'Bernie the Bolt!'

All I hoped was that she didn't see fit to mention it again.

She also had toiled in London during the war – and possessed no end of stories concerning young officers, battleaxe matrons and death-defying near-misses throughout the course of the Blitz.

'Oi'll tell you dis,' I remember her confiding, 'they can say what they like over dere in Oireland, Mr Meredith, sorr. But so far as auld Biddy Mulligan here is concerned, this country what is called England, it has done me nothing but a power of good. Aye, and plenty more like me. Looked after us, so they did, when there was plenty of others as wouldn't give you the stame off dere pish. Go into any doctor in London and you'll find yourself in a nice warm room awaiting your turn. When you get into the doctor, he'll give you to understand that you are a person, not a beggar. At home, and I've seen my share, you make an appointment to go and see the doctor, and you'll have to wait in an auld ruin of a house. Look all around you and all you'll see is poverty and despair and dirt on both the people and on the clothes. Sure, the doctor himself – he might as well be the landlord like as of old, in the auld times, Mr Meredith, sorr. With the people and their heads down, holding their hats – and them, God help them – shaking with humility. It's a bad situation. Don't you tink so, Mr Meredith?'

'I do indeed, Miss Mulligan,' I nodded in complete agreement. 'I absolutely do indeed.'

Out of nowhere returning in my mind to yet another of our back-bar assignations. There, in the daytime gloom of the old Scotch House. With, as generally tended to be the case, there being no one else present. As off wandered Plumm on yet another of his seemingly interminable, although admittedly well-informed, monologues.

'They blame us, the cheeky buggers, for the majority of their misfortune. A nation without towns or scientific architecture. No forestry to speak of, or fisheries, come to that. Delusional to a fault, every back-of-the-mountain man-jack of them. Even the so-called intellectuals and clergy. Perhaps most especially the clergy. Having somehow – why, man, it beggars belief! – persuaded themselves that, in a world jungle of rank material weeds, they may well become the saviours of idealism. And distracted foreigners driven to despair by the ever-multiplying complexities of the machine-driven age will try to relearn – from the tattered woman trudging all the way to the slum hospital to have her baby or from the peasant lost in wonder at the yellowing barley – the unutterable simplicity of living.'

Behind the counter, as I recall, Paddy Murphy was in the process of snapping one matchstick after another and lining them up in military formation on the windowsill. Releasing a long, low whistle as he observed the hailstones being randomly flung at the glass. Until opacity, finally, had claimed the pane.

'Fuck,' I heard Plumm groan, 'that I ought to have deserved a sentence such as this. Sometimes I think they're a nation of infants, Meredith. Such poppycock as is routinely peddled, whether from pulpit or in the senatorial chamber. But which in this daydream cradle of self-loathing, this gloom-constricted outpost, is swallowed daily, and by the truckload. Proceed in this fashion and there soon may be scant evidence of what once has passed for civilisation. Like the Mayans, maybe nothing else remaining but their pathetic monuments sinking into remote, lonely hillsides.'

He thought a long time, describing a series of circles intersecting, with a match.

Then he said:

'Although even that, I fear, may prove too good to be true. And yet at the same time, we're expected to be abject. Even offer reparations to these resentful, disruptive, wily-eyed ingrates. Who repay us, generation after generation, with an ever-replenishing shoal of glowering provocateurs, so many of whom are slothful, not to say murderous. As it has been across the centuries – side-swappers, bomb-throwers, border-hopping bastards – with no seeming end to it. With all of it now beginning to declare itself again. Or so it seems, idiotically christened the "Troubles". Except this time around, believe you me, it will be different. For there are many among us whose patience has run out. So there's only one thing for it, and I can tell by your expression you know what I'm going to say.'

'Void them,' Plumm continued, 'void the bastards once and for all. For ever,' he sighed, finishing up his drink. 'Only this time ensuring that, unlike the Mayans, even their monuments shall not remain.'

Chapter 14

Roll Over, Bubbles

'No, those monuments, God willing, they will not in the end be seen to prevail. Something, hopefully, they may have in common with their troublesome, recusant race,' seethed Henry Plumm.

Although I have to admit that such an impression might not have been your first.

If, that is, you happened to be in the vicinity of Dublin's Rathmines, the south-city suburb where the building called the Tramshed was located. And where *The Late Late Show*, Ireland's most popular television entertainment show, held its rehearsals every Monday and Tuesday.

Where I experienced my very first encounter with its genial, urbane presenter of legend – finding myself not a little impressed by his innate courtesy and general professional demeanour. Not least, also, his instinctive sense of humour. Which had been very much in evidence when, more out of a desire to make conversation than anything else, I had suggested that he looked not unlike Kenneth Williams, camp adenoidal star of the celebrated Carry On films.

'You're not the first to suggest it, dear boy,' he had brayed in response, 'and I dare say that you won't be the last. Now, if you'll excuse me . . .'

As off he skipped with his clipboard across the floor.

I had been requested by one of our agency's clients, a certain Ger Fitzgibbon of the Hibernia Players, to accompany him 'for moral support'. Something which I was glad to do, for I had always admired the fellow's solid if limited talent. And now that he was getting on a little, was more than happy to assist him in availing himself of whatever opportunities might come his way.

The towering strength of *The Late Late Show* – it really must be acknowledged there was nothing to compare with it on the mainland – was the manner in which it effortlessly combined the serious and the light-hearted. Weekly bust-ups on the panel had long since become routine – with this particular show featuring an ex-boxer lawyer who missed no opportunity for controversy, and regularly during the performance threatened to knock out the teeth of fellow guests. Although I have to say, in my own case, I found him most amenable. With it turning out, as a matter of fact, that he was an acquaintance of Henry Plumm.

'A grand old chap indeed,' he had proclaimed, before requesting my permission to excuse himself and going over to join 'some dear young friends' who had, just at that moment, arrived in the Green Room.

And who turned out to be the lively members of yet another radical fringe-theatre group, of whom I'd heard Clem Grainger speak, who were also known to Máiréad Curtin and affiliated with Trinity College. I was soon to become aware that there already had been a considerable degree of debate around this grouping. As to whether they would be permitted to appear on the show or not, given the extreme, controversial nature of the material they intended to present. The rehearsal had gone on well past its allotted time, but I have to say that at no point did I find myself bored. And, in any case, Ger Fitzgibbon had been scheduled to perform his offering last.

It transpired that the young activist group were based, in actual fact, in Belfast. With their five-minute slot proving to be nothing short of electrifying – irrespective of one's political views.

'However,' as the show host Gay Byrne pointed out later on, 'it was just as well that we had the funnyman Brendy Bon Bon lined up to go on directly after.'

Bon Bon was one of the most successful comedians in the country, and could often be seen cycling around the city streets dressed up in a green school cap and crested blazer – shouting out, 'Missus! Look who it is – it's me, Brendy Bon Bon. I'm a bleedin' cracker!'

Now he was performing a daft routine about a cat. Chuckling away like an overgrown schoolboy as he wrinkled up his nose, flinging a striped scarf over his shoulder. Approaching the punchline, he sank down onto his hunkers.

'Youse are all bleedin' laughin' at me, so youse are!' he whinnied. 'Especially you, missus! Will youse not have manners and listen to me story about pussens! Ah, puir pussens he's a darlint, so he is.

'The cat in question went by the name of Bubbles,' Bon Bon continued, 'and was owned, apparently, by a gentleman from County Kerry. By all accounts, there was nothing whatsoever that Bubbles couldn't do. Which was why all the neighbours from the nearby district, and indeed miles around, used to come to the cottage and gaze in the window. This was what gave the Kerry gentleman his cue.

'"Roll over, Bubbles!" its owner would instruct.

'And, sure enough, right over on his back would go the bold Bubbles. In time, as it happened, there came a rich man who wanted to buy Bubbles. Laying out a lot of gold as off he went, and him with the darlint bold Bubbles stuffed inside of a saddlebag – instead of all the gold he had brought to pay for him.

'When he eventually arrived at his rich man's castle, didn't he notice that Bubbles seemed to be a little bit thirsty.

'So what does he do?' said Bon Bon, chuckling away. 'Gives

him a sup, God bless us and save us, of petrol. Yes, hands the poor animal a sup of petrol on a spoon. "That'll do you good," he says to Bubbles.

'Only later on that very same night, waking up to hear this awful commotion below in the kitchen. And when the new owner of poor old pussens goes down to investigate, what does he find?

'Yes, what does the new owner find inside in the kitchen only the bold Bubbles and he running harum-scarum around the ceiling at what must have been a hundred miles per hour. And then, quite understandably, ladies and gentlemen, getting himself into something of a state! Weeping and wailing and gnashing his teeth, with him wondering what on earth he was going to do. Until, lo and behold, down comes Bubbles and lands with an unmerciful thump on the floor in front of him.

'"Oh God blessus, me poor auld Bubbles!" says your man. "Is it dead you are? Talk to me, Bubbles, do you hear me, God help you, child: is it dead you are?"

'And what does poor old Bubbles go and do then?

'Only opens one eye – that's what he does.

'"No," says the cat, "there's nothing wrong at all. It's just, I'm afraid, that I ran out of petrol!"'

Also scheduled on *The Late Late Show* bill for that coming Friday evening was 'Chesty' Buttivant, 'Ireland's foremost erotic dancer'. Who admitted that yes, there could be no doubt but that Ireland was a very repressive country, but that, however, things were changing.

'Like me and me husband,' she explained in a thick Dublin brogue, 'we enjoy a good old sex life. At it like rabbits half the time we are. Indeed it was me husband's idea that I start off doin' the dancin' in the first place. After all, he says, with a pair of beauties like what you've got there, there doesn't seem to be much sense in wastin' it – you know what I mean, Gay? So every Sunday morning when all of the likes of youse respectable people are thumpin yizzir craws at Mass, I'm down in Portobello shakin' me sexy auld booty to the sound of "Saturday Night Fever" and Barry White. It's great gas, so it is, Gay. Old-time Ireland is dead and gone – that's all me and the Boss has to say. That's what I call me auld fella, the Boss. That's him over there. Hi Davy! Hi! Ah, Jaze, he's lovely – I can't wait to get me hands on him whenever the pair of us get home. After twenty-five years of marriage, Gay!'

'Very good, very good, very good. Topping!' the host enthused, lowering his neatly combed, silver-grey head before continuing in a more sombre mood. As he prepared the audience for the next segment of the show.

'And which may shock some of you,' continued the suave compère, 'but then *The Late Late Show*, as many of you will be aware, throughout its long history has never been any stranger to controversy.'

The short dramatic excerpt, he explained, was simply entitled: *Ocras*.

'Meaning "hunger",' he explained. 'But then most of you, of course, will know that.'

It had been written, apparently, by a political prisoner in Her Majesty's Prison, Long Kesh. Also known as the Maze. Gay then affected a puzzled expression – holding up a ball of paper compressed to the size of the smallest marble.

Somewhat apprehensively, he cleared his throat.

'This, apparently,' he told the audience, 'is called a "comm", short for communication. On one of these, believe it or not, you can transcribe a message of up to one thousand words, perhaps even more. Quite a skill, I'm sure you'll agree. And one which, in recent times, has been raised to a fine art by a number of the inmates in Her Majesty's Prison. Many of these little gems have, by all accounts, been smuggled out of that grim institution over the past number of months. With some of them, I have been told, even intended for us here in RTÉ and other representatives of the press. Before we begin, I feel I must exercise something of a note of caution. And remind you that, as with so many aspects of the continuing horror that is the North of Ireland, there remains a possibility that some, or maybe even many of you here tonight, you may find the following performance offensive.'

The long-haired actors were all attired in the filthiest of prison-issue blankets. None of them could have been over twenty-five years of age – the average age of the hunger strikers themselves. *Ocras*, soon, was to prove itself quite a show.

The central performer – his eyes were fierce! – was clad in nothing but a drab grey tunic. You thought Theatre of Warsaw, Black Theatre of Prague, Harold Pinter, Jean Cocteau. One of the mounted billboards behind them read:

THEATRE OF CRUELTY: THE TRUTH!

'I am the Blanketman,' commenced the actor gravely, 'and I am the leader of a no-wash political protest on behalf of all my comrades. Who demand the right not to wear prison clothes, not to do prison work, the right to free association, the right to organise educational and recreational pursuits, the right to one visit, one letter and one parcel per week, and full restoration of remission lost through the protest.'

Out of nowhere, he launched himself from the spars of the rudimentary scaffolding – landing like some kind of otherworldly insect, caught in the blazing white glare of a swinging spotlight, which pursued his manic deliberations all around the floor.

'Ocras ocras ocras!' he screeched, adroitly skittering, spider-like, at great speed from one side of the studio to the other.

'But I didn't know nothing about hunger at that time. I mean I was only eighteen. But here – don't go away. Stick around a wee while and allow me the privilege of sharing with youse my story.'

He lithely ascended the rigging again, winding himself in and out. As a blast of rock music – some old nonsense called 'Whiskey in the Jar' apparently interpreted by a band calling themselves

Thin Lizzy – squealed and buzzed as it filled up the studio. His eyes were almost the same size as the spotlight – as he executed another goblin-style tumble. Fixing a clearly overwhelmed elderly couple in the front row with the steady and continued intensity of his manic gaze.

'There's this one time,' he began in the harshest of Belfast accents.

'I mean – fucking hell! Me and a couple of mates decided to take a trip down to Dublin. And of course, being from up there, neither of us knew very much about the city. Not to mention the fact that by the time we got there we were well-on bloothered! In the end, though, we managed to find the pub that we'd been looking for. And who did I meet there? I met this girl called Moon Maguire. Me and her fell in love, so we did. She, you see, was from Belfast too, the Short Strand, if you ever heard of it. You might think she was all into Irish traditional music, being she was involved in the struggle and all, but no way, man. No deal, sunshine. "Away to fuck," she says, "and let's get out of this pub. Let's go where we find ourselves some Thin Lizzy." Which is what we did. "What kind of music you like?" she says. "Thin Lizzy or maybe the Doors, aye, and Led Zeppelin too. Because I've had it up to here with that diddly-eye mountain music. I guess that might surprise some people."

'Us being Northern nationalists and all. And one thing for sure, that was what Moon Maguire, God love her, was. Wild brainy too – studied at Queen's University, so she did. History and all that there. Moon Maguire knew everything. Wolfe Tone, Robert Emmet and all them other Irish heroes. Anyway, we're talking away there about smashing the sham statelet that is the North of Ireland, and I'm there saying till Moon, "Up the IRA!" and she nods.

'Then she says – I couldn't keep up with her: "A whole generation of men has been ruined by it – have been ruined and destroyed by this iniquitous kip they call the North."

'I say, "The brave men of Ulster will finish it this time." Then I look up and there she is looking down at me – and I think she's going to say, "I agree, I agree!"

'Only the next thing you know: "And women!" she says. "Or maybe you have got a problem with that, have you? So come on then, sunshine – tell us the truth: have we admitted a fucking sexist into our glorious movement? Because if we have – !"

'Well, fuck me, man, she didn't half give it to me, that old Moon! She was a beaut, though, Jesus. To tell you the truth, I was stone fucking mad in love with her. She was killed in an own goal in Cappagh, seventy-nine. I'll still often think about her – try not to, but I do.

'On Thursdays I get the dole and come down here to sit by the river. I have trouble with the schoolkids shouting at me. Ocras, they call me – don't know how they came by the nickname. Because I wouldn't have thought they knew much about the hunger strike, too young. They'll sometimes chase me all the way from the dole office, firing stones and hiding behind cars. "Ocras! Ocras!" you'll hear them shout. "Why don't you go and cut your hair? Go on, Ocras – silly old hippy!"

'I agreed to go on the strike, early April eighty-one. This time it'll be till the death, I said.

'My mother wasn't fit for the struggle, I'm afraid – she died.

'It's funny because – at the start of it all you've got these wonderful images in your mind. Where you see yourself shaking your head like some kind of a noble king. Refusing food, yes waving it away, kind of imperiously, you know what I mean? As your eyes slowly close and you can see the black hearse nosing around the corner. Then you look up and see your coffin being carried high. Draped in a tricolour with a pair of gloves placed on the top.

'There are a couple of helicopters hovering overhead and five or six comrades in paramilitary uniform. With all of them saying, "Imagine, he lasted almost sixty-two days. You have to hand it to good old Ocras." And there's your mother in her Sunday wear looking on so proud. Except for the fact that she isn't there. Not physically, anyway – unless you count the grave next to mine.

'Here lies a soldier.

'His name used to be Ocras.

'I'll still sometimes think – what if me and Moon had got married.'

It was at that point the actor bowed his head and went silent. Then down came the lights with the studio going completely dark. After a pause which lasted around thirty seconds, a large spotlight burst into life on the wall behind, in place of the cruelty painted placards – the single word: Ocras.

Every single member of the audience looked stunned. With Gay Byrne himself seeming wrung-out, exhausted. Then the experienced presenter took the wise decision to alter the mood with a few well-chosen sentiments of levity and announcing the return of Brendy Bon Bon. Who, straight away, launched into another elaborate and unlikely story. Which turned out to be even more hilarious than its predecessor.

Making it all the more unexpected when, making my way across the car park, I became aware of someone following behind. And turned around to see nothing other than the green school cap. Which he'd been wearing all the way through the rehearsal, now tilted sideways.

I was on the point of congratulating him on a 'really terrific performance'. Only then becoming aware just how grave and actually nervous he appeared to be. He pressed a hardened pellet into my hand.

'I was told to give you this,' he said. 'It wasn't something I wanted to do. But you know how it is. How things have turned out to be these days. There are certain people with whom you don't argue.'

When I looked again, he was gone.

I continued to stand where I was. Before edging a little

trepidatiously – moving, gingerly, in the direction of the glowing streetlight. As delicately and carefully as I could, unwrapping the tiny, compressed piece of paper.

'What do you think you're up to, cunt?'

I couldn't make out where the voice had come from. I swung on my heel and looked all around me. But there wasn't anyone to be seen. I opened my fist and considered the hard little ball once again. Setting about my task – as I tentatively opened the bud.

Only to wish I hadn't.

When I eventually made out the spidery pencil markings on the tissue:

Don't think we don't know. Not for one single second, Mr Smiley.

Chapter 15

A Night out at the National

Whether or not the Nobel laureate's 'considerably smarter' brother Leonard, author of *Mr Harbinson's Delight, Not So Fast Bernie Wilkins* and many others, had ever, in fact, existed – and let us not be remiss here regarding the imperatives of dissimulation, inherent caution and maximum deniability – it would require no great leap of the imagination whatsoever to contrive the controversial ('communist' – at least according to Leonard) playwright 'old 'Arold' ambling along the foreshore of Woolsley Bay, with pencil poised and spiral-bound reporter-style notebook at the ready.

Employing, it may safely be presumed, that counterfeit trademark military gait which he had singularly made his own for the express purpose of intimidating anyone foolhardy enough to confront him, or challenge in any form, shape or fashion his meretricious drawing-room-style anarchy. What with it being the case that locations such as Woolsley Bay have provided the material for the likes of his startlingly original breakthrough *The Birthday Party*. Which I myself have actually enjoyed on a number of occasions, both in London and Dublin. And while I found Pinter's politics, along with his attitude and general demeanour, something approaching revolting, there most definitely are aspects of that microscopic concerto of chilling menace that I found comprehensively and undeniably gripping and compelling. Not to mention its deep and perceptive, quite unrivalled authenticity – particularly where the affairs of dear old 'Ay-Ruh' were concerned.

Éire, that is.
Potato Land.
Home of the Spuddies.
Conspiracy Central.
Good Old Watertown.
Neighbourhood of the Dead.
Soporific City-by-the-Sea.
Eyes in the Alley.
Amoral Atoll.
And all of the rest.

Where often the manners, and indeed the action – will call to mind the mood of *The Birthday Party*. Reminding one of that apparently harmless superficiality and bonhomie, yes that sweet and romantic hospitable land where, just as easily, you could find your throat opened in half a second.

Yes, in Dublin's fair city
Where the girls are so pretty
I there set my eyes on grim murder
First hand.

I pondered, abstractedly, precisely what the would-be communist and psychic poet Mr Pinter might have made of the occurrence which had taken place on that day in the middle of August 1979. What became known, subsequently, as the Narrow Water tragedy. Also commonly referenced as the Warrenpoint Massacre, in which eighteen British soldiers had lost their lives. And which, troublingly, had exerted a far-reaching effect on the previously resilient and resourceful Henry Percival Plumm. Who had been sitting with the newspaper opened in front of him as I arrived into the gloomy back bar of the Scotch public house. With the single most interesting aspect of it all, looking back, being the fact that he was stone-cold sober.

'This,' he declared imperiously, 'is the beginning of the end. After what they did to Dickie Mountbatten, the gloves this time are coming off, for sure. We'll hunt them down, every single last fucking running dog. And keep coming after them until, the cunting curs, they'll rue the day any one of them ever got born. And I mean it!'

The photograph of the Admiral of the Fleet and former Viceroy of India took up most of the front page.

'How did they know Lord Mountbatten had dandruff?' I heard him muttering bitterly under his breath, answering the question for himself. 'Because they found his Head and Shoulders in the water.'

A joke in very poor taste, which referred to a popular shampoo advertisement and had apparently been cracked by some amateur comedian up at the bar only moments before I came in.

Narrow Water, I continued thinking – considering privately the possibility that it might, in fact, provide suitable material for one of these activist-style Tramshed productions. Theatre of Cruelty par excellence. Yes, the real thing, I couldn't keep from tittering. Maybe I could persuade 'old Henry' to act as the star, I wondered as I sipped on my De Kuyper's. For now, it occurred to me – however he had managed it, he had somewhere acquired that eminence grise Max von Sydow look. As he sat there, stiffly shaking the *Evening Herald*. With that clipped moustache and the feathered trilby he happened to be wearing at the time, seeming every inch old Joubert – and not me.

Although nothing so much as a nondescript middle-aged man, exuding all the menace of a sinister Pinter marginal. Such a degree of suppressed and bitterly contained rage! Barely touching his full glass of Gordon's.

'Eighteen of our fellows blown to bits – but be assured that those accursed mutinous beggars will rue the day. They want a massacre? We'll give them one. In a way, of course, we ought to be somewhat grateful. Because there may exist now the possibility that, at long last, we can abandon this infuriating pretence. And if their authorities do not wish to comply with our wishes, then be it on their own intemperate heads. Perhaps now we may put an end to their inveterate Anglophobia and their stubborn shibboleth of neutrality acting as a brake on ambition, obstructing any meaningful or productive discussion with our people on recalibration of security arrangements with the UK. For that is all they have ever meant to us – are they really so stupid as to think we ought to be bothered by anything else? Not caring a damn, for heaven's sake – and never would, but for the fact that the so-called Republic of Ireland is perennially at risk of being compromised from within by any number of hostile actors. Geographical proximity, and of course the border, mean that Irish vulnerabilities are British vulnerabilities. Oh that we could, somehow, strike it once and for all from the map!'

Narrow Water – I repeated the name very softly to myself. Reminding me as it did, in some way, of one's alma mater, dear old Mandeville House. Perhaps on account of both calling to mind 'the End'. The ultimate – that we're all afraid of. Irrespective of whatever claims we might make to the contrary.

Not that you'd have known it from Henry's expression. But then, give him his due – he really was a master. I mean – he even fooled me. By now he was muttering incoherently and gnashing – vowing to commit to the recruitment of Mossad. Because of what the 'recusants and beggars' had done on this occasion – expediting one of their signature ruses. When, subsequent to the detonation of the first Narrow Water bomb, the 7th Parachute Regiment had, apparently, taken refuge in an abandoned outhouse situated close by.

Precisely as their killers had anticipated.

It was subsequently established that both devices used in the attack – which had represented, in fact, the greatest single loss of life incurred by the British military on Irish soil since 1921 – had been detonated from the southern side of the border, in actual fact less than a half mile away.

'Gloves off,' Plumm had seethed, sinking the Gordon's in one fell swoop.

'First off, Mossad – then maybe the Americans. With the time, without a doubt, having come to put an end to the whole infuriating farrago, once and for all.'

'To Louis Mountbatten,' I said, as I raised my glass. 'First Lord of the Admiralty – and to all others who perished on *Shadow V.*'

Which, of course, was the name of Mountbatten's beloved boat – blown to pieces in County Sligo's idyllic Mullaghmore Bay just a few hours before the Narrow Water bombs.

It was actually that very same night – acting on nothing other than a whim – that I found myself aimlessly drifting in the general direction of Dublin's National Ballroom. An impressive, almost regally colonnaded structure situated in the heart of Dublin's nightlife in Parnell Square – so named after 'Ireland's uncrowned king', Charles Stewart Parnell.

When, if the truth be known, he had been completely and utterly taken for a fool by the 'love of his heart', Katharine O'Shea. Who, having pursued him – perhaps on Gladstone's, the prime minister's, instructions – decided in the end to take matters into her own hands. By mysteriously dropping a rose at the feet of the so-called 'gifted' parliamentarian. Who, as Plumm had caustically observed on occasion, was 'nothing other than a damned bloody nuisance'. The fellow, anyhow, was instantly besotted. So, in the end, job done: Parnell ruined and the Irish Parliamentary Party torn from end to end. Game, set and match to the chaps.

'Impressive,' had always been Ambrose Roland's verdict – and, obviously, as we have seen – Henry Plumm's.

However, as I say, I found myself diverted towards the National Ballroom.

Never in my life had I heard of Burris-in-the-Glade. But the girl now hanging, as though for dear life, onto my arm in the middle of the sprung maple floor had right that very minute informed me, wholly unsolicited, that that particular village to which she herself belonged and had just forsaken was nothing other than a 'dump' and a 'kip'.

She couldn't have been more than seventeen. Working as a cleaner in some south-city, unspecified hospital. She had curly hair and a face devastated by an atom bomb of freckles. However, she was sweet. So slight I could scarcely believe it.

Almost as if she wasn't there at all.

'Just before the next dance,' we heard the MC announce from the rostrum, 'I'd just like to inform youse that the entertainment here next week is to be provided by the fabulous, one and only Altonaires. I hope you will all be in a position to come, for it's sure to be a night that no one can afford to miss. Then, after that, we have a special midweek presentation on Tuesday, which will feature Sonny Bannon and the celebrated Gowna Ceilidh Band. Commencing 8.30 p.m. sharp. So there you have it, folks – and now it's time for our very own evening's entertainment to continue. Here at the National, "Where many a man he will spend a pound / and many a man, God willing, spend two." Everyone now, without further ado, if you would take your positions on the floor. As we render Zambesi for youse heart's delight and pure contentment.'

'You seem nice,' I heard Freckles whispering into my ear. 'You look like a gentleman with money. Maybe you're from London. Are you from London?'

I told her she looked beautiful and, without so much as a single hint of protest, found myself permitted, without censure, to commence exploratory investigations between those sturdy country thighs. Nabla was her name, she confided warmly – I had never encountered such an appellation. Yes, Nabla Cooney, former resident of Burris-in-the-Glade.

'Do you want to come back to the flat with me?' I suggested – to which she replied that, to be perfectly honest, she really shouldn't ought to.

Oh, come now, Freckles, I thought privately to myself. Where on earth would you get such an opportunity? Let's cut to the chase – for you know you're going to anyway. Hmm?

'I really ought to go back to the hostel,' she explained. 'It isn't really all that far from here. It's in Granby Place.'

'Granby Place,' I murmured, enjoying the succession of cute little groans – as unseen among the sweating, heaving crowds, I set about subtly massaging her womanhood. Up and down. Her 'Mound of Venus' as they used to say in the books in Mandeville House. The ones that we used to read with 'Uncle' Leslie Courtney, in any case.

Yes, Mound of Venus. Up and down. We could have treats – perhaps some drinks.

She began to smile. Some expensive wine. Why – caviar!

'In that case . . .' she said, hesitating just a little. Before agreeing that – yes, she would accompany me home. And which she did – most willingly, I have to say. And was still fast asleep when I woke up to get a cigarette.

Smiling to myself as I thought of the caperings of the showband's lead vocalist earlier on – the Emperors, they were called. With the singer got up like Haile Selassie, complete with towering headdress, traditional robes.

These self-consciously eccentric showband acts were rather the fashion of the time: comprising a fantastically ludicrous roster which included, among others, the Zulus, the Indians – and, perhaps less memorably, the Bachelor Farmers. The Emperors ran through a variety of standard modern numbers, most of which I didn't recognise. Before launching into a rousing ballad: 'Nineteen Men', if memory serves – extolling the success of a recent, quite spectacular jailbreak from the Republic's foremost political prison.

It didn't take long before Nabla Cooney woke up – and she really did look fetching, lying sweetly there by my side. With the blanket around her.

'Nabla Cooney, you really are the sweetest of girls,' I said. And meant it.

As she kissed my earlobe and whispered ever so softly: 'I know I can trust you – because I can tell that you're a gentleman. Could, in fact, from the very minute I met you. Would you like to know the reason why I really left Burris-in-the-Glade?'

'Yes,' I replied as I squeezed her hand gently, 'yes, as a matter of fact I would, my own dear, sweet Nabla Cooney.'

'Because my father interfered with me. Over and over he did it, so he did. I hate him. He's a pig. And my mother too – she's a sow and all. I knew that I couldn't tell her. Because if I did – do you know what would happen?'

I shook my head as she rested hers upon my shoulder.

'She'd blame me,' she whispered. 'That's who'd catch it. Silly old Nabla here. She'd look at me and say: you did it. It was you what led your father on.'

It was extremely nice fucking her as she insisted that, even though she knew I was 'a little bit old', that nonetheless she would still be able to say that she liked me. And not be ashamed or embarrassed or anything. That was nice, I thought – plunging ever further inside of her lithe young body – incapable, however, of dispelling the recollection of Haile Selassie. The singing emperor cavorting in his regalia from one side of the stage to the other – swinging the microphone and clapping his hands. With it being absolutely hilarious now, to think of him appearing, completely blacked-up with boot polish, which he was.

There was some anniversary or centenary on, and of course he was compelled by tradition to pay his dues. Which he did, with some fervour, I have to say, Mr 'Emperor' Haile Selassie.

'Northmen, southmen, comrades all – Dublin, Belfast, Cork

and Donegal,' he had been bawling, 'always remember that we are on the one road!'

And that they wouldn't rest, he insisted, until every last single British soldier had been chased for ever into the sea. The crowd had gone wild when they heard that. As, somewhere to the back of the hall, a plate of glass, most likely the main door, gave in with a crash.

'But let's not bother ourselves thinking about that,' I said to sweet old Freckles – sinking my sword in as deep as it would go. While she conceded that she thought that perhaps she was 'falling in love' with me. And which I said was 'just fine'.

'Who do you work for – are you a banker or something like that?' she queried, running her nails with a little tinkle across my back.

'No,' I grinned, 'I'm gainfully employed by Em-Oi-Foive.'

'Oh, you!' she countered – hitting me this pretend little slap.

As I gripped old Percy, shoving even further inside of her – before finally stiffening and discharging whatever semen I happened to have left. Experiencing, you might say, what has historically been called 'the littlest of deaths'. In the service of Queen and country, obviously.

I never saw her again.

She wrote, and phoned – and, once I think, had even called into the Grafton Agency. Where Shivaun had followed my instructions to, in her own words, 'fob her off'. I had liked her though, poor little innocent thing – let there be no mistake about that. But 'Freckles' Nabla Cooney? For myself and her – that had to be, I'm afraid: The End.

Chapter 16

Biddy Mulligan the Pride

Biddy Mulligan, in her time, had also danced in the National Ballroom. I know that because she told me. There was nothing I enjoyed more than chatting to that old girl – and, boy, could Mulligan talk! Specifically as regards anything to do with her native city. The pair of us enjoyed some splendid chats. Not that, to be perfectly honest, she paid a great deal of attention to whatever it was I might have had to say. Being much more interested in getting on with her own story.

Yes, those blathering hoary old Liffeyside yarns of hers, of which she appeared to have an absolutely limitless supply. The seizured lips of puir auld Biddy Mulligan, I used to think.

'Wait till I tell you, Mr Merry, sorr,' she would continue. 'Mr Merry, sorr, will you wait a minute there till I tell you?'

Although, to be frank, there were plenty of times when she really did go on.

Not that that was surprising – being 'yet another characteristic of her race', as Henry had once remarked of some similar buttonholer, late one night just before closing time in Minty's.

'That off-putting blend of melancholia and sentiment – exhibitions of emotion in excess of the facts,' was how he had actually put it, as I recall.

'With the entire country belonging in one of the more

outlandish episodes of that lunchtime radio series *The Tumbletys*, which they all seem to be obsessed with. And which, at times, if you ask me – considering some of what I've seen ever since arriving in this mist-shrouded backwater – can often seem the perfect model of restraint.'

There was lots to think about when chatting with puir auld Mulligan. But then, of course, she would go and spoil the whole damn thing by irritating one again, tugging at the sleeve, repeating the same infernal story. Or being quite hopelessly and excessively amused by yet another of her own threadbare anecdotes. Along with squeals of: 'C'mere to me!' – and, 'Are you listening to me, Mr Merry?' Before releasing another mighty 'whoop!'

'Merciful hour!' she would hoot at the top of her voice. 'Amn't I only after nearly after forgetting for what it was I came down for! It was to give you this!'

I stared at her open hand and there it was. The same gold medallion engraved 'J' which I'd purchased for my darling Joanne Vollmann's birthday. There it was – gleaming. Resting snugly on Mulligan's palm. The very same gift which I'd so proudly presented – to my darling Jo, just a week before she took her own life.

Which is what happened, in spite of whatever rumours there may have been. And in spite of that idiot coroner, who had returned an 'open verdict'.

'I found this over by the cliffs,' beamed Biddy Mulligan proudly. 'I think you must have dropped it this morning when you were out for your constitutional.'

'Why, thank you,' I said. 'I suppose I must have done. Silly me – thank you, Bridget!'

She handed it to me and I slipped it into my pocket.

'I'd say the girl that owned that was a refined and lovely lady. Was she, Mr Meredith?'

'Maybe,' I replied, before turning away. For there are just some things that one simply doesn't want to talk about – or can't.

I could hear her wittering to herself behind my back. Mulligan, I mean – not poor dead Joanne. Although that could have been possible too. And has been, from time to time. I even saw her once – in the attic in Willesden. And which, with the reader's permission, I will delay until later. Joanne Vollmann standing beside a wardrobe. With her face a mask – a heart-shaped mask. Like something from a Theatre of Cruelty production. But all of that, by the by. As on droned you-know-who.

'Ah yes!' Biddy Mulligan continued. 'All the memories that we have that no one – not even them that's closest to us – will ever in their lives get to know about. Isn't that right, Mr Meredith? For what are we all doing, whenever you get around to thinking about it? Yes, because that is the truth. That when push comes to shove, there's not a single one of us living, whether here in Woolsley Bay or anywhere else, as is doing anything but performing for this very one last season on the coast.'

'That's right,' I nodded in agreement, adding as I did so: 'As a matter of fact, I was only making the very same observation to Mrs Dixon earlier this morning. Before she went for her evening snooze, ha ha.'

'Lord save us, master, but she's an awful old divil, isn't she, the same old lassie! An awful old divil, so she is, our Rosie!'

'One final season on the coast,' I sighed lugubriously, 'that's about the height of it, I'm afraid, Mrs Mulligan.'

'Ah yes!' she concurred, 'here at the Seafront Apollo in Woolsley Bay. With us all lined up to present our humble little penny gaff. Do you know what I'm going to tell you – I often thought of being one myself – a proper comedian, don't you know. Laugh though well you might, I distinguished myself once in this particular regard. During a concert that the nurses held for all the patients. Lord, it was a hoot! Will I tell you, master, what it was I performed back then? They said that they'd never heard anything like it – even Maddy Trilly, great old crabbit big fatarse that she was. Even she had to admit it. Do you know what I'm going to do, Master Meredith? I'm going to tell you a Biddy Mulligan joke. Because that's what I've become in this instant – the laugh-a-minute girl from way back there in the long ago. I'll bring the house down, that's what I'll do. Here she comes, the Pride of the Coombe!'

I couldn't have stopped her – even if I'd wanted to. It was something to do with a 'clown and a bag of apples'. I mean – God only knows. I wasn't listening to a word she said. With those entirely disproportionate bouts of laughter proving hopelessly tedious in the end. The fault, admittedly, being mine as much as hers. Mine, indeed, more, I think it would be fair to say. Bringing back Henry's words in Minty's.

'Their imagination,' I remembered him saying, 'whatever else it might be, it remains so entirely different to ours. And I would have to concede, however much it may gall me to do so, that when it comes to matters of levity and humour – there really isn't anyone to touch them.'

There were actually tears now flowing down Biddy Mulligan's face – as I rotated Joanne's medallion fondly in my hand.

'Mr Chenevix, sorr,' I heard Mulligan continue, 'it really was the divil and all, I got to tell you. This happened to an uncle of mine, I'm telling you. A fellow what went by the name of Pop Dan Dolan. So this Popsy, do you see – do you hear me talking to you, Mr Meredith? – wasn't he driving this very important visitor to a town called Ballytubber after the war. This would have been in the west of Ireland. Now this American, his name was Delancey, oh, and a very important dignitary surely. A tall, talkative man with sandy side-whiskers. Anyhow, doesn't this client remark to the bould Pop Dan, he says to him did he think perhaps that there might be a cottage nearby where we could have ourselves maybe a "sup", a "little drinkie". Because, after all, it had been a long journey, Mr Meredith.

'"Begorra, sorr," doesn't Pop Dan say, "you're in luck, because round about here there's a widow by the name of McGinn. As'd be a woman of my acquaintance, and I can tell you now that in that particular house of hers you can be sure of her having put a little something by. So let's go!"'

Drawing a breath as off she went again.

'Merciful hour!' Mulligan started screeching, 'but what do you think happened then, Mr Meredith? Didn't they only go and pull up outside an old thatched cottage there by the side of the road. And in skips Pop, with his cap in his hand.

'"Good evening, Mrs McGinn," the Yankee heard him say. "Haven't I got me a gentleman all the way from America. And him with a thirst that would trip a priest, saving your presence. So if you could, maybe, do anything for him, he would be more than extremely grateful. And I'd be inclined to be that way myself, to be honest. For I have a bit of a drought on me too."'

There ensued a pause as Biddy Mulligan twinkled, soberly collecting her thoughts – then off she went, emboldened once more.

'"Good evening, Pop," says the woman of the house, "and damn good it is for to see you this evening. For I knew your father and all belonging to him, and all belonging to them before that. So come ye in out of the drizzle, you and your fine young gintleman that's all the way from America. For don't I know it well that youse have had a tiring day. Only to say that it's sorry I am that all I have here for ye is a bottle of something – I don't rightly remember its name. Because I bought it with a bottle of whiskey and a dozen stout with the money that our Danny Midgie be's sending over every quarter from America. My neighbours have helped me to drink the whiskey and stout, but Ogie Coogan, the publican who sold me the other bottle, he tault me that all the gentry are drinking this partcular brand. So I bought a bottle, though I have never seemed to fancy it – and it is here with me still."'

By this stage, Biddy Mulligan was so doubled up with laughter she could scarcely get a word out. Continuing to slap those ample old thighs – creating a racket throughout which, unbelievably,

Rosie Dixon continued with her snoring. Which really was, by this stage, quite unmerciful.

'So up she climbs, God bless her, the widow McGinn,' enthused Biddy, 'yes, up she climbs on a kitchen chair, ordering the driver to "hauld it good and steady". As out of the thatch she produces a – wait till you hear it, master! – a bottle, can you believe it, of the finest Champagne de Pays, Veuve Clicquot. Yes, the sweetest libation imaginable, amn't I after telling you, sorr. Well, if it didn't become the talk of the country after that. Until it was time for his lordship to go back to America. And him saying to all as he strolled up the plank: "Well, I must say, it was a luxury for us! But I'm damned if I expected to come across such a thing in a place where even the poor old snipe might find things difficult!"'

By this stage, Biddy Mulligan had come perilously close to collapse. Resting her worn-out head on my shoulder, wholly incapable of any further articulation.

'Mr Meredith,' she squealed, 'are we not the divils all the same? Allowing that poor old American fellow to be going to his grave and all the time remaining oblivious that it was that same impish rascal Pop Dan that had stashed it in there. Aye – arranged the whole blessed thing, so he had. Had planted the champagne up there in the thatch. Saints alive – the things that us mischievous craythurs be's getting up to, you know? And I'm telling you not a word of a lie!'

But if Biddy had a few old yarns up her sleeve, 'well-suited to shortening the road', as she put it, I hadn't gone and spent the best part of twenty years by the banks of her beloved Liffey to be found wanting in that department, let me tell you.

Which was how – when I eventually got the chance, you might say – I came to regale her with my own little tale about Mickey Full Trickey, the so-called 'raparee rebel chanter', and his all-star band the Mighty Felons.

Who had kept myself and Henry Plumm up half the night in the – at least to my mind – astonishingly lax atmosphere of the

Shannon Great Western Hotel. Sometime around, I should think, the end of July 1976. Which was probably, as an unusually tired-seeming Henry had remarked when I picked him up outside the Gresham Hotel in O'Connell Street, the closest old Spudland had come to experiencing an all-out civil war.

And there we were, headed off straight down the dual carriageway towards the west, with Plumm at this stage knocking back tablets. Angina, he'd told me – but said little else about it. I couldn't keep from noticing the pearldrops on his forehead. Lined up, one after the other.

'Did you see the paper?' he said as we left the city.

'What is it now?' I said as we paused at the traffic lights.

He reached into his inside pocket and produced the *Irish Independent*. He smoothed it out, and in a grim monotone, read out the following paragraph.

'Shortly before 9.38 a.m., a stately Jaguar car drove through the ornamental gates of Glencairn House in South County Dublin. By a quirk of fate, the driver turned right rather than left. Just 317 yards down the road a 200-pound bomb was detonated. The newly appointed British Ambassador to Ireland and his twenty-six-year-old British civil servant were killed. The ambassador was on his way to his first formal meeting with the Irish Minister for Foreign Affairs.'

As we cruised at around 50 mph, an inane advertisement wittered away on the dash radio.

'Fancy a holiday in the sun? Very well, then – all you gotta do is join the JWT set. For all your holiday and vacationing needs, it's got to be Joe Walsh Tours: Yugoslavia from sixty-nine pounds!'

'This godforsaken hole they have the nerve to call a capital. I'll be damned glad to see the back of it, even if only for this weekend.'

He sighed as he mopped his seamed, fleshy brow – groaning a little in the limp dead heat.

'They're making fools of us, do you know that? I know who it was who did this – those bastards from Corrylough in South Armagh, contemptible land of the smirking hillbilly. But they won't be doing it for very much longer. That much you can be sure of, Meredith.'

We were headed for the western seaboard in order to catch the tail end of the Blind Raftery Summer School. Which we'd planned, on a whim, at the onset of the summer. I hadn't, in all honesty, known what we might expect. But felt that one or two surprises might be in store. And we weren't surprised.

'Because isn't that what it is?' Biddy Mulligan had chuckled. 'You can't be up to the Auld Sod for surprises!'

By the time we'd arrived and checked into the hotel, the venue was already thronged to capacity. With the main attraction being the live recording of *Dolly Bodley's Kitchen*, a hugely popular radio programme presented by the colourful Dolly herself – raconteur, journalist and all-round gifted musician. Following on from an apparently spirited debate, where the motion had been: 'Where to, Ireland?' and subtitled: 'The Battle for the Soul of Éire'.

The mood we found animated, to say the least. With the anger in the air, at times, being palpable. The Mighty Felons – 'all the way from West Belfast!' – had taken to the stage earlier than had been expected – considerably ramping up the fervour as a consequence.

Threats to bomb the hotel if the debate wasn't cancelled had, apparently, been received. And been taken very seriously. With the decision, however, having been taken to go ahead. Not that the discussion had passed without incident. Far from it.

The special guest of the evening was a nationally popular Sister of the Poor, spiritually and politically active in a number of different spheres, who had delivered a powerful and emotional speech.

'I won't pretend,' Sister Bree began, 'what with the way events have been going in that misfortunate province to the north of the island in recent times, to being surprised by the depth of feeling evident at the discussion here this evening. Because these are extremely contentious and difficult times.'

Already a chant had commenced down the back. It went: 'Chucky chucky chuck chuck chuck! Chucky chucky chuck chuck chuck! Rule Britannia – yes, like fuck!' From the very same group who, by all accounts, had earlier threatened the speaking government minister with violence. With one of them – a former political prisoner whose face I recognised immediately, around about twenty-seven years of age, being very much to the forefront.

'So what have you got to say for yourself, Sister?' he demanded, flanked on either side by lank-haired comrades in green camouflage.

'I want to plead for tolerance on all sides. I was present earlier on and heard what you had to say to the minister for justice.'

'I regret nothing. I'd say it all again. I'd say it again. I'll say it now. There's only one way to deal with the problems of Ulster – drive the British back into the sea. And, if it is to prove necessary, along with them all the privately educated, law-library running-dog lackies of imperialism!'

'There is nothing to be gained by excessive emotionalism or the type of language you and your associates were heard using earlier on,' Sister Bree shot back.

This prompted a cheer and a few verses of some bellicose ballad.

'I presume you are referring to the fact that I used the term "lice" when I suggested to the minister that if he were to encounter Ireton or Cromwell, who were renowned for using the term "kill the nits and there will be no lice", he would pull up a chair and do his best to reason with these Roundheads. But, of course – even if Cromwell or Ireton were interested, which they're not – they would kill the nits anyway, for that is their view of the world and the way of things. And, of course, their licence proceeds from a higher authority. Because we and the likes of us – we are perceived as unclean. Lower, in actual fact, than the dog.'

'That is not the type of discourse which inspires,' Sister Bree parried.

'But it's the truth. That is how the Protestants of Ulster feel about their Catholic neighbours.'

'You really believe that? Then I'm sorry for you. Because it simply isn't true,' the nun replied.

'Which of course is exactly what your predecessor, the minister, alleged. Because, of course, he doesn't know. All he can do is think and not feel. But feel, Sister – because I know. What it's like to be strip-searched, be an enemy of the state.

'To be an enemy of the state from birth. With the truth being that we've waited long enough. What kind of life, do you think, is it to wake up every morning knowing that there's no job and no chance of a job just because your parents have the wrong religion? I'm sorry, Sister, but we've waited long enough. We've waited now, my people – and the time, I'm afraid, for talking's done. There's only one way to resolve it now – like Machiavelli said, put the guns in the hands of the prophets, and believe you me, our comrades will soon conclude it. Because there isn't anywhere left to go. *Tiocfaidh ár lá*!'

A similar cry rose up on either side. 'Our day will come.'

As clenched fists defiantly batted the air.

Now Sister Bree had her eyes tightly shut – invoking Christ and the peace of all his angels. As the former prisoner conducted his revivified choir.

'Chucky chucky chuck chuck chuck! Chucky chucky chuck chuck chuck! Rule Britannia – yes, like fuck!'

The minister in question had appeared suddenly in the doorway of the partition seeming pale and exhausted. Then when I looked again, he was gone.

'Drive them into the sea!' bellowed the ex-prisoner. 'Every

fucking last British soldier, hang them from poles all along the M1! *Tiocfaidh ár lá*!'

'Who will release us from the burden of history?' implored Sister Bree with spindly arms outspread. 'Throughout this long life, for which I am grateful, I have looked on in dismay as everything I thought to be static and invincible has been swept away right in front of my eyes. Thrones have toppled, dictators arisen. Massacres, bloodbaths, purges, pogroms have followed one another with a ruthlessness and ferocity for which there appeared to be no precedent. Entire sections of society, in my time, have been mercilessly liquidated. And now here it comes, this horror, once again to revisit us in our poor beknighted homeland. Please will you listen to me – before God, let us join in prayer!'

But by now the young prisoner was at the bottom of a bottle of whiskey – whirling his jacket high above his head before redeploying it as an impromptu Starry Plough flag.

'A nation once again!' he shouted.

Before, much to the crowd's delight, being backed up by the various members of the Mighty Felons folk band – fiddles, bouzoukis and hand-drums at the ready. By this stage the shutters at the bar had been reopened. With Sister Bree already long since forgotten, railing helplessly against the cruel inevitability and insatiable bloodlust of history.

Which, later on, when we had retired to the relative peace and calm of our room at the back of the Shannon Hotel, a startlingly upbeat Henry Plumm had confessed to being 'more than a little impressed'.

'By both performances,' he had added as he sipped his gin.

'Haha!' I had chuckled, sensing myself rather tiddly by now – shaking my head as I regarded my friend with no small measure of affection.

'I suppose you'll be telling me next that Sister Whatyoumaycallher is one of ours as well.'

'Sister Bree,' he corrected, 'short for Bree-oh-nah.'

Before reaching in his pocket and producing one of his tablets. There ensued a bout of furious coughing – as he stood by the Venetian blinds, gazing out.

He didn't say anything else after that. Just swallowing the little that remained of his gin as he continued to consider the theatre in the car park. Which was still brightly lit, and where the long-haired ex-prisoner could be seen leaping up and down with his bottle. On the bonnet of the minister for justice's Mercedes.

'*Tiocfaidh ár lá*!' he roared out into night. 'Let's hear it for the Roundheads. Every last one of those imperialist fuckers – crucified, one by one, along the motorway. How do you like them apples, MI5?'

Just in case my remark as regards Sister Bree had been overlooked or unheard, I poured him another drink and, handing it over to him, repeating light-heartedly as I stood there beside him, 'I suppose you'll be telling me next that she's one of ours.'

Accepting the gin, he shook his head wearily.

'No,' he demurred, as he sipped at the glass of clear liquid and nodded towards the car park. 'Just him.'

By this stage the inebriated prisoner was in the process of scaling a lamp-post.

'Just him, dear boy. Being aware that, in Ulster, as in so many comparable theatres around the world, it pays to recruit them early.'

Then it was back to the beach – and myself.

'Surprises, Biddy,' I heard myself murmur. 'Indeed,' I added, with a giddy chuckle. Before looking up. Only to realise that my amusing Dublin companion – what had she done? Only turned on her heel and disappeared into the more hospitable and cool interior of the hotel building.

Abandoning me there once more – all alone with nothing to humour me but my thoughts and memories. Specifically of Minty's, *The Tumbletys* and all the rest. And just how accurate old Henry had been, when it came to that particular aspect of things.

That is to say – just how interwoven the real and the absolutely farcical life tended to be in Ireland. Why, even just thinking about McRoarty there with his script. Standing in front of the microphone, still semi-drunk from our carousing the night before – it was more than enough to bring a broad smile to my face.

'Howyeez ones all doin'?' he announced in that incomprehensibly thick West Donegal accent – the one I was more than familiar with. Having heard it so often being shouted up the Grafton Agency stairs. 'Are youse up there doing rightly?'

Then the next thing you know, he'd appear right there in the doorway, literally falling into the office. Looking every inch the caricatured rustic – with that electric-red hair like some Gaelic James Whale Frankenstein. A sort of brush-cut standing on its ends, with that Hapsburg lower lip and gap-toothed grin. Complete with that distinctively droll sense of humour and a profane vocabulary. In both his uncouth eccentricity and sheer rowdy doggedness, the acting fraternity had no equal in Hugh B. (for Barney) McRoarty.

With the only person who could seem to make any sense of what Hugh B. was saying half the time being his lifelong pal and 'butty', as he called him, the equally colourful Charlie Kerrins. Another of the city's popular character actors and a regular fixture at the counter in Minty's. Permanently clouded in a fug of thick grey smoke, interrupted only by occasional visits to the lavatory. In the direction of which he would often abruptly scuttle like a crab, in a flurry of thick Dublinese, which would later turn out to have been quotations from Oscar Wilde or Beckett.

Yes, all five foot three of the fellow. With his leathery face and mop of fierce black hair giving the appearance of having been painted on. Somewhat haphazardly, it has to be said – perhaps by someone like Brendan Behan, just for the hell of it.

'What back-of-the-mountain gibberish is that blasted idiot coming out with now?' lamented Henry one evening when I'd gone to see him in the Rathgar flat, blood rushing to his head as he tuned the transistor dial. 'This whole bloody country is in need of elocution lessons.'

Then back he went to hear the end of Hugh Barney delivering the last verse of part of 'The Dying Rebel'. Where the eponymous insurgent had just this minute entered upon the final stages of his demise – kissing the crucifix being proffered by his hoary-headed parish priest, preparing to forgive him all his sins. Which, of course, in the way of the lawless anarchist cloaked in the blood-saturated banner of patriotism, included the murder of who knew how many innocent people.

Henry winced at some of the more nauseating sentiments.

'Not that any of that ought to come as any surprise,' he observed, 'what with it being in their nature, as you know. Because that's the very reason Pat and Biddy from Ireland bother to ordain all these priests in the first place. In you go to the confessional box, back goes the slide – and, lo and behold, the slate is wiped clean.'

And that was the end of Episode 42 of the popular radio series *At Home With the Tumbletys*.

'Women and children blown to pieces, and not so much as a stain on their souls,' grumbled Henry irascibly as he switched the radio off.

'Charming,' I agreed, 'but, whether they know it or not, my dear partner – this time they are reaching the end of the road.'

'It would appear that way. Yes, that is true.'

'This time,' I emphasised, 'this time for fucking good. The Aden treatment, *vous pensez, mon ami*?'

'Yes, I do. And not a fucking moment too soon,' he said – retreating to the kitchen to replenish our glasses of gin.

Chapter 17

The Hydrogen Bomb

Yes, as I say, Madame Merciful Hour has gone and taken her leave – disappeared without a word into the deep, dark bowels of the hotel. 'Without so much as a by your layve,' as Charlie Kerrins used to say. No doubt, I am sure, to make it her business to tend to the needs of 'the Major' as she calls Henry. Who is really and truly in a bad way now – with almost all of his memories practically shot away.

That, at least, was what I thought.

Because, as you are obviously aware, this little interlude occurred prior to Henry smashing his head against a certain unwieldy, somewhat weathered spruce oar.

You wouldn't do that to an old friend, would you? He had seemed almost infantile throughout those final appeals. And then: Bash. Blub blub blub, and all the rest.

What was most surprising about the episode in the bathroom, however, was the sudden onset of clarity, after all those months of brain fog. Not to say downright incomprehension in his case – as regards everything in the world around poor old Plump the Bewildered, as I'd taken to thinking of him. In my own mind, obviously, of course.

And then arrives this staggeringly clear comprehension – albeit just for a few brief moments. Because vascular dementia, or in his case 'cortical atrophy', as it was called – it can really be quite deceptive. With shards of this abrupt lucidity being a feature – just when you're least expecting them.

But I still feel such a fool!

Having made such an awful mess of the place – and succumbing, almost Paddy-like, to an unforgivable weakness of emotion.

'Like something you might expect from the Paddies,' I can hear Henry say.

I mean, it had taken me almost an hour to clean up. Small wonder, standing here staring out, who I remind myself most of is not Max von Sydow or Joubert at all.

But the Notting Hill psychopath, the awful John Reginald Christie. You may remember I have mentioned him before. I even have the same grubby belted mackintosh raincoat – so familiar from those murky fifties photographs.

Which – and I wasn't going to tell you this, but I will nonetheless – is in actual fact the property of Henry Plumm.

He was wearing it that very first day when I met him off the Dún Laoghaire ferry. Because, in some ways, I suppose – I still can't be without him. Yes, myself and Plumm are indivisible, really.

It's almost as if Leonard – the more light-hearted, indeed arguably more life-affirming of the Pinter clan – has been summarily supplanted. Only this time for good. And we have been returned to that familiar landscape pioneered (with no small assistance from Franz Kafka and Mr Hemingway) in *The Birthday Party* and so many others. Where his audience find themselves captive in a twilight zone, observing his grotesque characters performing their unpleasant, ritualistic acts.

Not that I regret my actions. Not in anyway whatsoever. Because I warned him, didn't I? Don't write anything down, I cautioned.

And then what happened? He turned and gave me that treacherous smile.

'Even your own,' I whispered, 'it's hard to believe. But, even your own.'

And that was when I brought up the oar. Turned, as I say, into an unforgivably emotional Paddy.

But it's over now, and all I can think – thanks, in great measure, to my having been extravagantly uplifted by the tales, anecdotes and daily diversions of Biddy Mulligan, the Pride herself – is how pleasurable and invigorating it would be this minute to sail right over there to Mrs Rosie Dixon, snoring away in her chair. And to do nothing more untoward or inappropriate than fold her warm, plump hand in mine. And await that moment – that blissful few seconds just before you know the curtain is about to come down, and our show at the Seafront Apollo here in Woolsley Bay is on the verge of reaching its denouement.

For things most definitely would appear to be approaching some kind of exciting climax!

With the pain in my chest acutely increasing with every passing minute. Seems like the equivalent of a chain of fish-hooks being remorselessly dragged across the floor of one's torn chest. And I do apologise for not having mentioned this in detail before. Although I did advert to the consumption of a number of angina tablets. But attributed this to Henry. Which isn't, at least not strictly, true. With the prescription, in fact, having been made out to us both. Which generally tends to be the way with that old Plumm and I, as I'm sure you've already guessed.

Who would have imagined that we'd end up together – never to be separated, forever to continue our profession of watching – trapped inside a belted mackintosh raincoat, balefully gazing out across an empty strand? Perhaps John Christie ought to have been an agent? Unless of course, as we have seen in so many other situations . . . he was.

I've got that awful numbness in my fingers again. Which, no doubt – I mean the doctor told me to anticipate such a development – is attributable to His Majesty 'the old ticker'. But with no small amount of blame assigned also to that bastard Arthur Mullard, the so-called builder and his company of slope-shouldered, duplicitous vigilantes. Involuntary spasming, one confidently anticipates, being the next agonising step. All thanks to Mullard and his coterie of black-eyed, ingratiating inebriates. Who, just as I suspected from the outset, have arrived here in Woolsley Bay for but one reason and one reason alone.

To exact vengeance – as, I assume, instructed by their superiors. Army Fucking Council, or whatever. In order to ensure that I was consummately erased – wiped off of the earth. Without any further fucking ado.

They had missed me often enough, for heaven's sake.

And, like Ambrose had always insisted – dull-witted though they may be, Pat and Biddy are possessed of long fucking memories.

'If they want you, they'll get you,' he had said. 'The only sense of honour they have, poor bastards.'

So that was why they'd come here – it was more or less obvious from the start. But your safety can't, at all times, be guaranteed. As Henry, poor chap, discovered in the washroom. But he wasn't the only one – as I am going to tell you now.

I was pulling out Percy in order to enjoy a pee – when, suddenly, I looked up – all I saw was a looming shadow. One with the most enormous jug-ears imaginable – holding up a bottle. I couldn't make out what its contents were.

'Cunt!' was all I heard – and then he walloped me with it. As the door burst open and he was joined by Snudge and all the rest.

'A shooter's too good for him – we don't want to attract attention. I spiked what's in here good, so that ought to, jig-time, do the trick.'

What a crew! – as they say in the old-time shows. And what a performance they were setting about mounting now! Literally tearing all the clothes off my back – as Mullard himself began squealing with delight – directing operations as Alfie Bass held my mouth open and down went the bottle of finest Napoleon brandy. Laced with Nembutal, in case you didn't know.

Which – as if I didn't know – all along had been the sole purpose of their mission.

Mullard's Painters & Decorators – pshaw! I had known all along that something along these lines had been bound to happen – and had discussed the prospect regularly with Henry. Not that he seemed to care – with his back to me, still standing by the window, far more like Billy Bunter than anything resembling the eminence grise, Joubert. Never mind John Reginald Christie, bespectacled in his drab raincoat.

Not that it mattered, I can recall thinking to myself, because either way my poor old dreary tale is concluded. Or so it had seemed – as Snudge got a hold of a toilet brush and started battering and battering and battering – as Mullard upended the bottle of Napoleon brandy.

'Drink it, you spook fuck. Get it down you, every single drop!'

What a way to go, I kept thinking – just like the Americans say in the movies. After all this time. And all that I've been through, down the years. All that we've been through – myself and you-know-who. Billy Bunter, special agent. Ha ha ha ha, do you hear me now – it sounds like I'm becoming hysterical. Or maybe, like Henry said – that's the way that I've been all along.

Ever since my first days in the flat in Willesden Green. To which I'd been – at the insistence of one's superiors – strategically 'retired'. Well, some hope. Because never at any point in my career had I experienced anything to compare with this.

As Mullard hauled the bottle from my lips and instructed Snudge to hit me another 'wallop'. Which he did – the tip of a hobnailed boot in the face, as a matter of fact. You know those things that navvies wear.

'That'll do for now. Let's get the fuck out. It shouldn't take more than three or four minutes. And that'll be the last we see of this twister.'

Then they were gone. Saying goodbye as they scrambled

out the door. Leaving poor old Chenevix, RIP. But, as it happens – not quite yet. Because, after all – unlike Henry, I'm still here to relate the experience. What anyone, in their right mind, would justifiably describe as a 'fanciful yarn'. Or a 'two-foot-six-inches-above-the-ground fairy story', as Ambrose Roland, God rest his soul, more than likely would have categorised it.

I mean, it really must have resembled another episode of the Keystone Cops as those bastard Provisional IRA labourers flailed their boots and gave me – 'merciful hour!' – such a remorseless kicking as I lay there that it doesn't bear thinking about. It took three of the monkey men altogether to hold me down. And then they administered the last of the poisoned alcohol. Yes, the 'fatal liquid', as they might have it in the old-time stories. Except for the fact that poor old Paddy once again had miscalculated – never doing their preparation, you see!

Snorting and snickering and grunting as they stood there observing for, I suppose, maybe five or six minutes. As I spasmed and kicked, all the while clutching at my throat. Before eventually spasming and going completely rigid.

'Well, dere we are. Dat's de end o'de snakey bastard!' was the last I heard of Mullard's rustic drawl and Alfie Snudge calling back as he banged the door behind them: 'He had it coming – rot in hell, spook!'

I mean – what an end to the daftest of fairy tales! Surpassing anything Biddy Mulligan could have ever come up with – if she had ever existed, that is. At least in the form which I had granted her. And wasn't just a nondescript, dreary, old, pale-faced Agency employee, coming and going without so much as raising her head. All these agencies – I mean, honest to goodness!

But, Biddy Mulligan or not – it was she who found me and set to work stuffing my mouth to the tonsils up with soap.

'Don't be a damned fool, man!' I could distinctly remember Henry having warned me. 'They have people everywhere. You think we won't be identified eventually? Yes. Make no mistake, they and their people – they have eyes everywhere,' he went on to advise. 'Just as soon as you step off the boat.'

'You ought to have known,' I could hear Henry scoff. 'I mean, it isn't as if it hasn't happened before.'

Which it had of course – when I'd decided to revisit the 'old sod' after twenty-five years. Just out of curiosity, I suppose. In order to monitor events after my departure. To examine, perhaps, how the peace process had bedded in.

'No!' Henry warned. 'You are out of your fucking mind. Because the last time we got out by the skin of our fucking teeth and nothing more. Just as soon as you land, there'll be someone who will spot you. Because, even yet, they have all their ferries watched. With people of their own actually employed by these companies.'

'Don't worry, Plummsers,' I had jauntily replied. 'After all, this is the year 2019. Things have moved on a little from back then in 1965. They have aeroplanes now – I'll be flying Aer Lingus.'

'Well, is that a fact? Don't say I didn't warn you!'

It was a good laugh tricking Henry for, as Roland used to always say, 'For the likes of us in the service, old habits die hard.'

So there I was, up on the upper deck of the Munster, the foam like churning Guinness Extra stout spraying away underneath as the ferry steadily groaned on. Imagining myself – don't ask me why! – in the role so vividly rendered by Charlie Kerrins all those many long years ago, in *The Confessions of Brendan Behan*, so warmly received on its opening night in the Hibernia Theatre.

'I counted the spires,' I could hear him concluding in his flat Dublin accent, ably complemented by his partner in crime, the one and only Val McBoan in the part of the younger Behan. As he continued: 'From Rathmines' fat dome on one side to St George's spire on the other, and in the centre, Christchurch, I could see them . . .'

All of this had come to me as I lay there, sputtering, on the floor of the bathroom. As the 'former' Biddy Mulligan cradled my head and wiped me with a towel. Her name was Maudie, she told me. So sweet.

'Nothing but the best of agencies for Meredith,' I choked. Still feeling my throat dangerously closing in.

'Like rigor mortis, nurse – even though I'm still alive.'

Every digit on my hands was stiff as a board. What a way to go, sweet puppies, I couldn't keep from thinking.

'Don't talk! Don't think! Don't do anything!' urged the nurse. 'Leave it to me! Are you listening? It's important – trust me!'

But then, I reflected – how wise can that be either? I listened carefully for indications of a Spuddy-type accent. But my hearing was unreliable.

'Trust me!' she repeated – wiping off the remaining spots of vomit. The soap tasted awful.

'Trust me,' she repeated.

As I began to laugh, hysterically.

Knowing in my heart, and indeed from bitterest experience – as the reader now will know – that there are very few in this world, Paddy or Biddy or anyone else, that one can trust.

As a certain James Carey was to discover on board the good ship *Melrose* in the Year of Our Lord 1883, a year after the callous dispatch of the Lord Chief Lieutenant Frederick Cavendish, in the Phoenix Park in Dublin by the unheard-of – even for Pat! – brutal attack with specially purchased surgical knives. A transaction in which the eponymous traveller, or so it was rumoured, had been involved.

Now, however, as he sailed out of Dublin Bay bound for South Africa, he considered himself magnificently, gloriously free.

In spite of the fact that he had turned Queen's evidence – against all of his noble, loyal comrades in the most heinous band of assassins ever known even in the blood-drenched annals of infamy known as Irish history. Who had perpetrated the deed in question, namely the Invincibles.

'As roguish a band of psychopaths and cut-throats as even the atoll, in its time, had ever succeeded in discharging from the nether regions of its long-since contaminated bowels,' as Henry had memorably phrased it. 'As knavish a cabal as ought never to have been born, without exception.'

But now the sun had come out for the informer James Carey – particularly when he found himself befriended by a fellow countryman by the name of Patrick O'Donnell, who informed him he hailed from County Mayo.

'Where the crows ate the man!' the hearty, good-natured traveller declared, swinging his arm around the shoulders of the already fatally charmed James Carey.

As, once again – for such had become their custom – they ambled below deck in search of a jug of punch.

With it not being long before the eminent James Carey was once more consumed by bonhomie and fellow-feeling. Announcing 'how great' it was to meet a 'dacent man like himself', and 'as sweet a body as ever was encountered by a wanderer as would happen to be sailing upon the seven seas!'

'Yes,' agreed his companion, 'except, I'm afraid, that you won't be seeing them much longer.'

Suppressing a laugh as best he could on this, the occasion of their most recent assignation. When he had at last succeeded in getting Carey out of sight and shot his unsuspecting travelling companion. Who looked at him, lathered most copiously in blood, with his finger in his mouth, wearing an expression that almost seemed to say: 'Is it me?' As shot after shot was inflicted upon his by now fatally wounded person.

Thus did the informer Carey – reptilian traducer of 'the noble Invincibles' – justifiably meet his end.

'And it'll be the same for you, Chenevix Meredith, if you're not careful,' Henry had warned. And now it had happened.

But for the fact – thanks in the main to what turned out to be a genuinely trustworthy agency nurse, the loveliest English rose you could ever in your life imagine, sweetly named Virginia, from

Bath, in spite of the dedicated efforts of all those bomb-making bastards – I didn't, in fact, die.

Although I won't pretend my life didn't play out there in front of my eyes.

Because there I was in C Section back in Whitehall.

'These hill-dwellers that we're dealing with – nothing becomes them so much as the perceived authenticity of their grievance. The tedious validity of their so-called "incorrigible wound",' Ambrose Roland used to say. Adding, as always: 'We may not be permitted to treat fellow human beings as mere means to our ends. And it may well be true that practice of the "infernal art" of espionage may, in the end, corrupt us as human beings. But when the security of our island is threatened, as now – such ruminations tend to become superfluous, not to say self-indulgently tiresome.'

That very first winter of 1963 – when I myself had arrived in Dublin as a 'sleeper' – by common consensus had been among the worst in living memory. With an ice blizzard having practically turned the city into a skating rink. Roads and pathways had become treacherous, with the papers pronouncing 'King Winter' having arrived with a vengeance not seen 'since 1947'.

At Roland's suggestion I had attended the 'Holy Sacrifice of the Mass' in the Pro-Cathedral in order to familiarise myself with the terrain – and certainly, by doing so, had had my eyes opened. Never in my life have I heard so many prayers or experienced such an unctuous degree of craven subordination.

'Better get used to it,' my superior advised, 'for, believe you me, it can only get worse.'

They prayed and prayed for the salvation of the wheat crop, preached the powers and blessings not only of prayer itself but those of patriotism, volunteerism and helping one's neighbours. Every candle in the building was lit. When they came out, some people were so buried in tangles of clothing that only their eyes were exposed. The Guinness trucks seemed like great beasts that hauled their beer casks going down hard on icy streets, with an awful bellow and terror-stricken eyes.

That first Sunday morning I spent in Hollybank Road – when I looked out the window the entire city was silent and still as a white ghost town. The suburbs, I was later to discover, were the same – strewn with toppled telephone and telegraph wires, dangling electricity cables, fallen trees and broken branches that shattered roots and blocked roads.

'Let us commemorate in our rosaries the multitude who died during the famine,' intoned the priest in even graver tones.

'Jesus, Roland – they do go on,' I said, shaking my head.

'As I warned you, you had best accustom yourself,' I heard my superior reply.

Exhibiting as he did so that pose of amiable, disengaged worldliness for which he was justly celebrated, that agreeably louche but essential Englishness. Which, as he would have readily admitted, he was assiduously cultivating in my own good self.

'But never forget,' he would always insist, 'that when it comes to one's duty, the crucial task must always be to negate, subvert and monitor. But always, more than anything at all, my dear boy – frustrate!'

'At all times,' he would sigh, dabbing his lips with an oversized handkerchief.

We went up to the Phoenix Park, not far from the Vice-Regal Lodge where the under-secretary and Lord Cavendish had been murdered in the nineteenth century. We stood by the monument.

'This is where the Invincibles perpetrated their dirty deed,' I was told.

Like sparkling diamond earrings, the icicles all around us were hanging off lamps – everything we could see, in fact, was iced – streets, trees, railings, balconies, lamp-posts. Georgian fanlights. Great heaps of snow had been transformed into glittering, solid, silver-white ice capsules. There was a slashing east wind as we stood there by the pond.

'A boy was tragically drowned there last winter,' murmured Roland with tangible regret.

For obvious reasons, that was a topic I didn't want to discuss. Inevitably revivifying unwanted memories, as it did, of Goldengrove and Mandeville House. But obstinate Ambrose, as usual, forged onwards.

'I remember coming out here the very next morning after it happened,' he continued, 'and for the first time, as far back as I can remember, actually saying a short prayer for his poor immortal soul. Not that I necessarily believe in such things.'

I looked away. Because I just didn't want to hear.

'By midnight the pond area was empty and silent. The temperature had dropped to nineteen degrees – that's minus seven centigrade. Cold enough to create a new skin of ice on the hole in the pond.'

Once again, I made no attempt at reply.

In O'Connell Street people slipped, sprawled or simply plonked down on their posteriors. Others just toppled forward, then backwards – while their colleagues held on for dear life to a wall or building – even crawling a few feet, seeking better footing. The city had indeed been transformed into some sort of magnificent sculpture of ice, whose face was carved into frozen ruts, ridges, craters and human and tyre prints nearly impossible to stand on. Because of the circumstances, we – in common with a privileged number of others, newspapermen filing their copy and so forth – were permitted to extend our discourse in the Scotch House late into the small hours of Monday morning.

Over Hollybank Road the following morning, I could see that the first flakes were beginning to fall on Griffith Park. I looked down on the street below and could scarcely recognise it. Shop fronts, shop windows, hall doors had literally disappeared under a huge blanket of snow. An eerie silence hung everywhere, and there wasn't a human being in sight. There were drifts ten feet high.

And all I could think of, lathering my face in the bathroom, with the landlady downstairs calling out my name, was the grim implacability of Plumm's expression the previous night in the back bar of the gloomy, globe-lit Scotch House.

'Never has the climate seemed more appropriate and in sympathy,' he had sighed, 'for ever since my first day of arrival, that is exactly how I've always thought of it – like some lost village in Siberia. A crushing, ossified tundra of the soul. Another?'

My own prospective assassin's name – it had never been Arthur Mullard, of course. As I presume you now know. No, the ungainly obese painter in question, his actual title was none other than one Luke O'Brien. Apparently, O/C Southern Command of the Dublin branch of the IRA.

'Here,' he had said, approaching me on the landing, 'have yourself a snifter.'

As he passed me the already opened bottle of Napoleon. At which point – after all, I was supposed to be Em-Oi-Foive – I really ought to have suspected something! Don't you think? Unless, of course – I did?

'There you are, sorr,' he exclaimed, grinning broadly, 'for don't I know, in me waters, that it's gintlemen like you as is partial to a drop of the finest hooch. Like me auld father who worked in the auld times for Lord Givvens back in Balladine Hall, used to be always fond of saying: "Would you be after liking a drop of brandy, sorr? Would you like a drop of brandy, sorr?"'

'Here,' he said, 'there you are. It's all for you. You won't get better juice dan dat.'

As on he prattled.

'We have all the plastering done for her ladyship now, but there's no need for you to be bothered going to wake her. I'll leave the docket on the mantelpiece as we arranged. Do I want the rest of that auld Napoleon? Oh, not at all! You have it. Nothing but the best for a gintleman such as yourself. Well, I'll be off now, for I can see that the boys are waiting for me out front.'

And it was at that point I felt the cold barrel of a Glock pistol hard against my neck.

'Down the hatch – every last fucking drop!'

Luke O'Brien thrust the bottle upwards.

'Let's get out of here!' I heard his second-in-command bark. 'Leave him there like the Invincibles, the treacherous Brit fucking spook.'

After the slaying of Lord Frederick Cavendish, the murderers he referred to had escaped in a horse-drawn cab. But, true to form, as Ambrose had always insisted, it wasn't very long before the Crown found their rat. The snake in the grass who would give up all his comrades. It was James Carey, and he sent them all to the gallows. Before being dispatched on that steamer bound for the Cape, where he met that extremely genial fellow Irishman with whom he enjoyed a nightly drink and a bit of a smoke.

Only a few days later, when his pal and his chum was passing him over the jug and getting ready for to maybe launch into another rousing rendition of 'O'Donnell Abú', a defiant ballad which had become a particular favourite of theirs, what did the bold O'Donnell do, only produce a revolver and shoot the astonished Carey, one two three times through the head.

'Oh, God help me, but I'm shot!' squeals Carey, as Pat O'Donnell reloads and replies: 'Yes, that you fucking are. That's gone and bent your auld shuttlecock out of shape good and proper – hasn't it, hur hur hur? Yes, I would happily and confidently venture that it has!'

It was as vivid a dream as ever I've experienced.

'And who am I, Miss Nicholson,' I said to the Agency nurse Virginia, as she set about tucking me in, 'to try bucking history?'

'You are a very lucky man,' she said soothingly, reminding me a little – I know it's silly – of the actress Deborah Kerr in *Separate Tables*. Honestly, some of the things that come into your mind when you're a little bit out of sorts.

But – all the same, I meant what I was saying. With those being the last words I remember before drifting off – apart from a snippet of our old friends the Tumbletys.

'I mean,' I could hear old Plumm snorting derisively, 'just what on earth is one supposed to do with such a dysfunctional combination of Neanderthals – consuming Guinness Extra porter for breakfast!'

'Oi tink it's grate!' Val McBoan used to tease him. 'Bejapers, sure, don't we all know famblies da loike of dat here in Oireland! Jakers and becrakers, amn't I a bit like dat meself!'

In which, whether Val liked to admit to the fact or not, there was contained no small grain of truth.

Because, of course, back then, before prosperity reluctantly came nudging towards the island, the great majority of Catholics in Turfland were, it has to be said, hopelessly poor. Not to say undisciplined and unkempt – and routinely disposed to outrageous practices generally disdained by the rest of the civilised world. With *The Tumbletys*, however idiosyncratically, merely reflecting the unfortunate reality.

'Ah yes, the old Tumbletys,' Henry used to sigh, ruefully shaking his head. 'Whether we care to admit it or not, to my mind the Paddies are a sad old lot in the end. Aren't they, Meredith, in the end?'

I didn't say anything. As he gazed right into the bottom of his drink.

'Dullards,' he grumbled, 'a concatenation of malcontents and simpleton halfwits. We'd be doing them a favour if we dropped the hydrogen bomb.'

Chapter 18

Are You Certain It's Yours, Biddy?

By and large, the bar of soap, as I've said, did the trick. But we still had to wait over an hour for an ambulance. Don't, for the life of me, ask – but I woke up in the giddiest kind of stupor.

'Nurse, nurse, the screens!' I bawled.

'Hush!' urged Rosie.

Who, awakened by all the commotion from her gin-sodden sleep, had now joined the lovely Virginia 'Deborah Kerr' Nicholson by my bedside. Mulligan, of course, being long since gone. As was Luke O'Brien and his Dublin Brigade IRA.

One's nemesis, in other words. Whose insouciance, in retrospect, appears so effortless that it couldn't have been the first time he'd perpetrated such an operation – death by brandy and tablets, I mean. And who, for all I know, might have been connected to our former secretary Shivaun Carmody, regarding whom I had always harboured certain suspicions – as, indeed, had Henry.

Thanks, principally, to that malign bungler Lionel Harbottle, the Patagonian Banana Slug. Why, even the very thought of his sickly, pale yellow skin, those perverted beady eyes and long covetous fingers was enough to make me whoosh and projectile vomit all over again. It being that very same fool who, in the end, had caused most of the trouble which had plagued the Grafton Theatrical Agency – ultimately prompting near-disaster and single-handedly being responsible for its humiliation and eventual closedown.

Both Plumm and I had warned him on numerous occasions. Not just because at the time I had been deeply fond of Carmody, and respected her. I mean, she was one of the most pleasant, enthusastic and efficient secretaries I think I've ever known. But because practically everything about the Slug and his manner quite revolted me. Which was why, outside of the Grafton Agency, I'd done everything I could to avoid the loathsome cretin.

Except that, no matter wherever I went – there he'd be once again – whether standing up at the counter in Minty's, or squeezed into an alcove in the Manhattan, Mulligan's or the Lower Deck in Portobello. Acting the toff with yet another pair of floozies. The fellow was notoriously indiscreet. For all I know, he may even have been afflicted with some form of erotomania.

But compromising Miss Shivaun Carmody – that, I'm afraid, had been the last straw. Especially when working in tandem with that whiskery old warhorse Hildy Wyatt – someone who only dropped by occasionally, from the mainland. They'd raped her, apparently – subsequent to plying her with drink and overwhelming her with some form of self-declared 'sophisticated charm'.

When informed about it, I'd done my best to smooth things over. But she'd been so hysterical, actually deciding to hand in her notice, that I knew in the end it was going to be impossible. In heartbreaking floods of tears, she had described what had happened to her personally. What it was exactly they'd done in the backyard of the Minstrels' Rest, among some beer barrels.

Hildy Wyatt had held her down – and the Slug had 'obliged', as he put it – by unzipping his flies.

'Swallow that, you prickteasing little biddy!' he'd demanded, apparently.

'Dear little Cabbagehead,' Hildy had mocked.

It was not the first time – I knew that privately. Having been in the Slug's company a number of times, out in Aden. But I couldn't say anything – what with him knowing abut Budr Hussain and our crossbow. Bernie the Bolt, if you remember Gracie Urquhart's little quip.

Shivaun had sobbed out her heart for the best part of the evening – in the privacy of those soon-to-be abandoned offices housing the Grafton Agency 'Worldwide'. And it was only a matter of time before a furiously livid Henry Plumm – who had really taken it badly – relayed these latest, perilously compromising events to Roland, Petersen et al. over in the mainland.

It wasn't so much the anxiety that the newspapers might get hold of the information. More the fact that the two off-duty policemen who'd eventually called to Harbottle's house had not only threatened him with the ultimate sanction, but beaten the 'bejasus' – as they themselves phrased it – out of the overreaching imbecile. With the hostage to fortune, inevitably, of course being that one of them, in actual fact, was working for the Section. In a capacity similar to the Bowsy McAuley.

Roland, as soon as he heard, had flown over specially.

'That damned bloody fool!' he had seethed in the Scotch House late that same afternoon. As the exhausting rain ran in rivulets along the panes – with Paddy Murphy's narrowed eyes scrutinising something a very long distance away. The bells of Christchurch sounding muffled in the midst of the squall. As I watched Roland's fingers whitening around the rim of his whiskey glass.

'There isn't a thing he doesn't know about this city. Whether you or I tell him or not. Himself and Petersen – they have people placed everywhere. Nothing escapes him – absolutely nothing. Believe me.'

Don't worry, I thought, I believe you, Plumm.

Which was how it all came to light as regards the involvement in the above affair of Shivaun Carmody's brother. Who had been actively involved politically right throughout the seventies – before eventually sacrificing his life on hunger strike at the age of twenty-four in Her Majesty's Prison, known as Long Kesh or the Maze.

I had been apprehensive in the face of Roland's impending visit – I mean, there are things even yet which I cannot reveal. But what I can say for definite is that, as soon as he went back, not more than a couple of days later, I felt sure that the Slug wouldn't be bothering us again. Or, to put it in Henry's words: 'Good riddance, hopefully for ever, to the Patagonian Rapist Slug.'

Who won't, as a consequence, be performing in what I now must declare as the final and the most engaging act of our little 'Oirish Drama', here at the Seafront Apollo on the strand. With all the rest of their number, however, arriving up to do a turn – including, of course, Clem Grainger and Charlie Kerrins. Not forgetting Val McBoan and his old-time 'butty', Hugh B. Yes, that is to say Hugh 'Barney' McRoarty, boisterous egomaniac and flinger-outer of saxophones. Along with, perhaps, the cream of the crop, none other than Maurice 'the Big Man' Norton and, of course, his lovely wife Deirdre or 'Dee'. In the company of many others way – certainly at this stage – too numerous to mention.

So let's stick with Clem. With or without the Bertolt Brecht cap. Looking mighty impressive in furry bomber jacket and gold neck-chain. And there by his side – although, of course, they were never an item – sporting the most delicious-looking glossy auburn curls falling around those slim, narrow shoulders, folder in hand, stands the female equivalent *wunderkind* of her generation, Máiréad Curtin. Chewing on the stem of her shades, with the trademark volume of a Picador Beckett protruding out of her hessian shoulder bag.

And, just for a little variety, if I may be so bold – please permit me to introduce our unequalled star: yes, it's the glitteringly exquisite Grand Dame herself – Joan Collins! And, not to be outdone, probably her only serious rival from the seventies – yes, it's Kate O'Mara – sultry-eyed star of ITV's *The Brothers*. The panel-show compère Marti Caine has just arrived as well – with her allotted role being, or so she claims, 'to tell the truth'.

Marti ought to need no introduction – sheath-gowned idol of the popular series *New Faces*. Responsible for introducing Lenny Henry to the world, along with the soul band Sweet Sensation and many others. Including Gary Wilmot & Judy. Marti was carrying a folder beneath her arm – which she opened a little hesitantly, anxiously combing through a sheaf of notes.

'Now,' she announced in that distinct Geordie brogue – almost as indecipherable as Paddy! – 'the time has come for us all to hear the truth. From me, Marti Caine – and not from either of those two bastards Chenevix Meredith or Henry Plumm. Who, when it comes to facts or veracity, are about as reliable as Cannon and Ball. Eh?'

A declaration which clearly came as nothing short of a shock to everyone.

'What with the profession they're in, I wouldn't believe a word as comes out of their flippin' mouths. Either of them, right? You know what I'm saying? Because you want to know what I really think about their lies? They make me sick. Sick, do you hear me?'

Don't ask me why – but I flushed deeply, averting my gaze. Particularly when she mentioned the details of a north London funeral. That of a certain Joanne Vollmann, my one-time girlfriend. Who I'd been seeing after Bea's untimely death. You remember my wife.

Perhaps if she had left it at that – and stopped there. I don't know. Instead of reading out a further account of a private visit I had made to Joanne's bereaved parents. Both of whom lived, at the time, in Golders Green. Extraordinary people – and both survivors of the camps. She in Belsen, he in Treblinka. Having survived experiences which, to you or I, are unimaginable. Although, as Joanne's mother herself had put it, not being in any way certain that they'd find themselves in a position to survive 'this appalling tragedy'.

Which was the very same for me, I assured her. Leafing abstractedly through the manuscript of poor Joanne's now never-to-be-published novel. Which was entitled *Hegira in Jerusalem*. No doubt, had she lived, Joanne would have revised it to include details of a 'certain discovery'. Which would have been unfortunate – but I can't see any way in which I might have stopped her. Because, beautiful and highly educated as she was, poor Joanne, she could be so very headstrong. In so many ways like Bea – although their personalities were vastly different.

It was an ancient, washed-out Polaroid snapshot. From a crime scene, actually. Which, in retrospect, I ought to have taken greater pains to conceal. Like a lot of things, possibly, which oughtn't to have appeared in a 'forthcoming memoir'. I had actually secreted the Polaroid into the actual binding. But, being inquisitive by nature, Miss Vollmann had gone and made the mistake of discovering it.

In the circumstances, most unfortunate. It depicted, as you may have already deduced, the almost unrecognisable body of a certain undistinguished informant from the time we had spent in the Gulf. Taken, of course, in his cups, by Urquhart. Bernie the Bolt, lying dead there on the wharf – covered by what must have been a half-hundredwieght of packed ice.

Like I say, the Polaroid print was old and considerably degraded – which of course only piqued Miss Marple's curiosity.

'What is this?' she enquired of me, white-faced. When I'd made the mistake of arriving home unexpectedly early.

'Oh!' I'd replied, in the flattest of monotones, and laughed, 'that's just some old pansy from the Gulf.'

Urquhart, he had always had this 'thing' of – I don't know – holding onto 'trophies', as he called them. Little memorials he somehow got a kick out of. It wasn't any big deal to me, I had told her. As a matter of fact, I'd even forgotten I'd had it. With the worst thing being that Joanne – she just had to keep going on about it. Not only on that occasion when she'd discovered it first – but literally for weeks and months afterwards. What she had seen had horrified her, she said.

More than anything, I wish she hadn't interfered with my property. Not only because it's effectively intel, you know – more because it's my private property. Yes – I regret all that. The fact that she'd succumbed to the compulsive imperatives of curiosity. I mean – it wasn't as if I hadn't warned her. That such a thing could be – well, downright dangerous, as a matter of fact.

'But what is this?' she had kept on repeating. 'I demand to know.' Over and over and bloody well over.

It's impossible to say whether what happened was inevitable. With her body, not unlike the unfortunate Hussain's, washing up at dawn on Hammersmith wharf three or four weeks afterwards.

It was the loneliest time of my life, sitting there by the window in that Willesden flat – leafing disconsolately through the unpublished pages of her diary. The great majority of which formed part of her deeply moving, indeed compelling novel *Hegira in Jerusalem*. That very same manuscript, as I'd explained to her heartbroken parents, which she had so kindly offered to me not long after our first meeting in Charing Cross Road. With Ray's Jazz Shop, directly above Foyles Bookshop, being the venue.

'To Mr Meredith. Till Next Year In Jerusalem,' read the inscription on the inside front page.

'For some special people, this world can be just too much to bear,' I remember whispering to both elderly Vollmanns that sad morning in Golders Green – kissing each one, first on the hand. And then on the cheek as I eventually departed.

That had proved a distressing period for me – and was why I decided to suspend what had become my regular visits to Joanne's grave in Golders Green cemetery. Sensing instinctively – exactly as had been the case during the officiation of her actual funeral – that someone close by was taking a keen and profoundly unsettling interest in every movement that I made. An impression which transpired to be extremely accurate indeed.

As I was soon to discover – fatally, almost – in a godawful filthy Irish public house in Willesden – to which I'd repaired, after the ceremony, for the purpose of perusing my *Financial Times*. And, for my pains, ending up in Northwick Park Hospital. A development which had amused Henry Plumm no end – when he'd come to visit me, finding me trussed up in bandages and splints. Back in those days when the world still held some form of logical and identifiable pattern for him.

And he was still actually capable of enjoying one of my jokes.

'Nurse! Nurse! The screens!' I had laughed – but, looking back on it now, there was something faintly distant and unconvincing about his response. So I assumed the cortical atrophy had already begun to declare itself inside him.

Poor old Henry. All the good times and adventures we enjoyed together. To end up dead in a bathroom, blowing bubbles. But then which of us knows what the nature of our end is likely to be?

I didn't encounter him for some considerable time after that. About a year or so after my 'crisis', I suppose you could call it. Perhaps brought on by that beating I got in the West End – with a couple of the monkeymen having tailed me all the way from the cemetery.

With the nature of the assault being bound to affect me psychologically. I know that some of the neighbours had been talking. So it doesn't take long for the people who matter to hear. I wasn't in the least bit surprised when one morning two firm knocks came rapping on the door. Which I opened to discover three 'men from the ministry'.

To be perfectly honest, apart from one, they presented as nothing much more than wet-eared junior operatives – already pushing into my apartment and taking stock of the situation. It was quite a show, I'm afraid I would have to say. And not so much the lair of a Max von Sydow-style eminence grise as that of a desiccated, wholly irrational Gene Hackman. In what could have been the final reel of *The Conversation*.

'So this is who you are playing at being now?' remarked one of my younger visitors. 'Harry Caul?'

And I have to say that I was deeply impressed. Not only that, in spite of his relative youth, he was aware of the movie *The Conversation* at all – but that the character played by Gene Hackman was regarded as possibly the very best in the business.

Of top-level surveillance, that is. And was capable of recording practically any conversation in the world. There wasn't a single thing that Harry Caul missed.

'So far three people are dead because of him,' read the caption on the quad poster directly above my head. Which made me laugh – I mean, how could it not? As I counted them, privately, on my fingers.

Beatrice, Henry, Vollmann.

Vollmann, Beatrice, Henry.

The final scene of absolute wreckage in the film is often described as an 'expressionist triumph'. Whether or not that was the case with me, I couldn't really say. But I had spent weeks, indeed months – just lying there, crouched, playing 'Stranger on the Shore'. Which really is the most beautiful melody, you know.

It's that old tune by Acker Bilk from way back in the long ago, so mellow and fluid. Not to say uplifting, even in the most appalling of situations.

Which 111A Willesden High Road certainly was. As there I sat, no longer like Joubert or Henry but Harry Caul – rocking back and forth as I plied the pearly keys. Endeavouring not to think of Miss Vollmann as best I could – but which tended to prove almost impossible. Especially whenever I closed my eyes and there she would be again, large as life – my beautiful Joanne Vollmann, writer. Attired once more in that chic little embroidered yellow waistcoat that she favoured. With those great big jangling brass hoop earrings and that perfectly coiffured, glossy, *Cabaret*-style bob.

But then, of course – just as had been the case with Henry – once again it would all go wrong. And I'd let the sax drop the minute I became aware of that innocent face now contorting with what can only be described as the purest of loathing. Trying not to look at the loose pages of her manuscript scattered all over the floor – where it had fallen from her hands just as soon as she'd started trembling.

'Yes, Mr Meredith!' I heard her hiss, and it really did chill my blood. 'It is certainly possible that there may, at some time, be a *hegira* in the city of Jerusalem. But it won't be in the company of a wretched, perfidious bastard like you!'

As she sharply turned away, treating me contemptuously to a really most uninteresting view of her back. I mean, honestly, let's face it – what would you have done?

'Come,' said the younger of the men from the ministry, taking my arm, 'it's time that we were toodling along.'

'Don't you think?' said the older one.

I can't remember, but I don't think I said anything.

There followed a spell in a private sanatorium – prior to my 'rest cure' relocation here in Woolsley Bay. Where, to my delight, I had been informed that dear Henry – dear heart! – had already been in situ for quite some considerable time. For those who may be a little confused, there have always existed certain premises officially at the disposal of the government – locations which have an effective and functional purpose. When it is deemed imperative for certain persons to get off the stage, I suppose it might be fair to say.

'I'll be glad to see that old Plummsy again,' I'd called out to my designated taxi driver as we motored evenly along the south coast, 'to review old times, if you know what I mean. All our old and exciting adventures – so many of which now belong to the pages of history.'

I gave the glass partition a sharp rap with my knuckle. The taxi driver nodded as he pushed back his cap. Then I cleared my throat and began unburdening my thoughts.

'So what did you think of the Brexit vote? That's what they

always wanted over there, in bogland. They'll be happy now – having forced our hand over their accursed bloody border and made us look bad in the eyes of the world. There was always a temperamental contact with Paris and Italy, wasn't there, over there in that sodden, godforsaken dump. Just waiting for their chance to bypass the complex social preoccupations of industrial England. So what do you think, driver?'

I don't think, however, that he could hear me through the glass – or if he did, gave no indication. Before Woolsley Bay rose up for all the world like a fairy castle – everything paid for, and handsomely, by the authorities. With that being their wont, as I have explained, in such situations. And the entire operation being expedited with an efficiency I found commendable. Because, to tell the truth, it had been quite some time since I'd felt so – I don't know. At ease. Even, dare I say it, actually happy. Which was why, I suppose, I rapped the glass once again.

'Hey!' I called out – already aware that my designated pilot's country of origin was, in fact, Ireland. Just to 'shorten the road', as Val McBoan or Charlie Kerrins might have put it in the old days.

I was doubled up myself, with the laughing – chafing my hands. Heaven only knows what he thought of it, looking back.

'Did you hear what happened to Biddy Mulligan? She went home and told her mother she was pregnant. "Merciful hour!" replies her poor mother, taking down the rosary beads. "Are you certain, Biddy, that it's yours?"'

The driver made no attempt at reply. But I have to admit that I laughed like a fucking drain. Because, to be honest, I actually couldn't stop – for what remained of the journey, all the way to Woolsley Bay. Refuge of rogues and superannuated sleepers. Smiling in the rear-view mirror as on we drove along the coast road.

Thinking back on the days when teletext machines would have been racketing all over the world regarding the news of my apprehension and relocation. Or so I thought. Not to mention Big Ben striking ten as the latest mid-Atlantic incarnation of the *March of Time* narrator Westbrook Van Voorhis rearranged his notes and prepared to face the camera:

'Bip-bip-bip, here is the news. Major Meredith is on his way to Woolsley Bay!'

'I mean – can you believe it?'

'Everyone thinks it's a joke.'

'Her Majesty sending people like him over to Ireland, I mean.'

'And it really is – when you give the matter some thought, is it not?'

'Here is the news. Chenevix Meredith is off to the seaside.'

'Once more to reconnoitre with his old associate, Henry Percival.'

'Henry Percival Plumm OBE. (Not)'

'Her Majesty's representative, undercover Billy Bunter.'

'Bip-bip-bip.'

'We present *News at Ten*! Chenevix Meredith is travelling at sixty mph.'

'Coo-ee, what larks! If you'll pardon my French.'

Honestly the things that, while in motion, unexpectedly come into one's mind. Just as they'd done in the mind of Ian Fleming – perhaps the most inventive and resourceful employee of them all – in this business, I mean. Having originally conceived the idea of reinventing a deceased Welsh tramp in the role of a naval commander. In order, obviously, to hoodwink the Huns. Such tweaks and 'divarsions' as can often alter the course of a war. But which are, obviously, best kept to oneself.

Something which, I fear, Henry Plumm – after all these years – had omitted to learn.

The great big dundering fool.

'You are – what?' I had retorted when he had told me of his intention to 'tell his story'.

'Everything that happened to us both over there.'

It had actually made me feel unwell when he'd said it. But that was as nothing compared to when I had come upon the manuscript itself. I mean, it wasn't as if he'd taken any great pains to conceal it.

The Hibernia Files was the title he'd been considering. And upon which he'd been labouring now for quite some time. Complete with numerous little minnows of ornamentation – various distractions, I suppose not entirely unlike the account you are reading at this moment – specially inserted for the traditional purposes of distortion, confusion and, of course, plausible denial.

Initially quite shocked, I was ultimately relieved that many of these rhetorical flourishes which Henry had inserted, intending to garland the flat and essentially fact-based authorial style, served only to render the material even more unikely and obscure than it already was. To the point of laughable absurdity, in fact.

As I say, not in the least unlike the one you happen to be reading yourself. That, of course, is if I'm lucky, dear reader.

I flung them, one after another, over my shoulder.

'Ha ha, nurse – the pages, the pages!' I shrieked.

Before arriving at the chapter 'Assignment on the Border'. As off I went into the bathroom, turning the key. For a bit of privacy. Not wanting Mulligan or Rosie to come around bothering me again. Perching myself on the 'throne' as I turned yet another page. Of the soon-to-be blockbuster, by the soon-to-be-deceased Henry Plumm. The best part of *The Hibernia Files* yet, I thought. The most exciting chapter of the entire volume, without a doubt.

Concerning itself as it does – of course, without so much as even the most casual of requests for inclusion on the author's part! – with my eventual return, in the aftermath of the peace agreement. Entirely, of course, undercover.

Yes, back to the shores of dear old 'Ay-Ruh'.

Banba.

Fódhla.

Éire.

Paddyland.

With the Good Friday Agreement gradually approaching its conclusion – mid-1998, if you remember.

I'd been fed up thinking about the whole blessed thing, eventually deciding if I was ever to sleep properly again and erase its unfortunate psychological inheritance for ever, the only reasonable option on my part was to pay a return visit. Which I did – out of sentiment making the journey, as of old, by ferry.

I had scarcely been there for a day, ambling along Mount Street, having enjoyed a number of sweet libations in Mulligan's – the Scotch House was gone – when the silver Ford Sierra had pulled up alongside me at the kerb. And a young girl in a Dodgers baseball cap rolled the window down and looked out, a transistor blaring out at full volume.

'Amn't I after looking for McDonald's for to buy me a Big Mac, so I am,' was the first thing she said.

Before something struck me. Not a thought, as you might be forgiven for assuming – but a significantly blunt instrument, in actual fact. Right there on the back of the head. With the next thing I knew, I was being bundled into the back seat. As off we drove northward, at high speed.

And then, well blow me down if I wasn't being hung up by the heels in the darkened interior of a milking parlour, where the stench of cow dung was drifting out right across the farmyard. In a notorious hotspot which went by the name of Corrylough, County Armagh. Located somewhere in a godforsaken mountain district at the back of what had come to be called, in the time of the Northern Ireland Secretary Merlyn Rees, as 'bandit country'. What with it having been home – a situation which had prevailed right since the earliest years of the Ulster Plantation in 1603 – to every imaginable dissident and anti-Crown blackguard born to an excuse for a mother.

It was at this point my captors introduced themselves as the Bonner brothers – acquainting me as they did so of the fact that they had been waiting for this moment 'for a very long time indeed'. One was big and the other was small – kind of stocky. They were both masked, pestering me incessantly with questions regarding certain 'operations I had expedited on behalf of the British state'.

Amusing themselves, along with this latest arrival – who turned out to be paterfamilias of the dreary lumpen outfit, and to whom they demonstrated commendable deference, referring to him quaintly throughout as 'Daddy'.

Yes, drooling old semi-senile Daddy Bonner – gurning hideously – or 'girning' as they called it in Ulster – taking sharp pokes at me with a four-pronged garden fork. Which, for those of a more metropolitan inclination, would be more commonly known thereabouts as a 'graip'.

'Fillet him good and proper, the smarmy British bastard!' I heard Big Bonner snarl. 'Eviscerate his giblets, heel the fucker onto the ditch. For there's damn the difference talking to the likes of him'll ever make.'

'That's right,' agreed Wee Bonner.

'Because that was the way it was done in the old times,' observed Daddy Bonner, turning pale as a sheet. 'But now,' he elaborated, 'all these years later, since peace has been agreed between all parties, we have to adopt a – how shall I put it? – a more measured approach. Just get the fucking truth out of him. Dig into him and get it. But for the love of Christ will you make it quick!'

However, as Budr Hussain had discovered in Aden, things don't always end the way you quite expect. For one had one's own ideas, you might say. But right now wasn't the time. I was aware of that. So I just erupted into a bout of hoarse coughing – submitting a sympathetic, close to abject plea.

'What on earth do you hope to achieve by doing this? For heaven's sake, after all this time. There isn't any need for it, not now. There really isn't.'

Then, lo and behold, what does Wee Bonner do but produce a hand-held camera.

'You're making a mistake,' I continued, 'surely you can see that. Damaging the peace process – is that what you're intent on doing?'

'Just shut the fuck up and look directly into the lens. Get ready to talk, you slabbering Em-Oi-Foive fucker.'

So that was what I did.

And gave it to them pretty much as I remembered it. With a few elaborations and digressions along the way – as you might expect.

Chapter 19

Heaven's Gates

Bwooooagh! Gunk gunk-bwooooagh!
 Yes, that was all I had to say I'm afraid, as I remained there upside down in that foul-smelling cow byre – with ample time to go thinking back on all of my formative adventures. From Mandeville House College to the shores of old Erin. Concluding, as has become evident, on the sands of Woolsley Bay. Where, thanks to Arthur Mullard, Alfie Snudge & Co., all the chickens had come home to roost.

Not that it isn't amusing, looking back. With my face the colour of the most putrid green bile as, thanks to the doctored Napoleon, I had pitched forward violently, as though I had been the recipient of a godalmighty kick to the chest. A not-to-be-unexpected development which saw one's mood of alarm in no way alleviated by the helium-voiced squeals of a certain lady, Mrs 'Merciful Hour' Mulligan.

Not to mention poor old Plumm, who just at that moment had arrived on the scene – making a complete and utter ass of himself, to be perfectly honest. As he stood there on the landing, weeping his heart out.

'I've let you down! I've let you down!' was all you could hear – and it really did make me sick, I have to say. Because I'd never seen that side of him before. I mean, he looked pathetic, like some great big Billy Bunter ball of blubber. Which brought the worst out in me, I have to admit. Especially when he became hysterical.

Sangfroid, indeed.

With the only equivalent I could think of being the response of the housemaster in Mandeville House College – when he had learned of the tragedy which had befallen my old school 'pal' Peregrine Montgreve Masterson.

Or Masterson Maximus, as Uncle Leslie had called him – 'golden scion, peer without equal of Mandeville House'. Yes, that was what 'Uncle' Leslie Courtney, noted pervert, had christened his golden boy. In other words, at least to me, the drearily unimpressive Peregrine Montgreve Egotist.

Who had arrived at Mandeville House College around the same time as myself. To which I had been dispatched, without ceremony, in the tragic aftermath of the death of both my parents. During the Blitz. When a doodlebug had efficiently disposed of them both – within minutes of one another, apparently.

Subsequent to which a wealthy relative had seen to it that I was to become the beneficiary of a trust fund in the name of the family firm, Chenevix Plastics ('appropriately enough, given the pliable nature of some of your narratives,' as Plumm used to tease). I was handed over to the care of 'the Master of the House' – the ex-army veteran nicknamed 'Limp-Along' Leslie, because of his disability.

The leg which he had lost in the earlier conflict – having distinguished himself impressively, apparently, in Northern France.

Not on the battlefield, as it transpired later on, but as an extrordinarily capable and popular organiser of entertainments. Which he continued to be rather fond of during his time in Mandeville House.

Courtney Productions, he liked to call his concerts. Many of which saw Peregrine Masterson and I combining our talents in a variety of roles. Resulting in Leslie Courtney's taking what might be termed an 'extremely special interest' in us.

Pronouncing us both his 'ultimate, favouritest boys, tra la!'

'Let us have it again, my dear fellows!' he would announce, retrieving his tuning fork and striking a note upon the table.

'When you are ready – in the key of D.'

As we thrust out our chests and marched around the library in our vests and shorts, just as we'd been expressly instructed.

> What were you like as a boy? I say
> How did you play in the long-gone day?
> Did you ever think once that you would return?
> And there beneath the blue open Mandeville sky:
> Say farewell, old chums, and Mandeville too
> Sweet bonny Mandeville, fare thee well!

'Ah yes, the old school anthem!' he would sigh ever so fondly, with those familiar gleaming tears already showing in his eyes. Before erupting into song himself, lustily declaiming a Cossack nursery song which he claimed to have learned in Russia thirty-five years before. The effect was electrifying as he hugged us both and declared that, beyond all others, we were undoubtedly without compare among our peers.

With his only problem being, he went on to explain, that he simply did not know which one of us he liked the best. Or, indeed, even loved.

'Ha ha,' he chuckled, pacing the floor in a heavily perspiring condition. 'What fun we had yodelalay tra-la-la, down at the old Bull and Bush!'

Not to mention – when he was tiddly-eyed, rocking back and forth in his study chair. Offering one 'treaties' – which, on one spectacular occasion had actually included raspberry-flavoured vodka.

As, to the air of '*La donna è mobile*', he piped the refrain: 'Little boys are good today, gooder than yesterday!'

Before – I swear it – leaping across the desk to commence another episode of what he had termed the 'Mandeville wrestle'.

'Ow! You're hurting me, Uncle Leslie!' I could often hear myself complain. Not that it did a great deal of good, with those peepers of his ever so wide and those cheeks – oh so red! As, falsetto, old Leslie Courtney squealed yet again: 'Little boys are good today, much better than yesterday! Tee hee hee, yodelay-hee-hoo!'

It's obvious now what the deviant was up to. But way back then, one never suspected. Especially when he described it as 'old-fashioned, boyish fun'.

It was sad, of course – I won't pretend that it wasn't. For there can be little doubt that, right from the very beginning, I had endeavoured to do my best to ingratiate myself with 'our beloved Leslie'. To the point – it still sticks in my throat when it comes to the admission – of my having become almost insanely jealous of Peregrine Montgreve Masterson. Or 'Perry', as our housemaster preferred to call him. And who, with his delicate complexion and soft, fair, silken hair, a lock of which came falling down over his eyes, one might have expected to be of an almost otherworldly gentle and considerate nature.

But this was not the case, I'm afraid. Not a bit of it.

'My Winslow Boy,' Leslie Courtney used to call him. How I envied those looks he used to give him! Applauding vigorously: 'Very good! Very good!'

With his approval echoing tauntingly along the aisle of the empty library where, every Saturday afternoon without fail, we performed our rehearsals. When all the other students had gone off to play their rugby.

Not that I won't accept the numerous aspects of 'dearest Perry' – as Courtney addressed him – of which I myself was genuinely much in admiration a great deal of the time. However, as we approach the conclusion of this unfortunate and regrettable account, let us not for one moment fool ourselves. Because in spite of his unusually delicate features and lissome dancer's frame, the truth is that Peregrine Montgreve Masterson, deep down, he was little more than a complete and utter, absolute bully.

One, to boot, daily emboldened by the constancy and relentlessness of Courtney's excessive affections. I'm deeply sorry to have to acknowledge these facts. And which is why I know – irrespective of how I might try to forget that awful day, such amnesia is unlikely to be ever possible.

In the shade of the bower where I used to go to read my poetry, I looked up to see Perry appearing with some associates. Already they were bearing down on me.

'Just what are you reading?' I remember was what he said, adding acerbically: 'Master Meredith?'

As one of the others, disdainfully, relieved me of my collection – a small, gilt-edged volume which I treasured. For obvious reasons – it had belonged to my father.

The 'reader' proceeded in a flat, dreary monotone. The poem concerned, 'Spring and Fall: To a Young Child', had been authored by the clergyman Gerard Manley Hopkins in the year 1880.

> Margaret, are you grieving
> Over Goldengrove unleaving?
> Leaves like the things of man, you
> With your fresh thoughts . . .

Then they tore the pages out. No, not they.
He.
Peregrine Montgreve Masterson.
Tore the masterpiece to shreds as they scoffed.

Some time afterwards, it emerged that Masterson had been investigating my family history, in the course of which he had unearthed the fact that my father, something of a high-born aristocrat himself, was born of a long and distinguished line of military people – unhappily, he had fallen in love and married a would-be

Irish actress. Of a lowly stature. Whose name, Inspector Detective Masterson Junior had, apparently, discovered, was Isobel Soden.

Or 'Turf Sod' – as Masterson had now informed me 'was to be her new name'.

And with which he plagued me every time he encountered me.

Turf Sod Soden
Bad times are boding
Isobel Isobel
Legs apart Boden.
Ha ha!

Not being aware, of course, as so many who had no experience or knowledge whatsoever of the way things are done over in Paddyland, the truth was that she wasn't actually 'lowly born'. And that she wasn't, in fact, 'one of them' at all – but of good, solid Methodist stock. 'The Sodens of Baltimore Park', they were called – through a series of family misfortunes having fallen on hard times. Which had seen her ending up behind the counter in Lyons Corner House in Piccadilly – where, in actual fact, in the late 1920s, was where she and my father had actually met.

'Why, goodness me, fellows,' Perry Masterson would chime – in the hollow, echoing corridors or while perambulating along by the side of the lake: 'Why, if it isn't His Majesty, good old Turf Sod!'

I endured the persecution for as long as I humanly could.

With the final straw being, without question, the day Uncle Leslie decided to make his much-anticipated announcement. I had been absolutely certain that, without a doubt, I would secure the part in his forthcoming production.

'Not long now till showtime!' he used to say, every so often giving me this conspiratorial wink. There could be no mistaking the outcome. The inevitability that 'showtime', as he described it, was going to exclusively promote my abilities.

Yes, I had decided – the part was already, effectively, mine.

I remember when the day came, being absolutely electric with anxiety and excitement. Because it really was the greatest of honours. At least until Uncle Courtney assembled us all together. In the library, as usual – applauding smartly as he announced from the rostrum: 'I am delighted to inform you that – good as you all are, and believe you me, you are that – after careful consideration I have elected to offer the role of the Winslow Boy to our dear, dear comrade-in-arms . . .'

The atmosphere was unbearably taut. But he still waited another moment. Before announcing, with a flourish: 'And this term, the part goes to: Peregrine Montgreve Masterson!'

Very well then, I decided, suppressing one's rancour as best I possibly could – if that is the way that it has to be. So be it.

And there can be no denying that, in his way – Masterson had acquitted himself really quite well throughout rehearsals. Magnificently, really, if I'm to be perfectly honest. But oh how I wept as I stood there once more in the cool shade of the overarching bower – recalling what pathetic few words I could of the lyric I loved so much by my favourite author, Gerard Manley Hopkins. 'Goldengrove', in other words. Reflecting on how bitter and cruel all of it could be. Life, I mean.

'And me only after dying, bejasus and begorrah!' I could hear my mother's faint, pathetic cry – somewhere far distant among the universe's stars. As my father did his best to comfort his poor Isobel – in whatever way he possibly could.

And that was when the interior, the inner chamber of one's hopelessly bruised soul, call it what you will – ever so slowly began to ice over. With a stealth and commitment that was to prove both relentless and inexorably effective.

Mirroring as it did so the polished glass of Mandeville Lake – located on the perimeter of the college grounds, just beyond the woods. Where, if you listened carefully, you could hear Perry calling out, in that now practised and habitual way of his, much to the amusement of his fellows:

'Look! Why if it isn't Chenevix Meredith, our own little personal Laurence Olivier. Why so bitter, dearest heart? I mean, after all – perhaps next time Uncle Leslie might decide to cast you in the role of Cinderella. Because there's a rumour they might be producing that show next Easter. Which ought to be fun – that's if you haven't gone and killed yourself by then! But never fear – for I understand implicitly your humiliation and disappointment.'

That, however, wasn't the end of it.

'Poor old Merry! So inflated with his sense of himself and his abilities – and, in the end, amounting to so little.'

He really did know how to wound you, that Perry Masterson. Yet another of his many skills. Ha ha. That's funny. So many manifold skills of Perry Masterson.

So that, more or less, explains it, I expect. The accident, or however you might elect to describe it.

After that unfortunate development on Mandeville Lake, it was obvious there were going to be all sorts of investigations. But with the school's good name, just as I'd anticipated, remaining the paramount consideration throughout. To this very day, I still can't keep from thinking of that really quite miserable, regrettable afternoon.

One which, in its own way – had been defined, I suppose, by a certain poignancy expressed in the old-time music hall song that goes:

A little boy; a pair of skates; broken ice; heaven's gates.

It wasn't, however, as I'd anticipated, reminiscent of those adventure stories featured in *The Gem* and *The Magnet*. Which both Peregrine Masterson and I had enjoyed.

My father had used to read them to me also – initiating a longing for the Greyfriars or St Jim's-style boarding-school life. Where the boys all wore top hats and tail-coats – Arthur Augustus D'Arcy, the toff at St Jim's, wore a monocle. They had feasts in their studies. They sent a pie containing a boot to the bounder of the Remove. They strolled around 'the Quad' and rich uncles sent them money – largely in the form of postal orders, which they spent on more food. What a pity old Mandeville was in possession of none of these attractions. No, nothing but treacherous so-called 'friends' – who had brought everything that had happened, even something as tragic as their own death, upon themselves.

A little boy; a pair of skates; broken ice; heaven's gates.

Obviously, I could in some way have assisted. Being close by. Reached out and . . .
But one wasn't so disposed.
Apologies, dear heart.

Chapter 20

The Upside-Down Man

But all of that is a long way from Bandit Country and County Armagh. Where, what with the deployment of the video camera, proceedings were not a million miles from the fare one might have expected to be presented onscreen in the fabulous art-cum-grindhouse that was the Majestic Cinema, Mountjoy Square.

'Yes, the grindhouse presentation of the century, me auld segocias,' as Charlie Kerrins used to say – featuring a leading man hanging up by his heels in a milking parlour. Most accurately described, perhaps, to be honest, as what is now generally known as a straight-to-video affair. Largely on account of the lamentable inexpertise of the would-be auteurs: namely Daddy and the Bonner Bros. Inc.

Sooner or later, they were going to get an admission out of me, they hissed. By hook or by crook – come hell or high water. Everything. So that the truth at last would become common knowledge – known by everyone, even after all this time.

Yes, every single thing would be recorded, they explained. Daddy Director and Wee 'Fellini' Bonner. With the Upside-Down Man opening to static.

As a door opens and now who comes in? Why only 'Mammy' Bonner in her pinny. Would anyone like some tea, she wants to know. Nobody does. After which she makes her exit.

Wee Bonner can be seen struggling with the captive. Who screams and protests, but to no avail. They strike him – hard. And jab at him again with the graip. Very soon he goes quiet. As the camera goes down and, from its half-cocked angle on the stone floor, everything appears to be happening on its side.

Within my own interior world, as all of this was going on, I have to admit that it really was very difficult not to laugh. It being abundantly clear that they figured I was frightened and intimidated beyond belief, and on the verge of telling them every single thing I knew – dating back to God knows when. Way back to the beginning of the 'Troubles'. Or 'the War' – as they, amusingly, insisted on calling it. Ho-hum.

Home Entertainments South Armagh presents: the truth at last – regarding Chenny Meredith and his SIS cronies. Not that Federico Fellini et al. need have worried about that – as I have already indicated, their abilities as film-makers fell very far short of the mark. Stumbling and arguing over buttons and controls – banging into one another as their moony-eyed, shit-speckled cattle reviewed proceedings with their dead-eyed gaze. Contemplating poor old Meredith – topsy-turvy and now covered from head to toe in bruises. Talk about cheapo-cheapo productions!

Although it might have helped a little if they had adhered to their original pledge of civilised restraint. Instead of conforming to the national stereotype and throwing a Paddy.

'You bombed the Majestic Cinema in Mountjoy Square, didn't you? Tell us about Dublin and what happened there. And, while you're at it – all of those other operations you were involved in. You know what I'm talking about.'

Obviously, I did.

The operations in question were the synchronised destruction of a number of small towns along the border – including Midford, Longfield and Edenboro in the midlands. There were one or two others whose names I'm sorry to have to admit I forget.

Which is not all that surprising, for, as I told Big Bonner – who now seemed to have assumed the role of principal cameraman – I had only functioned as a peripheral, almost negligible participant.

'Really and truly,' I insisted, 'I swear. Nothing more than a "walk-on", really.'

But which may not, to be honest, have been how Ambrose Roland had perceived my role. Pronouncing himself 'satisfied' with not only the Majestic Cinema, but also the events now being, almost obsessively, referenced by the Bonners.

'Tell us!' shouted Big Bonner, elbowing me hard, full in the face.

'Give us everything concerning the Majestic Cinema!'

He slapped me again.

'Ow,' I said.

There was so much blood being discharged from my nose and mouth that he was forced, against his wishes, to switch the camera off.

'Easy, son,' urged Daddy, 'take her handy. There's a lad. We've got lots of time.'

'No we don't,' I heard his agitated son reply, 'no we fucking don't!'

'Come on, you evasive cunt,' I heard Wee Bonner snarl.

Finding myself so distracted and psychologically discombobulated, I suppose you might say, that I found myself releasing the tiniest, most infantile of chuckles.

Not, as you can understand, quite the thing to do in such indubitably arduous circumstances. Remaining throughout more concerned than anything that my interrogators would think I was fabricating even more elaborate falsehoods.

But not a bit of it. I can only say that I wish I had.

However, really and truly – even after all these years, and with all the objectivity provided by the clear-eyed passage of the years, was there any real possibility of finding the answer to this banal, indeed the simplest of questions? Which is: how, in all honesty, did so many otherwise reasonable and intelligent persons bring themselves to patronise material of such an appalling standard of crumminess as was provided on a daily basis (six shows per day) by the Majestic Cinema in Mountjoy Square, Dublin?

Blue Movie Blackmail.
The Texas Chainsaw Massacre.
Cries and Whispers.
Truck Stop Women.
120 Days of Sodom.

Showing tonight, 8 p.m. *Torso*, featuring Suzy Kendall. With grimy city streets and cheerless hotel rooms. Bare bulbs. Mugs of milky tea. Nicotine-stained fingers grasping a sad, pale breast.

Played out, as always, in a seedy, down-at-heel auditorium, which might itself have been inhabited by dowdily attired corpses. Resembling automatons themselves as they sat there in front of the screen, like mirror images of their twenty-foot-high simulacra. Shameful shadows in a flat, unflattering light – with lank hair and near-death complexions.

Even as I swung there in that Armagh milking parlour, dangling by my boot heels and with the top of my head perilously close to a mound of steaming, foul-smelling manure, those images continued obstinately unspooling through my head. Along, of course, with torsos scattered all along a Dublin street. Presenting as a really quite shocking, *giallo*-style *mise-en-scène*. Which made me retch, to be perfectly honest. Because if there was one thing I didn't want to concentrate on – it was that operation, the one in Mountjoy Square. The poor old Majestic.

I mean, I'd like to be able to say that there was just the slightest hint of downbeat, inner-city exotica that had, over the years, attached itself to 'the Maj', as the natives called it. Situated in one of the poorest and most blighted areas of what – architecture-wise – already gave the appearance of a post-war casualty. Except, as we know, and which both Henry Plumm and Petersen never seemed to tire of pointing out – the 'shirkers' in Paddyland weren't even in the bloody war.

Not that such an omission was likely to have bothered the young, up-and-coming theatre director Máiréad Curtin very much. Or, indeed, any of the other members of her little confrontational, anti-establishment 'art terrorist' ensemble. Who had just been distinguished once more – or disgraced, depending on your point of view – by their latest production entitled *Liffeyquake*. Described in all of its promotional material as 'this long-awaited assault on the moral hypocrisy of the Irish Free State'. With the result having outraged not only the Church, through the Archbishop of Dublin – but also many councillors the length and breadth of the country, along with the officials of Dublin City Council. Who had immediately demanded the closure of the theatre, and for its already meagre grant to be 'absolutely and categorically withdrawn'.

None of the members of the Rathmines Combination appeared to be in any way fazed by these strident objections. Certainly not Máiréad. Or, indeed, her boyfriend, Killian de Vere – also known as the Man in the Hat, an affectionate nickname which I myself had conferred upon him. In respectful homage to an arthouse feature popular at the time – David Bowie's *The Man Who Fell to Earth*. Featuring, as it did, a similar behatted, slim individual.

Killian de Vere – the ambitious young would-be unlikely star from some County Kerry village with a hopelessly unpronounceable name – had just become the hero of the hour. Or, considering the onslaught of criticism precipitated by *Liffeyquake*'s even more controversial second night, should that be the anti-hero? With his performance piece about the Church – and 'certain Dublin City councillors' who had dubbed him a 'corrupter of youth' – having seen him, by turns, vehemently denounced and lauded with lavish predictions of 'great things to come'.

'And for which, let me say it, or a great deal of it – I have only you to thank, Mr Plumm.'

Because it was Henry who had discovered him. I thought he was going to cry that day he arrived unexpectedly in the office.

'By far the best I have encountered in this city,' he had told me, 'ahead of his time. I don't pretend to understand it. All the same, dear Meredith – it is nothing less than magic.'

Poor old Killian. Yes, Killian de Vere. The once-rising star. The Man Who Fell to Earth. Because that much he had certainly succeeded in doing all right.

Which, I suppose – in common with the Bonners – is what comes from being born at the back of a mountain, digging up turnips and chasing cows all your poor, young, hopelessly idealistic life. What hope, realistically, did he ever have?

Surrounded by survivors of a murderous civil war, barren virgins masquerading as mothers and halfwits the likes of which were now attempting to capture me on film.

Bernie the Bolt, I sighed to myself. Soon your time will be coming, fuckers.

As the Fellinis jabbed me and asked me some more questions. But, by this point, I'd completely lost interest. Returning in my mind to Mandeville House – where one's destiny had already been sculpted in ice. As I stood there, silently, among the reeds, watching as the still water stretched out towards the trees. Without so much as a sound from the wind among the boughs.

Ice that had also been there that day in the Majestic Cinema. The Majestic Cinema, Mountjoy Square. Dublin. Second city of the empire, noble Georgian capital of Turfland. Where the soundtrack tended to remind you of a foghorn.

'Come to the restaurant where the service is fine and the food excellent!' it boomed.

With the adverts over, Robin Askwith filled the screen. His dirty, shoulder-length blonde hair reminded me of nobody so much as Roland's latest prized acquisitions – yes, the absolute dead image of 'my Scottish boys', as he called them.

'The Shortbread McClellands', as Henry Plumm described them. Two Robin Askwiths together. Complete with multi-coloured tanktops and zippered leather bomber jackets.

Askwith was grinning like a gap-toothed idiot, rabbiting on about 'sloshing his paintbrush in 'er shagging bucket'. Much to the delight of Máiréad Curtin – the feminist, if you don't mind! Literally stoned right out of her tree, as she sat there right in the front row of the Majestic. Passing the joint from hand to hand.

Something which they did every Monday afternoon, when they didn't rehearse.

Maybe its 'politics' and 'sexism' were suspect, as Máiréad had just been thinking – but what else could you do? Only laugh when that toothy young fool in his white painter's overalls poked his face through the spars of a ladder and announced that he was on the point of 'giving the audience some valuable advice!' Then he flung back his head and laughed.

'The benefit of my experience, mate,' he said – winking at Liz Fraser in her flimsy black negligée.

'Birds, eh? I could tell you some things about that lot, mate. But then, I suspect, that I'm not the only one. For them old nonces wot you sees 'anging round theatres – they got their secrets too and all, don't they?'

But Robin Askwith, he never did get as far as elucidating what exactly the rationale might have been behind his thoughts. Because no sooner had his mate, Tony Booth, stubbed out his cigarette on the dashboard tray, than half of Robin Askwith's head was unceremoniously removed from his shoulders. With blood everywhere, from the explosion.

An actual one – not one on-screen.

Followed by another horrendous blast, which seemed to have come from the back of the cinema. But there was so much panic developing now that no one could actually have said, not for sure.

This second explosion was succeeded by a third – an incendiary blast – a matter of a mere ten seconds later. Then, after that again – a fourth.

This, of course, being the occasion of the Captain's long-gestating 'spectacular'.

Intended, as Henry had put it one evening in the Scotch House, to 'force the hand of certain people', once and for all. When we'd been debating the progress, or lack of it, on matters of security – on the part of 'that recusant assembly'. Which was how he sometimes referred to 'the Dáil'.

These devices – the planting of which upon my solemn oath saw little or no direct involvement on my part – were an integral component of a change in policy as regards Roland's department. Involving, as it did, simultaneous 'wake-up calls' for both the authorities and the Irish public in general.

'The trouble with this place is that it's a bloody inconvenience. And always has been!' Roland had remarked that same evening in the Scotch House.

Having flown over specially to 'tie up a number of outstanding loose ends'.

The camera was still rolling in the milking parlour back in Armagh.

'That's the stuff to give the spook,' I heard one of them muttering as he jabbed with the fork, 'allowing him the exact same choice as he did our fellows.'

An assertion with which I wasn't really in a position to argue. And which can only prompt me to suggest that, had things gone the way they'd intended, it might have provided a neat conclusion to the proposed memoir of that silly bastard Plumm – in spite of what I'd fucking warned. Yes, *The Hibernia Files* – ending with me punctured like a pincushion, dumped on some lonely Armagh hillside, filled with holes. It didn't, however.

No, that's not the way his idiotic memoir's going to end. Because that has already been decided – with his backside in the air and the pages of his ill-advised account floating in a welter of soapsuds all around him. As I barked into his ear: 'Why on earth couldn't you listen to me, Henry? Look up, Bunter – can't you hear me talking to you?'

'Honestly, dear boy,' I heard myself murmur – and who was there then, smiling at me as I dangled upside down?

Why, only the delectable Jacqui Harpur, no less – legendary journalist and hostess of the TV show *Down Your Way* – where Killian de Vere had first come to public attention. Yes, it had been none other than Jacqui who had first brought the Man in the Hat into the spotlight. As the leading man of the controversial *Liffeyquake*.

What a really quite extraordinary acting talent he had been, I thought – for an innocent, inexperienced, back-of-the-mountain country boy like the Bonners.

Arriving, just as he had done, into our office at the Grafton Agency, carrying with him that air of unmistakable charisma. Inducing considerable gasps of admiration from all who were present. Including Shivaun Carmody, as he delivered an impromptu rendition of his trademark party piece, David Bowie's 'The Man Who Sold the World'. So far ahead of any other clients we had on our books at the time – why, they wouldn't even have known where to look.

'Bejapers, but you have to hand it to him all the same!' I remember Charlie Kerrins remarking, brushing away a swirling cloud of smoke. 'Yes, you have to hand it to the Man in the Hat.'

Of whom Jacqui Harpur, in fact, had written in *Starlight* magazine: 'Arguably the most scintillating talent to emerge on the Dublin stage in at least a generation.'

Which, as I have said, was more or less the general consensus among the Dublin critics, indeed the theatre-going public as a whole. Regularly delivering electrically charged performances on the tiny stage of the Little Matchbox Theatre – culminating, of course, with *Liffeyquake*. Aka 'the most shocking but truthful spectacle ever to be witnessed onstage in this country'.

The paper had also carried a photo of the frail but stunningly handsome youth with the braided locks and high cheekbones. Highlighting that strikingly individual expression of indomitable optimism as he demonstrated, yet again, his flying scissor-kick – the trademark of his 'art terrorist' combo Kabarett Noir. Which featured him attired in a variety of magnificent costumes, from whirling dervish skirts to Cossack blouses. Buckets of blood also featured regularly in their act, as did pigs' heads, along with intemperate denunciations of the Irish ruling class and clergy. 'Rosaries vs Ovaries, Long Live Kabarett Noir!' pronounced the flyers and posters pasted up all across the city.

This new Matchbox show had been put together over a period of six weeks in a former bus garage they used sometimes for rehearsal. I went out there occasionally and, as a result, had a fair idea what was likely to be on offer.

With the lights slowly dimming, out came the figure of a fully robed bishop, complete with gas mask. An image which drew sudden gasps of astonishment from the audience, with it not helping things at all when it became apparent that an episcopal representative – effectively the eyes and ears of Archbishop Augustus 'Gus' Hogan – had actually been present and been taking copious notes. His name was Father Martin Fleming. It was well known that he had taken a similarly keen interest in previous productions – getting out his trusty notebook when even the slightest effrontery, as regards public faith and morals, appeared likely.

But never had his commitment to his written observations seemed so comprehensive and committed as his response to Killian de Vere, now in the guise of what the programme had described as that of 'art-terrorist-cum-gender-illusionist' whose stage name – accompanying a lavish colour illustration of him in full Carmen Miranda-style regalia, including enormous fruit-laden hat and oversized strap-on phallus – was, apparently, Tallulah Babbie Chaste.

A photograph which those idiot mountain brothers had, for whatever reason, kept shoving in my face every time they jabbed me, asking, 'What do you think of this, you fucking English pervert!'

In my hideous bindings, I continued swinging to and fro. To be honest, they appeared more concerned with this representation of de Vere – whom I, and many others of my ilk, had, apparently, turned into a 'faggot'. Apparently, he was actually a relative.

It must be admitted that, in spite of their committed and unswerving efforts, both with their fists and a variety of implements, they never did succeed in establishing beyond reasonable doubt whether or not I had been directly associated with this regrettable calumny. Or, indeed, it must be adduced, with a great deal many other things. Including both my present and 'historic' adventures.

Much of which, I feel pretty certain now – what with her being wed to a politician – my old friend Jacqui was really quite aware of. Even if she didn't say it. I had always had my suspicions that it might have been her who'd initiated the rumours regarding myself and Henry and Grafton Partners. However much the poor beautiful dear might have attempted to pretend otherwise – which she always did. But then, of course – as we've established – they're all of them pretty much like that.

It was her, arranging, at various intervals, for a variety of elliptical hints, tittle-tattle and loaded stories to begin circulating about me and which, over time, began to grow considerably in number. The majority of them, as Jacqui well knew herself, contained about as much verisimilitude as Paddy and Biddy landing a rocket ship on the moon. Or walking in their big country boots to Mars.

Knowing, of course, that she was only doing it for a laugh – filling the pages, as she herself put it, 'in order to pay the rent' – I had challenged her about a story which she'd placed in the *Sunday Champion*.

'Oh, poppycock pip!' she'd chuckled gaily. 'I mean – who in their right mind reads that old thing?'

Only three quarters of the population, I thought. Already aware that she wasn't listening. Popping up her tootsies onto a table in Minty's or the Lower Deck in Portobello prior to the ordering of a brace of Martini doubles.

'It's the right one, it's the bright one – it's Jacqui!' I always used to laugh.

We rarely left those venues before dawn – always topped up to the gills with 'the right one'. Or, failing that, cool, crystal Smirnoff, which she also favoured. Sponsoring, as they did, one of her many columns.

Why such insouciance, I imagine I can hear you say – especially since events had advanced quite considerably in the milking parlour of old Armagh. With Daddy Bonner now reacting very badly indeed to my exhibition of unqualified disinterest.

If this keeps up, I could end up being the star of the very first Irish snuff movie.

Not that I was to any degree worried – not unduly.

Knowing, all along, that I had been under close surveillance. Ever since they had picked me up in Dublin, in the Sierra. And that Petersen – no matter how late in the day he appeared – he wasn't going to let me down.

Out of the corner of my eye – one's protective instinct never, not really, entirely fails – I had intuited furtive movement somewhere to the side of the outhouse. And the blacked-out face of a squaddie passing, fleetingly, by the window. SAS.

Which was more, I'm happy to be able to report, than those inebriated morons had done. Idiot fucking would-be 'terrorists'! Not to mention 'cameramen', ha ha.

'One more time. Precisely what you did when you were in Belfast, seventy-six. With the Captain, that bloodthirsty bastard they call McVeigh. Names, dates, times, et cetera. The lot,' grunted Daddy Fellini, stumbling over a pile of tangled cables.

What now is to ensue, I can but insist is to be apprehended solely by you, the reader, and your personal individual judgement. As Roland used to say: 'I have been instructed to inform you I have no authority to either confirm or deny the matters in question!'

A strategy which, as on so many occasions previously, has succeeded commendably – especially with regard to those damned irrepressible rumours regarding the Grafton Agency.

All hell broke loose, I suppose you might say, in the back end of those mountains in Armagh.

In the confusion, I could hear Petersen barking out a variety of orders – then succeeding in wringing the graip from the grasp of an astonished Daddy Bonner, before plunging it three or four times into his abdomen – in the process inducing such squeals as you can't imagine. Then giving it to his son in the face with the shaft. I don't know – one two three four five six seven solid blows.

Poor old 'Mammy' didn't escape either, because we went back up to the house and got her, after fixing Wee Bonner up good.

Much, as might have been expected, to the chagrin of Petersen – who had delivered an absolute bollocking to me in the Land Rover all the way to Aldergrove Airport. Where Ambrose Roland himself was waiting – implacable as ever, with the red tail lights of the RAF Hercules blinking behind him on the glistening tarmac.

'Who's been making a bloody comedian of himself then?' he demanded eventually as we boarded. 'Eh?'

Not that, even if I'd been in a position to do so, I would have attempted to argue with the man – for, looking back now on everything that's happened, Roland had been the most impressive of all. Having correctly predicted the emergence of an authoritarian government in Russia, the growth of Islamic fundamentalism, the rise of Iranian aggression and – perhaps most of all – the growing political and economic clout of China.

However cold, calculating and cruel he might have been, his political antennae had always been impeccable. 'Plausible deniability' was one of his watchwords – often to the point of obsession, indeed. Although, as he'd observed on our way to the screening room to appraise the video footage which had been retrieved from the 'South Armagh Studio', such concerns were unlikely to be of any particular relevance in this case. As he, personally, was going to oversee its destruction. 'Definitely Cert X,' he smiled wryly as we took our seats.

The only others in the room were Petersen and some scarcely interested fellow, youngish chap – from upstairs in D/Q.

And so it commenced, with a hand in close-up reaching for a meat hook, then the camera cutting to a long shot to reveal a naked man – guess who? – with his hands bound behind his back, hanging upside down with the top of his head a foot or two from the straw-covered concrete floor.

In the foreground, the camera constantly jostles from one image to the next as if, at times, striving to contain itself from rushing out of the room.

Cut to close-up of a meat hook being drawn across the man's naked stomach, then his thighs. Then another close up, a pulley device of some sort hauling him upwards.

Quickly the camera sweeps around to reveal more snippets of confusion and argument – and an elderly man ('A combat veteran, obviously,' sighed Petersen ruefully), swigging from a bottle.

'Talk, you fucking British spook!' he demands, as the whirring camera traces the captive's face. 'Before you end up in a ditch with a rubbish bag over your head.'

'Home Movies on the Border,' murmured the fellow from D/Q sarcastically. 'Given the circumstances' – meaning, of course, the peace process and the aftermath of the Good Friday Agreement – 'an absolute credit to all concerned.'

'You stupid idiot, Meredith,' groaned Petersen, fixing me with an accusatory stare, 'you rash bloody fool.'

And there wasn't a great deal one could muster by way of defence. As yet another slice of what might be described as *giallo* Hibernicus played itself out in flickering shadow before our reluctantly compelled gaze.

Chapter 21

The Rules

'The Longfield Affair', as reported in the *Sunday Champion*, had seen thirteen people injured with no one killed, but a considerable amount of damage inflicted on property.

Edenboro, which had exploded exactly eighteen minutes later, saw four dead and ninety others injured. McVeigh and his associates had driven the car across the border – it was a blue Avenger, which had been hired in Northern Ireland the previous day.

The second Edenboro device, roughly similar in size to the first, had been placed in a false petrol tank attached to a silver-grey Escort car, registration number 6951VZ, which had also been hired the previous day.

Given the fact that, on a number of occasions, to both Petersen and Roland at different times, I had expressed reservations regarding the wisdom of the involvement of 'the Scottish Boys' in any of this; now, however, I had to accept that I found myself humbled by the incontestable triumph of the Longfield Affair.

And, of course, the quite coincidental death of a junior cabinet minister. Ambrose Roland had professed himself 'most satisfied'.

'It's a fait accompli. I always knew I could count on those McClelland fellows – for no matter what anyone might have thought, it has to be conceded that they came up trumps on their own terms, in the end.'

The scenes in the Irish Parliament were compared by Jacqui Harpur, in a rare departure from her customary light-hearted commentary, to the final days of Rome.

With physical altercations breaking out in corridors and rivers of alcohol running down marble staircases and corridors.

'Look,' mused Henry, handing me the paper, 'what do you make of that, dear heart? I always knew that, in the end, the old Paddies wouldn't let us down. Thank you ever so much, as always, Pat and Mick. Always guaranteed to conform to the stereotype. But this time, I must admit – you really have done yourselves proud.'

The newspaper – not the *Champion*, in fact, but a more respectable broadsheet – carried a photograph of a beery, dark-eyed, overweight politician, replete with heavy, dangling, empurpled jowls – loosening his tie as he glowered murderously at the camera.

'And he,' smirked Henry Plumm, folding the paper neatly, 'is supposed to be their minister for justice.'

After five or six weeks in the Mater Hospital, Máiréad Curtin had eventually passed away. As a direct result of the injuries she'd sustained in the Majestic.

The device in question, and indeed the smaller ones which had succeeded it, having been intended as something of a red herring. Yes, a casual, largely unambitious side event when compared with the Petersen-orchestrated 'triple town' spectacular.

What is regrettable is the fact that her death might never have actually happened – had her rescue not been delayed for what proved a fatal period of time. Lying there in the darkness, trapped underneath one of the seats.

As regards the ordnance concerned, the device in the Majestic had been concealed in a small cardboard box, tucked away in an alcove close to the lavatory. The witnesses described hearing a sizzling sound close to them in the upper circle, just prior to the bombs going off. Followed by a cloud of dense black smoke spreading out in all directions.

It had – not unpredictably, as Henry had observed – taken an absolute age for the fire services to respond. Eventually arriving at a scene which might reasonably have been described as the quintessence of *giallo*. I mean, there was even – with an appropriateness best described as absurd – a fuzzy Fender piano playing the song 'Feelings', drifting through the window of an upturned white van. As the Dublin fire engines, close on thirty minutes later, finally made their appearance outside the cinema in Mountjoy Square.

Had that not been the case, it really is conceivable that Máiréad Curtin's life could have been saved. But, obviously, it's impossible to say – not, at any rate, for certain.

You know?

The 'coming star' of the underground generation, Killian de Vere, also known as the Man in the Hat, had not been present on that occasion. Having remained behind in the warehouse in order to paint a number of flats. It might have been better, however, if he had. With the stress of survivor's guilt, or something perhaps very similar, having the effect of making him return to the solace of narcotics. To which he had been formerly addicted. Heroin.

He had been found by a retired postmaster walking his dog, clad from head to toe in his trademark apparel of shiny black binliners, suspended from a rope under one of the archways on Portobello Bridge. Above a stretch of indifferently flowing water. With the only commentary I feel like making in that regard, being as it has a connection to both my own life and that of Henry Plumm – in the lyrical phrase of *Oedipus Rex*: 'Count no man happy until he's dead.'

'Free from pain at last,' guffawed Henry – all the while mocking me as I smashed him with the oar. Stumbling towards the bathtub as, yet again, I swung the sturdy, weathered implement.

'You think you can bury and annihilate me!' he protested. 'But that will never be possible, Meredith. Because, for all of the days that you have left to live, standing there like John Christie at your window, my shadow will always remain here in this very bathroom. Where you have drowned the pages of my manuscript – or think you have.'

Perhaps I ought to have mentioned that, practically all of his life, Henry Plumm had been what I can describe as a committed graphomaniac. A fact to which even the most cursory inspection of his intended memoir *The Hibernia Files* attested. I had finally located them in a secret locked drawer in his desk – the great bulk of which you are reading now.

Recounting, as they do, those lives as experienced by both of us, effectively beginning in the year of the big snow, 1963. But, graphomaniac or not – he really ought, as I warned him, to have curbed certain tendencies. And not gone blabbing about 'specific operations'.

It was a leather-bound manuscript, half finished, on impeccable vellum paper. A 'fictional memoir' was how he had eventually chosen to categorise it – regarding which, at this juncture, you may now be in a position to make up your own mind. I regret, however, to say that from my point of view there was very little he had elected to exclude. Even the demise of Dee Norton, for heaven's sake – not to mention poor old Val McBoan. Yes, there they were in stark black and white. I had to brace myself before turning the page. Poor Dee, I thought. Poor, poor Deirdre.

Then onto the stage in the little hall in Farnagh, County Donegal – came Deirdre Norton looking beautiful in her wedding trousseau. Well, actually, that's a lie, for if anything, her trousseau – it didn't look beautiful. Being as she had rescued it from a trunk – one she had used in the old days during her time as star female vocalist with the Witnesses showband. When they'd actually scored a hit, after years of trying, with a novelty number called '(I Gave My) Wedding Dress Away'.

It had taken a great deal of persuasion to coax the former chanteuse out of retirement – with it, probably, indeed, having been the intervention of her husband Maurice which had enabled it to transpire at all.

'You might enjoy it, for old times' sake,' he had suggested.

As indeed she had.

Which was how she came to be bumping along a winding old mountain-track dirt road somewhere in the middle of Donegal, on their way to a little valley town where the Farnagh Arms still stood – not having changed a bit since the band's heyday there in the middle of the 1960s. When the Witnesses had been the most popular showband in all of Donegal.

'It's great to see you, Deirdre, so it is,' said the elderly parish priest, who was still, after all these years, managing the parish hall. As he led her towards the ballroom where, 'just like in the old times', she and the Witnesses (or what remained of them, with two of them, sadly, having passed on years before) would be entertaining an 'ecstatic crowd'.

'The whole village is alive with excitement,' said the priest. 'Things still tend to be quiet here in Farnagh.'

But which was where, at approximately 1.04 a.m., in a hail of bullets from a Kalashnikov assault rifle, Deirdre Norton was to find herself pretty much cut in two. Done to death by over ten men (some of whom I knew had been dispatched by a battalion commander called McCausland, in concert with Captain McVeigh), none of whom had ever been apprehended.

Sultry Kate O'Mara was on the screen, sweeping through the lounge of their luxurious modern home and arguing bitterly with Frank Finlay in what was to be the penultimate episode of the television series *The Brothers* when the side door of the Farnagh Arms burst open and soon ten men in uniform were in the vicinity of the hotel's main ballroom. Where, by popular request, Deirdre had already assented to yet another rendition of her long-standing trademark novelty hit, tossing a bouquet (as always, she had brought along four) out into the middle of the packed, swaying crowd. Before pretending to weep, but in an understanding way, at the manner in which her younger sister had treated her. Actually going behind her back and seducing the boyfriend of three years standing whom it had been her intention to marry. Hence the beautiful cream-white organza wedding dress specially sewn with inlaid pearls.

'Everything I've ever wanted, she's always wanted too,' she lamented.

The men who had only just now rushed through the inner bar and into the ballroom where the dance was taking place were taken at first to be a British Army foot patrol. They were armed with self-loading rifles and sub-machine guns. Some wore berets and some did not. The leader was a heavy-set man, probably in his fifties, with a moustache, who was wearing dark glasses and appeared to be giving the orders. It was he who shot Deirdre – stood over her, laughing, as he tore her apart with bullets. Her crimson-stained wedding dress was shredded into pieces.

The whole operation took less than a minute – with three other members of the band meeting their end.

And as for poor old Val McBoan? What I had read about him almost made me – well, throw up, to be perfectly honest.

In his hand-tailored shirts, Val McBoan had always presented a dapper figure as he came strolling down Grafton Street. His handmade shoes shone and although it mightn't have been immediately apparent, his shirts were also always handmade in Tyson's. A tailored suit and overcoat were crowned by a jaunty trilby worn on the Kildare side, in the manner of his London idols such as Jack Buchanan and Noël Coward. In one of her reviews in the *Evening Herald*, Jacqui Harpur had described him as having a voice like 'melted caramel'. A description considered by most to be more than accurate, as he adjusted the microphone and, clearing his throat, commenced a rendition of the popular revolutionary ballad 'The Croppy Boy'.

Which was the title of the show, reported in the *Quacktown*

Bugle, that the repertory group had been performing on that particular occasion in Belfast. Not surprisingly, perhaps, given it was the height of the conflict, playing to largely empty houses. A state of affairs which had come to depress the sensitive actor considerably – leading ultimately, given his status as a former alcoholic, to his wholehearted and unfortunate abandonment of all restraint.

Which was why, hours before the show, the alarm had been sent out, with all of the company and a considerable number of police combing the city in search of him. With the more seasoned constables, although they wouldn't have dreamed of ever giving voice to such sentiments of dread, now that a considerable number of hours had elapsed, without success – being aware in their hearts that, given the circumstances, it might well be already too late.

It was.

What had happened was – a considerably inebriated McBoan had wandered blithely down a side street in the vicinity of East Belfast and, coming upon what looked like a warm, congenial hostelry with a little red neon sign in the window, above a Venetian blind like a kitchen, had struck up a conversation with a rotund man who'd admitted he'd been there all afternoon. But not only that, was more than glad 'for to meet a man like himself, all the way from the Irish Free State'.

'For, after all,' beamed Captain McVeigh – for it was he, 'in the end all of us's brothers, is that not the case?'

I won't elaborate, but that was how Val McBoan, at the age of sixty-five, came to be sitting in a porcelain chair, strapped around the waist, in a disused dentist's surgery in a deserted part of East Belfast – on the point of performing his very last role.

After giving them a few bars of his favourite song, which they had insisted upon – Dils Pratt principally, chuckling repeatedly that she 'loved a bit of singing' – described by Captain McVeigh as a 'special request', sharpening up his butcher's steel.

And who now was grinning from ear to ear, clad in an

ankle-length victualler's apron, touching Val's ear with the tip of the steel – as Dils opened up another bottle of wine and called out, giddily, 'Hang on till your hat's there, do ye hear me, Brother Teague? For it's showtime!'

Having completed my trip in the wooden dinghy around the lighthouse, I decided to confront Henry on the landing, outside the bathroom. With one thing, as I'm sure you can imagine, already leading to another...

'It really was most indiscreet of you, Henry. I mean you, of all people, ought to know the Rules.'

I hadn't, at least initially, had any intention of striking the fellow. Not, at any rate, with the oar. Which I still happened to be holding in the aftermath of my trip. I regret to say that he had now made that impossible. Impossible, indeed, to respond in any other way.

Bam!

At which point he fell – nearly tumbling over the banisters.

Bam!

After that, I'm not in a position to recall a great deal else. Apart from the comment he'd made about 'always having wanted to be an artist'. Which I'd heard many times before, of course. And requested that he not 'say it any more'. As he had done that day up on Howth Head – having delivered an impromptu speech as the sea breeze fanned our cheeks.

'It is I who am the Winslow Boy!' he had declared. 'And the devil take anyone who dares suggest otherwise!'

This time, I fear, it had all proved too much. So I struck him hard with the wooden stick once more. And again after that – not really knowing what I was doing until I discovered him lying there, motionless, in the bath. Surrounded by a soggy floating mush of papers – most of which I succeeded in drying out, and which hopefully you are enjoying now.

I've never been the same since I dispatched old Henry. It makes me sick to even think about it, to tell the truth. And as I stand here silent by the long window, whether resembling Max von Sydow, John Christie or anyone else – the longing I experience is always indescribable. Turning my face towards the white door of the bathroom. Knowing, yet again – that he'll never be there.

Because he is he and I am me.

And I am here by the tall Gothic window, alone. Representing the apogee of the eminence grise. Diligent espionage: only this time, after death.

Really, you know, when you think about it – a talent agency fronting 'Em-Oi-Foive'! What was it all about? Yes, indeed – you may very well ask.

??

!!!

As the plum-velvet curtain prepares to descend, bringing this final season on the coast to a close. With one's composure now largely restored, thanks to the ministrations of one's irreplaceable, fragrant English rose – Virginia Nicholson. The living image of Deborah Kerr – about as far from 'Merciful Hour' Mrs Mulligan and her clan of murdering IRA countrymen as could ever be imagined.

With not so much as a sound to be heard on the beach. Only that which might be conceived of as the long-departed ghosts of summers long ago – flitting between the battened windows and clattering shutter doors of what had once been the mightiest of provincial theatres: the Seafront Apollo. With those torn, faded posters pasted up on pebbledashed walls – and featuring such names as Al Martino and the Galloping Major. Along with Jack Jones in *The Love Boat*, and numerous other more minor artistes, a great number of whom are not even now so much as a memory. Including Bill Grounds, Barbara Cleave and Danny 'Two Step' Fletcher.

'Such ingratitude,' I remembered Virginia remarking as she tenderly daubed my cheek, 'but what's most upsetting, at least to my mind, is how charming and sweet these fellows seem when you meet them first.'

'I know, Miss Nicholson,' I had gratefully replied.

Even at that late stage, feeling immensely uplifted – simply through the good fortune of having encountered someone who appeared to – you know, understand?

I mean – some of the things that I'd been through.

All of which were bad enough without Plumm, in spite of numerous protestations on my part, going ahead and including verboten material in his self-aggrandising record. Until I'd no choice but to intervene. And although incipient cortical atrophy may have been the cause, or a part thereof, of the decision to include the account involving myself and a certain 'Mr Wilson' in Belfast – under no circumstances whatsoever could it possibly be countenanced.

What with Wilson's part in the strangling of the orphanage youth in Quacktown – although never properly investigated, it had somehow come to include me, however peripherally. Over time, things had become rather complicated in that Ravensbrook orphanage. And no one had wanted the boys' home to become centre stage – but yes, I did assist Wilson a little.

However, the actual organisation of the whole affair had been the responsibility of Roland and Captain McVeigh. I simply did what I'd been told had to be done.

But, for heaven's sake, Plumm – you don't go and write about it. I mean, the lad, for heaven's sake – he couldn't have been over ten years of age.

What was it that you wanted, Henry – another blundering, Mandeville House-style tragedy?

So be it, then – all I can say is, I've tried my best. And so he's gone to sleep – wafting away in the sweet old by and by, poor little lad. Just like Pergerine Masterson, my old ice-skating friend.

Ta ra! Tsk tsk!

One does what, regrettably, must be done.

The End.

All of which, inevitably, takes its toll. Which was how I ended up doing Gene Hackman 'Coppola' impersonations with my sax. Although credit must be given where it's due – with the fellows up in London taking care of the inquest and any other bits and pieces which might have been required regarding Henry.

For when they found me, I had been in no fit state to do anything. Spending my time grieving over Joanne Vollmann – in that squalid, filthy apartment at 111A Willesden High Road. A development which saw me degenerate into something approaching what, had Paschal Honan had been alive, he might have been persuaded to nominate as the 'fifth' Harry in his 'uproarious' drinking game of yore – Coppola's shabbily melancholic saxophonist musician and electronics surveillance expert – yet another now, presumably entirely forgotten, 'Special Ops' casualty, anti-hero of his film *The Conversation*.

Lurking naked in a corner of a damp and poorly maintained apartment – fingering the keys of the Selmer as best I possibly could, but producing little that might be said to be of value.

More like what Larkin, the poet – Henry's favourite – might have described in one of his *Observer* columns, in the course of a commentary on John Coltrane's phrasing, as the 'mental scribblings of a subnormal child'. Whatever one's opinion about John Coltrane, there being at least some measure of justification in my case for such demonstrations of atonality and crude assault upon melody.

Considering that, after my final visit to Jo's parents in Golders Green, one's degeneration had been seen to acquire a rapidity which – troubled though I'd been – had actually come to truly astonish myself.

Because I wasn't ready for it.

You'd think, after all that I'd been through, that nothing would faze old Henry – Plumm-Chenevix-Meredith. But that, regrettably, is where you would be wrong.

With it happening, really, in a matter of a few short weeks. As I lay there, huddled, having reconfigured some ancient copies of *The Spectator* and *Guardian* as blankets, in what was now effectively a midden.

Yes, a rat's nest, really, of chewed, rolled and discarded papers – piles of manuscripts, unanswered letters, empty cigarette packets, small stacks of political and literary periodicals, tradesmen's bills and publishers' brochures. With empty beer bottles lying around everywhere.

The rest of the time lying on the stark bare boards of the bedroom, shuddering as I monitored the seemingly interminable squabbles of the couple who lived underneath.

'What is love?'

'Love is death!'

'The day I leave is the day I begin to live!'

Such, it seemed, were their daily preoccupations.

Eventually discarding the Selmer altogether, I attempted to settle my own account with the past. To be honest, I suppose, in a way my own personal version of *The Hibernia Files*. Whose pages consisted not of vellum or even standard cheap publishers' mulch – but pieces of the Bible stitched together, along with assorted Rizla cigarette papers. Intended as a type of homage, I suppose, to the hunger strikers and other prisoners of Her Majesty's Prison, the Maze – also called Long Kesh, if you remember. Where the 'vermin of the lower depths', as Henry had been wont to call them right from the beginning of the 'Troubles', had ended up serving their time.

'Ocras' was the chapter I gave them – pencilled on a series of flimsy tissue-paper squares. Influenced, obviously, by that spectacular fringe-theatre *Late Late Show* performance. Comms, they had called them. Communications.

Who had first developed this unique system of messaging I

couldn't really say. But in this new situation, this 'self-built cell', which was how I tended to view my circumstances – I have to say that it suited me. Those tiny hieroglyphics scratched on barely existent scraps of paper – principally Kleenex and lavatory roll. With the latter, I found, being particularly appropriate to the task on hand. Being as each room – there were three altogether – was now decorated by a variety of human waste.

People had started to pay me visits. Not real ones, obviously – for not very many knew where I was. People such as Shivaun Carmody's brother, for example. Whose name was Emmet – after Robert Emmet, the insurgent hero. And who had finally ended his life in the Maze after fifty-five days, all told, on the strike. Without food or water of any kind. I drew a picture of his face on one of the comms. Before inserting it, initially with some difficulty, into my rectum.

Which I did with a lot of them, actually. Squatting on my hunkers in that ever-expanding pool of filth, dazedly fingering the Selmer as best I could. Yes, wanly perusing those once so beautiful, now encrusted, inlaid pearl keys. Before composing yet another masterpiece of historical accuracy – and depositing it, just as before – deep inside my rectum.

Which is scarcely a period or a pattern of behaviour that one is motivated to justify and certainly not defend. But, really and truly, ever since Joanne's sad departure, I had long since passed the point of actually caring. Because, I mean – if it hadn't worked out with her, then who on earth could it possibly . . .?

'Yes,' I scratched on another tiny paper stamp, 'I have ended up being Harry Caul.'

Before changing my mind – and scribbling it out.

'Except that is where you are wrong,' I wrote, 'because Henry and I, we were once the glorious English princes of Dublin. Yes – like it or not, that was what we were.'

Endeavouring as best I could not to dwell on the memory of our very last day in the city. When all our clients had arrived en masse at the Grafton Agency. Where a farewell drinks party was to be held among the packing cases and empty filing cabinets of Grafton Mews. And where glasses were to be raised, no doubt, to the nearly twenty-five years of continuous occupation there by myself, Shivaun and a number of others, including the Slug. Cheers, as always, to the men of the moment, Henry Plumm and Chenevix Meredith!

Except for the fact that neither of us were present.

The following morning the removers had arrived, and the Peter Marks Hairdressing Salon was duly ensconced – with the Grafton Theatrical Agency Ltd, Dublin, officially being no more.

I set it all down in one's new-found, distinctive hieroglyphics – an entire little world of biographical and extremely sensitive information, regarding the adventures of a certain Mr Chenevix Meredith. Formerly of Mandeville House College, and once upon a time theatre and entertainment scout. In that little land where they like to grow potatoes. And, of course, breed irrational cold-blooded killers.

Late one afternoon when we had finished our debriefings – fortified by gin, we stood there in the middle of a rainswept O'Connell Bridge. From which you could see the spire of St Laurence O'Toole's and St Barnabas, and not so far distant, the chimneys of the Pigeon House. Plumm seemed lost in a world of his own. Which wasn't all that surprising, as it was a crisp autumn evening, with only the slightest of drizzles beginning to fall, and with a strange kind of peaceable quiet slowly beginning to descend on the emptying city.

'I feel guilty sometimes, you know – over some of the things that I've done and said about this harmless little place.'

You could smell the brown pungent aroma of hops from the Guinness brewery lingering powerfully in the air as he collected his thoughts.

'In a way I wish I had never come here. In my dreams it's like a city made out of glass. Above which a fragile, diamond rain begins to fall. And then when I look again, around the people, who always seem to be dripping with rain, some with coats thrown over their heads as they make their way home, hurrying through the traffic, it gets so I can hear the beat of the rain so hard that the street and the very bridge, indeed, upon which we are standing – it becomes like a dance of the most beautiful glassy shapes. Kind of like the circles that you can see in any of their churches – the shape of the blackened spokes on those candle shrines which hold the penny candles. I wonder, do you know what I mean? Do you, Chenevix?'

He paused.

'Don't answer if you'd rather not.'

I didn't.

Even as he'd concluded, the thin light rain had resumed once more.

'Poor old misbegotten Paddyland,' I remember him sighing wearily, 'where the likes of you and I must endure our purgatory in the hope of bringing some semblance of peace to this distracted nation of born agitators.'

As off he went, not entirely unlike John Christie in the rain. I remained where I was for a few further minutes. The clock above the Scotch House showed a minute after seven. You could see the lighted globes glowing warmly inside the front lounge. It was extremely tempting not to return. On what was clearly going to be another damp, drizzling, wet evening – with the Liffey now already at high tide, and the seagulls shrieking high above Liberty Hall, as though in collective protest.

'Éire,' I murmured. 'Ay-Ruh!'

Not without some strange kind of wrench, which I suspect was comparable in character to Henry's, 'Soon it will be time to say goodbye.'

Throughout those last few months in the Willesden apartment, my mind had become overheated to such an extent that nocturnal disturbances of one stripe or another – they had become an almost daily occurrence. With perhaps the most alarming 'visitation', if that's what you want to call it, outside of Shivaun's brother, being the Ravensbrook Boy, as I called him. And who reminded me of the Milky Bar Kid.

'You did this,' he said, showing me the burn on his neck. 'This is what you did to me. I don't know why. Because I did nothing.'

Then he was gone.

With Shivaun's brother Emmet returning. Laughing – same as he had done on a number of previous occasions. Laughing, if you don't mind. As though he hadn't a care in the world. And certainly not giving the impression of someone who had undergone fifty-five days of mental and physical torture. Before finally expiring in honour of the comrades who had preceded him, and for love of his country.

No, he hadn't given that impression at all. I hadn't even apprehended him as an entity, ghost or however you might wish to describe it. Which is an indication of just how far I was actually gone. But, then, ghosts can assume all sorts of forms.

They can even arrive as Marti Caine in a figure-hugging one piece. Complete with that trademark Geordie accent.

'Welcome to *New Faces*. So how are you all doing this evening, my lovelies – it's Marti Caine here. This week on the show I'm delighted to present to you the fabulous Harry Caul and his beautiful golden Selmer. On which he's going to accompany me in my other persona as the emaciated hunger striker, the one and only Emmet Carmody. What was he doing in prison at the tender young age of twenty-seven? Well, why don't you ask him.'

'Hello there, I'm Emmet. Yes, you might well ask that question – what was I doing torturing my healthy young body by going on hunger strike? But talk about a comedy, lads and lasses, regarding what used to go on in there from time to time. Hit it, Harry.

'Did I tell you what used to happen whenever we'us all on the blanket? Such a laff! Yeah, we weren't wearing nothing only a tatty old blanket, our protest, you see, for being denied political status. No wonder that you're putting all of 'em things, I say, Harry, up your bum – all them leaves of your forthcoming autobiography and everything. No, since you ask – I am not one little bit surprised. Because, back in Long Kesh prison, why everything used to go up your botty. It really did, lads and lasses. We'd roll the fags in our hands and cram the papers into a biro casing. You call over one of your mates and up it goes. The lads always made sure that it was well up so that nothing would show when the screws, they would search you like they always did after Mass. It's quite a laugh what you can manage to fit in up there when you want to. Go on now, why don't you try it. Stick all those comms up your silly old fatty bum bum. One bloke, I remember, you know what he did – he brought out three pencils that way, and another hid a pen, a comb and a lighter. You don't feel it unless the casing is too long, but you do bleed all the time and sometimes pieces of flesh come off. As you can imagine, everyone has piles. You never expect that someone who has been on the "dirty protest", as we called it back then – that they'll end up on a show like this. But you tended to get all kinds inside of the prison – all different kinds of talents. Why, some of those blessed buggers, I'll tell you not a word of a lie – while they was darkening those walls with any dirt they could lay their hands on, and scrawling political slogans on the white walls, you never knew how they were going to start amusing themselves. One bloke in particular, I remember, he went and got it into his head that he was Picasso or something – and starts painting all these flipping palm trees! It were a laugh, though – with the rest of them starting into singing all these duets. Which I suppose is how they ended up here on *New Faces*!'

I remember looking up after that to see the Slug – admiring his fingernails in that sly old shifty manner.

'Tell me about the maggots, Carmody,' requested Lionel the

Patagonian Banana Slug, 'because I should like to hear a little more about those, if you would.'

Emmet Carmody now seemed really quite matter-of-fact. Tired and irritable – somewhat frustrated the panel-show participant concerned didn't seem to quite fully comprehend the matter of his narrative, if you'll please excuse the pun.

'The battle of the bowels,' explained Emmet, 'hotted up when the prisoners started throwing their faeces out the window. In spite of the deployment of firemen's hoses, the maggots nonetheless continued to multiply. You'd wake up with them in your hair and your nose and your ears. You'd lift up the mattress and there they were, crawling under it.'

'Yeuch!' winced the Slug, before hesitantly adding: 'Please, if you don't mind – I wonder could we possibly move on?'

As – just for the hell of it – Marti blew a single note from the Selmer.

B'durp!

Not very musical, one has to concede.

As she flipped the pages of her clipboard and continued: 'And now we come to the rape by two policemen. Have you anything concerning this which you might be of a mind to share with us, Mr Carmody?'

'Yes,' began Emmet, 'that was my sister. Meredith and his crew arranged that to happen. To ensure she never again interfered. She'd been nosing around, you see – unwise.'

A shadow fell across the Selmer.

'You didn't have to do it,' I heard Emmet saying, 'because our Shivaun, and well you knew it, had never been involved in anything political. She may have been, to some extent, a sympathiser. But that was all – why couldn't your people just have left her alone?'

'It wasn't me,' I replied, somewhat unconvincingly. 'I couldn't possibly have ever condoned that.'

'Is that so? In any case, what happened in the long run badly affected her nerves. She's been in and out of places ever since.'

'I'm sorry to hear that,' I said.

'No you're not,' said Marti Caine, lowering her clipboard – and, quite unexpectedly, beginnning to cry. It was a shocking moment. But not as much as what happened next. When I saw Leslie Courtney emerging from the shadows – wearing that silly cricket jumper of his. And that equally silly, nauseating smile.

'Come over here and sit upon my knee,' he said, 'I long to hear some of your elegant verse.'

I shrank away – but still he pursued.

'Will you oblige?'

?

?

!

And, as always, that was what I did.

Lifting my head as I began to clear my throat.

Leaves, like the things of man, you
With your fresh thoughts care for, can you?
Ah! as the heart grows older
It will come to such sights colder.

Then he whispered into my ear – pressing a freshly pencilled comm into my fist.

'Goldengrove,' it read, 'I implore you, don't leave us. Because all of this will be forgotten in time.'

'But of course it will!' I found myself chuckling. 'Because isn't that the strategy? Just like it was with the Brothers McClelland!'

'Those quite indispensable Shortbread Twins', as Petersen used to call them.

Robin Askwith on-the-double. Who had been selected for operations in Dublin precisely on account of their status as 'wide boys'. Making it their business to mingle with as many subversives as they could, many of whom were billeted in caravans along the border. Preparing operations or fleeing from this or that.

As the *Sunday Champion* had revealed when they were eventually apprehended, the McClellands had been involved in petrol-bomb attacks on police stations, actions intended to reinforce a view that an already vulnerable Irish southern state was now on the verge of being entirely overwhelmed by anarchists and malcontents of every conceivable political stripe.

Of which, lo and behold, Clem Grainger now, apparently, was one – having thrown in his lot, however temporarily, with the Shortbreads. Paying regular visits to the caravan, where political discussions continued far into the night. With arguments over divisions, counter-divisions and strategy.

'The war on the people will be turned into a people's war,' Clem Grainger was fond of saying.

It had never, however, become public knowledge that he had been in any way involved with the Shortbread Bank of Ireland robbery – for which he had actually driven the getaway car.

When – talk about a laugh! – the McClelland brothers, in the process of filling up bags with banknotes, had referred to one another throughout as major, corporal, sergeant and so on. It was obvious to the bank staff that the robbers had not taken a great deal of trouble to disguise themselves. Such was the relaxed atmosphere in the bank that the robbers discussed with the staff a boxing match which had been televised the previous evening and included the British fighter Joe Bugner. Even the antiquated telephone system of the 'hilarious' Irish Republic had, apparently, come in for some trenchant criticism during the course of the robbery. Which had netted, in total, £67,000.

From Roland's point of view, the entire affair was hopelessly petty, quite obviously a smokescreen. But, nonetheless, he had professed himself pleased.

It was to be some weeks later that Clement Grainger received a message from one of the brothers requesting that he pay a visit to the caravan, which had been rented for a while by one of the Shortbreads. And where they had – foolishly, as they readily admitted themselves – left some incriminating 'stuff' behind. Would he mind very much going around there to collect it? It was hidden in a duffle-bag located directly underneath the sink.

'In the McClelland tartan,' the message had joked.

Clem was more than happy to oblige, he made clear in his prompt response. Probably enjoying himself thinking about all the many conversations that had gone on in that very same mobile home – what was going to happen to Ireland, the manner in which the struggle was proceeding, the inevitable redistribution of wealth, etc.

It remains difficult to credit why someone like Grainger – whatever else, an intelligent fellow – valued the McClellands' opinion of him, certainly to the degree that he did. But such appeared to indeed be the case. Not that, in the end, it mattered a great deal. When – having located the stipulated item, a tartan duffle-bag, just as soon as he was locking the caravan door behind him – what did it do? Only go and blow up in his face. Killing the poor fellow instantly.

Which just goes to show – you must be so careful whenever you decide to become involved in things. You really and truly do.

That's what I was thinking as I sat there on a bench by the side of the Lower Deck in Portobello, having bade goodbye to Henry 'Bunter' Plumm and wondering might he, in turn, nurture comparably ungracious sentiments as regards myself. Considering, as he strolled back towards the suburb of Rathgar, whether the individual whose company he'd just left was not in fact Chenevix, but the cold-eyed egghead who had murdered so many defenceless women – accomplished player of panic, selfishness and malice. Namely John Reginald Christie, eyes shining like the smallest malignant marbles, cardigan-wearing ghost of London's Notting Dale. As it had been once upon a time.

An individual always at one remove from those around him – who knew something we don't but would never blab. The ultimate inscrutable, cold warrior. Unfurling one's umbrella and stiffening as the falling drops of rain began to patter – and, unlike Mr Christie, I'd find myself accepting just how hard, in our way, we had been on poor old Dublin down through the years.

That rainy old ancient settlement by the bay. On whose uniqueness even Henry had, from time to time – however reluctantly – remarked. A city where one never gets dehydrated, and where there is always a breeze blowing from the sea.

'Not to mention the mountains,' I could remember him observing, almost wistfully, 'always within one's reach – those blue remembered hills of Glendalough. Never far away. Where there seemed to be an air of sadness.'

Without my realising that he was vaguely recalling some lines of Philip Larkin.

I remembered the people coming into the pub as shadows. And the sullen buses pressing onwards through the swathes. Right up until closing time, when Paddy Murphy at last draped the towels over the pumps. Watertown, I remember he had called it. And I almost wept as, lying there on the paper-littered floor, I scratched out yet another comm.

'Harry Harry Harry Harry Harry,' I wrote.

And, on the wall, like the strikers, in excrement: 'I am not Harry Caul!'

Followed by: 'Signed Chenevix Percival Meredith, late of Dublin and Mandeville House College.'

Along with a number of places, I chuckled, that I really feel it unnecessary, at this point, to mention. Yemen, Indonesia, the Gulf, etc.

Then I stood up on a chair and inscribed, as best I could, with a flourish: 'Joanne Vollmann Loves Anthony Newley.' Which she did – through me, of course.

Yes, Joanne Vollmann had really loved all of my stories – especially those concerning him. There had even been talk of that particular song-and-dance man arriving over to Grafton Partners to 'do some deals' with myself and Henry. Anything seems to have been possible in those days. With our agency, on behalf of Máiréad and the Little Matchbox Group, having actually already contacted Newley's management.

Regarding possible productions of *Stop the World – I Want to Get Off* and *The Roar of the Greasepaint – The Smell of the Crowd*. But in the end Newley himself had telephoned and regretted that it all had proved impossible. So that was that – no Dublin extravaganza for Anthony, revered progenitor of so many London-based hits of the period.

It's really such a pity that Anthony Newley never made it – because I think he would have triumphed with the version that I had in mind. With the bulk of the story comprising the once buoyantly beautiful, not to mention quite impossibly tender, love story that had proceeded between myself and Joanne Vollmann.

Beginning with the very first movie we had gone to see, in one of my favourite London venues – the Columbia Cinema on Shaftesbury Avenue, which in later years became the Curzon. Where, in common with so many others at the time, we'd hopelessly enjoyed *Cabaret*. Starring Liza Minnelli, whom I loved more than anyone. Because, of course, she reminded me of her.

And why I somehow became putty in her arms – explaining also, perhaps, why, in the end, I told her everything.

Just like I'd done with dear old Uncle Leslie. Yes, Mr 'Trust Me' Courtney. We all know how that ended. So I suppose I ought to have really had more sense – and realised where all of it was likely to go. Just like Mandeville House.

'Not that you helped things, Plumm,' I remember on one occasion saying to him just before he became debililiated, 'for you ought never to have mentioned my name in connection with that cretinous little Protestant bastard Mr Wilson. You broke the cardinal rule, my friend.'

I was right – and Henry knew it. But he wouldn't back down. And, cortical atrophy or not, I couldn't allow myself to take any further risks. Bam! That's why I did it. I'm sorry, Henry, but you left me with no option.

'It was you and Wilson – you and that Ravensbrook boy!' he had blurted out of nowhere one day.

So heaven only knew what he might actually write, commit to paper, unguarded, some day.

Bam bam bam!

So, is it any wonder? That was what happened – I hit him a good sturdy slap with the oar, before heading back to London to tidy up a few loose ends. Involving Mr Arthur Mullard & Co.

I was singing all the way up on the train – mostly a number I'd learned during my time in Ireland. Where, as we all know, there's no shortage of amusing tunes!

'Merciful hour!' I called out aloud – and you ought to have seen the looks I received. But that was hardly going to bother me now.

The pub Mullard drank in – it was called the Case is Altered. But first I had an important call to make. The owner of the brothel was called Mrs Moloney. Yes, Mrs Bridget 'Coddle' Moloney – not actually from Dublin at all, but County Clare.

Who professed to being 'surprised' that 'not in a power of blessed months' had she seen me.

'Layvin' us to ourselves!' as she'd put it. 'But you're very welcome, so please will you come on in.'

The girl that she provided for me, she didn't seem a day over eighteen years of age. And a great deal better looking than, say, the likes of Freckles from the National. For a start, she didn't have a pasty complexion like an uncooked Fray Bentos pie. I was wearing my Ashenden linen jacket and black-banded Panama hat. I'm glad to be able to report that, in spite of her youth and inexperience, Miss Mulgrew didn't give me the impression of seeming the slightest bit nervous at all.

'Merciful hour!' I remember her actually saying. 'The gintlemin that does be coming in here!'

'Hush!' I whispered – as I retrieved my spiral-bound notebook and proceeded to outline the Rules.

Which is why I describe her as a 'prodigy'. And why, like I say, she brought tears to my eyes. Young Miss 'Arsagaun' Mulgrew – she really was a natural. Everything that I seemed to want or need, somehow she seemed to instinctively understand, not to mention comply with. Comprehending, in her very DNA, the necessity of rules and their essential nature. I wiped my eyes and squeezed her preciously pale, sculpted hand.

'How much is it going to be then, Miss?' I said.

'Mr Meredith, it'll be ten pound.'

She really was charming. 'I'm sorry, sir,' is all she kept saying. I could only imagine Plumm's reaction.

'Neither civic order nor practised self-restraint. Like children, really,' I could hear him sigh.

Which she was, I suppose.

'Very well then,' I said, 'I'll get you a drink.'

I had some gin stashed away in my case.

'Now we'll begin the Rules proper,' I suggested.

As she drank and drank, chucking it down, like so many of them – like water.

'Do you want to kneel?' I said – and she did.

I slipped the iPad out of my case – pressing the button as the strains of Spotify began filling the whitewashed cellar. And all I could think of was having drinks with Jacqui Harpur, back in the day when – at times, at least – the Minstrels' Rest might have been situated in the Riviera or Monte Carlo, and not in that grey old familiar glum outpost of provincialism. As my 'Peggy', just like Jacqui in her cups, began to croon – speaking the words I'd given her rather than singing them.

Which, in a way, was how the chanteuse herself, Miss Lee, had originally delivered them – curiously flat and in a near monotone.

'This is perfect,' I said, 'keep going.'

As I bent over, double, and released a protracted groan,

whether of pain or pleasure or both I cannot be relied on to say for sure.

And I'm glad to say – experience, you see – that, unlike Bridget Moloney, my obliging performer did exactly as requested. Saying nothing until it was time.

Until it was completely and entirely appropriate. In order, I suppose, not to spoil the dream. Fracture it in even the smallest, most insignificant of ways. Or seemingly insignificant. So as I could convincingly imagine her there in her very own study, astride a blonde Steinway piano with her white bookshelves all around and chandeliers hung on either side.

The sight of her in her fur-trimmed gown, easing herself onto the instrument's glossy white curve, crooning that particular favourite of manipulative, invasive, drama-teaching housemasters: 'Rum and Coca Cola' by the Andrews Sisters, an explosion of black-beaded fabric and ostrich feathers, with a foot-high black plume rising out of her wig. Having the effect of making a lump swell up, almost monstrously, in one's throat.

'Is That All There Is?' I asked her to say that. She did.

'Is that all there is?'

Executed with the specified delivery – eerily emotionless, oddly flat.

'What do you remember?' I asked her then. 'Please tell me what you remember.'

'I remember being a little girl,' she said. 'Then I remember our house going on fire.'

'And what do you remember when your father gathered you up?'

'I'll never forget the look on my father's face,' she said. ' "I should have known," my father said. "It wasn't as if I hadn't been warned. Both women and men – unreliable as veal. They simply can't be trusted," he said.'

'And – ?'

'As I stood there shivering in my pyjamas.'

'And did you watch the whole world as it went up in flames?'

'Yes,' she nodded, 'Mr Meredith, I did.'

'Very good. And what did you say when you knew it was all over? When you realised that this was the end?'

'I said to myself: is that all there is to a fire?'

'Excellent. But now you must tell me about when you were twelve years old.'

'When I was twelve years old my daddy took me to the circus.

'"The greatest show on earth," he said.

'And it was.

'There were clowns and elephants and dancing bears and a beautiful lady in pink tights flew high above our heads.'

'Perfect. Yes, my dear. And what did you say then?'

'I said: is that all there is to the circus? Because if that's all there is, then let's keep dancing,' she said.

As I heard myself murmur — at least that was how it had seemed to me. But then I hadn't even noticed that I was, in fact, standing up — pale and rigid.

'I didn't mean to do it — why did you make me do it, Plumm? Plumm, you idiot — answer the question! Can you hear me, Henry?'

Before embarking on a private dialogue with myself.

'Good day, Mr Plumm. It's extremely good of you to drop by, for I know how difficult it must be — having agreed at my request to disclose the truth, the awful news.'

'That I don't exist, you mean?'

'Precisely.'

'No, for you see — I'm simply doing my duty.'

'Very well, then — explain to the girl.'

I turned from the wall to which I'd been addressing my monologue.

'There is only Henry Meredith,' I said soothingly, 'what with old Plummsers, sad heart, being little more in the end than a convenient diversion. Or "divarsion" as old Hugh B., in his cups, might say.'

I waited for some time – and then, when she gave no sign of responding, exasperatedly struck the wall.

'For heaven's sake – what on earth is wrong with you people? Don't you understand anything?'

It was then I noticed that she was shivering – looking so pale and ghastly that it actually frightened me. Like she was becoming afraid or something. At which point I tired and told her that was enough – and that all it had been was a 'silly old story'.

'I'll maybe see you next week,' I whispered softly into her ear, 'but right now I just have one last bit of business to do.'

As she nodded compliantly – lowering, as instructed, her willingly abject eyes. A really lovely young lady, all told. Someone who knows, understands and accepts 'the Rules' without question. If only the rest of the world was like that.

As good old Plumm – ha ha, do you hear me? – used to say, long ago. Yes, before old Billy 'Bubbles' Bunter went and broke the Rules.

I produced a book and, ever so softly, began to read. I hadn't heard those lyrics in so long.

> Margaret, are you grieving
> Over Goldengrove unleaving?
> Leaves, like the things of man, you
> With your fresh thoughts care for, can you?
> Ah! as the heart grows older
> It will come to such sights colder
> By and by, nor spare a sigh.

'Who am I?' I asked her, sotto voce.
'Sir, I don't know,' I heard Mulgrew reply.
'I thought I told you what you were supposed to say.'
'Sir, I don't know, sir, I forgot.'
So then we repeated it – went through the whole thing again.
'Very well, then,' I said. 'Who am I?'

'You are my lord and master, sorr.'

And it really did tickle me, the innocent and entirely trustworthy way she said it.

'Again,' I whispered, 'say it again.'

'You are my lord and master, sorr.'

'And I must do whatever is demanded.'

'And I must do whatever is demanded. Because you is the Master.'

'Because I is the Master.'

It was wonderful, sitting there listening to her – thinking back on that first time.

And why, even if I'd wanted to, I couldn't possibly have dissociated myself from the growing impulse to experience that very same feeling – of love, really, to be honest. What, in all likelihood, might be the very last time.

'Goodbye,' I said, 'goodbye to you, my sweet and lovely Mulgrew. And goodbye, Goldengrove.'

There wasn't so much as a sinner on the High Street when I came out. Blinking in the light as I headed briskly towards the Case is Altered.

Chapter 22

The Man from Del Monte

So that was that, then.
The curtain was about to come down at last. Last show tonight at the Seafront Apollo. I couldn't remember ever feeling so happy. Not to say capable and totally 'in control'. With my heart still pumping – but with possibility, not apprehension, as I made my way – still whistling 'Biddy Mulligan' – towards the Case is Altered. Where – with my fastidious enquiries proving accurate – I was informed that the 'party' was indeed due to start later on, as advertised. At precisely nine o'clock on the dot. With old Mullard – or, to accord him his proper 'military' title, O/C Southern Command, Luke O'Brien, Dublin Brigade – well, any moment now he was scheduled to appear.

But, true to form – as of course I had anticipated, given the unimpressive history of his race regarding matters of dependability – the obese cretin was already over fifteen minutes late. Allowing one's expectation, I have to say I was in no way discommoded. With the device I'd placed on the underside of the lavatory cistern primed for precisely five after ten. Being well aware that O'Brien would get drunk and, without a doubt, stay the course.

I must say that, in spite of everything, I found myself calm enough. But, as bitter experience has demonstrated to yours truly over the years, a certain degree of apprehension in such circumstances has to be permitted. Is inevitable, really. Doing the best I could to attract no attention. And with some degree of success, I might add. Even though, in truth, my mind was a lot more 'busy', shall we say, than I would have preferred.

'Why,' I could hear myself chuckling somewhere in the distance, 'it's like the feeling you used to have before being called into Uncle Leslie's study.'

'Pray commence, Master Hopkins!' he always used to say.

I ran through the lines as I waited there in the corner, alertly observing the door of the pub.

> Margaret, are you grieving
> Over Goldengrove unleaving?
> Leaves, like the things of man, you
> With your fresh thoughts care for, can you?
> Ah! as the heart grows older
> It will come to such sights colder
> By and by, nor spare a sigh.

Then I went out again, checking and securing the duct tape one final time. The device itself was rudimentary but functional – comprising, basically, one pound of C-4 plastic explosive – considerably more powerful and far-reaching, in my view, than Semtex. Now safely and securely affixed – I was more than satisfied. Before returning to where I'd been positioned – directly, as it happened, under a bleached portrait of a smiling Ben Jonson in his ruff.

By this stage, the sweaty boisterous venue was heaving. In spite of one's protestations of discretion, I really must admit – that what with one's banded Panama hat, coloured cravat and sunglasses, I did to some extent stand out from the crowd. And without a doubt, not very long after making my entrance, had found myself being scrutinised very closely indeed by yet another central casting-style builders' labourer. Who – sigh, such predictability! – looked like he hadn't washed in a week. So I have to admit that I did stiffen somewhat.

'Who are you, friend, if I may ask?' I heard my narrow-eyed scrutineer enquire. With a less-than-guarded hint of disapproval, indeed containing something even close to malevolence. 'For somehow I don't recall having seen you around here before.'

'Oh, that's because I'm a silly old flibbertigibbet, a quite irresponsible refugee from the world of dear Somerset Maugham. If you've ever, perhaps, heard of the Ashenden stories. Which indeed I'm sure you haven't, being as it's a world that has long since vanished. And which he himself so lovingly invoked, a near paradise composed of parasols, punka-wallahs and Panama hats. I'm like something you might find in the pages of *The New Yorker*!'

Becoming, I have to say, ever more convincing as I thrust my walking cane upwards to align with his Bud Mulholland-style chest. Which I impishly tapped.

'But one's actual name, since you have been so kind as to ask, is none other than Henricus Percival Plumm.'

'Is that a fact?'

I nodded.

'P for Percival, isn't that right, dear?' I continued, addressing my cane – before positioning it mischievously between us.

'The Hush-Hush Men, always at your service!' I told him in my best Tony Hancock voice. 'Isn't that the case, Henry?'

I swear to God, out of sheer force of habit, almost actually expecting a reply. From someone who, obviously, wasn't even there. And, perhaps, had never been.

My companion grunted a bit before muttering indistinctly – reaching out his big gorilla arm for a pint. But even that didn't dissuade me.

'What a to-do in the Case this evening!' I heard myself declaring in falsetto, 'reminding me in its way of those evenings when we would all collect around the Bechstein in dear old Popsie's studio. With its scarlet walls, emerald ceiling and huge black pouffes, to sing about jolly ploughboys, tarry sailors and milk-maids dabbling in the dew.'

'I hope you're not one of them fruity boys,' I heard him grunt sourly, treating me to a studied, aggressive shove. As I started up an impromptu verse of the old favourite, 'Biddy Mulligan'. Which appeared to have the effect of making him dramatically reconsider, scratching his head as I fulsomely explained that he needn't have to worry a jot about me.

'Or the likes of me,' I added gaily, dabbing my brow with an embroidered silk handkerchief.

'Because all I am in the end is silly old "Billy Bunter" Plumm – a poor fellow who is far and away too imaginative to be taken seriously in almost any respect – if, of course, he even exists, ha ha!' I informed him – plainly to his evidently growing satisfaction. 'And hasn't been some fictitious, over-imagined understudy to *The New Yorker*'s Eustace Tilley all along, tee hee hee.'

Humming inside – 'like so many of our profession', as Ambrose Roland had occasionally observed – with the giddiness of my genius.

'I mean, I'm such an old idiot,' I confidently continued, while in the process of loudly clearing my throat, 'I even expected people, when I was domiciled over there in your capital city, to believe that I actually ran a bona fide theatrical agency. During a period – I mean, such impertinence! – when, in fact, I was actually occupied in the execution of some seriously important and perilous tasks of extreme significance to the realm and Her Majesty.'

He thought that was amusing, he told me.

'In fact,' he went on, 'I think it's the best yet! You're the best of a man now, with all these different voices that you have.'

'Yes,' I agreed, 'I like to think of myself as a "gentleman in a world of players".'

'You are that, surely!' he replied, beaming good-naturedly.

Before adding that I was a 'grand old topper'.

'Sit up there, Henry!' he said. 'And I'll buy you a drink. Never let it be said that Neilus Bunyan from the great, grand city of Cork ever neglected to buy a reasonable and dacent Englishman a drink. Sure them auld "Troubles" we used to have over there in the old sod – they're all over! Don't we have the peace process now and all of that, sure, after all!'

'We do indeed,' I fulsomely agreed, as he clapped me heartily on the broad of my back.

And I found myself simultaneously stiffening and turning cold all over – in the mirror suddenly descrying a hugely distinctive figure with enormous ears standing right there in front of me in the doorway.

'Hullo. Yus, it's me, Arthur Mullard! And just to prove it, oi've arroived!'

Already in the process of hauling his considerable girth across the threshold, bent on engagement with an expectant agglomeration of thick-necked collaborators.

Searching all around him with those evasive little brown piggy eyes. Before assuming his position on a high stool at the counter – as always on display that unappealing builders' crescent-moon crack.

It was obvious from the start that he wouldn't be expecting to see me – having had his little joke on the beach some considerable time before. However, all of that was history now. Retribution, vengeance – settling of old scores, blah blibbity blah blah blah. As I listened a little further to the great big fleshy unwashed fool blithering away – discoursing tediously about football and racing and how the country was 'going to the dogs'.

It was obvious, of course, that he wouldn't be expecting to see me – after what he'd presumed had been their 'successful hit'. And I myself really didn't have the time or inclination to enlighten him. With only a very short time now to go before what McVeigh would no doubt have described as 'curtain up'. A mere fifteen minutes, in actual fact.

I looked around – and my spirits soared even further – for who had joined O'Brien at the counter? Only another well-known renegade who had, apparently, only just been released from custody. And in whose honour the so-called 'party' was being held – in recognition of his efforts in the now concluded 'war of liberation', ha ha. That 'barnyard bunfight', Henry would often call it.

As the music swelled further – if you could call it 'music' – a torturous cacophony of fiddle and flute combined.

So we're off to Dublin in the green – shouldering the rifles of the IRA!

With Mullard's comrades at the counter continuing to bestow further slanders upon Albion – and all she had ever stood for, slamming their fists down hard upon the counter. I grabbed my opportunity, pushing impatiently in between them.

'Do I know you?' began O'Brien darkly, looking askance at the white silk scarf semi-covering my face, along with the Panama hat and dark glasses. As another baboon-headed associate strained as best he could to catch a glimpse of me across his shoulder.

'You do indeed!' I smiled, seizing the initiative and gripping him firmly by the lapels. 'Perhaps you might even be aware of my forthcoming memoir. *The* ha-ha-ha-ha *Hibernia Files*, in other words, by one Henry Percival Meredith. And whose pages contain a no-holds-barred account of political life, subterfuge and subversion in Her Majesty's Speshul Intelligence Shervish in that laughable rathole you have the audacity to call a country. Ah, but bejasus, sure amn't I only joking, and don't I know well you know dat, Mr O'Brien, sorr, your lordship!'

I released a mischievous shriek as copious tears came spewing out of my eyes.

'I'm an awful man, amn't I, Mr O'Brien!' I sobbed into his face with both shoulders shaking. 'Hopelessly amoral and unreliable, just the very same as Mr Noël Coward has always said – a great big blessed lump of veal is all that I am.'

'Do you know who you remind me of in that stupid straw

hat?' his bleary-eyed companion offered without even being bothered to cast up his eyes. 'The Man from fucking Del Monte, so you do!'

'Is that a fact?' I returned with a cheery, ironic smile. 'Well, I have to admit that I'm pleased to hear you saying that. *El dice que sí!* And, since you're so funny, I'm going to accord you the privilege of enjoying the most hilarious joke.'

??

!!

'One that I made up myself, in fact!' I continued. 'It's even better than *The Comedians*!'

As the big discommoded idiot kept on scratching his buzzcut head.

!!!

???

'Oh yes!' I told him, examining my fingernails. 'During the "Troubles" in Belfast, this fellow comes strolling into the bar. "Oi!" says the barman. "What have you got in that bag you're carrying?" "Oh nothing," says your man, "just the usual six pounds of Semtex!" "Well, thanks be to God for that!" says the barman. "For a minute I thought you were going to say a tin whistle!"'

Then the last thing I remember being the blast blowing the lavatory door off its hinges – but, curiously, in the process making a sound no louder than the average crushed paper bag. With practically the entire back wall caving in, along with most of the windows, whose curtains were so filthy they were ready to disintegrate anyway.

I mean, talk about *giallo* Hibernicus and *Torso*! With no shortage of those either, you can be assured – for all the world lying there like livid sides of bacon. Scattered willy-nilly across the floor as bewildered drinkers bled profusely, pawing their way as best they could through swirling clouds of masonry grit and dust. Coughing and choking helplessly as the bells of Christchurch Cathedral seemed to ring out somewhere, increasingly further away.

How could they possibly have done so? But they did. And somewhere, also, those fine sentiments I'd depended on – and loved, for goodness knows how long, in the past. Before everything went so pitiably wrong.

> Nor mouth had, no nor mind, expressed
> What heart heard of, ghost guessed;
> It is the blight man was born for,
> It is Meredith you mourn for.
> And why, sweet Goldengrove,
> I now must say 'so long'.

Lying there, contentedly, underneath the portrait of Benjamin Jonson in his ruff – as though another recusant regrettably, but necessarily, voided from the realm.

Acknowledgements

In the writing of this book I have made liberal use of authors such as Gerard Manley Hopkins, James Clarence Mangan and others, whose works – after the manner of traditional ballads, however inaccurately – would have been familiar to those of a certain generation, very much a part of what is commonly referred to as the oral tradition.

Unbound is a publisher which champions bold, unexpected books.

We give readers the opportunity to support books directly, so our authors are empowered to take creative risks and write the books they really want to write. We help readers to discover new writing they won't find anywhere else.

We are building a community in which authors engage directly with people who love what they do. It's a place where readers and writers can connect with and support one another, enjoy unique experiences and benefits, and make books that matter.

This book is in your hands because readers made it possible. Everyone who pledged their support is listed below. Join them by visiting unbound.com and supporting a book today.

Matthew Adams	Rune Berntzen	Matt Callow
Lulu Allison	Sean Berry	Elizabeth Card
Meg An	Neil Best	Fiona Carpenter
Kirk Annett	Beyond The Zero Podcast	Pat Cassidy
David Archer		Andy Charman
Armchair & Rocket	Daniel Bolger	Lavina Chu
	Steve Bowbrick	Jeff Cieszkowski
Sabrina Artus	Tom Bowden	Natasha Clark
Ed Baines	Carolyn Braby	Anne Clarke
Gordon Baird	Elle Bradley-Cox	Joseph Clarke
Jason Ballinger	Richard W H Bray	Lucy Coats
Andrea Barlien	Nick Brown	Steven Cockcroft
Maria Barrett	Brian Browne	GMark Cole
Sebastian Barry	Sean Bullis	Noreen Collins
Ben Bartosik	Caroline Butler	Kate Colquhoun
Larry Beau	Sarah EC Byrne	Joe Cooney

Lucy Cooper
Ray Cornwall
Eileen Corroon
Aileen Courtney
Matthew Craig
Jessa Crispin
David Cronin
Simon
    "BawdyMon-
    key" Cross
Tony Cross
Daniel Cullen
Patrick Cullivan
Matt Curran
Shane Currid
John Darnielle
Michael Delaney
Paul Dembina
Stanislaus Dempsey
Barry Devlin
John Dickson
John Dineen
Laura Dobie
Philip Doherty
Jennifer Doig
Maura Dooley
Declan Drohan
Adrian Duncan
Bilge Ebiri
Rob Emmett
Penelope Faith
Ciara Ferguson
Conor Ferguson
Helen Finch

Anne Fleming
Kaylen Forsyth
Rachel Francis
Lisa Frank
Matthew Frost
Richard Furniss
Orla Gallagher
Mark Gamble
Elizabeth Garner
Matthew Gilbert
Rina Gill
Peter Gowen
Andy Green
Sarah Greene
Darren
    Greene-Ryding
Jessie Greengrass
Phil Greenland
Gregory Grene
Sian Griffiths
Patricia Groome
Martin Gunn
Lindsay Haney
Tim Hanna
Fionan Hanvey
Alan Hardy
John Hardy
Shelley Harris
Barry Hasler
David Hayden
Sanjay Hazarika
Helen Gillard
    Healy
Tiernan Henry

Gina Herold
Alex Hewins
Jeremy Hill
Daniel Hillman
Tony Histed
Thomas Hodgins
LeeAnn Hollister
Bridget Houlton
William Hsieh
Andrej Huesener
Rob Hughes
Nicholas Hurter
Nicholas Hussey
Gav I
Iestyn & Corinne
Gavin Irvine
Ruth Irvine
Maxim Jakubowski
Michael Janes
Dave Jeffords
Dan Jenkins
Alice Jolly
Deb Jones
Sam Jones
Neil Jordan
Matthew Keeley
Joe Keenan
Zach Keenan
Bob Kelly
Hilary Kemp
John Kenny
Tim Kerr
Kate Kerrigan
Brian Kimmey

Jacqui Lacey
Mit Lahiri
Nicola Lancaster
Margaret Lavery
Ewan Lawrie
Alison Layland
Enda Leaney
Kim Leech
Stephen Lehec
Robert Lennon
Marian Lewis
Brooke Lieghio
Toad Loathley
Jim Lockhart
Rachael Loftus
Kevin Longrie
Mary Lynch
Patrick Lynch
Russell Mackintosh
Kendall Mallon
Michael Marsh
Paul Marshall
Miss Nora Mawe
John McArdle
Mark McAvoy
Barney McCabe
Ben McCabe
Ellen McCabe
Eugene McCabe
Evelyn McCabe
Katie McCabe
Patrick McCabe
Eugene McCague
Patrick McCarthy
Ted McCarthy
Barry McCrea
Páraic McGeough
Robert McGrath
Kieran McGuigan
Padraig McIntyre
Gregory McKenna
Brian McKeon
Gary McKeone
Paul McLeman
Katy McLister
Alan McMonagle
Stephen McNamara
Eoin McNamee
Dermot McPartland
David McRedmond
Mary Megarry
Dwight Mighty
Roger Miles
Andy Miller
Sam Missingham
John Mitchinson
Aaron Monaghan
Ian Mond
Alexander Monker
Eddy Moore
Jonathan Morgan
Mary Morgan
Orla Morgan
Daniel Mudford of Balham
Adam Murphy
Brian "Rat" Murphy
Cillian Murphy
Laura Murray
Tiffany Murray
Carlo Navato
Anna Neill
Pedro Neves
Jim Nolan
Keith Nolan
Gerry O Boyle
Marianne Gunn O Connor
Pat O Loughlin
Joe O'Byrne
Ben O'Connell
Rebecca O'Connor
Alan O'Donnell
John O'Donoghue
Timothy O'Grady
David Constant O'Neill
Mark O'Neill
David Oconnell
Chris Odonoghue
Kevin Offer
Christopher Owens
Daragh Owens
Jack Page
Jan Page
Michael Paley
Parker

Richard Peace
Gordon Peake
John Perkins
Mark Phillips
Tara Physick
Kenny Pieper
Brian Powell
Tracy Powell
David Proud
Steve Pyke
Catherine Quinn
Margot Quinn
Pat Quinn
Terry Quinn
Dearbhla Quinn-Hemmings
Celia Rafferty
Leeds Reader
Michael Regan
Jillian Reilly
John Reilly
Mick Reilly
Aaron Reynolds
Anthea Robertson
Alistair Rush
Patrick Ryan
Mark Sanderson
Alan Scanlan (Harolds Cross)
Anda Schippers
Ramona Schneider
Ronald Scott
Bill Scott-Kerr
Barry Shanahan
Jude Sharvin
Jimmy Shaw
The Sheehab
Robert Sheehan
Chris Sheridan
Lorna Simes
Duncan Smith
Valarie Smith
Peter Somers
Nikolaos Sotiriadis
Spider Stacy
Peter Steadman
Andrew Stocker
Matthew Storer
Darcy Strand
Ander Suarez
Annie Szamosi
Ewan Tant
Paul & Bridget Taylor
Philip Taylor
Laura Thompson
Niall Toner
Dave Tormey
Natalie Trotter-King
Cade Turner-Mann
Jon Turney
Ben Tye
Maize Underwood
Richard Vahrman
Hannah Van den Brande
Fabio van den Ende
Barbara van der Swaagh
Gary Veirs
Mark Vent
Annie Vincent
Guy Ware
Tom Welch
Bill Whelan
Jonathan White
Enda Whyte
Rosetta Whyte
James Widden
Deiniol Williams
Rosamund Williams
Joanna Willmott
John Wirkner
Tristan Wood
Tom Woodhead
Peter Woods
Vincent Woods
David Yarrow
Jeff Young
Murray Lachlan Young
Geraldine Zechner
Thomas Zechner
Karen Zumhagen-Yekplé